BACK ON THE INSPECTOR

BY

HOWARD WHITE & IAN SLOAN
(Cover design by Jonathan Dolan)

All The Best

Ian

Copyright © Howard White and Ian Sloan, 2020.
All rights reserved

Fun + love from

Howard

The right of Howard White and Ian

Sloan to be identified as the authors of this work has been asserted by them in accordance with the Copyright, Designs and Patents Act, 1988 and all international copyright laws

About The Authors...

Ian Sloan met Howard White at the Royal Flying Corpse training school in Netheravon, near London, in 1915. Having survived being shot down by Manfred von Mann, the infamous but colour-blind Pink Baron, Ian was immediately drawn to Howard, by a horse, that later went on to power the World's first horse drawn air force.

Little is known of their wartime exploits, and what is known has been vigorously denied by both of them and a Mrs E. Stoat of Chichester.

However, having had very positive reviews for their humorous articles and sketches in "Signal", the Wehrmacht's satirical magazine, Ian and Howard went on to further successes at Stalingrad, which got jolly good reviews.

After the war, Howard and Ian had a trial separation, they chose the Nuremberg trial and split it 50/50.

Little was heard of either of them for a while, until during his rift with McCartney in the post Beatle years, John Lennon stated that Howard had written all of his satirical and drug-induced songs, which got far out reviews

And then, in the late 1990s, Ian wrote a series of critical articles about the Cream night club, which led to rave reviews.

It was then, while both were noticeably not writing Inspector Morose novels that Howard suggested as nobody else was doing so, there might be a gap in the market – Ian subsequently found someone had parked a Fiat Uno in the gap in the market, but they decided to give this Morose thing a go anyway.

Eventually, Ian and Howard concocted a story that they had met in the 1990's at a bus depot in Birkenhead and vowed to keep their very long-winded warmongering history a secret. According to this official version they shared a love of

Spike Milligan and Viz magazine (as if!) and also shared a laptop to write with. No one believed them or bought either of their first two books, apart from those people who did.

Despite all this, we now present their third volume of stories about Inspector Morose, the miserable bastard.

Canny good like.

Ian is still a lizard and has no further wish to be invited to parties with princes or given the title HRH.

WITH THANKS TO...

Ian thanks...

Mary, Shiraj, Mum, Linda & Terry (no, not *that* Terry), Julie, Todd & Caitlin. We've all been there for each other through the difficult times, losing Dad xx

Thanks also to Big GB and Sharon two lights in the darkness.

Howard says...

To paraphrase Lemmy: Two types of people in this world, those who are there to pull you up out of the gutter, and those who put you there in the first place.

To the first type I say thank you, I never say it enough and I do mean it. I love you all.

To the second type; well, it's not fucking well working, is it? Ha! Ha! Ha!

Always thanks to Joe, Nick, Andy, Pete, John, Marty, Marg, Degs, Alan n John n Francis, and the rest.

Special thanks to Vic, Grim, Midge, Drooper and Tabatha; to cousins Viv and Jane and families, the staff and supervisors at Rock Ferry, the others at Laird St, Prenton Way, Cleveland Street and Hooton Green, and the many friends I've made along the way. You know who you are.

No thanks to those whose skulls I shall hollow out as drinking vessels, in the after-life. You also know who you are.

We both wanna thank the following, without whom much of this would not have happened: -

Mr Lee Fitz – Keep winning those fights, mate x

Mr Jon Dolan – Without whom our books would be very floppy. Check out Jon Dolan Animation & Film on Facebook –

your eyeballs will love you for it!

M.A.N.U.P. on Facebook – If you fight the black dog, check 'em out!

Russell Woodward – thank you for your support and encouragement

To all on our Facebook groups and everyone who has visited Offensiveghosts.com

Vic – thank you for putting up with us both, our moans, complaints, coffee and proof reading

Vel, the crow

Carlsberg Special Brew

Craig Manning at Wirral Globe

This book was prepared with the aid of Sparks, Talking Heads, Squeeze, Fiat Lux, Stranglers, Bauhaus, Blondie, Leigh Heggarty and Ruts DC, Dead Kennedys, My Chemical Romance, Motorhead, Status Quo, Kreator, Idles, Creeper, Meet The Robots, and Melwood go and see 'em!

ALSO AVAILABLE BY

HOWARD WHITE & IAN SLOAN

Being Morose

Raise A Glass To Inspector Morose

"It's all bollocks!" – Victoria Ledsham

ERRATUM (big word!)

Foreword By Russell Woodward	9
Chapter 1 – Deceived By Shyte	10
Chapter 2 – Spoiling It For Everyone	58
Chapter 3 – Dead On Line	101
Chapter 4 – id Theft: The Case Of The Fake Sergeant 'n' Shit	
	156
Chapter 5 – It's All Over	209
Chapter 6 – 12,000 Mile Service Of All The Deaded	258
Chapter 7 – In Nomine Patris	311

FOREWORD
BY
RUSSELL WOODWARD

When I wrote the foreword to Raise A Glass to Inspector Morose, I really thought I would be left in peace. However, I was compelled to agree to compose a second after receiving a written request that began with the words, 'we have your dog.'

What can I say about the authors? Like many creative people, Mr. White is a very emotional man, witnessed by myself in the local curry house when he was inconsolable after being informed that his naan had slipped into a Korma.

Mr. Sloan is very slow to embrace modern technology, highlighted by the Tippex on his laptop screen.

Both have that determination to see everything through to the end, no matter how long it takes. A good example of this being last Saturday when they spent six hours counting the steps on an escalator.

Despite all of the above, they are both gifted story tellers with now three wonderfully crafted and funny books under their belts. Back On The Lash With Inspector Morose is composed to the same exceptional standards as their previous works and I tell everyone who will listen to me, "Just buy this book. You won't regret it."

Russell Woodward

CHAPTER 1 – DECEIVED BY SHYTE

"Surr, we had an agreement!"

Robbie stood in his now inappropriately named sitting room – there was nowhere to sit. Superintendent Colin Weird occupied two thirds of the sofa, while the rest was taken up with box files stacked up to the ceiling. The floor had a myriad selection of filing cabinets, a front desk, three phones, an intercom system, and five free standing doors that seemed to lead nowhere.

"Estimates matey! You know the job always takes longer than it should."

Robbie put his foot down, hard; and nearly dislocated his ankle tripping over a black box flight recorder, that had just been handed in from the plane crashed into Oxford Town Centre toilets.

"How long, Surr? Ma wife wants her house back. We can't cram anymore prisoners in the downstairs shitter, man!"

"Yes, about that, I was wondering if we could annex the upstairs er, shitter…"

"Ohhh no way, Surr. It's the only place we can…"

"Good that's settled then, and could I possibly install a gateway to the er, golf club somewhere unobtrusive, say… the back of the fridge?"

"Tell ya what, Surr, I'll get the missus for ye! Ya can ask her y'self!"

"Now look here matey, there's no…."

"Claudie luv, can ye…."

"Mr Harrissss…."

"Sergeant to you, Surr. Yes luv, can yer just pop yer head here...."

"Sergeant Harrissss...."

"Make that CHIEF Sergeant Harris, aye, the boss here wants a word wi' ya, man."

"Look for fuck's sake don't involve....."

Claudia Harris' huge tits appeared slightly ahead of her voice, and followed closely by her rest of self.

"Fuckin what now, ya fuckin sponge?"

"MRS Harris, my dear...."

"You're after something, aren't yer?"

"Ha ha, never under-estimate a woman, they say, and you've just proved it...."

"Cut the shit an' out wi' it ya fookin gimp."

"I was just curious as to....."

"If this is about...."

"Well I was just mentioning to your lovely husband...."

"Out wi'it!"

"We need your permission......"

*****

As he picked up the remaining pieces of what had been his files, and still–Sergeant Harris did his best to revive Jampton, Soames and White, and Jessica switched off the extinguisher that had put out his suits, Weird reflected with a slight pain in his black heart, that even demons need to beware of female humans and their territorial instincts. True, his eyes now matched his black heart, but now so did his shins, and that dentist had better be on form tomorrow.

"So you're setting up shop, er, where, now, sir?" asked a

slightly resigned Harris.

"Get that piss bucket Morose on the blower."

"Aye man....."

Harris pressed 'call' on his posy new phone and the ring tone came through on loudspeaker. There was a click and a "NOW what, you cork muncher!"

Harris couldn't help the smirk as he said, "The Chief wants a word, Surr."

"He can f....."

"Morose?"

"'kin what?"

"Do you have a postcode?"

"Yes."

"Well what the cack is it, man?"

"It's OR41 5EX"

"Right, tidy up, we're moving in til the pen is re built."

"You can....."

Weird pressed 'end call' and, hailing Satan and a cab, swept up the remains of his office and as the taxi swept the lot away, so Claudia joined Robbie and Jess on the lawn, and observed,

"Well that'll stop his farting in church."

"Aye Mum," observed Jess, "Well doon, I can get me One Day International cricket back on the box, now!"

"Ah! " cried Robbie, "Glad you reminded me, I wonder how the match is goin'?"

*****

In the room which now served as his own office,

Endofleveldemon Morose was busy twiddling with his knobs. He pushed, pulled, twisted and wrenched, but still couldn't get "The Friday Thrash Show with Kate Middleton", on "Death FM", the station for all the latest in violent metal. To make matters worse, that useless bog snorkeller and northern whingebag, Harris, had just walked in, and was undoubtedly going to drone on about some insignificant shitty crime. What a tosser.

"Howay, man, can ya get the ODI match on that antique?"

"Fuck off, I'm busy."

Harris surveyed the cold concrete walls of the pillbox, and the lack of any files on anything.

"Busy doin' what? There's fuck all in here!"

"Correct, and that's how it's staying, I'm busy doing precisely fuck all. Sweet FA. Zilch. Zero. Jesus' tomb. Richard Hammond's no claims bonus."

"Aye, I get the picture. Can ya put the ODI on, then? England's bowlers are gan like a camel's fanny in a sandstorm, an' them Sooth Africans are ganna be well up shit creek soon....."

Morose spun his chair round, no easy manoeuvre as it had four legs. Picking their smashed legs off the floor, along with his smashed self, he looked Harris in the eye.

"Is there some horrible upper class Tories only, cricket match on, then?"

"Well as it 'appens...."

"Well you can swivel on your own cock. I'm busy interviewing."

Harris looked around the bleak room.

"Surr.....interviewing?"

Morose looked Harris in the mouth for a change. "I'll

find someone."

"I'm sure you will eventually sir, but in the meantime, who are you interviewing?"

There was a knock at the door, and Jampton stormed in, flattening Morose into the wall behind the door.

"Hi Rob, 'ave you seen that fuckwitted shithole, Captain Dick Cheese today?"

"I'm behind the door, you wanker," muttered Morose into the concrete wall.

"Aw shit surr, sorry. Just as well I never said nothing against you, isn't it!"

There was a ripping sound as Morose removed his face from the wall, and, stretching his balls, which went back into place with a loud, reassuring "Twang", he addressed Hugh.

"You fucking useless dog humper, why can't you wait til I'm out of the way?"

"It's urgent sir, them couple of nice gentlemen who I'm not in the least bit homophobic about…."

"The fire claimants from book one?"

"Aye, that's them, they're out front demanding to speak to yow again."

"Why? Do they need burning out again?"

"They say their bookshop's been torched, and you are wanted."

"To investigate?"

"No, as a suspect."

"Who's investigating this, to name me as a suspect then? I've not heard anything."

"Aye Surr," jumped in Robbie, "We've been assigned the case apparently."

"Who by?"

"That's why I came in," Jampton grinned.

"Since when do you assign our cases, Jampton?" Morose was not amused.

"Sir, Superintendant Weird is outside the pillbox..."

"Sty"

...Sty, and he can't squeeze in, so he told me to tell you..."

"This is ridiculous, I'm going to have to find somewhere else to doss. Where are my former neighbours then?"

"They're outside waiting to lynch you. Seem a bit afraid of Weird."

"That's natural, I'll come out then."

The phone rang. They all paused for a second. All three then made a grab for the phone.

"Get off!"

"It's mine!"

"It's my phone, you idiot!"

"Give it to...."

"Argh! My face!"

"Get you finger out of my eye!"

"Give me the fuckin....."

"You bastard!"

"My new teeth!"

"My teeth!"

Sandy grabbed the handset. "Hello, inspector Morose's office? Oh? .....Yes, he's just here."

He punched Morose in the face, adding "It's for you."

"Morose."

A voice on the line, "Do you fancy dinner later?"

"No, I fancy dinner now. My brother's pub, the food's shit and the beer is wank, but it's free."

"Free?"

"I always walk out before he can catch me."

"I see."

"Great, see you then."

"Don't you want to know who I am?" asked the slightly hurt voice.

"No. But just in case I'm murdered, my Sergeant can make a note of the name."

"Okay, it's Anthony Doom."

"Do I know you?"

"Yes, we were at college together, St Basher's."

"I'd hoped you'd died by now? But okay, you can pay."

"Fine! See you then."

Morose handed the handset back to Sandy, and punched him out. Next he addressed Harris.

"Sort this pair out, I'm off."

"Aye sir....... Any messages for the Chief?"

"Yes! Tell him to fuck off, from you."

*****

Morose sat eating his snail and chip, with his old college chum Anthony Doom, who was tucking into a twiglet and water, as they sat on the ducking stool outside, admiring the view over the Isis.

"You see, Anthony, when Morose invites someone to dine, they dine in the style to which they are accustomed."

"But I thought I was paying?"

Morose did a massive double take. Mopping it up, he shouted,

"Fuckin ace!! I'm having the steak and Special Brew pie, easy on the steak, two skips of chips and four pints of Special Brew."

"Okay...." began Anthony.

"And for the main course...."

"You've not changed since college days, then," Anthony tried his best to laugh.

"I'll just tell my brother Geoff."

Morose threw a rock at the pub's grade one listed front window, and sure enough, Geoff Morose came out, with a cheese wire between his hands.

"Fuckin what? You grassing stoat."

"Five pints of Macallan and an unnecessarily large amount of chips, mine host! Have one yourself!"

"Are you taking the piss?"

"My friend here has a credit card?" he said conspiratorially.

"Yes sir, Mr Morose sir! God bless you and free enterprise!"

As they tucked into their steaming cold chips, so the conversation turned to happier times.

"Do you cook?" asked Anthony.

"Are you calling me a puff? Christ in Gaza strip, man, that's a woman's job."

"Still single too, then?"

"Yes...... I did have a microwave in the house once...."

"Any good?"

"No, the sex was awful. Do you really think that I've missed out, I mean, being married?"

"No, your bandaged hand really suits you. Just imagine this, back then, eh, me a solicitor, you a pig, both of us hated by everyone who comes to us."

"No change there then?"

With a gesture to Geoff, Morose called for the bill. Geoff answered by cutting the rope on the ducking stool and they plunged into the icy depths of the river. They re-emerged a few minutes later mostly dead, but not quite, to see Geoff's pleasantly smiling face.

"Ahh, Mr Doom. Your credit card needs authorising apparently. American Excess said it was a staggeringly large amount, and that they may have to approach Barclays for a small loan themselves."

Anthony swallowed hard, "I know we've been, well, your brother has been, a bit liberal with the sauce this evening, but it was hardly the national debt."

Geoff picked up a passing duck, and with a marker pen he took from his jacket pocket, he proceeded to draw crossed lines over its beak, "I've checked the bill. Yes, all seventy five sheets, you'll find it's all correct. My brother and I had an agreement, next time he came here he would have to settle his tab."

"S'true!" murmured a semi-conscious Morose.

"I've been very generous, normally I add a ten percent service charge..."

"...and I normally tell you where to shove your service charge, Geoff..." Morose added.

"I've left my Winchester behind the bar, but if you wish

to dispute the bill?"

Doom authorised the payment and wondered which was quickest, slashed wrists or an electric heater in the bath. He had every intention of finding out, however, they still had a walk back along the river to attempt. Maybe the river bank was safer?

Morose asked his friend, "Was there anything you actually needed me for? Other than to bankrupt you, which, let's face it, you deserved, being an oily solicitor?"

"Why do you ask?"

"Oh, all a bit out of the blue, really."

"Well...... things look different when you get to our age."

"The filth look younger?"

"Well, that and well, I just wanted to see my old pal again, since I'm here for the cricket reunion."

"Oh, that boring shite?"

"Yes. Meet up with an old pal. Have a chat. Chew on the fat."

"H'mmm, you can chew on this," growled Morose, and let rip a genuinely offensive plate of air biscuits.

"Nice. Do you have any Brut?"

"No."

"Get some and decontaminate this part of the swamp. I had a book about Buddhism that quoted a wise man, saying that he who bashes the bishop, needs a fresh table cloth for Sunday. Think about that."

"I will. Good to see you."

"You too."

"And you."

"Yes, lovely to see you."

"I must say I've had a delightful evening"

"Yes"

"This wasn't it"

"No"

"Still, it's been"

"Hang on… are we stuck in a perpetual loop here?"

"I rather think we may be."

"I've had a simply wonderful evening"

"Look, just fuck off and we'll call it a night."

"Yes, probably for the best. Can I just say…"

"Fuck off!"

Leaning to one side, Anthony made his way back to his temporary lodgings at St Aardvark's College, where it seemed all the cricket freaks were circling like vultures round a thing vultures like. As they do.

Next morning the vultures had a target.

Morose tore up the street but the arresting officer let him off, and he made for the address given to him by Jampton. Harris let him into the room at St Aardvark's, with a heavy face.

"Why the heavy face?" asked Morose.

"New plate in my head," replied Harris, "Sir, wasn't this your mate?"

Morose looked at the corpse.

"Yes. A brilliant mind and a superb bank account. Saved my arse up at Geoff's, I can tell you."

"He rang late last night, asking for you."

"Did he? Did I answer?"

"No sir, you were out."

"Out where?"

"Of it."

"H'mmmm. And now he's dropped off the twig?"

"Well, threw himself off it, sir, looks like he electrocuted himself with his microwave."

"Was he missing his wife?"

Harris looked puzzled. "I'm puzzled," he said.

"Good," replied Morose. "I need you to get the lab boys, the C.I.D, the Air force, and Mrs Stella Quats."

"Why her?"

"I love a dirty woman around, and my microwave is on the blink."

"Very good sir. Now get someone else to do it, I'm on leave an' that, so up yours you boring old clapped out prick."

"Haven't the Tories banned holidays for northerners yet? Only reason I voted for them."

"Bit of a swing to the left for you, voting for the Conservatives, sir?"

"Well Heidrich wasn't standing in my constituency....."

"Anyway," grinned Harris with a grin, "I'm off. Bye!"

"Wanker," snarled Morose, buzzing a photograph in an iron frame, at him. It was no use, the northern turd was already out of the door, down the stairs, out of the front door and revving the bollocks off his car, before the picture hit the floor.

"Looks like suicide to me," growled Max, as he walked into Morose and sent him head – first into the back of the door.

"Inspector Morose!" shouted P.C. White, as he opened the door and flattened Morose against the wall.

"Aye, this wall can go," shouted a workman as he put a pick–axe through the panelling, and followed it up with a big tin of masonry paint, which left a permanent impression in Morose's skull. Morose wearily got up, dusted himself down, and after spitting out a few teeth, addressed Max:-

"Suicide my arse, all he had to do was stand anywhere in this room and he was dead meat!"

"Well anyway," Max continued, "He appears to have electrocuted himself on his microwave, bit of an odd way out if you ask me!"

"Sir," White continued, "I've got Mrs Doom here, is she okay to see the chargrilled, burned out corpse remains? I mean, they've put me right off the barbecue; only she's part way through her radio show, and needs to be back after the massive commercial break."

"You can't knock that wall through, you soft shite, the whole room will fall in!" said the foreman, also carrying some emulsion.

It was getting a bit crowded in the room, what with workmen, Max, that wanker White, the body, a few C.I.D work-dodgers, AND the dead body. Just as well that monkey hanger had gone, reflected Morose.

"Ah, Mrs Doom, I knew your husband."

"Ah yes, he didn't mention you, ever."

"Can't blame him. Look, sorry about the mess, we seem to have the painters in. Can we step outside?"

Stepping out of the second story window, they were soon on the lawns outside, and landed on two blokes in cricket whites, one of whom was pushing himself along in a wheelchair.

"And which window did you walk out of?" asked Morose as he was run over.

"Good God, it's Morose!" shouted Davros.

"You should look where you're going!" they laughed at each other.

"Are you here for that cricket match, too?" heaved Morose, barely able to face the answer.

"Of course – do you have a radio? I'd love to know the latest on the cricket."

"The latest on the cricket," snarled Morose, "is that you're a man down. He's dead. Carked it. Dropped off the twig. Settled his account."

"I'm his wife!" grinned Mrs Doom, extending her hand, a trick not many of us can pull off.

"I'm not married, you dick," cried Morose.

"Not you, the corpse!"

Then she remembered and went back to being a widow, she gave a quick sob, blew her nose on Morose, and explained to the cricket team manager,

"I'm afraid your number four batsman has died, Roland."

"What, Anthony? Dead? Does this mean he'll not be playing tomorrow, at 'The Pillow Boys' reunion match?"

"Unless there's an improvement in his condition, no," Morose interjected, "By the way, who did you say you are?"

The disabled man struggled to his feet, and introduced himself.

"I'm Roland Law, don't I know you? Aren't you……"

"Morose," sighed Morose, "We were at college together….."

"By God, yes, 'Plague' Morose, ha ha ha, what a peasant surprise!"

"You mean pleasant?"

"No, not in the least. This is Vince Cranberry, he's our number two."

"Yes, he looks like one."

"No, two."

"Fucking whatever. Look, I'm halfway through the day and not even remotely off my tits, and now this death to look into, and......"

"And you're looking into the death of Anthony? Are you a pig, now, to top it all?"

Morose smiled wide enough to reveal his over sized, and oddly hollow, canine teeth.

"Yes. I'm not sure it was suicide."

"Jesus," muttered Law, "Well, good luck with that! Come on, Vince, we'd better get the radio on and check out the latest in the O.D.I."

"Can't any of you watch something interesting?" muttered Morose. Then he remembered Mrs Doom next to him, and, turning to her, snarled, "Come on, dog face, we need a few pints and anyway, I've got a few questions about your husband's death,"

"But my radio show?"

"They'll have to run a few more adverts."

"It's been half an hour now!"

"Good, they should have got the hang of it by now!"

Morose could hear an advert promoting the reopening of a recently burned out car dealership. He'd have to drop in. With a few cans.

He took Mrs Doom to the nearby students bar.

"We're shut," said a spotty four eyed geek of a barman.

"Fuck off," said Morose, and rammed his head into the sink. "Mine's a massive one, and a pint of wine for the hog here."

"Fucking pigs" said the student, as he added a little floater to Morose's quart.

Morose fixed Mrs Doom with a stir, well she looked hungry and Chinese was a quick snack.

"I suppose you want to know why they nick named me 'Plague'?"

"No. Look, I'm in a bit of shock about this death. Anthony was a very special woman...."

"I thought he was your husband?"

"Yes, that's why he was special. I just can't believe he's popped his own cork, like this."

"Why would he kill himself?"

She lit up a small cigar, "Anthony had no reason to kill himself. Do you really think it was suicide?"

"Well, microwave in the bath won't really wash as 'natural causes', will it?" laughed Morose, and as the air turned frosty rapidly, added as an afterthought, "Anyway, there's always murder."

Mrs Doom cheered up at once, "Oh goody, when can we start?"

"No, you muppet, I mean, he might have been done in."

She sank the last of her second pint. "Do you think so?"

"Maybe, or this story is going nowhere. Why would he have a gun?"

"He didn't."

"There was a gun under his pillow."

She looked a bit taken aback. "A gun? He hated guns.....

what kind of gun?"

"An anti aircraft machine gun."

"Must have been a fucking massive pillow."

Roly, freshened up and on the pull, joined them at their table.

"Plague, old boy," he began, "Why would Toners pull his own plug? 'The Pillows' will be a man down!"

"I was just wondering that," bubbled Morose into his second vat of Special Brew, "Is there any chance he might have been murdered? Just to make my presence worthwhile?"

"Er…."

"Excellent, cos I think he was killed. Bloke comes up to Oxford for a dullards cricket reunion, carks it, and sleeps with a point – five chain gun under his pillow."

There was a scream from Mrs Doom, as her forgotten cigar burned through her lips.

Roly ignored her. "Do you have any suspects?"

"Eleven. The whole team."

Roly went a bit white. "Ten, surely?"

Morose chewed his napkin. "Eleven. I'm including you."

"Oh, how exciting!" exclaimed Roly, "But this won't stop "The Pillows" from playing their match, tomorrow?"

*****

It had started out as a beautiful day at 97 Trilby Avenue. The Sun had put in an appearance, Robbie had told the paperboy yet again he didn't want that filth delivered through his letterbox. Then as dawn broke on a scorcher of a day, Claudia seemed to have temporarily forgotten their dazzle ship painted house. Thus, the tins of paint stayed in the shed, while Emily made her famous French toast; Jessica then scraped it out of the pan, and fetched the extinguisher. Claudia had a very therapeutic cry, before pouring out bowls of cornflakes for five.

Yes, five.

No, Mr Chopper had not taken up a Kellogg's inspired diet.

No, in fact Jessica had, on her way to the bin with the scrapings, found a visitor, a very smelly visitor.

"Never made it home last night, Robbie. I was looking into a death, well, murder hopefully, at the golf club…"

Harris went pale, "The golf club, Surr?"

"No, do try to listen, you knob! I said the cricket club. Well, not actually the cricket club, but you know, one of their Johnnies. Bloke I got wrecked with the other night, he's stopped breathing. Anyway on my way back I was thinking of all the people I know who owe me a favour. And a bottle of Jack Daniels I briefly knew very well suggested I speak to you."

"And did you?"

"No. Jack found your house ok, and even volunteered to throw himself through your bedroom window, but you slept right through it."

"We didn't hear anything, Surr?"

"No, well it turned out Cleveleys Road looks very like yours in the dark. Apart from all the broken glass. Don't you worry, I gave Mr Daniels a very stiff talking to. I have no idea what happened after that until young Jester here pulled my head out of my own yak in your bin. Any more of that burnt bread going?"

"Aye probably Surr. Claudia's just preparing wor breakfast now Surr. What do you mean I owe you a favour?"

"Ahhh yes, you love me don't you? Do anything for me in fact. Course you would, why wouldn't you?"

27

"Surr... I..."

"Don't get all sentimental Robbie lad, just go and get your cricket uniform or whatever it's called. You're playing in a couple of hours. Oooh! Tell Mrs Geordie-pig not too much sauce on my fry up. I hate spicey yak."

"Aye Surr, too much sauce already."

Morose bit into a cut off piece of bin. "I suppose you're wondering why I'm here?"

"Not really, you were off your face weren't you?"

"Well yes, but also, you're back on the job."

Harris blinked in disbelief. "You've stopped my holidays?"

Morose gave a particularly violent sneer. "Yes. I don't see why you should have a great time with your missus if I can't."

"You utter ......you fuckin'....... You..... you....."

"Robbie, you whingebag! Just think, you'll be out of re-painting this bloody awful house you live in!"

He ducked to avoid a flying coal scuttle, and then ran like fuck to avoid the whole family.

*****

Breakfast eaten and Claudia's cricket stump removed, Morose made his way to see Mrs Doom. An enticing prospect! He made sure that he'd make a good impression, he had his clean sock on, his shirt was freshly sponged (off a tramp), and he was wearing his best cologne. Harris' words still rang true, though..... a pair of trousers would be advisable....

He pulled up outside Mrs Doom's; and after again being let off with a caution by some career minded piglet, who he pushed under a truck for her efforts, he made his way back out of the hedge and up to Mrs Doom's front door. He knocked firmly on the bell.

"Hello," she breathed.

"Wibble" said Morose. He was back on familiar ground.

He took in the house, he took in the hallway, he took in the kitchen, and finally he took in his trousers. As she poured him a fresh mug of steaming water, he asked,

"So, was it you?"

She looked blankly back at him. "Was what me?"

"Killed your husband?"

"No!"

"Good, I'll stay a bit longer then. Did your husband have a vast number of enemies?"

"No..... I can't imagine who'd want him dead. No work problems, no money problems, he was fuckin' minted, no vengeful criminals cos he worked in patent law, not anything interesting."

"Bit of a boring turd, then?"

"Aye, maybe a bit more."

"Was he jealous because of your radio show success?"

"Only for the extra drugs and sex I get."

"Any idea about the gun?"

"No. He preferred flamethrowers."

There was a pause, as Morose choked on his drink.

"What the fuck is this mongoose piss? I can't get trolleyed on this!"

She smiled. She liked him. "He had the key to the drinks cabinet Inspector. I'm afraid it's all I can offer you."

He looked horrified. "Mrs Doom, I will make it my personal mission to solve this dreadful crime. All of Oxford Police will be prioritising your sorrowful situation. And if there's time we'll look into who knacked your husband too. Now before I go off to Threshers, he was quoting some hippy Buddhist crap about peace and being nice and other gayness, any ideas?"

"He got that from one of my books.... Is it important?"

"I don't know. It's likely to be shit anyway. I use anything for clues. I spend a lot of time stumbling around looking for clues...... usually off my face....."

She was still smiling. He thought about it. Then he thought about something else.

"Anyway, fuck this for a lark, the pubs open in an hour and I'm camping outside one." He put what passed for his coat back on, and stopped. "Simple lock on the drinks cabinet is it, or is it a proper lock with trip wires and tear gas, like my supervisor... and my sergeant... have both had installed... with retina and fingerprint scanners?"

"Just," she thought about it, "just a simple key job... I think, my husband dealt with it more than me."

"It just goes to show you, you need to plan for these moments. You always need to ask yourself if my husband throws his cards in, will I be able to get at the giggle sauce? Now, important question, before I arrange to come back with some safe blagging tools, I know a former Blue Peter presenter, he'll have some, I'm not going to open this happy piece of furniture and find it empty am I?"

She smiled, "Stuffed to the gills, man. You've won the lottery here!"

Morose left a trail of drool as he walked out of the window, well, there's another repair bill she thought, as she swept up the shards of glass.

*****

Meanwhile, that snivelling northern nancy boy loser, Robbie Harris, was quickly learning the new role that Morose had assigned for him. The college cricket team had been planning on using the college porter, Mr Baker, as one of their attack bowlers. Now Baker was rapidly showing Harris the ropes as a porter while he was 'inexplicably away on urgent business', actually ducking out of the way while Harris got a place in the cricket team to have a snoop about, make an amazing discovery, and solve the case! Well, that was the theory, anyway, thought Morose, just watch the little prick mess it up and announce himself as an undercover cop on his facebook page, or some limp shit like that.

Already Harris had learned how to pass keys through the slit, he'd learned that off a page on the dark net. Also he'd learned which person wanted their room key, and where they all were. This was fun, being Mr Baker the porter; and he wondered how Mr Porter was getting on as a baker, too.

"My keys, please, you peasant pleb," spat a cricket team member. Out of sight, the real porter, Baker, pointed at the right keys, and Harris got them, wiped his knob on them, and with a lower middle class smile of hate, handed them to the visitor.

"Piece of piss, isn't it," grinned Baker.

"Do y' get many toffee nosed rats like him?" asked Harris.

"All the time," grinned Baker.

"No nice people?" asked Harris.

"Sometimes," grinned Baker, "Here's one now."

"Ah, Mr Scum, you're the new chap we patronise, aren't you? Don't worry, it's just a bit of laddish ragging. My keys please, tosser, I've left mine in my room, you Commie plonker."

"Aye man," snarled Harris.

"Oh, and any mail for me?"

"Any name, sir?"

"Yes, Carling."

"No."

"Okay, wizard, I'll bring these spares back when I've got my own back."

As he slithered away, Baker grinned, "See? They're all different grades of privileged cockheads."

"Aye, man, who was he? Shifty looking muck, if you ask me."

"Claims to just be a visitor, who's taken rooms with his wife," grinned Baker.

"Claims?"

"I'm not sure she is, maybe you should do a bit of detective work, you know, like you pigs do?"

"Aye, I needed a dump anyway, I'll follow him and if he asks, claim I'm off to drop a log."

"Good idea," grinned Baker.

Harris looked straight at him. "And stop fucking grinning, you dozy freak."

"Ah, sorry," said Baker with a smile.

Harris, unable to take any more, shut the porter's lodge with Baker's hand in it, and followed the strange man.

He followed Carling to the room Carling was staying at, and then almost at once, was back to following him as Carling crept upstairs to the room of another cricket team member. Good God, he was going to Roland's room! The utter wank stain!

He crept back to the porter's office and, releasing Baker's crushed hand from the door, re – opened the window as a new visitor arrived.

"Ahhhh, Baker baby, how's it hanging, you useless ape muncher?"

"Fuck off Surr," he replied to the alcohol stained voice of Morose.

"Yes, be that as it may… keys please, Baker did we say?"

"Aye Surr, Baker. Which keys did you want?"

"Which room houses the girl with the biggest tits, or maybe has the best non water supply?"

"I think you want Mrs Carling's room Surr."

"Is she stacked is she?"

"No Surr, but I think you'll be interested anyway," he winked conspiratorially at Morose.

"Don't wink at me homosexually" spluttered Morose. "I've told you about that before, Sergeant Harris."

"No man, it's Porter not Sergeant Robbie Harris, I've no idea who he is, man!"

"Oh right, I forgot," Morose tapped his nose knowingly, "for the benefit of these gentlemen queuing up here, I'll call you Porter, Harris. Now, don't forget when you get back to Oxford sty put in an overtime form. Gentlemen, you'll remind him won't you? His badge number is 75390 in case he gets lost. Sergeant Robert Harris. But keep it dark eh gents, he's undercover. Scouts honour and all that knobrot. That alright for you Robbie?"

"Aye sir, I think my cover's been blown harder than JFK's knob by Marilyn Monroe."

Undeterred, Morose made his way to the rooms of the

mysterious Mr Carling, and his well stacked wife.

Morose's voice rose from his usual low pitched growl, to comprehensible words, like a vulture pulled out of a storm drain.

"Mrs Carling?"

"Who is it?"

"My name is Morose."

"We can still be friends."

"I'm with the Oxford and District Police."

"Maybe not, then."

"I'm investigating a murder, can we have a chat?"

"Gosh, a real live murder, how can I help?"

"Was it you?"

"Of course it wasn't, you tosser!"

"That's another line of enquiry fucked, then. About your husband, then."

"Is he dead?"

"No, but I've been checking names and reasons for visiting the college, and I was wondering if we could have a chat."

"You seem to do a lot of chatting, inspector."

"Yes, it's what comes of being a nosy wanker. Your phone number in London?"

"What about it?"

"Is it still the same?"

"Is it still the same as what?"

"Is it still the same as you wrote in the visitors' book?"

"Unless we've been disconnected?"

"Sour Hill 344 142?"

"No, that's Pammy the Prostitute's Pimp Line."

"You know her?"

"Is this really important?"

"No. You look worried, Mrs Carling."

"Inspector, you guess too much."

"It's my line of work, makes you nervous?"

"No, it's just I've not opened the door to you, yet."

Morose looked stunned at the door.

"Confound it, I'll get you for this, you slag."

"Go away or I'll call the pigs."

"I *am* the pigs. By the way," he continued, "If you're seriously here for the cricket, you'll be at the game, tomorrow?"

"Yes, and you'd better be good at your cricket knowledge, or you'll be answering questions – to your boss! So huge dog's cock to you!"

Realising he'd met his match, Morose pissed through the keyhole and stumbled off, catching his knob on the stair bannister.

Meanwhile back in the room, Mr Carling emerged from the wardrobe.

"Well done," he said with a stern look at the door.

"Thanks," said the door.

*****

Robbie, still acting the part of Baker the porter, was about to make his way home, when his phone rang.

"Aye man, what?"

"Robbie, it's Hugh down the station," came the voice of Sergeant Jampton, "While you're playing cricket an' that, we've had a report of a possible break in at the cricket club. Since you're down there, I was just wonderin….."

"Haddaway an' shite man, I'm tryin' to get home fer mah tea an that!"

"It's only a little break in."

Harris sighed. "Aye man, I'll take a peek on me way like."

He drove the new Triumph Mayflower that he'd been so lavishly equipped with, to the cricket club, and took a quick look to see if anyone was about. No. No signs of forced entry. No window open. No door open, no wall missing. Roof still on. And most important, no one could see him, either? He had a quick slash and was about to return to his car, when he spotted a shadow move in the locker room.

"Aw well that's just cannae grand!" he muttered to himself.

Quietly getting through a low window by kicking the shit out of it, he crept in to take a closer look. Nothing moved. He moved toward the door to check it, and just didn't see the axe handle descend on him. He saw the fog and felt his legs give. Then he saw nothing til Jampton found him, a few hours later.

*****

As the team, nicknamed 'The Pillow Boys', prepared for the cricket match that absolutely no one dared to care about, so one player shouted above all the jolly banter,

"Hoy! What clap hangar has been going through my locker?"

Harris looked up, "What was in the locker, Surr?" He felt the huge lump on his head, and tried to ignore it.

"Some vital stuff I'd rather not discuss. Was it you? You've been acting all strange lately, Baker!"

"No!" Harris cried his innocence.

"That's a nasty bump you've had, looks just like a locker door hit it!"

"Well it didn't. My wife was up on ramps and I said a wrong thing. Just as well that new plate in me head was there, Hahaha."

"I think you're some grassing rat of a cop, spying on us."

"Aw come on man! But out of interest sir, what appears to be missing from said locker?"

"Some very high quality bus porn, some top notch Cockney hard core filth, and some Illegal strength Dutch weed. Oh yes, and some very good quality potcheen."

"I'll have a look around Surr, but it's probably gone by now."

"You'll do no such thing, Baker. Get into your cricket uniform, or whatever us tossers call it," snapped Roly, "We've got a game to win! Come on the pillows!"

"I want to know who's knacked my locker!"

"Oh stow it, we've got a match to win!" yelled Jamie, Roly's nephew, "Come on Uncle, don't forget, we may need a bit of help with the pitch!"

Roly frowned, "I can't show you any bias, my position as umpire is one of trust, and the same goes for our opponents from Exeter St Slob's."

"Boo! St Slobs are brats and spoiled plebs!"

"They're known as 'The Curtains' cos they're always trying to kill off their opposition!" laughed Jamie, then, as a sudden hush descended upon the room, added quickly, "Oh, er, sorry, I didn't mean.....I mean, after the death of.....oh, ignore me....sorry guys."

"Aye, never mind man," consoled Robbie, "I've slipped up a few times like that recent."

"You certainly have, telling us you're a porter AND a copper," laughed almost everyone.

Harris, aka Baker, smiled through freshly gritted teeth, and joined the general rush out of the door and onto the pitch.

Outside, there was an enthusiastic crowd, alternately calling out

"Come on, the Pillows!"

And "Come on the Curtains!"

Somewhere, someone really needed to think these names out afresh.

*****

Morose sat on a deckchair in the early afternoon sun, his face hidden behind some quite superior Bus Freak Monthly magazines, and smoking a very pleasant roll-up, while the ice clinked in the freshly topped up glass at his feet.

He was beginning to nod off, the opening of a dream about young Dennis, the star of page 17 of the periodical, when his slumber was disturbed by a ripple of applause from the spectators. Automatically, Endof reached to check his flies, no problem there, he could feel the nesting crow behind, who gave him a playful peck and coughed up a worm. Happy that everything was in place, and the cage was closed, he turned to see what was happening.

There was that muppet of a sergeant, Harris. What was the stupid fucker doing? He was supposed to be in work. Morose would see to it that he got a roasting for this!

"Come on Robbie!" he shouted, just to let him know he'd been seen.

A half brick bounced off the end of Morose's nose as Roly shouted, "No Sir! We can "Come on The Curtains", we can "Come on The Pillows", but we do not "Come on Robbie", it's simply not cricket."

"Aye Surr," shouted Robbie, as he continued to follow his team on to the pitch, "Whoever this Robbie fellow is!"

Morose was aghast. Obviously poor Robbie had been hurt worse than Morose had thought when he decided to investigate that locker. Poor chap had concussion, couldn't even remember his own name.

Now, what had that moose at the hospital told him? Best cure for concussion is another blow to the head. Like a factory reset. Yes, he was sure that was right. The trouble was, he mustn't embarrass the poor lad by drawing attention. Best thing, just hurl some bricks back at him until one connects. Shame to leave the good stuff though. He necked the last of the hooch, and with the huge joint still sticking of his mouth, he found an ideal hiding place and threw his first brick.

Harris instinctively caught it, not quite a textbook catch and it did dislodge his two front teeth, but he'd learned the basics quickly.

"Get up!" hissed Roly, "We can't afford any more missing players, we've no twelfth man as it is!"

Groggily Harris rose and as his vision cleared, so he realised The Pillows were supposed to be batting anyway, and made his way to the bench. The bench furthest from Morose.

Morose meantime had met up with Mrs Carling, and taking a quick drag herself, she settled down next to him.

"I didn't know you like cricket, inspector?"

"I don't. It's cack. But I'm here for the piss up and free food after."

"Oh come on, inspector, it's like war, but without guns! It's really exciting?"

"Perhaps you could talk me through it, then , as battle commences? Er, 'ang on a second, this weed is stronger than I thought, won't be a mo….."

There was the usual Liz Hurley session and a few gasps of pain as his lungs ruptured, but aside from the sudden invasion of flies, no one seemed to have noticed his little slip up.

Mrs Carling looked sternly at him.

"If you don't mind me saying so, inspector, that doesn't half ruddy well honk, shall I spread some Vosene on it?"

Morose's crow came to the rescue and offered its own sachet of Harmony Hairspray. Morose accepted the gift and hoofed the little fucker out of the park.

Mrs Carling took another drag of Morose's spliff, and once her vision had returned, and the sensations had returned to her body, she took Morose's hands off her, and explained the rules of cricket, as the match proceeded.

"Now there are two teams, obviously; one goes out in the field to be in, and the side which isn't in, goes out in the field. The men of the in side, they go out to be in, and stay out til they are out, then they go back in the pavilion. The side which isn't in, get each of the side which is in, out."

"…And that's when DPD try to make a delivery, when everyone's out?"

"Well, sort of. When the side who are in are all out, the side out in the field then take their turn at going in, til they are all out also." She broke off for a huge fart. Morose replied in good measure, so much so that the ground subsided.

"Hmmm, I think I see, now, what about the offside

rule?"

She sighed, "That only applies if the pink is on the blue spot. You really are a thick Jeremy, aren't you? Anyway, when both sides have been in and out…."

"Do they shake it all about?"

"…..and you count up their runs and include the no balls and not outs, they all go off and get utterly wankered, and no one cares who won!"

Morose looked at her in disbelief. "I'm going home now."

"Wait, you can't go yet, two of Roly's team have already been dismissed, and your sergeant who isn't really a copper at all, that pig, is going in, to bat! Come on, the Pillows! Come on Robbie!"

Morose tried to leave but his belt had been cunningly wrapped around his deck chair. It was too much. He managed to grab someone else's pint, and settled back to watch the utter lack of drama unfolding.

Harris, meanwhile, was about to face his first ball. Roly, umpire at the bowler's end, welcomed Robbie,

"Welcome to the crease. The bowler will be coming over the wicket."

"The filthy swine, and with all these pigs here too."

"Would you like your guard setting?"

"Aye man, that's cannae grand man."

"Middle…..that's leg side….."

"Aye man, aye man…."

"A touch to leg…… you've got it."

"Aye man. By the way, which direction is the bowler coming from?"

"Play."

There was a man in the distance with a ball. Harris wasn't sure, but he did seem to be rather large. He certainly was far away, but less so now, as with a bellow of vengeance, the bowler – for it was he – began his run up. Spittle frothed from his mouth and steam flew from his ears, as turf flew up from his run in, and a dog in the pavilion had a nosebleed.

Harris tried to shelter behind his bat, but it was no good. With the sound of an impending express train arriving, the bowler drew alongside Roly and a small planet was dislodged from his hands. The ball – for thus it was – approached like an airborne missile. Harris raised his bat and ducked his body, there was a horrible crunching sound, and the ball flew to the boundary at double the speed it had been delivered at.

Shaking all over, Harris smiled as the ball decapitated a fielder and rolled over the boundary rope for four runs.

"Jolly good shot!" came a few derisory cries, and a ripple of applause echoed around the ground.

"Aye well, thanks, lads!" smiled Harris, "I'll be off for mah tea, then."

"Stand your ground!" hollered Roly, "Next delivery coming up."

"You mean I've got to go through that again?" Harris paled white.

The bowler, halfway down the pitch, glared at him. Static electric played around his horns.

""YOU," he vomited, "Are fucking dead."

He stalked away with his stalk, as the sunlight reflected off the ring through his nose.

A safe distance away reached, but only for a second, he turned, hooves pawing the grass.

"Actually," Morose said to Mrs Carling, "This is all very

interesting. Do you think that bowler will actually kill my sergeant? He's got a great career with me if he does!"

"Play!" called Roly.

The earth shook and the pavilion tilted a few degrees. Flames spat out from the bowler's nostrils, matches burned in his beard, and the forked part of his tongue lolled around, picking up worms as it went.

"Haaaaagggh!" he ventilated, as the ball hit the ground halfway down the pitch, rose up as a really vicious bouncer, hit Robbie in the forehead, and knocked him clean out.

"Fuckin' ace!" Morose was on his feet applauding.

The bowler continued his run and stopped only when he'd jumped up and down on Robbie's head a few times. The ball trickled into the stumps and a single bail fell off.

"Out," noted Roly. "Though I must warn you, bowler, about your sledging."

"Suck me knob," replied the bowler.

Robbie's nose bled lightly on the ground, the bowler, trying to mask his violence, breathed heavily on the red stained grass.

"Offside!" Screamed Morose, "I can clearly see pink on the blew spot!"

At the far end of the pavilion a shape shimmered into existence, ripping a hole in the fabric of the ground to make way for him. The shape settled itself into the now familiar, but none the less displeasing manifestation, of Colin Weird. Weird slowly turned his head to the left and watched, fascinated as a second apparition moved slowly into reality alongside him. The second figure, once fully corporeal revealed itself to be a projection of a female, a female that had clearly known times of darkness and destruction. The many cuts and tears to her body exposing pink, rotting flesh underneath spoke of tragedy and endless suffering. She raised an arm towards the wicket, and poked what was left of her rat gnawed index finger, towards the bowler. The finger once pointing now beckoned.

The bowler looked around at Roly's awestruck face, "Me mam says I've got to go in for me tea."

"That's okay," replied Roly, "That's your over finished. See you later if you're playing out?"

Back on the grass, the match continued, and back amongst the spectators, a new development was occurring. Fresh from her radio show, Mrs Doom, trying to make a play for Morose, came face to face with Mrs Carling. Morose looked at one, then the other. They both glared at each other. Impasse.

As Harris was stretchered past, groaning quietly, Mrs Doom said, "Bitch."

"Slut," came back the reply.

"I'm glad you know each other," Morose smiled weakly, like a Chris Trauma stuck between two mistresses, again. "Mrs, er, Thing here, was just explaining. The rules of engagement. You see," he offered to Mrs Doom.

There was a smattering of applause as another batsman was carried off unconscious.

"Yes," sighed Mrs Doom, through gritted teeth.

"Why don't you join us?" Mrs Carling asked sweetly, adding, "Spunk bucket."

"No thank you," replied Mrs Doom, "I never park near a bike."

"Shall I keep score?" asked Morose weakly.

"It's okay, you were just leaving to do that, weren't you, Mrs Trollop?" To emphasise the point, she yockered one out, "Pick the bones out of that on your way, moose."

"Do it yourself, you're the main scrubber here, whore," came the reply.

"Slag" they both said together.

Mrs Doom waddled out of the ground and went over to Morose's Heinkel, stifled a sob, muttered "I was only hoping......" and hit her hand on the side panel. The little car fell over, disgorging a flight of spare crows.

Back at the match, Mrs Carling was starting the crowd in a chorus of "We are the Barmy Boys", to the confusion of the Japanese tourists who made up most of the crowd, as all the English males busy watching the Sumo Wrestling on Channel number nine. The last wicket fell and with a respectable score of 110, two hurt and one missing in action, The Pillow Boys made their way out into the field, as The Curtains came in to go out. Morose had decided to lay on some "half time entertainment", and, suitably tanked up, had gone off on a quick streak across the pitch, but caught his arse on the wicket and in some pain, was helped off by a pair of Health & Safety officials, who made a note to shut the whole game down in case of further arse catching.

The Curtain Men's opening pair got off to a fast start, but the park warden caught them both, and they returned abashed to play their innings. A couple of boundaries in the opening over saw them settle in, in fact they got so comfortable on the pitch, that they broke open a can of Trolls Cider and threw it at the piss awful opening bowler.

Then a change in the bowling.

"Mr Baker, one bouncer an over, no over stepping the mark, and no running down the wicket, please."

Harris gave the umpire his sunglasses, pullover, cigarette and his warrant card, adding, "Yes, I'm not Sergeant Harris, never heard of him." He took a few paces back, and, pulling the pin out, ran in and bowled. There was a medium explosion and the batsman's shoes stood smouldering in the crease, while the rest of him took out the stumps and several spectators.

"How is heeee?" screamed Harris, raising his finger at the remains of the stumps.

"Out," sighed Roly, "Mr Harris, do l need to warn you about your sledging now?"

Harris smiled, "No man, just thought I'd make an early impression, like."

"Well you probably have made a permanent mark on the batsman."

"Aye man," said Harris, "Should l take a new ball, too, like?"

Morose was rather enjoying the game, a fact he pointed out to Mrs Carling who had ironically fallen asleep with her third bottle of the day.

A few rather more legal deliveries later, and Harris had his second, was told off by the increasingly irate park keeper and also took a wicket. He was about to knock the shit out of The Curtain's vice captain, when suddenly there was a huge, and blood curdling scream from the pavilion.

Robbie looked round to where Morose had been sitting. Remarkably he was still there, "Surr, what have you done, said, or left behind, that caused that scream?"

Morose shrugged his shoulders.

Everyone else looked round. The screams continued as Colin Weird floated out of the pavilion.

"Ooh, that caught me by surprise, matey's. It seems a bit redundant while Sergeant… sorry not Sergeant Baker is killing people at the stumps, but there's another dead body in here. Does it belong to anyone?"

Morose staggered up, "Until the real filth arrive, I'm

taking control of this." He reached for a particularly powerful looking unopened bottle of Geordie Strength Vodka on the pavilion table, "And while I'm here I'll have a go at this new murder too."

He marched into the pavilion, Harris just behind. They were confronted by the grim sight of Mr Carling, flat on his back, with a pair of scissors pinned right through him, holding him to the floor.

"Fucking Hell," muttered Morose, "Just as me Vodka's run out, too, the Carling's gone!"

"Shit," muttered Harris, "I'll stop Mrs Carling coming into the room."

"Good idea, Harris."

"I'll stop everyone else too, I'll get them into the 'Away' changing rooms and we can get to work at once, sir."

"Great idea, Harris."

Harris went to leave and get a few Scene of Crime types up, but stopped, turned round, and went up to Morose.

"And, er, sir…"

"Yes, Harris?"

"I'll get your clothes for you, too."

*****

"Everyone's either ootside, or next door man, er Surr" over geordied Robbie.

"Is Max going to want to have a look at this fellow?" Morose pondered.

"Probably not Surr, but it's his job."

"If he turns up keep him busy, keep hiding the body when his back's turned, or kick it halfway across the room while he's examining it."

47

"Fer God's sake Surr, why?"

"Some of that Swiss fellow's Macallan never turned up. I bet it's in the boot of Max's car. I'm going to crow bar it open."

"You don't have a crow bar, Surr" Robbie stated.

"No, that's true. But I do have several very enthusiastic crows in my trousers."

"You can fuck right off," snarled Max from behind the lockers, "I got here early before the murder, and parked up far enough away to stop you breaking into my car."

Morose slid over to Max with that annoying sneer on his face, "And where have you parked, you fucking buffoon, so that I can't get to it?"

"Wolverhampton, I had to get a train in," Max sneered back, "What a bastard having to stuff a corpse in the bogs to avoid paying for the extra train seat."

"Most commendable that you got here before the murder, then," Morose said, "I'd like to see them do this bit on television."

Robbie scratched Max's knob. "Hang on Surr, what body? You've only just got here, and the body's doon there."

"Not that body, and leave my knob alone. Remember the Moyes case, I was having another look at that."

"I was only giving it a pull to test it didn't fall off the front of the suitcase," whined Harris, clearly not gay in any way whatsoever.

"Anyway, who's the stiff?" asked Max.

"Well not any of us, obviously," muttered Robbie.

"Mrs Carling's husband," said Morose.

Mrs Carling put her head round the door, unusual as the door was closed at the time. "You'll be wanting to interview me, inspector?"

"Oh yes," said Morose, "What did you do with all the booze, eh?"

Mrs Carling sat down on Max's suitcase knob. "Look, you hopeless turd, you may as well have the truth."

"About time too! Robbie, make some notes."

Robbie got a piece of chalk and scrawled all over the walls.

"You see, inspector, Mr Carling isn't my husband."

"Is he your wife?"

"No."

"Your French poodle?"

"No."

"Your pet Stegosaur?"

"Sir," interrupted Harris, "That's two sides of the gallows and the noose drawn, you've not got many guesses left."

"We're Customs & Excise police."

"Fuck me, the coastal pigs!" screamed Morose and ran into the nearest locker, slammed the door, and the whole lot fell over.

Max, having been dragged away from kicking the shit out of the locker, stood it upright and the locker too, and dragged Morose out of the air vent. He dragged him by the dick back to the chalked interview, sat him down, and had to be dragged away again by Harris, as he screamed, "I didn't take your fucking booze!"

"You see, " continued Mrs Carling, "We're on the track of one of the cricket team, who's been using the cover of the team as a means of smuggling narcotics, Macallan, a donkey or two, and we think several stuffed alligators."

Morose raised a quizzical. "Why are they smuggling stuffed alligators? "

Now it was Mrs Carling's turn to see her arse, "Oh come on, inspector, why does anyone smuggle alligators? Anyway, the smuggling fits the pattern of the cricket tour exactly."

"Where exactly are they going on to next?"

"A one day international in Amsterdam."

Harris spoke up, "Aye, that's fuckin great, I'll be able to play in the ODIs after all!"

The rest of the teams trooped in.

"Look, can we go? We were all on the pitch, we can't have done anything," sighed Roly's nephew.

Morose looked them in the eye, not easy when there were 23 of them.

"Oh really?"

"Oh come on old bean," piped up Roly, "Surely the tour can go on? It can't have been any of us done him in."

Morose pondered, "Really I need to run it past my superior. Has anyone seen Superintendent Weird?"

Roly had a slightly puzzled look on his face, "Yes, one of the chaps said he was outside, practicing his bowling. The poor fellow made a dash for the toilet after that, haven't seen him since."

"What, *exactly*, did he say?"

"Just that he was outside practicing floating."

Morose drew a deep breath, "Okay, you can travel as planned," he said, "But that means all of you, my sergeant, who isn't really a piglet, will have to go with you."

Roly beamed, "That's the spirit, 'Plague', old chap!"

Everyone made a rush for the door and the lockers, knocking Morose over again. The door slammed shut. Morose stood up. The door was flung back open, flattening him again.

"And thanks, old bean, I've got some shit hot stuff to get through customs, couldn't have done it without you! We'll all be on the Dover steamer tomorrow!!"

Morose looked at Customs officer Carling.

"Anyway, we've got to find this smuggler."

"Yes," she sighed, "He's covering his tracks well, whoever he is."

Harris and Max concurred with a "H'mm" apiece.

It was promising to be an interesting trip to the coast.

*****

Morose stood at Kate Doom's door with a couple of armfuls of flowers, which he'd taken from a nearby accident hotspot. Using his teeth, he managed to knock at the door. She opened it at once, leaving his dentures on the door knocker.

"Yes?" she asked, glaring at him.

"I'b cub to gib you dizz," he managed to say.

"Come in, loser," she replied, taking the opportunity to remove his teeth from the door, and ram them back halfway down his throat.

They sat in slightly strained silence, til Morose loosed one off.

"Look, I'm sorry Morose, but I didn't expect to see you with that tart, at the match."

"Which tart did you expect?"

"None. Just you and me. That SLAG wrecked my plans."

"I'd only met her the day before, she was talking me through staying awake at the cricket."

"I thought she was trying to get you."

Morose changed the subject. "Have you got a vase for these? They'll need water."

She went to get a vase. He cast a look at her bookshelf, and his eyes lit on a little book of Buddhist quotes. Intrigued, he crept over, and opened it. The writing inside. An address from a lover? A thousand kisses til we meet on the Dover steamer? What?

She returned with a tall vase, and Morose put his teeth in with a sterile tablet.

She put the flowers in, on top of them.

"Phuck my wuck" muttered Morose.

But at last, he had a clue.

*****

Harris was bored already. He had just finished an article in the BBC History Magazine, in which they discussed the first text message sent by Alexander Graham Bell, telling his assistant to "Will U ansa the bstd phone cos it keeps going to v/mail, angry face pending".

All the bits of the crime puzzle fitted together. Obviously the shifty looking chap from the cricket team was smuggling the drugs and the alligators. Anthony doom had electrocuted himself with his microwave and his poor DJ wife was shadowing Morose, cos she fancied him. This all made sense. But where did that shifty looking Geordie, pretending to be a porter fit in? And why couldn't he find Wally in this picture of the Moon? Four eyed wanker. His police radio kept relaying messages to all of Oxford Police, domestic disturbances, a riot in the Swindlestock Tavern in Carfax - a bit delayed that message - and a large number of turds left on parked police cars in the Woodstock area. It was becoming increasingly difficult to get anyone to believe he wasn't a police officer.

He looked behind the bus, at the rest of the team pushing it.

"Don't worry lads, one big effort and we'll get to the crest of the hill that overlooks Dover, put ya backs into it!"

"Fuck off!" came the unanimous reply.

Morose followed behind in the squad car with that pair of gormless muppets, White and Gonemad. Not bad going for the poor little Austin Ruby, it had been powered by Morose's booze most of the way, as the petrol had run out just outside Milton Keynes, having been syphoned off earlier by, er, Morose, once he had finished off the minibus's diesel on draught.

"Come on Roly man Surr, give it a good push," urged Harris

Roly looked down at his own four wheels, "I don't know if you've noticed Sergeant, I'm at a bit of a disadvantage here. Possibly we could freeze the road and slide down."

"No sledging Surr."

As the bus made the brow of the hill and Dover lay ahead of them, it began to accelerate. The rear platform vehicle was easy for most of the team to reboard, poor Roly struggled however and ended up stranded in the middle of the road watching as the aging bus accelerated away from him.

In all, seventeen vehicles were involved in the pile up of traffic attempting not to put Roly in orbit and from behind the jenga of vehicles a small Austin Ruby, treating the collision as a roundabout, steered carefully through – one of White's better pieces of driving.

"Oi fuckwit! Get off the fucking road, you're going to cause an accident if you're not careful," screamed a passing nun on a steamroller.

Morose head-butted a paramedic who was paying far too much attention, and turned back to Roly. "If we stash your wheels on the roof, you can come with us, better yet, put you and your wheels on the roof, that way I don't have to move my crisps off the passenger seat."

"We've ran out of fuel Sir!" White reminded Morose.

"Ahh, I might be able to help you there," exclaimed Roly, "There's a secret compartment, in the back of my wheelchair, there's a couple of gallon of unleaded in there, under the drugs, help yourselves."

"Fucking marvellous!" beamed Morose, "We might get there on time now."

"Where exactly?" asked Roly, unclipping the back of his chair.

"There's some fucking drug dealer on the bus, we're going to nick him at Dover. Bastard doesn't suspect a thing."

"Whizzo!" cried Roly.

The coach managed to drag itself to the Dover Steamer Terminal, and the passengers piled onto the coach, got their baggage, and piled off again. Harris took Roly off the roof of the Austin Ruby, which now had a permanent indentation in the cloth roof, from Roly's wheelchair.

"Thanks chaps!" beamed Roly, "I've been touching cloth there for far too long!"

"Aye man, now then, we've just got to get you on the Steamer, and ya can shat the whole lot out."

"Be a close thing, I don't want my drugs cushion filled with my own dung."

Harris wheeled him toward the Terminal Room. He just had time to say a passing "Hi!" to Mrs Doom, and wonder how she got there, when suddenly a horrible thought struck him.

"Surr!" he bellowed at Morose, who had just taken up position to see the party off with a prolonged mooning and cock – waving session.

"Fuckin' what?" Morose bellowed back.

"It's him!"

"Harris, you freak, what, is who?"

"Whom, you uneducated knobhead, and it's HIM!"

"WHO?"

Roly had got to his feet to avoid a trouser embarrassment, when he suddenly realised his cushion was in fact stuck to his arse. Underneath the stuck cushion were two alligators, clinging on for dear life. Morose stepped forward, and, glaring at Roly, took a big package out of the hole for the cushion, labelled "NEDERLANDER SMAKKEN".

Morose was going almost dark red in the face.

"It's been you all along!"

Roly tried to make a run for it and promptly fell over. His nephew stepped forward to pick him up, and Kate Doom stepped forward to pick Vince up.

"Well, here's a pretty pickle!" gasped a totally bewildered Morose.

"She is NOT pretty," retorted Customs Official Mrs Carling, "She's a SLAAAG. I did tell you."

*****

As they sat in the public bar looking out across the howling hurricane that had blown up, sinking the cross channel ferry, Harris relaxed his grip on Morose's throat, and asked,

"So when did you begin to suspect, well, any of this?"

Morose drained Robbie's pint. "I've learnt Robbie, never to suspect anyone. No, that's not right, suspect everyone, that's it, that's better. You're on empty Robbie, fill 'em up. No, it all came as a bit of a shock. I just thought he was one of those benefit scroungers the Tories keep telling us about. You know, gets his smack on the NHS."

"It's always the ones you least suspect Surr."

"Roly has been smuggling alligators to the Netherlands for almost a decade. The drugs were an after-thought."

"But where does his nephew come in?"

"Yes, shifty little turd, isn't he? He made the mistake of doing in Anthony Doom, on Kate Dooms' orders after Anthony had stumbled across the drugs on the team coach, coming to Oxford. Anthony had been threatening to leave her cos of all the stars she took liberties with, in her job as a DJ, and he'd have taken custody of the kids too, she was never home."

"So if she'd never fancied you as next on her list, we'd have never caught them?"

"Arse bollocks, you snivelling Geordie toad, she only wanted me for the crows."

"Ah, I see," said Harris, not seeing at all. But anything for a quiet life.

*****

Returning to Oxford, Robbie had dropped Morose off at the pill box. Jampton was the only one on duty. Apart from the dumping on police cars and the domestics it had been a quiet day. The riot was supposedly at 13.55 and two constables had arrived quite promptly at 14.03 to find no sign of disturbance, in fact no sign of the pub, just a branch of Santander. Couple of students causing trouble probably.

It was a cold night as Morose pub crawled his way back into town. Passing Oxford Road Sty he noticed a light still on in the reception. The builders working late he thought.

"Hello?" he called, walking up to the new reception

desk. It was bigger than the old desk, Hugh must be putting weight on.

"Closed guv!" shouted a voice from the back, "Not re-opened yet."

The foreman of the works walked through.

Morose waved his very old warrant card at him, "Chief Inspector Morose, you look almost finished?"

The foreman scratched his head, "I'm knackered to tell the truth, guv."

"No, I mean the work, all finished?"

"Oh yeah, just needs a signature really. I was going to ask to see the big boss in the morning. Bit of a funny smell, and some odd laughing coming from the Superintendent's office, but otherwise…"

"No need to bother, I'll sign, just give me the papers."

Within minutes Morose had in his hands on the keys to the new station. A warm new station. A cosy new station… that no-one else knew was finished.

What a great new apartment, and right across the road from Oddbins.

Fucking ace!

CHAPTER TWO - SPOILING IT FOR EVERYONE

Right eye open.
Just the right one.
Start gently.

Left eye open
Ooh too much!
Close right eye first!
Easy... gently does it.

Start again
Both eyes shut
Left ear open.
Swivel ear round, RADAR style

Not hearing any glasses clinking
Or jukebox sounds
Or...

"Ahh, coming round are we sir?"
There was nothing for it, he was going to have to give it another go...
Both eyes open.

Morose looked blearily around the room; he saw bar stools, bar floor, and a bar top that looked chronically free of anything alcoholic.

He casually vomited on a convenient carpet that someone had very kindly displayed on a rack of some kind. Strange interiors some places have, these days.

"I take it you are still open, mine host?" He dabbed his mouth clean with the other chap's lapel.

"Well, yes sir, closing shortly, which is why I thought I'd better get you up…"

"Very good, what do you have on the silly shelf?"

"Silly shelf?

"Yes! Look, if you're near closing I'll need to head back to that awful sty. And there's sweet FA to drink there."

"Sweet…"

"Fuck All! Come on, hit me with something that'll make my kidneys confess to all sorts of crimes."

"Sir, I think you've mistaken…"

"Always guaranteed a good night at The Tap and Sediment. I was only saying to my… my… myself the other day…"

"Sir, The Tap and Sediment has been closed for a few years now."

"Funny, I can normally trust my booze satnav."

"We've been getting a lot of this since TomTom stopped doing automatic updates. This is the site of said pub, but we're a furniture showroom now."

Morose took the room in. It was true. It was bastard true.

"You must have kept some juice back…York!… for old times sake if nothing else?" Morose's puppy dog expression didn't have its usual effect, possibly due to his involuntary hurl, mid-sentence. Quite incredibly 98% of it finished in a convenient toilet.

"Before you carry on Sir, can I advise you that shitter is for display purposes only."

"Yes, I see. Looks a bit more realistic now though, doesn't it?" For some reason the assistant found himself offering up his sleeve for Morose to have a really good clean with.

Morose always enjoyed a shopping trip, he always found someone to help him out of the store, and this was no exception.

"Get the fuck out, and don't come back!"

The kids playground via Victoria Wines, that was what was called for.

*****

In the event Victoria Wines was closed. Morose therefore decided something new was required. He had found a taxi driver who didn't have a picture of Morose in his cab, preferring instead the Pope, and was seemingly happy to take Morose to Oxford Airport.

Having arrived at a point within staggering distance of the flying bus park, and within an ace of the point at which the taxi driver was about to lose his sanity at, the cab pulled to a stop.

"Can you get out now please sir?" requested the taxi driver, who had spent the entire journey being out-offended by his passengers' racist remarks. "That'll be £28.50 please."

"I take it you'll be adding the usual cab cleaning fee?"

"Of course."

"And I will, naturally be playing my warrant card. I will be reporting that you are carrying passengers in an unsafe vehicle."

"Nothing wrong with it!"

Morose had a good look around the inside of the vehicle and watched as the cabby did the same.

"Mr Hackney, as I will now call you, can you honesty say this public service motor, is ready to receive another passenger?"

The cabby shook his head.

Morose stuck out his hand and coughed

"What?" the cabby whined.

"What about my tip?"

"I'll get that scraped off later."

Reluctantly the cabby realised Morose's meaning and passed him a £20 note.

*****

Back at the pillbox, Robbie and Hugh were having a kickaround. It was quite handy being stationed at this out of the way location, no-one seemed to know exactly where the Police Station was anymore, and since all the phone wires had been chewed through by, well, something, it now seemed they were incommunicado. The residents of Oxford were now finding it much easier to solve their own crimes. True, according to the Oxford Gazette, vigilante crimes had risen by exponential numbers, but no-one could say by how much exactly, as no-one could find a Police spokesperson to speak to, or speaks person to spoke to.

Just as Robbie nutmegged White, delivered an inch perfect pass to Jampton, and positioned himself on the edge of the penalty box, a strange thing happened; a phone rang.

"Oh bastard!" tutted Brewis, "You know what this

means? Weird has got us wired up again. Sorry lads."

"Oxford temporary sty, how can I help you?" offered Hugh.

"Hugh," whispered Robbie.

"Not now mate!" said Hugh, returning to his conversation.

"Hugh man," whispered Robbie, more urgently, "the phone's inside, you need to answer it first."

Hugh looked at his empty hand, swore, and plodded inside the pillbox.

"Day one stuff that, man" called Robbie.

*****

Endof had found a comfy place to sit and was necking his seventh of the day. This was absolutely perfect, why had he never thought of this before? Loop Farm Roundabout, he could sit here, and get completely off his face. He reached for another bottle, discarding his last in the vague direction of a double decker bus, negotiating the junction. Somehow, he must have disturbed the fabric of time or something, as his phone chose that moment to start ringing. He checked the screen display, it showed a picture of a camel curling out a length of bad cable. That meant only one thing.

"Robbie baby, how the devil are you?"

"Not now Surr, where are you, and what are you up to?"

"I am just getting trolleyed, found a handy place near the airport."

It was true, his warrant card had gained him the full supply from an Easy Crash passenger fight to Tibet (west) and his newly acquired duty-free trolley was now propped up in the centre of the roundabout, where Morose had made himself very comfy, by fashioning a seat out of an upturned Volkswagen Beetle.

"Aye Surr, well stay there. We're on a case."

"Stay where *you* are! I'm on my third case of champers now!"

"No sir, a criminal case."

"Fuck off, I'm busy."

"We're ganna have to come an' get you....."

"Oh, what a shot, that bus isn't going to Woodstock now! They'll have to get the last one."

"I'm sending White and Franks over."

"For me?"

"No, to protect the traffic, they're a pair of useless pricks who'll get in the way, long enough to get you."

"I'm not going. Hup! Christ, there goes another cyclist. No use pointing at that camera, sonny, your helmet's in the lorry tyre. As are you! Loser!"

"And another thing, sir, please stop chucking stuff at the....."

"I'm going to have to stop you there, Harris, there's....."

"White and Franks will be with you soon...."

"I'm just....."

"Oh fuck sir, there's me other phone......hello? Someone's just bricked your car, Franks?"

"Harris!"

"Sir, some bastard has just thrown a brick at White and Soames' squad car!"

"Oh shut it, listen, when they get here, will you make sure that they bring a fresh supply of bottles of port? I've had to resort to throwing bricks at passing pig cars."

"Sir, you mean you've....."

"'ang on, I've just thrown a cobblestone at a police van."

"That's Brewis, you hopeless turd!"

"And.....just coming into sight......"

"No more please sir!"

"Just this one! It appears to be an army lorry full of nuns! Take that, ya Catholic shite!"

There was a pause.

"Sir?"

"Yes?"

"That army truck full of nuns was a transfer of penguins to Oxford Zoo."

"How do you know?"

"They've just managed to round them up after the mass escape a few stories ago."

"Well they're on their way back to the Isis again!"

Suddenly the line went dead, as did Morose's brain.

They had caught up with him, then.

*****

"So, what's the crime, dog toffee?"

"Good morning, Surr. There's been a murder."

"Have the decency to be Scottish next time you say that. Who has been murdered?"

"Errr, well, a panda man, at the zoo like."

"A panda man?"

"No, I mean a panda, at the zoo, surr. But you're sort of right too."

"If you think I'm cancelling my road trip because a panda's carked it… wait a minute, the zoo you say?"

"Aye man"

"Hmmm. I might be able to make that work, first round's on you though."

"Surr, I'm taking you to a crime scene not a pub."

"Aren't these zoos full of bars then?"

"Only to hold the animals in, man!"

"So! The animals get on the lash more than we do?!"

"No, well aye, maybe! Look man, it's a people panda."

"I am NOT investigating a dead animal. I only investigate dead people. Preferably with a decent stock of booze, or I find that the case goes cold, very quickly."

"The local community police johnnies…."

"Harris, have we got to go through all this again? They are not the local community police, what are they?"

"Well according to you, sir, either 'The plastic pigs', or 'That bunch of job losers', or 'the muck'. "

"Just get it right, you pathetic turd."

"Aye sir, the muck, sir, have put the whole zoo out of bounds…."

"Not much point going, then, is there?"

"…..except to us, as we have been selected to investigate the apparent murder, sir."

Morose couldn't hold it back any longer. After he'd released his massive burst of wind, he shouted,

"This is madness, Harris! I've been asked, even ordered, to investigate the, I can't believe I'm saying this, the murder of a bloody bear?"

"Aye sir. Orders from above, 'an all that."

The air started to get colder.

Morose spat.

"Oh fucking hell. Okay, we're on our way."

*****

As the zoo was closed, Harris climbed out of the car at the gates, and shouted:-

"Ahhh Hellooo! Anybody there?"

Morose crawled over from the passenger seat and rolled the car back about twenty feet.

"It's Oxford Police, man. If anyone is like…" Harris continued while Morose rammed the pedal to the floor and ploughed into the gates. The car still accelerating, hurtled across the empty car park towards the turnstiles. Morose decided this would be an ace moment to test the handbrake on Robbie's vehicle, and, at a speed approaching 80MPH he yanked the handbrake on.

As the car left the ground, Endof considered his own safety, and while it attempted a triple somersault he tried to buckle his seatbelt.

Robbie watched as the car rolled forwards once, twice, three times before hitting the turnstiles and taking them completely out, before it came to rest on its roof; and on the roof of the staff building adjacent to the entrance.

As the noise finished, Robbie became aware of the short, balding man standing next to him.

The man spoke, "Can I help you Sir? Only we are actually closed today. There's been a murder, in a Scottish accent."

"Oxford Police," said Robbie, offering his Oxfam Clubcard, "We're here about the murder."

"Well, you are a little late it's already happened."

"Can we have a look anyway? Just to keep our boss happy."

"Of course, just follow me past the trashed Police car. Will you be taking that with you?"

"Aye man. So where is the stiff, like?"

"Which one?"

"Well the panda, man. Y'kna, the murder like."

"Ahh, that's what you're here for? The deceased is in the snake house, just keeps nosy people at bay."

"Won't the snakes try to eat the body?"

"Sergeant, do you think I'm a complete berk?"

"Nah, ya daft sod! Just mostly."

"Well the snakes I've put him with, are vegetarians."

"Ah, cannae grand that."

As they walked past the ticking, pinging wreckage that had been the police car, so Morose managed to prise open the driver's door, and stepped out, falling 20 foot, and breaking his arse. The zoo man and the sergeant man ignored him, and his yells of pain.

"Nice day for a trip to the zoo, sergeant?"

"Aye man, shame we're here on business, like."

"Would you like a look at the elephant house?"

"Nah, let's get to the deceased one."

They got to the snake house, and Harris knocked. The zoo man laughed.

"Sergeant, they're snakes, they don't have arms or hands to open doors."

"Aye, got their own pass codes, then?"

They went in.

"Now where did I leave that body? Er......"

Harris had a quick look around while the zoo man tried to remember what he'd done with the corpse. This was a shifty looking bunch of snakes, he decided. They all had eyes like Weird, for one. They were mostly asleep, for two. Just lazing around, no effort anywhere. What would the Works and Pensions people say?

"I'm sorry, sergeant, but I seem to have made a bit of a schoolboy error."

"In what way?"

"I've put a schoolboy in the vegetarian snake tank."

"So where did you put the murder victim, ya soft shite?"

"Well I'm not sure, but I think he went into the non-vegetarian snake tank."

They walked to the next display. An extra fat boa constrictor looked guiltily at them.

"Ah shit, too late!" gasped Harris.

"Never mind, he'll pass it out soon enough."

"Aye man, but it'll be in a damaged form! We must have the un-damaged body!"

By the time that Harris had reached his arm down the snake and brought the dead man out again, who thanked him profusely before dying all over again, something occurred to Harris.

"By the way, I thought we were investigating a dead panda? Just a thought like."

"Ah, well. You see, a lot of the zoo animals ran off in that apocalyptical couple of days that mysteriously occurred here in Oxford. Remember? Back in book 2, still available on

Amazon. We had to replace them with people, dressed up as animals."

"Wow, that's great man!"

"It is?"

"Well, yes! You see, we're not really animal murder police, we only investigate people murders, an' shit! Why aye, y'knaa!"

"Well fuck my old boots, sergeant, this is your lucky day!"

"Here, bring that body chap along, I'll go and tell my inspector the good news!"

Harris opened the door to the snake house just as inspector Morose had managed to crawl to the door, getting his fingers run over, with the door, for good measure.

It was turning out to be an interesting day for them both.

*****

Weird hovered over his desk.

"Well?"

"Aye, cannae grand man, thanks for asking!" enthused Harris.

Morose stopped the sergeant with a well-aimed boff.

"I think that the Superintendent, you wank cloth, is asking about our progress."

Harris tried to smile, but his jaw seemed to have locked.

"Aye, well, er, sorry sir, y'see, we've cleared up the missing schoolboy case."

Weird frowned. "He was given to you in the snake tank,

you fucking oaf."

"Aye well, we cleared that one up, eh?"

Weird's eyes pierced the sergeant's soul. "Sergeant, you are boring the arse off me already. Maybe the rank of sergeant doesn't suit you?"

"Ah well, I have passed me exams, like!"

"I mean, as in, 'here lies the body of Sergeant Harris.' If you get my drift."

Morose cleared out another blockage, and spoke.

"I think that what my dickhead of a flunky means, sir, is that we're finding this new case to be a fresh and interesting challenge."

Weird now took time to dribble one out, before asking,

"You mean you have no idea what to do."

The two more humans in the room, looked uneasily at each other.

"Well I wouldn't go that far…." began Morose.

"I would. You are a pair of useless bird turglers. I need results, and I need them soon, or you can both book your coffins now! Pair of gormless pricks."

They spoke together. "Yes sir. Very good, sir."

They both ran like fuck for the exit and slammed the door behind themselves.

"Aye sir, fuck off sir" they said together.

Morose finished off his last drop of fart, before adding,

"Anyway, we need to take a few other pigs with us, get those useless bull milkers Brewis and Collier, they never do fuck all these days."

"Sir, they're working on that really traumatic sausage machine murder at ASDA."

"Ah fuck that off, tell them we need their lack of expertise, come on, we haven't got all day!"

*****

Harris and Morose watched as Collier and Brewis showed up promptly two hours late.

"Where have you pair of trouser snakes been? I'm wasting valuable trolley-offing time here!"

"Sorry sir," offered Collier, "DC Brewis here had to deal with a smashed window case."

Morose went apoplectic. "A smashed window? What the fuck are the C.I.D. doing investigating a smashed window?"

"It was on the front of our car, sir, apparently some drunken tramp wrecked it earlier this morning."

"Ah," said Morose, "Well now you're here, put everything out of bounds and arrest everyone."

"Everything?" asked Brewis.

"Everyone?" asked Collier.

"Yes. I need a bit of quiet, I can't hear myself wank with all these zoo types pissing about."

As the two CID twerps went on their way arresting everyone, so Harris asked,

"By the way, sir, how many animals in this zoo, are actually people dressed up?"

"Er….. well, er, rather a lot of them, Harris."

"Any idea, why? It's all a bit, y'knaa, a bit strange, like, isn't it?"

"Robbie, the way I see it…er….ah. Actually, forget that, I don't actually see it at all."

"WE need a motive," suggested Robbie.

"Got it! My motive is, I'm in need of a few pints, let's use that to fuck off for the day!"

Harris managed to stop him by a karate chop to the neck.

"Haddaway, ya soft toss, we can't just fuck off like that!"

"Can't we? Isn't that in my contract of employment or some soft arse human rights act, somewhere?"

"We need to find out who murdered the panda, and why."

Morose glared at Robbie, "Brilliant. Find out who did it, and why. All this time I've been in the filth, and I was wondering where I'd gone wrong."

Robbie snarled, "YOU, sir, went wrong when you slithered out of the pub that day into the job centre, and found the ad saying, 'join the filth', sir."

Morose ignored the insult and kicked Robbie in the balls, before continuing,

"Are we seriously investigating some lovers tiff, or a gambling debt, or a game of Pokemon gone wrong, in a fucking zoo? Have we been relegated to this?"

They were interrupted by Collier hurrying up to them.

"Sir, sorry to bother you, but could you just come down to the wildebeest enclosure?"

"Found my sister, have you?"

"No sir, but there is something we feel you ought to see."

*****

In the petting zoo, a small crowd of zoo staff had

gathered around the rabbit enclosure.

Inside, two of the bunnies were going at it hammer and tong. The crowd were cheering enthusiastically.

Collier approached followed by the two incompetents.

"Just a minute, we'll want to see this first gents."

All three peered over the crowd, who were baying enthusiastically.

"Robbie," Morose questioned him insightfully, "Didn't I say *all* of the animals are actually people?"

"Aye man.... Oh Christ!"

"Just walk on, Collier, where is this wildebeest enclosure?"

"This way gents," he led them on.

Morose looked back at Brewis, "And arrest them for gross."

Brewis looked confused. "Gross?"

"Yes, just gross."

"Very good sir."

*****

They arrived at the wildebeest enclosure to find one of the residents was hooves up. Morose took a long, hard run at the gate, and managed to get through without falling over, but sadly slipped on a massive turd and twisted his thing muscle.

Harris gave him a hand. When he'd finished clapping, he got Brewis and the two rabbits to help Morose up, "I'm not touching that prick again" Harris offered by way of explanation.

Wiping the excess off, Morose waddled toward the

inert mammal. He frowned.

"Is it really a man dressed up?"

Collier frowned, "I'm not totally sure, but if I unzip it, we may find out."

Collier unzipped the wildebeest and found, as suspected, the dead body of a man, therein.

"So, who's this tosser?" asked Morose, as he took a quick selfie with the corpse. As no-one spoke, he rolled his eyes to occupy a few seconds. "Come on, who's that little guy who showed you in?"

"The zoo-keeper Surr? One Colin O'Scopy, I reckon he's deep in this shit Surr."

"Hmmm. Well he should know who was on wildebeest duty shouldn't he? I mean, do they have a rota?"

"Most zoos don't actually need a rota," offered Collier, "They have real animals."

"Most police forces have real pigs, now fuck off and get me an answer from O'Scopy before my next breath!"

Collier returned a few minutes later, just as Morose was turning blue, with Mr O'Scopy, who had been on his lunch, a terrible mess he'd made of it too.

"Fuckin' what?" he asked, "I was just on me....."

"Stow it! There's been a fresh murder, and we need to know who this dead person is."

O'Scopy took a quick gander, and they both had a look at the dead body lying in the wildebeest suit. He staggered backward in horror while the goose fainted.

"Oh, sire, what evil is this, that lyeth in yonder wildebeest suit? Forsooth, would that mine eyes deceive me, yet 'tis Ye truth! Fie, fie, cursed be me that I ever lived to see this day, I would still rather have been snatched from mine mother's womb and…..."

"Oh, stop being all dramatic, and tell us who it is, you monkey spanker."

"It's Mr Trick, the president of the zoological society!"

There was a tense pause, finally Morose let it go, and everyone moved to the next enclosure. Morose scrutinised Mr O'Scopy with a deep, searching scrute.

"Mr Trick, you say?"

"Yes sir, man and boy I've known him, well, other way round actually, boy first, then man, but you know what I mean don't you sir?"

"And he's president of the zoological society, you say?"

"Yes, that's him."

Morose's eyes lit up as he turned to Sergeant Harris, "By Christ, Robbie, you halfwitted Geordie toad burglar, this is more like it! Not only is this someone well connected and at our level of the social pecking order, but he's bound to have a happy room, stocked to the roof with loony juice!"

"Aye sir, just a thought man. All these animal people dying. Could it be something in the feed?"

O'Scopy coughed, "Yes, well, we've just had a supply of feed dropped off, Sergeant Harris. Possibly you'd like to check it in, you could examine it then?"

Harris thought about it for a moment, "Canny good like, I'm just off to log a drop then!"

He went to leave but Morose chinned him one, "Look you Berkley Hunt, I need you here doing useful things like taking statements and arresting people and other dull arsed plod work, while I go off for a tug or something. Got it?" He chinned him another for good measure.

"Sir!" Harris spat out several teeth, "Stop chinning me

one, or I'll come round to your pillbox and shit on your living room floor."

"I wouldn't bother, what difference does one more make?"

"Whatever sir, but you see, when this is over, we're goin' tae pagga!"

"Pagga?"

"Police Authority General Grievance Applications."

"Knob off."

As the shocked and emotional Mr O'Scopy was led out of the enclosure and battered unconscious by Brewis and his vegetarian snake, so Harris called to Constable White, to shift his lame arse and get his "murder in zoos" examination kit out.

"Right – oh!" shouted White.

"There's no need to shout, you useless arsewipe, I'm next to you," sighed Harris.

"Sorry Sarge," said White, "But this is jolly exciting, tis the first time I've been able use my 'murder in a zoo' forensics kit."

Morose took Harris to one side.

"See this wall of the building? It's one side." he informed him.

"Thank you, sir, fuck off," snorted Harris.

"Sergeant Harris?" It was that wanker White again.

Harris sighed, "Aye man, what is it, you hopeless turd?"

"I think I've found something."

"What is it? A piece of straw? A nail?"

"I've got the murder weapon."

White was knocked down in the rush to see the offending item. Picking himself up, he held up a fresh boa constrictor.

"I found this wrapped around the dead man's throat."

"Shit," muttered Morose, "How did we miss that?"

"Now hang on, White," cautioned Harris, "A large number of the animals that seem to be here in this zoo, are actually people dressed up as animals."

White looked confused. "And?"

"Well, is this murder weapon of yours a very tall, very thin person, dressed up, or a real snake?"

White reached for a zip fly at the back of the boa, and got a slap in his face for his efforts.

"It seems to be a real snake, sir. Albeit one with hands."

Morose took charge of the situation, "Okay, White, I want you to go into the reptile house and arrest all snakes, that are real snakes, and not humans dressed up as snakes."

White skipped off and after only a short time, was on his way to hospital, with ten different types of deadly snake poisoning.

*****

"We've got the lab report on the bodies," shouted Brewis.

"There's no need to shout, I'm next to you," sighed Harris, "And when you say 'Lab Report', are you sure its from a genuine Labrador, or is it another bloody idiot dressed up as a dog?"

"Lab" retorted Brewis, "As in laboratory."

"Let's see it," grunted Morose, and blew his nose on it, "Sorry chaps, that blocked nose has been pissing me off since breakfast."

He opened the paper and read it.

"Some wanker has smudged the ink on this report, if I find him, I'll ...."

"Can you just give us the fucking report!" howled Harris.

"Sergeant Harris, you don't seem yourself today. Why don't you go and take a walk down the M5?"

Harris, now being held back by Brewis, Collier and the rabbits, foamed heavily at the mouth while Morose put on his specs, and addressed them.

"Pathology report on two deceased at The Zoo, today, today's date."

He cleared his throat for effect.

"Well?" they all asked.

"Deceased share similar DNA and is assumed they are related. Advise to beware further murders within same family. PS Morose is a wanker. Gentlemen and Harris, you know what this means?"

"Yes, it means you're a wanker," shouted the whole throng.

"God, there's no need to shout, I'm in front of you," groaned Morose, "Now look, you lot go and do police things, and I'm off to the pub with my trusty sergeant."

"Sir," protested Harris, "should we not take DNA samples from the rest of the staff as a precaution, to send them off to the lab and get the low down on the likelihood, that anyone else here is part of the same family?"

Morose thought long and hard about his answer.

"No. Get your keys. We're leaving."

*****

"Right Robbie, this is the plan." He raised a finger, "Military precision's the thing!"

"Surr," started Robbie, "Can't we just…"

"Pinscher manoeuvre, Robbie!"

"I think you mean pincer manoeuvre, Surr…"

"No Robbie, Pinscher manoeuvre. If we get this wrong, Geoff will set the dogs on us."

They were waiting just at the side door of the Worm and Hammer, Endof's brother's pub. The main entrance was 'too obvious' apparently. Robbie rolled his eyes, he'd seen someone else doing it successfully earlier.

"You go and distract Geoff, buy a few rounds of drinks or something. I'll take out the jukebox, so we don't have to listen to any of that retch factor shite!"

"Surr, he's taken precautions, man. After last time he's had the jukebox removed. He has a live band on now."

"Good! A moral victory Robbie, while you're getting the round in I'll smash up the band then. It'll be like my days with The Who."

Robbie was stunned, "You were in The Who Surr?"

"Well, not according to the judge I wasn't, but I still had fun smashing up their instruments. They just said my timing was a bit out, I should have done it *after* the gigs."

"Aye Surr, so I'm just getting the roond in?"

Morose nodded, "Roonds, Robbie, roonds."

*****

"So, what did you want to talk aboot, man?" Robbie took the top off his pint, anticipating his boss would finish it.

"I've not really had much chance to speak since we got back from the end of book two."

"Aye man, can you not just say from our time travel adventures, the readers don't like it when we keep reminding them it's a book."

"Just as you wish, Robbie. Any sign of Geoff back yet?"

"No man, he's still filling out insurance forms next door, no wonder he hates you, man."

"He never was as robust as me. Still, now we know why, eh?"

"What do you mean, Surr?" Robbie took another slurp.

"Well, you weren't in on the meeting. Remember Weird wanted to speak to me after our little time travel escapade?"

"Victorian Oxford..."

"Yes, end of book two."

Robbie masked a groan with another slurp, "Aye?"

"He told me, that Spring Heeled Jack was my father."

"What? That jumping feller?"

"Yes Robbie, that jumping feller."

Robbie reached for one of Morose's pints, "So did he live a long time then? A mean, Victorian times, man?"

"No, I have lived a long time, so has Weird. We both began in the force back then. I apparently the son of a demon."

"Fucking fuck me!" Robbie drained Morose's next pint and started on his whiskey chasers, while Endof continued to talk.

"I mean I've tried the fire breathing, nothing yet, but I have managed to set fire to a few good farts. And I have managed to leap a few cars. Not quite daddy's level yet, but still..."

"Awww man!" Robbie looked at all the empty glasses on

the table, and noted Morose still cradling his first. "I'll just go and top us up, like." Saying that, Robbie slithered gently to the floor.

*****

Harris arrived home that evening to be greeted by the front door, which for once, was more than his brain could cope with. He fumbled with his pocket, trying to find his keys, and at once scared off a couple of visitors from the Jehovah's Witnesses, who thought he was having a crafty wank outside. He found his keys a short ten minutes later and found to his horror that the lock had been changed. Funny, the key was the right shape for a key. He sat down on the step to examine the key, and realised he'd never had a proper look at the step, before. It was a nice step. In fact, it was his favourite step. He could stay here forever, no one would notice! His arse sat just nicely on it, look! Ah, that felt good, but what didn't feel good, was that he was in dire need of the toilet!

He needed to get the right key. Now, which one was it? God, why are doors so difficult? He studied each key meticulously and alighted on the one that had "Front door" on it in bright pink. Now, where had he left his legs? Ah, there, in front of him. Need a wee. Stand. No, not walk off the step, stand! Must look as if I'm upright! Mustn't show any sign of weakness, no one will notice, they were all women after all.

He tried the key. It would turn, both ways, but somehow the door didn't want to pull toward him. He gave it a good talking to, and, trying again with the key, gave the door a firm pull toward himself. No. The fucking little shit. Always worked before. He addressed the door sternly.

"C'mon yer wanker, I need a fuckin' slash, like!"

He decided to take the key out and try from the top. He took a few paces back, steadily, in a really straight line, so no one would suspect anything. He lowered his head and held the key as if to stab the door.

Watching from the front room, Mr Chopper, the family Guinea Pig, poked his head back round the curtains and pointed outside. Jess, Robbie's eldest and the local brainy goth, turned to her Mum and muttered,

"Dad's back and he's pissed off his face."

"Aye, Jessie man, I've been kinda suspecting it since he fell through the gate, twenty minutes ago."

"Should we help him, like?"

"Nah, he'll only get upset an' shit."

There was a crash and Robbie fell through the door, and landed on the glass ornamental table in the hallway, toppled the grandfatha clock on top of himself, and swallowed the chime.

"Aye, the fookin' door was open the whole time, the soft shite," observed Claudia, switching the channel on the telly to avoid that bunch of tossers on "The fookin' Voice".

Three of the household slept in beds that night.

Robbie kept waking up as he rang the chimes out each hour, as he lay in the glass on the floor, against the nailed up front door.

The next morning was bright and fine, and Robbie was enjoying a hearty breakfast, of heart and beans.

"Daddy man?" questioned Emily, the younger offspring.

"Aye man, pet, lass, wor Emily?"

"Well, you know, y'came back last light off ya fookin tits man, and slept like a fookin wankah in the clock and all that?"

"Aye what of it?"

"An' now, yer havin a like fook off massive fry up an

beans man, and double cream in ya coffee?"

"Aye man, Emily man?"

"How d'ya do it?"

Harris broke off to chime eight o clock. He wiped some glass off his nose.

"Ah, well, that'd be tellin'! Have you done your homework?"

"Aye Daddy."

"Has Jess done hers?"

There was a crash outside the kitchen door as Jess fell over the prostrate clock, gave it a good kicking, and punched her way into the kitchen.

"Fookin clock! Daddy, will ya get the fookin thing up an outta the way, ya drunken old toss rag?"

"Aye, just getting me breakfast like, have you done your homework an' shit?"

"Aye man, both."

"Ah that's cannae grand. What was the homework?"

"Aye Daddy, it's like this, we was doin' that science cack about the human body an' how it's like really complicated, and the DNA structure of cells and genetic an' hereditary characteristics and stuff."

"Oh aye?"

"Aye, we had to find a common ancestry of some mammals, like. I got the cat an' the fookin dog."

"Better than say, the lemur and the hippo?"

"Aye that was given to Michelle Slagly, I don't like her."

Harris drained the last of his drain fluid into his coffee and drank the lot, "So, what did ya' find out, pet?"

"Aye well, the common ancestor of the cat and the dog,

is like, a Cog."

"A cog? Wow, who'd have thought it?"

"Aye man, an' there's more! There is an ancestral side line called a Dat!"

Harris took a long look at his eldest daughter.

"Don't tell me, there's also one called a Dis?"

Jess dropped her spoon in amazement, "How the fook did ye know that, Dad? Have you been readin' my secret research before I woke up? 'cos if you have I'm gonna fuckin knack ya!"

"Steady, wor Jess, ya daft whore. Don't go getting all het up an' shit! It just seemed like a logical step, like. Emily, what was your homework?"

"I did a bit of study for my 11 plus Dad, I was readin' up on the women's movement in the early 1900s, that Emiline Pankhurst, worra guy she was!"

"Aye man, but what about poor old Mr Pankhurst, eh?"

"How d'ya mean, like?"

"Well, poor man, man, Who made his breakfast the day after she was killed, like?"

"Oh shit! I never thought of that! What a cow!"

Robbie was just seeing the girls off for their bus, when he had a sudden thought.

"Jess?"

Jess turned back.

"Aye daddy?

"The common ancestry stuff. In the DNA, you said?"

"Aye Daddy."

A penny fell into place and Robbie's mind turned one pace further forward than usual.

He paused.

"Shit!"

He ran back in, and shouted to Claudia,

"I'm off ter see Morose, double quick, like!"

"Not til you've had another piece of toast, to soak up all that booze you had last night!" she admonished, "Or they'll be pulling you for drunk driving!"

He rammed more toast into the toaster, and thought about the possibility that Claudia had common ancestry with the honey badger.

*****

Morose opened an eye, strangely it wasn't his own.

This old codger was propping up the reception desk and had disturbed Morose's sleep. The old man had been ringing the reception bell constantly for the last 10 minutes. Eventually Morose had given up on the idea that the old duffer would realise the police station wasn't open yet, and fuck off somewhere else, but no. Morose had to make his way up from the cells to the front desk and now the fucking fossil couldn't even be arsed to be conscious!

"Oi! Can't you fucking read? This police station isn't rebuilt yet! If you want to report a crime go to my old pillbox on the A5… and stop dripping blood on my new counter. Someone who gives a shit will need to mop that up!"

The elderly tossbag stubbornly refused to wake up. Morose looked at the knife sticking out of the ancient fucker's back, if it was Morose he'd want to stay awake and get that looked at, but this geriatric old fuckweasel seemed content to pass out in the reception area.

It did present Morose with a problem though. Either

the senile delinquent was alive, and in which case needed an ambulance, or he was dead and that needed a police investigation. Either would alert the authorities to the fact that the police station was finished and ready for occupation and service again. Knob cheese! That would mean giving up his lovely new home. Oh coitus, he thought.

The cackling voice from the as yet unoccupied superintendent's office did nothing to help resolve the situation.

*****

Robbie's toast was just turning black and inedible when a phone rang. As it was an iPhone that posed a problem.

It's a funny thing, when people buy any other type of phone they change the ringtone, but for some reason not iPhone users. So, whenever an iPhone rings on say a train, or a bus for instance, everyone checks their phones.

Or in this case at the Harris breakfast table. It wasn't Claudie apparently, or Jess, or Em. Mr Chopper checked his but again nothing. Therefore...

"Hello, Sergeant Harris, Oxford..."

"Never mind all that arsewipe, Robbie. Come and meet me at the swimming pool. And bring Claudia's Jag. We need to deal with a stiff."

"You mean the pool next to new police station, that they're taking forever rebuilding, Surr?"

"Yes, that's the one, no news on that yet. Anyway, I've dragged a... I mean I've found a corpse by the pool. Come and help me shift it."

"Surr, we shouldn't shift it, man. Call forensics, get Max on the scene, he loves shite like that."

"Oh fer fucks... alright Robbie, but come and get me,

and bring something off your top shelf, and I don't mean another Do – It – Yourself mag!"

*****

The ring of police cars around the Happy Days Leisure centre and Health Spa (formerly council owned and funded swimming baths - There was no material difference, except to shareholders) gave a hint that something was amiss. A bigger hint was the Mini Moke and the Isetta bubble car, rammed into the side of a brand new armoured police vehicle. To the untrained eyes gossiping on social media, there had been a road crash, and a subsequent chase of a heavily armed suspect, into the swimming baths, foiling a terrorist plot to assassinate the whole Royal Family.

To the trained eye, Max had turned up to examine a corpse, still pissed from the night before; and Morose had added his own car, to make it seem that he'd come from anywhere, except the inside of the new police station.

"Interesting!" hollered Max, "This body seems to have dragged itself from at least 70 yards away, to this part of the swimming baths, stabbed himself into the marble floor, from behind, and all the while dead from 8.30 this morning, before the baths opened?"

"Very odd," Morose managed to say.

"Even stranger, he seems to have a police desk bell in his hand!"

"Aye, some odd shit goes on in Oxford," sighed Harris.

"Complete mystery to me," added Brewis, "There's no other building in vicinity except the police station, that they're re building."

"Yes well he can't have come from there, its locked up," stated Morose, remarkably quickly.

"Yeah, and no ones got a key anyway, so we're off to do some detective work on the zoo," added Harris.

"Yeah, can't win 'em all, eh, come on Harris, lets fuck off," concluded Morose.

Harris tripped over the body as he went to run out, "Just move him to the mortuary and stick an ad in the 'lost and found' bit of the paper," he suggested.

Max looked at him incredulously, "Which paper?"

"Aye, any paper, bye," gabbled Harris.

"Morose!" shouted Max, after the rapidly running pair. Morose stopped and bellowed back,

"'kin what now? We're busy esc....er... getting on with the zoo case."

"Aye, the zoo, its urgent, there's a bat lost," agreed Harris.

Max stumped over to them, and brushed the shoulder of Morose's flasher mac.

"Don't you see!" he scolded, "There's a load of dried blood here, you'll look a right dick walking around the zoo covered in dried blood."

Gonemad walked over, you could see the cogs turning in his brain. He looked hard at Morose and Harris.

"Inspector Morose, I'm not happy with...."

"Fuck off," hinted Morose, giving Gonemad a further clue, with a baseball bat.

"Aye, we're just off," repeated Harris. They half ran to the bubble car, had a fight over who was getting in first, and drove off.

"What would we do without them," mused Max, to the assembled scene of crime men.

As the little car wound its way toward the zoo, Harris

managed to update Morose on the subject of D.N.A.

"It's like this sur, y'see wor Jess was workin' on some stuff for her science homework, an it seems that all that D.N.A. stuff can be traced back to individuals and ye' can trace whole generations back through time, an stuff, like."

Morose took a bite out of Harris' toast. "And?"

"Well don't ya see?" sighed Robbie, "You had that DNA report yesterday, about the deceased at the zoo, sharing common D, and N; and probably A as well."

"And?"

Harris took a bite of Morose's fingers. "I think there's more D, and N, and probably A, need sorting out there."

"Harris?"

"Aye sir man?"

"You really are a boring bastard, just drive."

Harris was amazed. "Me drive? I thought you were doing the driving?"

"Me? I haven't touched the bloody thing all journey!"

"Then who is driving this out dated sieve?"

Morose thought long and hard about the answer, before stating, "You know, I get the horrible feeling that……"

"Too late, we're here, anyway," noted Harris, climbing out of the forward – opening door.

"I'd like to see them do this in the television version," observed Morose, as they left the little car in the zoo car park, strapped on its feedbag and strode toward the turnstiles.

*****

"Good morning, gentlemen," grunted Mr O'Scopy, "Two

day passes, is it?"

"Stick your passes," snarled Morose, and rammed O'Scopy's head into the turnstile wheel.

"Aye, alreet man," smiled Harris, in that annoying way, "Have you noticed any unusual occurrences since we were last here?"

"Such as?" asked O'Scopy, between bats of the turnstile paddles.

"Well y'kna, any like murders or attempts on any animal's lives? Or people dressed as animals, or the other way round, whichever came first?"

"Well let me think," mused O'Scopy, as the paddles came to a halt, "There was a murder in the hippo house, and two violent stabbings in the giraffe enclosure."

"Did anyone ring the police?"

"Yes, I sent some old bloke to the police station in town that's just been rebuilt, to let them know. He's not come back yet, though."

Harris smiled, "Aye, when he does, tell him to pop up an' see us?"

Morose nodded "Yes, and by the way, the Police station isn't open yet. So, he probably went to the leisure centre next door."

O'Scopy groaned, "Oh, don't tell me that I've sent him on a fool's errand? He already thinks I've got the knives out for him."

"Don't you worry," soothed Harris, "He'll be fine."

The two police made their way toward the hippo house, and got about halfway there, before a very large realisation dawned on them both.

"Shit!" they both said.

WPCs Franks and Soames looked at them with bleary eyes.

"Ah, didn't expect to see you two in the Hippo House" grunted Morose, without any hint of sarcasm whatsoever.

"Fuck off sir," they replied by way of a greeting.

"We've been up all night and the one place that we weren't able to cover, there's a bloody murder!" complained Franks.

"We even had an undercover man working in the giraffe enclosure, he's the only one who prevented a double killing there," sighed Soames, doing her best to look as pretty as she could after a night in hippo shit.

"Would you mind keeping the bastard noise down in there," called a voice from outside.

"Fuck off, we're the filth!" helped Morose.

"Well, we're the bastard sodding BBC. So, you fuck off!"

That voice sounded familiar.

"Shall I go an' chin him Surr?" Robbie had his jacket off ready.

"No, we'll both pop out in a moment, give them time to start filming first. Might make Newsround on C-Beebies!"

"Soames, where's that giraffe? We need a statement off him."

"He's just sleeping off his tranquiliser dart, sir," smiled Soames, "First chance I've had to use my zoological taser all year!"

The voice from afar was now much nearer. They all turned to face him, as he ignored the presence of the police, and talked at the camera that some goon was carrying and filming him with.

"....Here, in the very darkest depths of the hippo house,

we find that the scandal overtaking the Oxford City Zoo has plumbed new depths, not only has there been a further murder, involving a male of the species and injuring his partner, but also, that awful bore, "The Copper", has turned up after, as it were, the stable door has bolted."

They looked incredulous at David Attenborough and his editorial team, accountants and solicitor. Morose spoke first.

"Fuck off."

Attenborough droned on, "The greeting this primeval being gives us is not the friendliest, but then, he is a member of the Oxford City Constabulary, and therefore, a bit of a shit."

"I said, fuck off. Take you sodding camera with you."

"If I refuse to make eye contact with him, and stand perfectly still, he cannot see me, as his vision depends on movement."

There was a brief scuffle and an agonised scream. Then a painful pause.

"The male of the pack appears to have hoofed me in the balls, and my teeth have been forced out. Hopefully this is not going to turn into one of their ritualised mating rituals."

"Aye, now fuck off, an proper" concluded Harris, pausing to punch out the cameraman.

"Sir, I've got the giraffe here," said Soames, leading the lanky legged beast into the hippo house.

"Take your stupid costume off, and tell us all about it," muttered Morose.

The man in the giraffe suit just stood there, swaying slightly.

"Come on, man, we haven't got all day," scowled Morose.

The fool just leaned over and took a bite out of Brewis' toupee.

"Stop it!" hissed Harris, exasperated, "Shit man, this is serious stuff, get that head off an' talk man, we've not got all day!"

In reply there was a bar-rattling fart and a quarter ton of excrement flew out of the back end of the giraffe suit. The assembled police took a long hard look at him.

"Sir, it's a real giraffe," observed Harris.

"Well book him!"

"Book him? For what?"

"The Christmas party, the kids need more than a shitty bouncy castle and a pissed up Santa this year."

Morose took Harris to one side.

"This is getting hopeless. Three deaths and no witnesses, some old fool carked in my pad – er, outside the pool – and our only witness is a fucking giraffe! What will Weird say?"

"He'll blub about not being able to go to his golf club, for fear of being laughed at, again," suggested Harris, "Anyway, I think we should take a D.N.A. sample from the lot and test them."

Morose looked witheringly at him. "You really believe in that poncy scientific stuff?"

"Aye man, all the rest of the police forces across the planet use it."

"Well my arse on it, nothing like old fashioned policing, Harris, you mark my words, the murderer is amongst us, and no amount of U.D.A. can avoid that!"

So saying Morose collapsed into a nearby hippo turd, exhausted after his longest stretch without a drink for years.

"Aye sir, I'll get on with it, an' ye might want to scrape the D.N.A. off your suit when you come round, the flies are already alighting on you."

*****

They re-grouped at the former armoury cupboard in the pillbox.

Weird, fresh from hanging his washing and a few souls out, got out his vacuum cleaner, and a chair, and hoovered menacingly in the background, as Harris stood to speak.

"Aye well, its like this see, I wanted to get a D.N.A. sample of all the people in the zoo posing as animals, and also, all the people who've been like, bumped off an' shit, in the zoo, whether they were animals or not."

There was a muttering of consent from Brewis, Collier, Epstein, and Weird.

There was a cry of "Wanker!" from Morose.

"An the results are like, really interesting, mans."

More consenting mutterings, and one "Tosser!"

"Aye, anyway, they all match up."

Weird broke the silence that followed.

"Meaning what? Look here matey, you've lost us all now, a damn fine exhibition you're making of yourself, I'm going to look a right dicksplash at the golf club again, and….."

"Meaning, sir," continued Harris, with that awful patronising look, "That they were all closely related, to one man, who was the father of rest of them."

The Cockney Brewis spoke up. "As the station's token cockney, I have to ask you straight! Who's the daddy?"

There was a triumphant gleam in Harris' eye, as he said,

"The president of the zoological society, man."

"What!" squarked Weird, "You mean that chap Mr Trick? But he was a fellow at Saint Carbuncle's College, he was sent down nearly twenty years ago!"

"Aye, well, that's the connection, gents."

Morose got to his feet, felt sick, and got back to his arse, before asking, "Very good, Harris, you northern bore monger. And where exactly does this get us?"

"Well surr, I found by a bit of your old–fashioned policing, and a quick break in at a solicitors office, that the person who stands to inherit the lot, is the president of the zoological society's estranged wife, Mrs Trick."

There was another pause.

"So she killed off all her own children to inherit what was probably coming to her, anyway?" fumed Weird, "Are you taking the piss?"

There was an extra-wide and extra-annoying beam on Harris' face.

"Nah, not really, y'see, all them kids were fathered by Mr Trick, out of wedlock. She gets rid of them, and there's no one else to stand in her way!"

Weird, for once, lost his menacing demeanour, and relaxed enough to attempt a smile, as he said,

"Well done, sergeant! And all without the help of your superior! Which cell is the suspect in?"

Now it was Harris who lost his composure.

"Er…… ah….. well, y'see, it's like this. We've not actually arrested anyone, yet. I just wanted to run it by you, Sir, y'see. I sort of forgot the, er, wrapping the case up, bit, like."

Outside the pillbox, an audience of crows and hedgehogs watched with interest, as a small pall of smoke in the shape of an atomic mushroom, appeared over the pillbox roof. This was followed by an internal iron door, some teeth, a succession of bodies, and a lot of screaming.

Harris emerged with his suit in tatters and his hair very badly on fire. Morose followed, wearing his seat around his neck, and his prize sock stuffed up his arse.

There was a very loud voice.

"Fucking get it right!!"

The damaged people left the scene very quickly on foot and in cars, one of them managed both. The cloud of vapourised gas dissipated, and the hedgehogs and crows returned to their peaceful routine of eating and shitting.

*****

All morning there had been a constant trail of vehicles leaving the zoo, as the various animal impersonators vacated, and a trail of trucks arriving, as the new selection of creatures arrived. The keepers, who were left, were kept occupied by introducing the animals to their new enclosures. In each case the staff would show the animal their bed, their food trough, the multichannel Sky package, and give them the wifi password. Only the panda offered a tip, the rest were just animals.

The TV people were setting up outside, ready for the big announcement that the zoo would be fully re-opened today by its new owner, and chief shareholder, Mrs Abigail Trick; who, until last night had been occupied, between killing sprees in the hyaena house. All she had to do each night was get past that unfunny prick White - she couldn't believe no-one had picked up on how quiet the hyaenas were – and once through, she had the run of the place and the ability to bring herself higher up the list of inheritors of the zoo. One more to kill, in the deer enclosure and she'd be officially in charge.

The deer house then, for the final instalment of Kind Harts and Coronets.

Ah, the relief of getting to the end of this whole unpleasant business! All of Humphry's sprogs by those 'other women', zoological secretaries, student zoo keepers, and aspiring zoological vet girls. Tarts! Tarts and harlots, the lot! And their bloody sprogs, that Humphry had fathered, and got jobs for in front of their legitimate offspring! Humphry, the former mild mannered zoo keeper, then the rising star of the world of rare animals and pungent shit! The double crossing, womanising, toadying muckraker.

And now, she, Abigail stood to inherit the chair, and all the huge grants that flowed in from around the World! She didn't have to bother having all the slags and harlots bumped off. She could hire other people to do that!

Pulling the Rhino head over her own, she made her way past that loser PC White by showing her bus pass ("Aye, that'll do, ma'am" he had said), and then to find the final illegitimate child, still in there somewhere posing as a crocodile, she'd heard. Her spy in the camp, that fool O'Scopy's old and doddery friend, hadn't got back to her, yet, as to which crocodile; but how many crocodiles would be likely to answer the simple question, "Hey mate, want to make a quick thousand pounds for us?" Where HAD that old fool got to? Never mind. This should be a piece of piss.

The rhino, quite unusually seemed to have decided to go for a dip. Equally unusually, it had decided to take a rifle with it. This not only alerted the crocodiles to the possibility that their new mammalian visitor was, maybe, not all she was cranked up to be; but also that she might be on the lookout for one of their number. Maybe it was that human who had run off the previous night? Intrigued, they silently slipped into the water, and thus almost submerged, advanced.

Abigail looked around at the crocodile enclosure and

was surprised to find it seemed deserted. Bloody reptiles! Still, what can you expect from the last survivors of a species that not only had been there with the dinosaurs, but also made quite exquisite handbags?

*****

Morose and Harris managed to park the Messerschmitt vaguely on the lawn of the late Mr Trick, and purposefully strode up to the front door. They knocked at the bell. They rang at the knocker. They shouted through the cat flap. They buzzed a few bricks at the upstairs windows. Eventually, Morose leant on the door and fell in, it had been open all the time.

"Hello? Mrs Trick? Are ye there, like?" whispered Harris.

In reply was a sort of strangled cry, from the kitchen. The cook?

They cautiously opened the kitchen door. Young Charlie Nook, 15, who had just discarded his crocodile suit, lowered the revolver he was aiming at them, and whispered,

"Are you the pigs?"

"Aye man, are you the last of the kids that Mr Nook hired to stand in, as animals, at the zoo, like?"

"Yes."

"Well you're safe now," grunted Morose, "There's a couple of pigs on their way to get you to safety."

"Are you sure they're not animals dressed as pigs?"

Morose turned to Harris, "You see what messing with their heads has done? This little prick doesn't even call me 'Sir', take that you little shit!"

Harris helped him up, and between him and the kid, they got him back on his feet, the drunken bum.

"Sir, stop takin' a swing at the kid, he's traumatised enough."

"He'll be traumatised even more when he finds WPCs Franks and Soames are looking after him."

"WPCs?" asked the youth, "Have they got good hooters?"

"Not today," said Harris, sadly, "They had to give the owls back."

"And their wild tits" added Morose.

"Look, Charlie, where's Mrs Trick? We need to know for her and our safety."

Charlie thought before answering.

"I think she's probably gone to find and kill me, at the zoo. I was standing in as a crocodile."

"Ah," said Morose, "You mean, she's after you there, when you're here?"

"Yes."

The two coppas looked at each other.

"Shit!!"

*****

"What's all that noise?" asked Morose as he and Harris left the house.

There were several ambulances and police vehicles flying past with sirens and blue lights in use.

Robbie shrugged, "They seem to be slowing down over there, man. Put that whiskey back in your pocket and let's have a look."

They wandered over slowly. By the time Robbie had

been served at the hotdog stall and Morose had found some popcorn to tease the penguins with, Max had arrived on the scene.

"Oi!" Morose got Max's attention by throwing the now empty bottle at his head, "What are you doing here? They're all animals now!"

Max looked up from the deeply savaged dead rhino that had been pulled out of the water. "Not this one Endof old chum. This one was a human apparently, despite the disguise. Seems like the crocs enjoy their barbecues rare, gents."

"Aye, so who was it?" smirked Robbie. "Nah, ah know really, just wanted to see that look of disbelief on that arse-holes face" He pointed at Morose.

Morose summed it up, "silly bint went for the croc thinking it was our young Charlie and instead she became a proper Charlie."

"Fuck off sir" observed Robbie.

CHAPTER 3 – DEAD ON LINE

The telephone engineer put his tools to one side, and turned to the community nurse, who was stood nearby.

"Yeah, that's fixed love, it was only a wire pulled out, got time for a quickie?"

"Test it, just so I can see that it works."

"Well that's an unusual chat up line, but….."

"The telephone."

"Oh. Ok."

He dialled a number and sitting back, lit a tab.

The connection was made. A muffled voice asked "Hello?"

He cupped his hand over his mouth, "what are you wearing?"

"What?" the muffled voice replied.

"What colour are your knickers? OOOOH!"

As the voice on the other end shrieked, he replaced the receiver. "Yeah, all working fine."

The phone rang back.

" 'kin what?"

"Are you taking the piss?"

"Who is this?"

"This is the Right Reverend Brian Squire, Michael, I dialled 'last number', you hopeless spunkguzzling prick. You know very well I always go commando. I shall be contacting your employers about your malpractice."

"Spoilsport!"

"And mine's a pint at the social club later, you idiot."

Michael turned to the nurse again.

"Yeah, that's all working just great."

The nurse smiled, "Ace, I can get my wifi back now!"

"So how about….."

"I'm married."

"He doesn't need to know!"

"To a woman."

As Michael trudged out, and dodged the various items thrown after him, and the paint thrown at his van, he reflected on how fickle women are.

Nurse Clarke turned back to her employer, and smiled.

"I'll be on my way soon. I've got a concrete mixer lined up to push at him, at the end of the road!"

"Thank you," smiled the worn out, shattered bodied man, whose house this was, "I'm just ringing Katie." He pressed a few buttons. "Hello? Katie? Yes, lovely day. Good luck with your knickers exhibition later."

Nurse Clarke quietly closed the door, got her Austin Healey Frogeye revved up, and sped off with a spray of stone chippings to the concrete mixer. She'd get the little prick before the vicar!

*****

"Aye well I'm off home an that!" shouted Harris, across the pool table. Well, I say pool table, it was actually a flat stone sitting on a couple of tree stumps that Brewis had set up, bringing a bag of pool balls with him. Every time he tried to get a game started the same cry went up. In this case from Harris - "Aye well I'm off home an' that!"

"Mr Morose?" hissed a voice from inside the Police Pillbox.

Robbie looked around but everyone else was pretending they hadn't heard the voice of their Superintendent, Colin Weird.

"Errr, I think he's gone, said he couldn't be arsed workin' today, man. Said it's POETNF day!"

"It's what?"

"Piss Off Early Today's Nearly Friday, Surr."

"It's Tuesday, Mr Harris."

"Aye... well..."

"Right everyone. In the Police cars, and follow me." Weird vanished.

Harris, Brewis, Gonemad and Jampton looked at each other.

Weird reappeared. "Sorry, Oxford Road, site of the old station, meet you there." He vanished again.

*****

Four police vehicles pulled up in the car park of the station.

Robbie looked around, "Hey lads, it's not lookin' bad, from the ootside a mean, canny good!"

A voice like a snake on the X factor whispered behind him, "It's not looking bad from the inside either, Mr Harris. It's looking perfect, ready to move in you might say. A fact your supervisor neglected to tell us. Unfortunately for Mr Morose I have.... Inside contacts, you might say."

Morose stood in the doorway, "Twatting Jesus!" he muttered.

"No, though the similarity is, as you might say, non-existent, matey. As you will be, when I'm finished with you."

"Anyway, like I was sayin, I'm off home, like," and with that, Harris reached for the door. He was flattened against the wall by Desk Sergeant Jampton, fresh off his fresh desk, who asked,

"Has anyone seen Sergeant Harris?"

"Behind the door, you fucking nit," came the reply.

"Oh right, hello Robbie, you can't leave yet, there's been a shooting."

"Arse and wank and bollocks."

Harris breathed in, got his general body shape back, and addressed the door.

"Can't it wait?"

"No, the bullet has arrived at its destination."

"Aw fuck! White, get a camera and follow me."

"Okay Sarge," grinned White, happy to be of use to something at last.

*****

"Max, you old horse fondler…" shouted Morose.

"Can ya wait until we arrive, before ya start shouting at Max, Surr?" groaned Harris.

The car had barely pulled out of the car park.

"Just practicing young… no, you'll have to tell me your name again."

"Harris, surr!"

"No, I'm not getting this, Harris. I'm going to have to call you something I can remember."

"Surr it's barely opening time, and you can't remember my name, man?"

"Just concentrate on driving, you gormless prick, and…..by Jove, yes, that's it!"

"What's it?"

"Just pull up here by this letter box, I've got something to post."

Harris, or whatever his name was today, dutifully pulled over almost alongside the bright, red, phallic shaped object that people used to pop all sorts of paper in, before the invention of the internet.

"Just be a mo," grinned Morose.

Harris watched with initial fascination, then resignation, as Morose got to the Post Office letter box and, leaning against it, threw up through the aperture; finished his hymn to the great god Huey; and, pausing only for his finale of a quick slash – "Look at that Robbie, all in! Not a drop missed" - returned to the car, wiping his vomit encrusted mouth with a mail sack. He got back in, fastened the seatbelt round his throat, and, turning purple, instructed Harris,

"Carry on, crow."

"Is that the best name you can come up with?" sighed Harris.

"No," replied Morose, "Over there! I can see one! A carrion crow, my first of the day."

"Sir, if eating carrion crows has that effect on you, I suggest you stop, man, that probably didn't half ruddy well honk."

"Bah, it wasn't the crow toastie this time, it was the 13th can of Special Brew. Always my unlucky number."

"Heavy night at the booze, man?"

"Night? That was my breakfast. Anyway, that off licence looks unattended, I'll meet you at the scene of the shooting in a few minutes."

Harris dropped his boss off at the unguarded Victoria Wines and, checking with him that he had the wrong address, drove off with the windows down and the windscreen wiper fluid nozzle bent round into the car, to get rid of the smell.

It didn't take long to get to the scene of the shooting. He flashed his card at the new kid on duty at the door, who saluted him with a fascist full arm salute, and hurried in to find that idiot White already at work, with his camera.

Harris, upon entering, noticed at first a certain pathologist hard at work, or what passed for work anyway.

"Robbie!" shouted Max, "how are you doing? Frog still on the Tyne, eh?"

"Aye Surr, a message from the Chief Inspector, he says 'Max, you dead horse fondler' there was also a mention of something vile you do with wombats, but I can't remember that!"

"Probably for the best. Young White here has been taking some photos. Got an art project on or something."

"Not enough light," muttered White, and, going to the curtains, pulled the lot off the rail.

"Still not enough light," White muttered, and, grabbing a fire axe, demolished the wall adjoining the window.

"That's better."

As the plaster and brick dust settled, Harris asked, "Didn't you bring your flash, man?"

"Sorry sarge, I forgot. And I forgot the vim, too. All those blood stains, and nothing to get them up with!"

Methodically, he photographed the body, the gaping wound, the blood on the carpet, and the position of the corpse in relation to the rest of the room, in relation to the city of Birmingham, and finally in relation to the planet Saturn.

Then he called the rest of the coppers over, and took a photo of them at various angles with the corpse; posing like hunters with the corpse; and finally, a group shot and selfie.

"Now one just me and my wife!" he called, sadly his wife was in Australia, anything to get away from him, so he had to be photographed with W.P.C. Soames, providing further ammunition for his wife's forthcoming divorce case.

"And now, can I have one with the murderer?"

There was a pause.

"Ah well, just an idea."

"Bright young man, that," observed Max to Harris, "I saw what he did there, trying to snare the killer."

"Aye man, he'll go far in the force," replied Harris, adding to himself, "Hopefully the further the better, like Siberia."

There was a crash outside and a large ornate plant pot, designed by Capability Brown, fell over and shattered. There was a cry of "Fuck that piece of shit!" and then a "Whoops, there goes the rose bush!"

"Okay lads, pack up soon, Morose is here," sighed Robbie. He knew Morose didn't like messy, bloody scenes like this, and went outside to greet his boss.

Morose clapped an arm round his sergeant, and, thus managing to keep upright, asked,

"What have we got here, Mick?"

"It's Harris, sir."

Morose sobered up at once. "Jesus! What has happened to Harris?"

"No sir, it's...."

"If any spineless bastard has touched a hair of my sergeant, I'll plant his face so far into his head, that it'll fall out of his arse!"

"Sir, I'm...."

"Where is he, is he safe? Talk to me, you blithering idiot!"

Harris punched his boss in the face, the boss mysteriously fell over. Morose's brain fogged a bit, then cleared, and he saw...... miracle!

"Harris baby! I thought you'd been done in! That cretin of a sergeant who looks just like you, said you'd been blotted out."

Harris played along, anything for some peace.

"Aye, I'm here, and so are you."

"Well that's splendid! Let's get pissed to celebrate your return."

"We're here to take a peek at a shooting sir."

"Oh yes! Well let's go in!"

"We think its suicide sir, and its all a bit messy. Looks like a vampire's picnic, man!"

Max looked up to officially note Morose's arrival. "No chance of our doing the vent act, Endof. We still haven't found most of his head! Young Gonemad is having a go at reconstructing but... no Saul, that's his cat's bowl not his cranium." He tutted and took a quick glance around the room. His eyes eventually caught Morose's. "It all has to be within wheelchair reach, but I can't find it yet."

"I'll get the old booze sniffer onto it." Morose, doing a remarkably good impression of a blood hound, sniffed around the room, out into the hallway, and the back of WPC Soames trousers for some reason. "It's no good, I'm drawing a blank here."

"Aye surr," uttered Harris, "possibly we could get on with the case then?"

"It's just our luck," muttered Max, brushing some bone splinters off his overalls, "First really good carking we've had in ages and the cunt's a teetotaller!"

"Tell Weird unless he gets some top quality hooch down here we're not solving this one. I can easily start a good fight at an off licence, or down our Geoff's place. Quick frame up and all you can drink. Hey! Make it Geoff and I might inherit…"

"Aye Surr, shall we just have a look at this one first?"

"Well I'm going outside for a game of conkers. There's no murder and no booze. This is a shit party. You coming Max?"

"Only if I can use my 99'er Endof!"

"You soaked that in vinegar, you cheat." So saying, they both left.

Soames, White, Gonemad and the SOCO team all looked at Robbie.

Soames coughed, "Sir, can we…"

Robbie gave in, "Aye, just for ten minutes mind and then it's straight back to work. Don't make me come and get you!"

Conkers at the ready, they joined Max and Morose on the lawns outside.

Robbie was left alone in the room. It was true, there was no murder here, this was suicide, poor feller, very sad, but there you go.

So, the routine side of the job began. He entered the kitchen to find Nurse Clark cradling a cup of coffee and staring vacantly at a wall.

"I'm sorry miss, I just need to ask a few questions. You found Mr errr…?"

"Kramer, Joseph Kramer, yes. I popped out to throw a brick through a Telephone engineers windscreen, I had to chase him some distance and when I got back I found...this..."

"Aye, when you say you found this, I take it you found it *like* this, I mean half his bastard head blown off, blood all ower the walls like, brain and bone caking the floor."

She gulped back a tear, "Yes."

"I mean it's fucking awful in there, man."

"I know Sergeant, I discovered it."

"I'll be having fucking nightmares tonight me. Puts me right off me pie and mash that!"

"Sergeant!"

"I'm just saying like. Couldn't you have tidied up a bit, man?"

"No Sergeant, you and the forensics people have to come in first."

"Aye, I suppose so. It doesn't help matters when you come in to work to that, man! So, who was he anyway? Any reason he felt like redecorating the walls, like? Knocks me sick that!"

"It didn't do him many favours either Sergeant!"

"Aye, his choice, but!"

"He was terminally ill Sergeant, he had a progressive illness, let me give you his doctors details."

"Terminal? Nothing contagious? Only that room is caked, I don't know if I said"

"I don't think you can catch the bullet that killed him sergeant. Take his doctor's details."

"Aye well, I'm throwing these overalls right out, man. Our Claudie's not washing these. Covered man. Fuckin' last, man."

"His doctor's name is Dick Blake."

"I'll be sure not to go to him with a sore throat, look what's happened to his last patient! All over the fuckin walls man."

"……and the name of the unfortunate man here who has killed himself, after struggling with a progressive illness that I was his named community nurse for, is Joseph Kramer."

"Aye man, miss, I'll be off now before I catch anything off any of this!"

"You can catch this on the way," she observed, and punched him nearly dislocating his jaw.

Clutching his knob, Harris opened the French windows and shouted,

"Time!"

…and the conkers match broke up with a mixture of complaints about it never being ten minutes, and what a cheating cow Soames is.

"So, who's the stiff?" snorted Morose with a waggle of his undamaged jaw, just to piss Harris off.

"One Joseph Kramer, he….."

Morose took a huge step back, that ended when he fell back out of the French window. He climbed back in, shaking and barely able to speak, which was welcomed by everyone. He did, however, manage to whisper,

"Joseph Kramer?"

"Aye man, it seems….."

But Morose had already apparently lost contact with everyone. He stood and looked out at the ducks in the pond. They all had alibis, just in case the silly git tried to pin it on them.

Harris tried the soft approach.

"Did you know him?"

Morose dropped a veritable inflatable balloon worth of stomach gas, before replying,

"And don't mention the smell, I've already eaten a bar of Brut soap. Should be perfect. Yes, I knew him. His brother in law is Dick Small, lives at 23 Partridge Grove. Kramer's wife is in London, runs a knickers emporium. She has a flat."

"Nearside rear?"

Morose gave Harris his best 'fuck off, Harris' look, and continued, "Fuck off Harris, I don't know the address of her flat in London, get one of the piglets back at the sty to look it up will you, I can't be arsed. Oh, and Slip around to Partridge Grove will you, and tell Small his brother in law's croaked at last."

"At last?"

"At the last time we saw him."

*****

Harris knocked at the door of a hideous 1960s outside bog.

"Anyone home? Ah could do wi' a shit, an' that!"

The back door to the equally hideous 1960s house, opened. A butler with the look of Max Wall peered out, and asked:-

"Do you have to peer out of the door? There's a bloody bog here!"

He walked like Max Wall too, as he came up close to Harris he gave that famous Max Wall sneer. "It's just, I have to mop it up"

"Aye, am going in for a crap just now. While I'm doing that, is Mr Small in?"

"No Sir, he's in the house."

"No, I didn't mean in the shitter man. Plenty of paper in there?"

"In the house?"

"No, the shitter man!"

"Oh yes, I keep it well stocked. Well, you never know do you?"

"Aye, listen. While I'm in there, dropping the otters off at the pool an' that, can you go an' speak to Mr Small."

"I can just stand back and whistle if you're embarrassed."

"No, can ye' tell Mr Small his brother in laws carked it."

"I can promise you I cleaned the toilet this morning!"

"No, he's dead man."

"Is Mr Small expecting you?"

"I divven't kna' man, just give him the message. I'm going in now, I may be some time."

*****

Harris flushed and emerged feeling a lot better.

In addition to Wall the butler, Harris could see another gentleman stood behind him. For some reason that gentleman had dragged a large piece of gym equipment into the garden behind him. It was a saddle attached to a sort of rodeo ride device. Mr Wall was busy trying to run an extension cable back into the house. There was an embarrassed pause, and then a relatively minor explosion; a great pall of blue smoke emerged from the door, and Wall, skin freshly bleached and hair now set three foot higher than before, announced,

"Right you are, Mr Small, its plugged in now."

"Whack – o! " cried Mr Small, who jumped on the fucking ridiculous contraption, pressed a couple of buttons on a control panel, and the whole thing shook, blew vast amounts of smoke everywhere, and fell to bits.

Small picked himself up, "You should try it, it keeps me fit."

Harris, trying not to laugh, grinned back, "I wouldn't know where to put it."

"I think this one's for the incinerator," replied Small, "Now, who are you, and what do you want?"

"My name is Sergeant Harris of Oxford Town and Country Police, sir, I'm here to tell you your brother in law has shot his brains out all over his room, right fucking mess it is too, I mean you can hardly call it a living room any more, God, you wanna see it man!"

Small scratched his knob. His own knob that is. "Is he dead?"

Harris took a go at his own, as well. "Aye man."

"Shot himself?"

"Aye, aye, man."

"But doctors said he had a year to live!"

"Bullets don't travel that slow, sir."

"True, you are quite correct. Are you sure you don't want my horse simulator?"

"Positive, the simulated hay would cost a fuckin' fortune. Have you got his wife's address in London, like?"

Small put on his smoking jacket, which was, indeed, still smouldering.

"Wouldn't you prefer it here? London's over fifty miles away. I've got her address, yes, but better than that, I'll drive down and get her to Jos' place right now. Are you pig fellows at the house now?"

"All except one, sir."

"Oh? Where is he?"

"Interviewing some loon with a horse fetish, sir."

"Capital! I must meet him, sounds like a top bloke! I'll get Katie right there as fast as poss, what ho!"

"Thanks man. Can you get her to bring her vacuum cleaner, too?"

"Whatever for?"

"You want to see the state of the place man, it's a right fuckin mess! Bits of fuckin brain all over the shop, man, its......"

*****

Three police cars screeched to a halt outside Oxford Police Station as six policemen bundled three criminals through the main doors. One, still wearing his balaclava screamed, "You'll never get me to confess, pig!" before receiving a sharp kick to the nads from one of the plain clothed officers they bundled them in to the station, this all looked very exciting, which is a pity, because it's not connected to our story at all.

*****

Two hours later, a Range Rover arrived outside the station, and two people got out. The first person, we have already met, Mr Dick Small. He held a hand out to support his sister, who had one hour ago been told the dreadful news of the death of her husband.

Inside, Robbie was going over the fine details of the case with Colin Weird.

"Oh man, the state of that room! I've only just finished throwing up!"

Morose looked up from a Victoria Whines catalogue, "If I might say, young Robbie, it ruddy well honked!"

"Aye, I'll pour some industrial strength bleach on the next one shall I?" He turned back to Weird, "Honestly Surr, if you're ganning to send us out to scenes like that man, I'm going back on the buses."

Jampton popped his head around the door, a neat trick as he was stood at front desk, eighty yards away, but then he was a very gifted officer. "Sorry lads, err Sir, that wall decorator's wife has turned up with her brother. I've popped them in Interview Room 1…"

Morose tore his eyes away from a very nice looking special edition Jack Daniels, "what was wrong with interview room 7?"

"Brewis is interviewing some pensioners in there," shrugged Hugh, "While I remember, they've parked their Range Rover in the disabled bay. As soon as the interview starts, I'll get Terry to tow it away. When you're done we can go to the waste ground by Milligan Way and practice doughnuts!"

"There's a restaurant there now, opened a couple of years ago," said Morose, "We'll go up Bentine Close, there's a lovely abandoned piece there, by the old dog food factory, where the fallers at Newmarket went to."

Thumbs up from Jampton, to the disgust of everyone else. Weird made a mental note to have a word with Hugh later. That word was 'don't'.

*****

Robbie entered Interview Room 1, followed by Morose. Katie turned around to face the door and, on seeing Morose, almost collapsed. Her brother steadied her as she whispered, "Endof!"

"No just before start of," Robbie switched on the new microphone system, recently installed by a couple of children, "Interview commencing 19.54, in attendance myself Sergeant Robert Harris, Chief Inspector Endofleveldemon Morose, Mrs Katie Kramer and Mr Dick Small…"

Katie looked slightly puzzled, "Am I under arrest, Sergeant?"

Robbie looked up from his papers, "Oh no man, gerraway! You've enough to worry about redecorating that study after your husband had a go. No, this is just a formality like." Robbie looked down at his notes again, "Perhaps I could start by asking, what luxury you would take to the island?"

Katie looked first at Robbie, then her brother and finally in desperation at Morose.

Morose cleared his throat, and as an afterthought his back passage, "Robbie, you're doing it again, you're not hosting Desert Island Discs, you never have."

"Oh sorry, I keep doing that lately!" muttered Robbie, "Has your husband ever tried the shotgun mouthwash trick before? Or you know, dangling from a light fitting, toss himself off the Pier, took a swim in the Tyne, that sort of thing?

Katie looked cold, "If you mean has he ever attempted suicide…"

"Aye?"

"Then no."

"But you've caught him looking longingly at the pill cabinet a few times, eh?"

"He was terminally ill, Sergeant. It's not completely unexpected."

"So, you think it may have been suicide?" asked Morose.

"Yes!" they all shouted back at him.

Morose turned to Robbie, "Sorry to waste your evening out."

*****

The Coroner's Court in Oxford was hardly the sort of place to make one feel good. Today, just to add to the misery factor, the inquest into the death of the late Jos Kramer was proceeding....well, staggering....along, just about.

Nurse Clark was finishing her testimony.

"......it was after I'd clouted the bastard with my concrete mixer, that I finally got back into my 1200 cc Frogeye, and that was the last I heard of it til I got the call off the fascists."

"And what time was that?" asked the droll, monotonous tones of the Coroner.

"Oh, definitely before the evening, I was only onto my third glass."

"Thank you Nurse Clark, I shall not be needing to ask you anything else. Can I call the next witness? Sergeant Robbie Harris of the Oxford city Police Force Protection Crew."

Harris took the stand, to one side of the court, and began.

"Well I was on ma way home an that, an we got a call to attend a shootin', like, and when we got there it was fuckin vile man, I almost threw me hoop up, there was like blood an snot an all like gory shit, all over the fuckin place, I mean, worra fucking mess, this twerp had no consideration for others, how anyone can do their job in those conditions is beyond me, I...."

"Yes, thank you Sergeant Harris, that will...."

"It was fuckin RIPE man, it well honked...."

"Yes thank you, Sergeant, can I….."

"…..an the curtains? Don't get me started about the curtains, man, they were positively DRAPED in…."

"Get this frothing clown out of here, Mr Grimley!"

Mr Grimley, a huge, seven foot man with seven feet, lifted Robbie up by the scruff of the arse, and carried him out. There was a thud and a shout of pain, followed by the sounds of stairs coming up to meet a body. Mr Grimley returned and sat down by the door, fondling a large club with spikes in the top.

"Next witness, can I call the wife of the deceased, Mrs Katie Kramer."

Kate took the stand back to the correct place and began her testimony.

"Er, I had a phone call off my brother to say that he'd have to consider selling his mechanical horse as it was all done in, and by the way, my husband had died."

"Were you at all surprised by this news?"

"Not at all, the mechanical horse had only ever brought him piles, and a sprained testicle."

"What about your husband's death?"

"Well it was expected, wasn't it? He knew he was dying and had always said that when it got unbearable, he would take the necessary steps."

"The necessary steps?"

"Yes, the ones we keep in the shed to get my brother back on the mechanical horse. He always considered others like that, which is probably why he shot himself, he didn't want to be a drain on us."

There was a scuffle at the courtroom door, and a voice shouting,

"Well he didn't consider me very well then did he, I hate that sort of blood thing man, Jesus Wept, I've had nightmares about it....."

There was a crash from Mr Grimley's club and a loud groan.

"Call the next witness, Mr Max Pathos."

Max took the stand and examined it carefully, before realising everyone was watching him being a prick.

"Just checking for clues. You can never be too careful."

"Mr Pathos, you are the police pathologist?"

"Yes."

"Can you describe your findings?"

"Well there was blood all over the place, it was utterly horrific, like something out of a Victorian bloodfest, I've never been so insulted in all my life......."

The Coroner sat back, closed his eyes, and tried to think of Nurse Clark without her clothes.

*****

Morose stood outside the court with his 75-er conker, waiting for Max to return to carry on their match. Max did come out of the court, head first, still struggling with Mr Grimley and his massive club.

"Max! I hope you've not forgotten why we're here?" He pointed proudly at his conker.

Mr Grimley took a swipe at Max, missed, and utterly flattened the shit out of Morose's conker, which was scattered to the four winds in several thousand pieces.

"Well up yours, then," muttered Morose.

Katie Kramer emerged from the Court, and Morose went to offer his condolences.

"These are my condolences," he said, showing her a handful of Special Brew cans, "Is there somewhere we can go?"

"Probably," replied Katie, "There's got to be somewhere on this planet."

"We'll try to find somewhere I'm not barred from," muttered Morose.

They walked slowly, they had to, the pavement hadn't set properly yet.

"So, what happened to you after you dumped me, you heartless moose?" Morose barfed.

"I went to The States with Jos, he lectured, and I took a crash course."

"In what?"

"Crashing speedboats. We had two girls. The elder died in a car collision after we'd returned from the States."

"Yes, I do remember the case."

"What about you?"

Morose thought hard, "What about me?"

"What did you do after you threw me out, you heartless wankbag?"

"I joined the army."

"Was that good?"

"It was til someone shot me. I left after that. Very quickly. They still haven't found me. Instead I joined the filth and worked my way up the trough."

"Did you marry, yourself?"

"That's been illegal til recently. Well, in public anyway. That court appearance just now, that must have been difficult."

"Yes."

Morose stopped, thought long and hard, and then, and only then, broke wind.

"If you don't mind me saying so," she commented, "That doesn't half ruddy well ronk."

"H'mm. This isn't the time but if we get the time, would you consider a bit of time?"

"I won't be much company."

"That's why I ditched you, you boring cow."

"Perfect. I'll ring you in a few days."

She slipped on her coat, well it was covered in grease after all. She got into a taxi and drove off, leaving the irate driver behind.

Harris sidled up to Morose.

"If I'd lost a girl like that sir, I'd also be a miserable, flat faced, pissed up, washed out, tossrag of a badger's arse."

Morose looked him in the eye, not easy as he was facing the wrong way.

"Harris?"

"Sir?"

"Suck my arse."

Harris smirked and, robbing another cab, left the miserable git with his tins and another taxi driver, at high speed.

*****

A noise of someone rustling, alerted the orchestra that they were not alone. The conductor looked around, to see there were actually three people in the audience.

It was Mrs Jephcott who had made the noise, the brown paper bag on her knee rustled loudly each time she reached in for another boiled egg or a walnut.

Mr Jephcott wasn't making too much noise, since he had the nose band fitted his snoring hadn't been too much of a problem.

Technically there were three people in the audience, although as Mrs Double-Topp had died, she could be dismissed from many people's idea of an audience; this wouldn't be discovered until after the performance, which was a pity as it would have livened the night up no end.

Bert Cross-Ply, the conductor and part time taxi driver, looked over his shoulder as the door at the rear of the hall opened emitting a stream of light from the ticket office, where Gladys Peastreamer was counting up the nights taking.

The door had opened to admit two late comers – that pissed police officer, and that bit of stuff that had nicked Bert's taxi last night.

Endof walked Katie down to their row and escorted her to her seat.

"Will you excuse me a moment please, Katie?" whispered Morose, "I never feel right at these events without a..."

"Ahh, a program? Will you get one for me too?

"I was going to say without a gallon of silly syrup. If they've got a list of runners and riders I'll bring it back, most important is the sauce."

"Thank you," she mouthed as he left to sniff out the special stuff. "And a bag of pork scratchings?"

For an amateur performance, it wasn't too bad. It was a little irritating the way the conductor kept looking over his shoulder mid adagio, and telling everyone who he had in the hall last week. And blaming immigrants for the lack of good baritones in this country during the sonata. If you could ignore all of that though...

There was a loud noise from the direction of the foyer. It made Katie quite nostalgic when she remembered she was back on the lash, with 'Dead-Eye' Morose. Yes of course, he would be trying to get the barman to leave him the keys while the barman could take the rest of the night off. Old habits die hard. And of course, following the refusal there was always the obligatory punch up. Yes, Morose had been gone about twenty minutes, you could set your clock by him, although some preferred to set their dogs on him.

There was a crash during the intro to the finale. The conductor – cum – taxi driver looked in his rear view mirror, to see a body hurtle through the double doors to the auditorium, and land in a heap on the floor, God knows who left that heap there. Morose climbed out of it, brushed the shit off, and straightening his jacket and tie, looked menacingly at the double doors and stormed back through them. The music wafted about like the smell of a turd in a train lavatory just before you raise the lid for a slash. The conductor threw his arms around like a windmill in a tornado, and was now sweating like a bastard, as the quintet, playing madly for the end, approached the last page. The viola player actually managed to break all four strings and saw through the instrument, such was their concentration no one noticed. Mr Crossply, sweat now pouring off him, trickling off the podium and toward the edge of the stage, paused, for full dramatic effect, and the quintet paused accordingly. A second body flew though the door and hit the conductor in the small of his back. The last notes trailed off, and the audience members able to move who hadn't died of boredom, applauded politely and quickly dashed for the exit, in case some moron tried to shout "Encore!"

Morose, one black eye and his wig pulled down over his mouth, staggered back in, and gathered up his coat. Katie rose from her seat, and, hovering, proceeded out with Morose, pausing only to give the barman a good kicking on the way.

They proceeded to dinner. Avoiding the Worm & Hammer, which tonight was playing host to the Harris tribe, they had a light meal at The Horse's Arms, a new family friendly restaurant – pub chain horror, that Morose hadn't been barred from quite yet.

As he finished off another waiter, with a headlock and the removal of a few teeth, so Morose leaned over to Katie and asked,

"Er, your husband's GP wanted to see me tomorrow, says its something to do with something. Any ideas?"

"It may be to do with something," she replied, "Mind you, it could just be nothing. End of?"

"Yes?"

"Did you hate me when I left?"

Morose thought a few seconds, "To be honest? I think hate is a bit of a gentle word."

It all went a bit strained after that.

*****

Next morning, Morose turned up at the GPs surgery.

"Dreadful business, this," sighed Morose.

"Yes, but it pays the bills," replied the secretary, who was doubling as the wife, a first for an English doctor, who usually has at least two of each.

"Did you know Mr Kramer?"

"Not really, just his son in law." She didn't seem very happy about that, and Morose's brain immediately thought, "I'll bet there's loads of sex I've yet to uncover here!" The doctor cut across his thoughts.

"Are you chattin' mah wife up?" he shouted.

"No," replied Morose.

"Why, are yer a puff, man?"

"No," sighed Morose, "I'm here about the suicide of Jos Kramer. Did you do it?"

"No!"

"Pity." Morose crossed a name off his list. "Your hound of a secretary booked me a chat with you, cos you wanted to see me, or did you just want to take the piss out of a total stranger?"

"Aye, well man, It's just I don't think he could have stoved himself in, like," said the doctor.

"And why not?"

"He was so far gone, an' that. He couldn't have lifted his own willy, never mind keep a fuckin great shotgun and rinse his tonsils with it. If you see what I mean, like."

"So, you don't think it was suicide?"

The doctor glared at his wife, as he replied, "Not my job that. I just think it wasn't what it's been reported as."

Morose left the doctor with a sample on his carpet, and tried to get Harris on his mobile phone. After the fifth attempt he gave up and, flagging down a school minibus, dragged the driver out, and drove round to the garage where Harris had driven Weird's car. Sadly, Weird was also there.

Weird studied him, as Terry went about dismantling his car for spares, for a 'Ford Specialist' in Liverpool. Weird studied something else, as he addressed Morose,

"If you're going to drone on about some shit, go away. I'm on leave."

"Where are you leaving to, sir?"

"Anywhere to get away from you."

"Before you go, sir, just a quick update on the reported

suicide of that chap the other day."

"Don't tell me you've made an arrest?"

"No sir, but I may be about to. Kramer's son in law sounds a right dodgy toad, and I want him banged up for it."

Weird sighed. "It's all a bit tenuous. This chap is now prime suspect in a suicide, before we even have a case against him? I'm going to look a right knob at the Chief Constable's golf club."

"Look sir, you go and have a nice play with the Chief Constable's club, and while you're polishing him off, I'll get this dick wipe of a son in law."

"Just watch it, matey."

"I have been doing that, sir, and its given me no pleasure."

As they walked out of Terry's garage, to the resounding sounds of a car being fire axed up, Harris joined Morose to tell him,

"I've already spoken to Max about it."

"What does he say?"

"He agrees that you're a droning old shit. Also, that fella Kramer, he could na ha' held a fuckin gun if his life depended on it! All sounds a bit like, sort of wrong to me, like."

Morose looked Harris in the eye, and walked into a lamp post.

"Go round to this chap Tom Jenkins, the son in law, and let him know we're interested."

"Interested?"

"Interested."

"Ok. I'll nail a note to his window, or his forehead, or something."

"That's the style, Harris! We'll make a fucking pig out of

you yet."

And with that he remembered walking into the lamp post, and fell over.

*****

"I know how I'll feel about your leaving," said Morose, very seriously. "It won't feel good."

He paused for a moment.

"But if that's the price I have to pay for your comfort, now......"

He stared into the middle distance.

"......then, that's something that I'll just have to deal with."

With that he took a last look at his bottle of Jack Daniels, and swigged the last quarter down in one go.

"I have no right to expect this of you," said an emotional Kate Kramer.

"I have the right to make that choice," said Morose, in a final sort of way, before shouting over to his brother, "Oi, shit-house, two more JD's, you're slacking!"

And that's how Morose got another bottle over his head.

*****

"Hello? Shop?" shouted Robbie as he looked around the small antique shop. It was a fruit shop, but very old.

Robbie picked up a melon, "Oi! Shop!" He shouted, throwing it through a mirror.

"Do you mind stopping that?" asked the man stood in front of Robbie, "You've been ignoring me for fully five minutes now, what on Earth are you here for?"

In reply Robbie threw a bag of potatoes at the man, "Are you Tom Jenkins?"

"No, he runs the antique shop next door."

"Oh, fuck this then!" said Robbie, leaving.

*****

"He's lying, surr," reported Harris.

"That Jenkins fellow?"

"Nah sur, the bloke in the fruit shop, he's lying down after I threw a bag a spuds at him."

"Must be a scouser, Harris, it's all they ever do, lie around, waiting for the work to come to them."

"Aye sur, an' I'm not sure about that Jenkins fellow either, he apparently rang the ambulance at 5pm to report that he'd found Kramer splattered all over the fuckin room, like, real like just DEAD an a right fuckin mess at that!"

"Yes, I am aware of the details. Get to the point, you piss gargling Geordie knob flopper."

"Jenkins said he'd rung his fatha in law to arrange to see him, at the house, at 3pm."

"And? Was there no 3pm that day?"

"Nah, yer stupid fuckweasel! Ya see, the phones all over the house were out of order til 5pm."

Morose stopped to look his sergeant in the eye.

"Nab him."

"Aye sir!"

Harris ran off to get his car, shoving an elderly priest into the road in his haste. Morose looked up to see that there were no lamp posts around, and, finding none, walked off to meet

Kate, and fell down a manhole.

Kate looked stunning as she finished off her game of Russian roulette with the local Towns Women's Guild, there was applause from the spectators as Kate and her partners walked off the pitch, and polite applause for the ambulancemen who lifted the damaged losers into the back of the ambulance, that had been on standby since midday. She made her way to the deckchairs arranged around the lawns, and reflected that there must be an easier way of raising funds for the church roof.

A pile of rags blew into the chair next to her. It smelled of an eclectic mix of beer and badger's arse.

"Hello Morose," she smiled, "You've missed the main event."

"I decided to skip the Russian Roulette bit," replied Morose, "Seemed a bit close to home after recent events?"

"Oh shit, you're right, silly me! What a faux pas! I'm such a dozy whore."

"Yes."

"Anyway, you've not come over here to ogle my tits again, have you?"

"Yes."

"I knew you hadn't." She became serious. "Its about Jos again, isn't it?"

"And the tits."

"Go ahead." She smiled, adding quickly, "About the case."

Morose changed tack at once. "What were the financial arrangements you and your husband had, with young Tom Jenkins?"

"We'd made him a loan at family loan shark rates, for his antiques rubbish that we'd got him established with, but Jos had cancelled that recently."

"Any reason?"

"We needed it for my knickers emporium. Jos could be pretty ruthless like that."

Morose thought hard for a minute; then thought better of it, and continued,

"When was this loan arrangement cancelled?"

"The day before he killed himself."

Now Morose took an interest.

"The day before?"

"Yes. Tom must have been pretty upset. I could hear them arguing about it on the phone."

"Even though you were in London?"

"It was quite a disagreement."

Morose lapsed into thought. Surely even Weird could see that this was fast becoming a water-tight case?

"How did Tom take the news?"

"Not well. Jos said he made a vague threat to come round and redecorate the walls with him. I'm sure he was only joking Morose, you must not take that as meaning anything."

"Just the same, I think we should have another word with him."

"Well, I'm sure you know best..."

*****

Harris escorted Jenkins into the station. Jampton told him to leave the escort outside and just walk in, so they did.

"Interview Room 7 free, Hugh?" called out Robbie.

Hugh looked on the computer, "Earliest I can do you is next Friday."

"Awww man, I had me heart set on interviewing this gimp tonight! No offence Mr Jenkins."

"You really should be booking the rooms on TrapAdvisor now, Robbie," suggested Hugh, "and book early, they're getting great reviews."

"What can you give me, man?"

"I can offer you Interview Room 8?" Hugh perused the computer, "coffee making facilities, unusual view, no wifi…"

"8?"

"That's one of the new rooms, accessed via the portal in Superintendent Weird's office. It'll be alright, he's off today, looking for a replacement car or something."

"Aye man, send the others through will you."

Harris made sure he'd got the recording equipment right this time. While the assembled throng watched, he prepared the memory stick, got the backup disc loaded, the microphone plugged into the correct socket, and had a stack of pound coins ready for the meter, just in case.

"Reet, you lot!" he sat back beaming, "Music's ready, when it fades, grab a seat and we'll…."

"Harris, you're doing it again, you are not in charge of musical chairs."

"Ah shit, sorry, I keep doin that recently." Harris pressed a sleek control button. "Er, okay, aye man, interview chamber eight, present today there's me Sergeant Harris, an' also Inspector Morose, an there's P.C. Gonemad…"

"Hello!" beamed Gonemad.

"…. An' there's also what looks like a malevolent bat hanging off the top of the gallows in the corner, and yes, the condemned man, sorry, interviewee, Mr Jenkins."

"Now look," Tom was taken aback, "What's all this about? What are you trying to pin on me?"

"Aye man, all in good time. Now, you said, in your statement, that you'd spoken with yer fatha in law on the phone, an that, to see him about yer business goin' so well, and that more money was on its way. He called you at 3pm to finalise it, and when you'd got there, it was all dark like, an that's when you discovered the fuckin rank mess of an abattoir that was all that remained of...."

"Yes, thank you Harris, we get the idea," interjected Morose.

"I'm tellin ya, it was fuckin the utter pits man! Couldn't you have at least cleaned up a bit?"

"I think what my sergeant is trying to ask," smiled Morose as he headbutted Robbie out of the way, "Is, you went to see Kramer on your usual monthly meeting and found him dead?"

"Yes," Jenkins was cautious, "Why? What's this all about?"

"I put it to you, Mr Jenkins, that you went to kill him cos he'd cancelled all his support for your poxy shop, and made it look like suicide."

"No, he was terminally ill, why would I...." Jenkins' voice trailed off.

He suddenly saw a trap closing.

"I never! There was no cancellation of the loan! He wouldn't do that to me!"

"And Mr Kramer's bank agree, cos they had his orders to cancel it, that morning."

"Never! He phoned me!"

"The phone was off til 5pm."

"He rang me! You're all scum! Let me out!"

Morose turned to Gonemad, "This will make a cracking tape, for "You've Been Framed Up. Make sure a copy goes to the editors tomorrow, there's fiver hundred knicker in this!"

He thought about what he'd just said.

"Five hundred quid. Not knickers. That's the business line. Knickers. Aw fuck it, lets go for a pint, Robbie. Robbie? Get off the floor!"

He grabbed Harris by the chest hairs. Despite the screams of the prisoner to get out, Harris to get his hairs back, and Gonemad to get the CD out, Morose still managed to trip over the doorstop. The door clicked shut and locked them all in. It was going to be a long day.

*****

Hugh had just finished telling an elderly lady that if she wanted to report a robbery in progress she'd have to book an appointment, they were far too busy to see her right now. He gave her the appointment line number and advised her she'd need to leave a message on the answerphone service and someone would get back to her within the mandatory 28 working days.

He replaced the receiver and went back to looking at naughty pictures on his computer, the sort his Mum wouldn't let him look at, at home. Those pictures of kids... throwing bricks through windows, drawing faces and writing 'clean me' in the dirt on filthy cars. His Mum always said looking at those kinds of things would give him ideas, and no child of hers was going to be put on detention. Mum... that reminded him, he had promised to do a bit of online shopping for his Mum. He logged into the particular website and as he keyed in his account number, he glanced at the 'About Us' section on the home page. Underneath the picture of the proprietor of the business - with a crow on her shoulder, and a can of Stella in her hand, for some reason – and was struck with a thought. Wasn't that... Without even a thought for Data Protection he ran down the corridor towards Superintendent Weird's office.

The usual sensation of a sickening twist in the dimensional fabric passed quickly, he was starting to get used to it. He headed for the space where the invisible portal to the Dark Realms should be.

This was the part his soul wasn't used to. Although Hugh wasn't aware of it, the only time he had come into the gravitational pull of the Gateway previously, his id had been protected by the presence of either Morose or Weird, either of which could dampen the soul draining effects. This time he travelled alone, unprotected, as it were.

A cloying, dreadful darkness permeated poor Hugh's soul as something tried to rip out the very essence that made him Hugh Jampton. Parts of his past life were scrutinised by demonic imps as his embodiment was shared amongst very hungry dark forces. It felt like something deep within him was slowly bleeding to death, when he became aware that something was reaching out to him, and the darkness lifted.

He found himself standing in a large building with masses of desks ahead of him, the queues to each desk seemed to reach back an eternity, possibly infinitely. Each thing queueing – they were not all human – seemed to be carrying large writhing cases, for some of them the cases were getting bigger, they appeared to be far too big for most of them. Hugh looked to the front, to the creatures at the desks. They seemed to be having their parcels examined, in some cases they were taken off them and passed through to a conveyor belt behind, but in most cases the impish figures behind the desks seemed to take great delight in rejecting the parcels and sending these damned creatures to the back of the queue, to wait another eternity.

"Can I help you?" hissed a voice behind Hugh.

Hugh spun around to see a creature that looked more like a seven-foot-high image of what Gerald Scarfe would make of a dragonfly.

"Ye – yes… Where am I?" Hugh stammered.

"Why, this is Purgatory, Mr Jampton."

"It's looks more like Manchester Airport!"

"The one is based on the other. I'll let you decide which came first. After where comes why. Why are you here? It's not your time yet."

"I'm looking for Interview Chamber 8?"

"Don't distract it!" said a creature more human than the dragonfly. If it wasn't for the glowing red eyes, the fire cascading from its lips and the constant cackling from behind the flames it would be able to pass as human.

It leapt over several queueing creatures, much higher than expectedly and seemed to stumble slightly as it landed. Using Jampton to stabilise itself, Hugh felt the razor sharp claws at the end of its fingers dig in to his shoulders, near the base of his neck.

"What have we here?" It asked. "An Oxford police officer, in my realm, how tasty!"

"Please… I just want…" Hugh stuttered.

"Interview Chamber 8." The jumping thing screeched. "Help him, Idris." So saying, he bounded off.

The dragonfly thing pointed vaguely away from the desks, to Hugh's relief, and flew off.

"Over here Hugh," shouted the familiar voice of Morose, "For fuck's sake what are you doing?"

Hugh ran slowly at first, then faster and faster, til he crashed into the wall at the back of interview room eight. Morose and Harris stood looking at him; Harris simply said,

"Now look, that's why we don't allow running in the corridors, you should know matron doesn't like that."

"Keep your eyes open," agreed Morose, "We'll never make a proper swine out of you like this."

Hugh opened his eyes and immediately asked, "Is this still interview room eight?"

They looked at him blankly, and carried on.

"Mrs GP woman rang me earlier," Morose informed Harris, "Wants me to meet with her and give her point of view on the suspects for suicide that we've stitched up. You coming for a laugh? That tosser is guilty as fuck, anyone can see that."

"Nah sir," said Harris, "I'm off to find out who's been left what from the will. I wanna see just who has benefitted from what."

"You got anything to add?" Morose addressed Jampton.

"Well actually, I've found this website about Mrs Kramer's knickers business, I think maybe you ought to have a look."

"You realise we can be on a disciplinary for that?"

Hugh eyed him with an eye, "No, you daft tool, it's the addresses and stuff. Something you maybe really ought to see."

Morose conceded the point, "Okay you pathetic waz bag Hugh, take this up to the front desk while you're going?" asked Morose, and jumped into Hugh's arms.

Hugh sighed. It was better than Hell, but, not by much.

*****

Sandra Blake, the good doctor's good wife, sat on a tombstone waiting for Morose. She wore black – black overall cardigan, black leggings, black shoes - not because she was in mourning, it just suited her general demeanour. A hard-faced dog, she looked like she once had an allure about her, but she seemed to have left that allure at a railway locker one day, and lost the key. Her one colour was her grey eyes.

Morose appeared, looked at the woman in black sat on the tombstone, and muttered, "That's a miserable crow if I ever saw one." He extended his hand, and it fell off. Immediately he produced another hand, and walked over to Mrs Blake, and shook her gently by the throat.

"He's innocent," she began.

"I'm pleased to hear it," he replied, "That almost wraps the case up, but out of interest, why is he innocent?"

She turned her blank, grey eyes on him, "Because he didn't do it. Tom wouldn't have knocked off his own father in law."

"Well, that's all the detail I need. However, I might need more than just a character reference, to get the chap off this charge we've trumped up."

"Well, that's all I can say."

"Nice hands."

"They were burned in a bonfire."

"What a dreadful accident."

"Not really, I needed a new set of fingerprints."

"Well I'm glad you got them. I've got a life to get on with, I'm the fuck out of here, you boring crow."

Morose's phone began to ring, he reached into his pocket and tore a hole in the lining, all his change fell out and was stolen by a tramp who had been loitering nearby. He tried again, and found that the phone had been in his other hand the whole time. Wrenching it out of his other hand, with his first hand, he answered it by pressing it with the former holding hand, and then using the current holding hand, to hold it to his ear as he spoke, not many people can speak with their ears but, this was Morose.

"Yeff?" he asked.

"Oh awright sir," said Harris, "I've just found oot about that will, an' that."

"Web dub, Horris."

"Er…are you okay sir? Your voice is a bit, well, shite, sir."

"Wang on….." Morose made a dull farting noise, before starting again, "Sorry about that Harris, my ear was blocked with wax. I can speak better now."

There was a pause while Harris took this notion in, thought better of it, and then continued,

"Aye well its like this see, Kramer left his mad bastard brother a truckload of dosh, and the rest of it had gone to that G.P's charity fund.

"WHAT!!"

"Aye man, are yer still with the G.P's wife?"

"She's just left, having landed me a right hook, for being unkind to her."

"Ah. Pity. Anyway, now we can really hit the murderer with it! I'll come an' pick you up an that."

Morose pressed the 'off' button and made his way quickly out of the graveyard, and toward the nearest off licence as fast as his partly repaired legs would carry him. Back in work and it's not 2pm? No bloody chance!

*****

"Interview commencing. Time 18.43. The Bombay Army led by Major General Sir Charles Napier has just defeated the Turkish..."

"Harris!" shouted Morose.

"Aye sorry Surr.. Time 18.43 present are Detective Sergeant Robert Harris, Chief Inspector Endofleveldemon Morose and the vile murderer Thomas Jenkins."

"Hey!" started Jenkins.

"Alright Surr, if you are going to waste our time protesting your innocence. No skin off my nose. I hope you know we're sending the cleaning bill to you. That place was disgusting, man. Made me fetch right up. And our Claudie had made a lovely mushroom soup too. Even the pigeons outside were hawkin' up man, it was ripe..."

"Thank you, Harris," interjected Morose.

"Alright well, am just saying like, it's disgustin' that's all. Just want it noted."

"Why aye pet!" sneered Morose.

"Ok, first question, Mr Jenkins – did you kill Mr errm, you know, the dead fella?"

"I didn't."

"Can you prove that rather unlikely statement?"

"I can't prove it, but I'm being set up."

"Do you know who would want to set you up, Surr?"

"I don't know but.."

Morose had been watching this exchange quietly. At this his ears pricked up. Robbie shook his head quietly at him, "We need more Surr."

"What do you mean?" spluttered Jenkins, "What have I said?"

"Don't you know?" asked Morose.

Jenkins lowered his head and replied, "No"

Harris rang a bell, "Oh well done Surr! I'm sorry Mr Jenkins, you failed to avoid saying yes or no in the minute, so you lose. Next!"

Jenkins bowed his head and left the stage, accompanied by three topless nuns, playing saxophones. As Morose and Harris applauded, so WPC Franks, wearing a sequined tutu, grinned her way onto the stage. Morose presented her to the audience.

"Welcome, Miss Franks, and your starter for ten, is......"

"Sir?"

"'kin what?"

"We've just let our chief suspect in this suicide case, loose."

The two men looked at each other, and said together,

"SHIT!!"

Chasing the audience out amid a chorus of bleats and grunts, and quickly decontaminating the room, Franks and Jampton ran after Jenkins and beat the shit out of him, then dragged him back in. Harris sat on the desk lighting a fag, which Morose took off him and smoked himself.

"Tell us about the scene, when you found the body, Mr Jenkins," sneered Morose.

"It was hard to see, the curtains were shut....."

"They were open when Nurse Clark left the room."

"I know, I was watching her change."

"Sir," interrupted Harris, "Saul opened the curtains."

Morose exploded. Then he got rather upset as well, and spoke his mind.

"Now, you bally well listen to me, young whippersnapper. What the blazes do you think you're playing at disturbing my trumped up charges? By heck! I'll be jolly mad if you don't make amends soon. And get your hair cut, too!"

"Fuck off sir, I wanted to see the scene of the crime for meself, like, an' White had to take the photos, or else we'd have no evidence except a load of blank photos."

Morose ripped another one out, adding, "Eat that. And while you're at it, find out from the General Post Office Telephones, when the fault was fixed."

"I can help you with that." Jenkins momentarily brightened up, "When I arrived, the engineer asked me to help him. Someone had dumped a cement mixer through his windscreen."

Harris checked his notes, "The fault was reported at 10, and fixed at 5, but it was only fixed at 5 cos the customer – the dead guy, like – had requested it to be fixed then. He could have had it fixed any time, cos he was priority, like, being a bit near dead, an' that. Apparently, he has his own parking space at Morrisons?"

"Really? I didn't know he was a single mum?"

"No Surr, y'kna? Blue badge gadgee? Wheels of steel? That sort of thing!"

Morose pondered, "And you met him leaving, Mr Jenkins?"

"Yes!" Jenkins nodded.

"Well that's your alibi fucked,"

"Cack!"

Morose snorted a quick line, and got his single sheet of blank paper together, as he led Harris out of the interview cupboard.

"Well I'm off to meet Mrs Kramer and try out my 'Deal or

No Deal' game."

"Aw sir, no! Don't show her your photos of that place in Kent."

"And while we're getting it away, Harris, go to London and have a look at her knickers will you?"

"While she's in Oxford, Surr?"

"Check out the knicker emporium in London. I want phone records checked, speak to her neighbours, find out if she's got a bit on the side. Dammit, man, I want answers! If Jenkins is going to protest his innocence we need to have checked all avenues before we get him sent down."

"Canny good," offered Harris writing something rude in his notebook.

Morose turned back, "Just one more question, Robbie."

Harris doodled a pair of balls and a cock, with all spunk on the end in his book, then looked up, "Are we pretending to be Columbo now Surr?"

"Knob off Harris, you're not funny. How did the dead man report the phone fault if he was already deceased."

Harris looked up from drawing a biologically impossible image of a naked woman in his notepad and stared at Morose. "No Surr, he reported the phone and like died later, man"

"Hmm…" muttered Morose. There was something not right here.

*****

The next day they assembled at Weird's office. Weird looked out over his horn-rimmed face at the shadowy collection of shady looking mother fuckers before him.

"Well this is just ridiculous!" he spat, "We have a man who is determined to die, possibly by his own hand; a GP who supports him at killing himself; and the chief beneficiary of the deceased's will, is the GP's own charity."

"Sir," they all said together.

"Well it's fucking ridiculous. We'll be finding out that the other beneficiary, is some cloth headed tit who rides a mechanical horse, next! Ha! Ha! Ha!"

There was a pained silence.

"You really are a bunch of humourless self fisters", growled Weird.

Morose dropped a silent one, as he spoke up.

"The beneficiary does indeed match that description, sir."

There was another pained silence. Weird glowed a sort of dull green, before speaking.

"Get it sorted, matey."

"Matey," muttered the others, and left before they were turned into frogs.

Harris, however, popped his head back round the door.

"Ah, just one thing, sir," he began.

" 'kin what?" growled the green apparition.

"Hope y' don't mind me sayin so, like, but that noodle sucker Morose, he's getting a bit too close with the widow in this case."

"I thought that was all over decades ago?"

"It's restarted, sir."

"He really is a useless tool. Keep an eye on him, Harris, and if you film any of it, it'll be worth a few quid on 'You Wank' or some other porn site. Don't forget! A good copper blows his mates up out of a sense of duty."

"Aye sir," replied Harris, and shut the door on his hand.

Morose was indeed getting a bit close. Mrs Kramer, dear ex-girlfriend that she was, had taken to spending long evenings with Morose. Okay it was only ten minutes over a glass of water and a couple of twiglets, but it always FELT like a long evening, with Morose.

But today, Morose was meeting up with the increasingly shadowy figure that was the GP's wife. He'd been going over his old files again and couldn't help noticing, that the car crash that had taken the Kramer girl, had occurred startlingly close to the residency of the GP. The police photos showed a burned-out car, and a list of casualties had included Sandra Blake with burnt hands. Had she rushed to the scene to help? If so, why? Did she know who was in the car? Why was she so sure that their main suspect, Tom Jenkins, was innocent? He ran this train of thought round and round in his head, until it fell off the tracks at a level crossing. Bloody cheap foreign shite.

This needed careful handling of a sensitive woman, and he was the man for the job.

"What really happened that night, moose?" he began.

"Er...."

"You've let me almost get the wrong man, haven't you?"

"Er....."

"You'd rather see an innocent man in gaol and your reputation safe, wouldn't you?"

"Erm..."

"Those burnt hands weren't for new fingerprints for some past petty drugs dealing, were they?"

"Mr Morose..."

"You'd rung Tom Jenkins' wife out of spite to come & see him at yours, where he'd spent the whole week, 'cos you two had had a row! And when she saw him there she drove off in a huff having battered the shit out of you, and then she made a mess of her driving, and ended up around that tree in a fireball!"

"Mr Morose..."

"Shut it, dog face. I've got some serious shit to get sorted now, quick, or else I'll never get to our Geoff's to smash it up tonight. You've not heard the last of this, or your lizard like husband!"

He closed the letterbox and fell off the step, tearing his trousers on the railing. By Christ, that clot Harris had better have some good news on the telephone situation.

*****

Harris had already found out a few interesting things. He hadn't even had to leave Oxford. He sat with Sergeant Jampton who had been rattling on and on about the bloody knickers emporium, and how it didn't add up, and why was there a phone number for this emporium in London, when the number was for Oxford? It wasn't making any more sense.

"Fuck it," he said to Hugh, "Ring it. See who answers."

Hugh dialled the number and it began to ring.

"Hello?" said a voice.

"Hello Robbie, I'm waiting for someone to answer the phone," muttered Hugh.

Then the ringing stopped and a woman's voice answered, "Hello?"

"Ah, alright there luv," droned Hugh, "I was just wondering, what colour are your knickers? I mean, for women? Not for me, you see, I wouldn't be buying women's panties, cos that's not really a cool scene, is it?"

"Of course not Mr Jampton, do you want it on the same account as last time?"

Harris tried not to smile as Hugh suddenly turned deep red. Then, a horrible realisation crossed his mind.

"Hugh!" he whispered, "that voice! Get her name!"

Hugh covered up the speaker, "Are you feeling lucky?"

"No, you daft stoat nosher, just do it! Don't let her hang up!"

"Hello? Same account, Mr Jampton?" came the voice down the phone.

"Hello, yes, great idea love! Thank you for that! Er, erm, by the way, are you the same girl who I usually speak to?"

"Yes, it's my office you've come through to."

Harris resisted the urge to shout "Her office!" and instead urged Hugh, "Keep her talking! Ask if she knows the manager! Ask if she says Mrs...."

"Ah that's just great luv," Hugh was playing this for all he was worth, "Just for my records, sorry, my Mum's records, who did she.... I... me, yes, who did I speak to?"

"Yes, that's fine, it's Kate."

Hugh was well into his act now. "Oh, I thought it was either you or, er, Kylie."

"Definitely not Kylie. I don't employ a Kylie. You should know that by now."

Harris had already run out of the building and was leaping into his Ford Anglia estate before Hugh finished,

"Oh, not Kylie then? Sorry, just wishful thinking. Thanks."

He hung up.

"Hey Robbie, she says her name is.....Rob? Robbie?"

*****

It was important to get to Morose quickly. Find him, explain to him and get the case solved. It was Tuesday evening at 8pm, where would the Chief Inspector be?

A Renault Megane pulled up outside The Worm and Hammer, and Harris got out.

"Thanks for that pal, I'll get my car dragged off your driveway before morning man. Very kind of you."

"And the other…" asked the driver.

"Aye, I'll get your parkin' tickets looked at too, man. I can't promise anything about the Windrush thing, mind. Mind you, if you go to Jamaica they won't chase you for the parking tickets."

"Not the point."

"Aye man, we'll do what we can. Thanks again."

As Robbie approached the main entrance all the signs were there that he'd come to the right place – A bubble car 'parked' half in and half out of the Thames; the door hanging on by a single hinge; two ambulances with the lights flashing parked up, and a wall mounted modern jukebox occupying the space normally reserved for the pub signage. Yes, it looked like Geoff was having a family reunion tonight.

Inside the scene was initially very quiet. This was the eye of the hurricane; half gone, the other half presumably to come.

Harris looked around the surprisingly nearly empty room. Of the twenty tables only one was upright. The chairs had all been stacked on top of each other, not vertically – horizontally, they were positioned ready to be pushed through a window. The bar could no longer in truth be referred to as a bar. All signs and bar taps had been removed, several were decorating the face of an unconscious Geoff. Chief Inspector Morose himself was atop the one remaining table, he had hooked a bottle of industrial strength something, cleaning fluid possibly, and was decorating his tonsils with it while crooning a very twisted version of "Love Like Blood". For some reason he was jamming pound coins up his own arse and demanding a different tune.

"Surr," began Harris, "are yer busy?"

Morose swayed slightly, as he teetered on the verge of playing a fresh record he'd swallowed. He seemed to believe that the pound coins would play them. He looked at one of the Robbie Harrises before him.

"You again! You always call at the most inopportune moments, Mick."

"It's Harris, sir."

"Harris, you camel felcher! What have you done with Mick?"

"He's dead, sir."

"Good, I hated that shit. I suppose you've come to bore me with something, that can wait til next week?"

"Not quite sir, its about that Mrs Kramer person."

Morose sobered up very quickly.

"Katie? What have you done with her? Has she run off with Mick?"

"No sir, but you need to know that she's not….."

Morose grabbed his sergeant by the throat, "Not what? Alive? Lord Rothmere? Everton's goalkeeper? Playing bass in Status Quo? Answer me!"

Harris kneed him in the balls before he turned blue, and after Morose had retrieved them, he explained.

"Mrs Kramer, your ex bit, she's in charge of the….."

"Now you listen to me, young Harris. While you've been trying to frame up my ex, I have found out that her husband, the room respray expert, had deliberately framed up Tom Jenkins, who I always believed was innocent, as some sort of twisted revenge on Jenkins....."

"Sir, your ex..."

".....AND furthermore, that dodgy GP fellow with the hound of a wife, was his helper and partner in crime, and...."

"Sir, your ex...."

"Don't you see? That splatterbucket Kramer got them, to frame up Jenkins! We've got to get him! Get my car here, now!"

"Sir, you're in a pub."

"My natural environment! Its where I do all my thinking. I was going to...."

The sentence was never finished, as an aluminium beer barrel flew through the air and knocked him clean off the table, into the line of chairs, and thus out of the window, where they all landed on top of him.

Geoff Morose, peeling the beer labels off his face and the tap from up his nose, leered into view.

"And stay out, pig!" he managed to say, before sliding back down onto the floor again.

Harris ran outside and, despite his best efforts, failed to keep Morose under the pile of matchwood that had been Geoff's furniture.

"So, knowing all that, sir, what about Mrs Kramer?"

"We'll have to tell her. Get me into that waterlogged Heinkel of mine, and let's get up there. She'll be taking this quite badly."

"First time for everything," muttered Harris to himself.

*****

The police claxons were going ten to the dozen as five cars full of armed officers tore down a normally quiet country lane just outside the city of Oxford.

"I wonder where there all off to Surr?" muttered Harris

"Can we just get to Katie's place quickly, Robbie. I'm desperate for a piss."

And so, they kept pushing the bubble car up the hill.

*****

Finally, having got the bubble car started, they got it to free wheel down the hill, toward the Kramer household, running over the telephone engineer on the way.

"Serves him right, hiding in the bushes waiting for that nurse to return," muttered Morose. Skilfully pulling up just a few yards inside the garage doors, Morose and Harris had to batter their way out of the little car as it had a forward opening door. Morose used Harris' head as a hammer to break the glass with; and Harris obligingly left a severe dent in Morose's forehead as a repayment.

They ran up to the front door of the house, and then caught sight of the lizard- like Doctor Blake's car, parked up outside the house. Morose's jaw dropped. He quickly affixed a replacement jaw, and spoke.

"That's that newt wanker doctor's car. What the fuck's he doing here? Katie!" he called out.

He held his finger on the doorbell button, not getting an immediate response he began headbutting the door panel, and then began hitting the glass pane at the top with his other hand. Harris reached forward and turned the door handle.

"It was open all the time," he observed, with barely a hint

of amusement.

"I know that, you pantie liner. What has that gimp done to Kate?"

He tore in and made for the lounge, Harris putting the lock on the door, in case there were any burglars around. Didn't want the police dropping in as well!

A familiar figure met them at the door to the lounge.

"Too late," sighed Derek Small, Kate's mad brother, as he carried his freshly singed mechanical horse out of the room, "I had called round for a cuppa and a quick gallop, but, too late."

"What do you mean, 'too late?'" blurted Morose. He pushed past the madman and into the room. Kate's body lay draped across her favourite chair, holding her favourite sherry, and wearing her favourite slippers.

Harris joined him, and after a respectful pause, asked,

"Why is that bottle of sherry, wearing Kate's favourite slippers?"

"This is that lizard's fault," seethed Morose, "Come on, I'm going to batter the shit out of him!"

"Do you think that's wise, sir?"

"No, but it'll make me feel better, move it, you Geordie loser!"

*****

Morose hammered on Marriot's door with a hammer.

" 'kin what?" asked Marriot, opening the door, shortly before getting a hammer in the face.

Morose grabbed him by the throat, and dragged Marriot back into his own waiting room.

"Wait here!" he shouted.

"How long for?" asked Marriot.

"Til I'm ready! See how you like it!" retorted Morose, "You gave Kate those pills so she'd do herself in, didn't you!"

"Mr Morose..."

"You've been responsible for all these deaths and now, you get one over on me!"

"Mr Morose...."

"I'd been trying to keep her alive after Henry blew his arse all over the house, and you've killed her, 'cos she was all that stood in the way of you and your bastard inheritance from her will!"

"Mr Morose...."

"And another thing, your wife is a fucking hog!"

Sandra stuck her head through the office door. "Did someone call me?"

Marriot stood up, and said,

"I prescribed her suppository tablets, cos she was complaining about you being a pain in the arse. If she's taken too many, that's her choice, not mine."

"You callous shithouse! Couldn't you at least try to talk her out of suicide?"

"Whatever she saw in you, if she wouldn't listen to you, why would she listen to anything I'd said? Her choice. And I've gained nothing. She left everything to the Amazonian Bushbaby Nose Flute Tribe Aid Fund."

"Oh." Morose sat down. He picked up a magazine. "So when can I see you?"

"For what?"

"A prescription for a quarter ounce of weed?"

*****

The Mazda 360 drove slowly down the gravel driveway to Katie's house. It pulled up between the two police vehicles as the door opened and the rotund body of Max Pathos emerged grumbling quietly to himself.

He passed Derek Small and Wall – his butler – sharing a healthy fag outside the door. Max didn't know them too well, so he kept on grumbling to himself as he entered the house.

"Aah White, Gonemad, good. Evening Soames. Is the stiff in here?"

Without waiting for a reply, he entered the first door he came to. It was a study, or in actual fact an office – the official office for the Oxford branch of www.katiespanties.com. The walls were covered in promotional pictures of G strings, fuller panties, some split in strange places also garters, basques, suspenders, bras of all manner and description and even a 'gentleman's section'.

As Max took a second to scan around the room his ears became attuned to a regular beeping noise. He passed a stack of www.katiespanties.com catalogues and a mail out tray with a box addressed to Hugh, at the station, for some reason, to find a small, 1990's answering machine, the kind with big blocky buttons and a switch you used to turn it on. If Max remembered correctly this model used an old music tape, like he used to use to record Tommy Vance back in the good old days.

Sure enough there it was, and the beep and flashing light indicated a message left unplayed.

PC Gonemad entered the room just as Max was about to press play, "No Sir, the body's in the other room."

"Yes," muttered Max, "No ice in mine..."

He pressed play. The tape rewound itself back to the

start of the message and began: -

"Hello? Katie? Yes, lovely day. Good luck with your knickers exhibition later."

"Hmm, nothing of interest there, young Saul. I was hoping to find a clue somewhere in that message. Do me a favour Saul, pop that into a bin for me. Where did you say the body was?"

CHAPTER 4 – ID THEFT: THE CASE OF THE FAKE SERGEANT 'N' SHIT

There was a hint of romance in the air. Jessica and Emily Harris had both picked up on it, excused themselves, and gone to bed early. Now the sweet smell of candles and scented oils, and just a hint of champagne, wafted gently around the Harris household. Claudia lay back on the sofa and let her head take itself a legal ride. Well, they'd had to pack up the real stuff since the girls arrived. Also, it didn't look too good with Robbie going in to work stinking of weed, any more.

Robbie gave his underpants a final blast of air freshener, and, remembering he wasn't wearing undercrackers, tried his best to fight back the urge to scream and writhe in pain. Claudia might enjoy that bit.

"Is yer phone off, pet?" asked Claudia.

"Not quite pet, I've put it on 'aircraft' mode."

"What's that all about?"

"I've thrown it out of an upstairs window."

"D'ya think you'll be able to find it tomorree mornin', like? Just in case there's any shit goon' doon on the toon tonight, pet?"

"No crimes left unsolved in the whole of Oxfordshire, pet. We've been told we can take games in tomorrow. I'm takin' Kerplunk"

"Just in case pet, y'phone?"

"Aye well, should be easy enough, as long as that fucking gravity stuff doesn't take it out of reach of the window."

"Have y'seen my stockin's pet?" Claudia shouted through

the bathroom door.

"They were in Mr Chopper's cage last time I saw them, luv. He was making a bed out of them"

"Oh no! Sorry pet, I might smell a little bit gerbily tonight."

"It's alreet pet, leave him with them."

"No, I've got them. Little bastard's laddered them, mind."

"Aww, give him them back, I can hear him whining and knocking on his cage."

"No luv, that's not him, he's on his X box. Oh, by the way hun, can we leave his cage downstairs tonight?"

"You mean, you get a little cagey when he's in the room with us, like?"

"No, it's not that so much, it's his sarcastic posts on Facebook."

"Hmm, hey pet, if that's not Mr Chopper, what's all that knocking and whining then?"

"You know he gets very frustrated when he's playing Stereotypical Italian Plumber 7."

Harris listened again, then asked his wife,

"How long has the little prick been playing on his X Box, outside?"

"I don't know luv? Was it still connected to your phone?"

"Well if it was, he's had an interesting flight to the ground floor!"

"That knocking is sounding really angry now sweetheart. I don't think he enjoyed his flying lesson. Can you change the setting to roaming?"

"Not from here pet!"

There was a pause while both of them listened out for any

further sounds. As if in answer, there was a huge fart like two dolphins slapping the sea. Robbie asked, carefully,

"Was that you, pet?"

"Who me? I'll fuckin knack you when I've got this hairnet off.... And, no."

"And 'No'?"

"No, that eruption wasn't me and no, it's not Mr Chopper ootside. He's just bidding on ebay for a combine harvester, for some reason."

"Take that laptop off him!"

"I don't like to pet, he's got the highest bid and only 5 minutes to go."

"Aye ok, but no more after that. He's already had a bid in for some Stranglers collectables earlier."

"That's canny grand, but he just sends them on to Susan Boyle with a note, 'do it like this'."

"While you're at nothin', can you get him to stop knockin' and whingein', and shit, like?"

Claudia slid down the bannister and, forgetting to brake, uncovered an alien skeleton behind the plastering in the wall opposite.

"Ah look at what you've done now, ya soft whoo'er!" wailed Robbie, "That's the third dead UFOnaut this month! What will we do with this one?"

"Stick him in the wardrobe, hung up with the other seventeen."

"Aye, I'll put him on hangar eighteen, then."

There was another urgent knocking. Claudia grabbed the door handle, and almost wrenched the door off its hinges, with a snarled:-

"Fuckin' what?"

"Ah, Mrs Harris," soothed a familiar voice, "Is your wonderful, fantastic husband, my dear Sergeant Robbie, at home?"

The two stood looking at each other. Claudia took a step forward, in a way that suggested extreme menace. Taking the hint, Chief Inspector Morose took a step back. Claudia took another step forward, grabbing the fire axe reserved for unwelcome visitors, off the wall. Morose took another step backward. This continued, slowly gaining in pace like an asthmatic steam engine starting up, down the front path, through the gate, and down the road, while Robbie watched with a mixture of fascination, foreboding and puffins.

There was a ping, as Mr Chopper's bid won the combine harvester.

There was another pinging sound, that of an axe bouncing off a tin helmet, which echoed back up the road and back up the front path.

"Robbie!" wailed Morose, "I've just had an accident and I've come for your help!"

He managed to slam the door behind himself, and leaned against it to barricade himself in.

"No," sighed Robbie, "You're not having another pair of my trousers."

"Not that sort of accident!" cried Morose, "A REAL accident ..... Jesus wept!" he added, as the panelling behind him was smashed up like firewood, and the axe head swept past his back, missing by part of a gnat's pube.

"Sir," Robbie continued his enquiries, "When you say a real accident...."

First a hand, then an arm, then the rest of Claudia Harris, battered through the remains of the front door and swung the axe back, in a sort of 'now, you die' way.

"Some knob has rammed my car off the road, and I'm injured!"

With a screech of brakes, the axe stopped part way to its target. Robbie stepped forward a pace, and took the axe off his wife.

"Aye well, in that case, you'd better come through and give me a statement," said Robbie.

"I'll get us some tea," snarled Claudia, still unsure if her sudden humanitarian approach was the right one. After all, she could always poison the tea.

*****

"Mom, I'm telling you, I didn't!"

Hugh breathed a huge sigh, as he recognised a need to tear his attention away from the computer screen, and back to the phone.

Something sounding like a highly irritated potty, from Michael Bentine's Potty Time (look it up, why should we do all the work?) was shouting at him from down the phone.

"No Mom, I've not even been home today"

More high-pitched squealing.

"You know that's not my website, Mom"

Squeal. Angry disbelieving squeal.

"Katiespantysuk.com. You know that."

Squeal, but slightly calmer.

"Yes, and I'll find a new site next time, the knickers are coming through, Mom."

Squeal!

"That's why I ordered you some new ones."

Squeal of confusion (that's what the world is today, hey

hey).

"Why would I ask for your card details Mom. I have a secondary user card."

Conciliatory squeal.

"We'll look into it tomorrow. I've got a few hours off before pulling another 96 hour shift"

SQUEAL

"Hero hours contract Mom, got to go, a little man with a small seventies moustache and a bowler hat is waiting. Painfully thin."

Hugh replaced the receiver, with a lobster. Across the police station counter, a painfully thin short man with a seventies moustache and a bowler hat, was waiting for his attention.

"Yes, you're him, aren't you?" muttered the said man.

"I'm sorry," said Hugh, pointedly pointing at his sergeant stripes, "Shall we try again?"

The man cleared his throat and looked like he was going to clear Hugh's throat too. "You're Jampton, aren't you? Hugh Jampton? Should I say Sergeant Jampton?"

Before Hugh had a chance to reply the man started again. "I believe we are going to be having an important meeting later, and I would value your thoughts."

"Yes?"

"Yes. You see, you are going to kill me tomorrow, Sergeant Jampton, and I'm understandably curious to know why."

*****

"Do you have your insurance documents, Surr?"

"What?"

"I said, do you have your…"

"Yes, yes, yes… Robbie… are we making up words now? What is this in… something?"

"Insurance Surr… you must have… I mean didn't you start in Traffic?"

"Well, I once kicked off in the middle of the M42. I think Mr Jim Beam directed me… I didn't begin my career there though, if that's what you mean? I'm sure I was born at some point…"

"No Surr, you used to be a traffic policeman?"

"Yes, I was briefly a Road grunter, it was much easier before the invention of the car, Robbie."

"Surr, you must be aware cars have to be insured."

"Well frankly, if the car needs to be insured, shouldn't the car take care of that itself?"

"Surr, if you are the legal owner of the vehicle, you have to insure it. Simple."

"Well that's okay then, I'm pretty sure the man I stole the car off, has had it insured."

"Aye well that's alreet then….what?"

"Well good God, man, I can't go around buying and owning a car, when there's important things to do like fight crime and get pissed all day! What would my bank manager say?"

"You have a bank account?"

"Don't be a berk, Robbie, of course I haven't! But if I DID have one, and a car as well, what then?"

Robbie struggled with this concept for a moment, before asking, with a slight worry,

"If you don't mind me askin' with slight worry sir, man, how do you get paid, an' that?"

"Badly. Same as yourself. No one likes you fucking pigs."

"No, ya stupid, thick arsed, Exeter graduate type! I mean, wi' you not having a bank account, why – aye?"

"I really don't know! Chief Superintendent Weird gives me some petty cash on a Thursday and tells me to fuck off, that any use?"

There was a knock at the door.

"Daddy!"

"Aw fuck, yes, Emily?"

"Can I interrupt?"

"Aye pet, what is it?"

"Nothing, I just want to interrupt."

"Aye, that's canny grand lass. Now look sir," he continued, shutting the door on Emily's face, "who did you steal the car off?"

"Oh, some gormless turd who lives in a cave near my pillbox."

"Not that fuckin idiot Terry?"

"Ah, that'll be the chap. Awfully agreeable, when he's not threatening me with his sawn off."

"Sawn off what?"

"I'm not sure, but I'm pretty certain that it's been sawn off."

Harris took Morose by the pubes and they stepped outside. The Lada Riva did look a bit like a car, in parts. Several parts, actually.

"He won't like it, sir."

"Do you think he'll like it better if I smash the windscreen? These youths like that sort of thing?"

"No. We'd better get it back to him. I'll drive. You man the rear turret."

And so, they drove the car back to Terry's cave, leaving it showing its good side, and a note on the windscreen saying 'slight traffic damage to entire vehicle after collision on the M40, ashtray looks in good nick."

As they started towards Morose's pillbox, Endof made an observation, "You know Robbie, you really didn't think this through. I'm nearly home, you've now got a long walk back to humanity. I'd wish you a safe journey, but I don't particularly like you, and besides, that bypass is a death trap. I'll wish you a good… no fuck it Gary, I can't be arsed!"

"Aye Surr, can't stand you much either. By the way, not that I give much of a shit, but what hit you exactly?"

"You're going to have to be a bit more precise, Mick. I've been hit by lots of things in my time."

"What hit the friggin' car, Surr?"

"Oh that, a lovely sporty number. Didn't really see the driver but I did spot a couple of things."

"Such as?"

"Well, a sticker on the back window – Sharks Motors. Wasn't that the lovely chap we had the pleasure of spending a bit of time with, a while ago?"

"If by that, you mean destroy his livelihood, accused him of murder and burn his business to the ground, yes."

Morose smiled nostalgically. "Ah, we did have a laugh over that."

"And the other thing?"

"Oh yes! I got his number plate."

"At last, a lead! What did you write it down on?"

"No time for that Jackie! I got out, and took the liberty of ripping his number plate off, by way of an introduction.

He then sped off for some reason, shouting something about 'please go away, you fucking cunt'."

Morose produced the plate from down his trousers. A crow pulled it back in. There was a brief scuffle and a few screams, which ended when the crow threw Morose down in a classic judo move, but Morose retained the number plate, as it was by now embedded in his arse. Smiling sadistically, Harris curled it back out; and, pausing only to give Morose a good kicking, turned and headed back home.

It had been an eventful evening so far. No doubt Claudia would be waiting for him with a glass of something strong, like mercury. He rang Hugh Jampton at the station, and asked him for a lift. Hugh drove out in his pool car, he had to kick two lads off and pot the last few balls himself.

They returned in silence; the engine didn't work. A handy supply of 50 pences kept them rolling long enough to get back.

As they went, they were cut up by a Porsche 711. Robbie caught a quick glance of the driver, as the registration plate seemed to have been torn off. The driver looked strangely familiar.

"That driver looked strangely familiar," muttered Hugh.

"Weird!" said Robbie.

"No, he's back at the station, frightening students."

"Everyone should have a hobby, come on Hugh put your back into it."

"Hey Robbie", Hugh puffed, "I've had a bastard of a day today. You know the sort of day when someone says you've killed them, and they're standing right in front of you?"

"We get all the nutters, don't we? Did you tell him he's not dead?"

"Nah, didn't want to spoil his fun. I just nicked him. Can we interview him tomorrow? You be good cop and I'll be murdering cop."

"Fair do's mate. Drop us at ours, eh? Claudia will think I've gone off with flappy arse for the night."

"No, Franks is off tonight. Ah, is it this one with the gap where the front door should be, and a fucking great combine harvester in the drive?"

"Aye," Robbie sighed, "That's it."

*****

In a dark room, an infinite distance from Robbie Harris's home and yet easily reachable from his place of work, a figure sat, pondering his next move.

Phase one appeared to have been completed moderately successfully. Possibly it might require a bit more subtlety from the homunculus, but it was in place, and had even confused the victim's matriarch into releasing her barter tokens.

The prime homunculus was free and unchained, tonight.

Of course, the figure understood, one could not win the war alone. His unbidden army waiting in tanks for their call to life. It merely took preparation.

Like all good battles, it took knowing your enemy to win. And yes, he knew his enemy. He smiled. He had followed the movements of his enemy, as the one who commands his enemy for a very long time indeed. He smiled again; the imp perched on his desk giggled, the funny sight of the miniature giggling daemon caused him to laugh, and when he laughed billows of flame cascaded from deep within his throat and vomited out into the world. It made the imp dance, which made him laugh more.

He looked deep into his heart of darkness. The time was coming for a family reunion.

*****

Hugh Jampton's mother, dear old Enid, meantime, had become aware that something was amiss. Hugh had arrived back from his shift, unusual in itself as he often stayed at work for weeks on end, and only came back to check that Enid was still alive and well. But now, he had arrived back and was confused, perplexed, and uncertain.

They sat in silence over a cup of tea, each wondering which was going to fall in first. Very big cup. Very high budgie perch. Hugh eventually spoke.

"I'm not happy about this bank statement, Mam."

"Well neither am I. I can understand the money going out for the new pants, but not for the new Porsche, and not for the 100 bottles of champagne, either."

"Well, it's not like you, is it? The fast cars and bubbly isn't your sort of thing."

"Do you think my account has been hacked? You hear so much about it, in the papers."

"In the papers?"

"Yes, that's where you hear about it. Ooh, it is awful, all these famous people and even royalty and that, having their bank of twitter or WhatsApp savings hacked, and people leaving rude notes after emptying their accounts."

"Well you're not famous or rich, really, are you Mam. You're just a retired teacher living on the profits of all the dinner money you stole from the poor kids. You're more like royalty, in that sense."

"Oh, fuck off our Hugh! Don't you start giving me your anti royalist rhetoric."

"Well, it's true mam." Hugh puffed his chest out and

was about to launch into another tirade, when his mother launched him into the teacup.

"I'm bored now, Hugh," she offered by way of an explanation.

"You know I'm not allowed to get tea on my uniform, Mam!" Hugh splashed.

Enid stuck up two fingers, but quickly pulled them out when she remembered her son was still in the room. She threw him the life boat, and hobbled off to make a fresh cuppa.

*****

Back at the Harris household, Robbie had successfully parked the combine harvester on his neighbours Audi S5. After showing it to Mr Chopper, the Guinea pig had insisted on going straight onto the laptop and leaving a favourable review – 'incredibly quick delivery, 5 stars' – unfortunately, he had left the review on Twitter which made no sense and lost him 700 followers. He was a very tired guinea pig.

Robbie put him back in his cage and welded the door closed.

"Come on Robbie, I'm waiting," came the sweet, screech owl tones of his wife.

Taking a moment to drop his trousers, so that he could be seen to be ready for action, he bounded up the stairs. Ripping his shirt off, he approached the bedroom as naked as the day he was born. He was born with Y fronts and odd socks, by the way. Then he stood on Mr Chopper's roller blades (one of last week's successful eBay bids), and to his horror, went skidding straight down the corridor, through Jessica's bedroom, approaching the window at a speed that the Health and Safety people would say was inappropriate, smashing right through the glass, and falling through.

"B2" said Jessica.

Why Jessica said "B2" we will return to shortly, meanwhile it's probably more important to discover what had happened to young Robbie. He had gone straight through the window, snagging his testicles on the shards still attached to the window frame; and was currently dangling by said sack, out of the window.

To avoid confusion, Robbie shrieked, "Ooh, me knackers!" loud enough to wake his neighbour, he of the Audi S5.

"D8" said Emily.

"'Ere!" shrieked the neighbour, "What's happened to my Audi S5 with DAB radio reception, Milano leather upholstery, Bluetooth interface and free kinky topless nun? It's got a fucking combine harvester off eBay parked on it!"

Just to remind everyone of the problem, Robbie again shrieked, "Ooh, me knackers!"

"Sorry, there's no square for S5" muttered Emily. For, verily, they playeth "Battleships," while their father hung from his knacks over an Audi S5 with naughty nun, and combine harvester without such optional extras.

"Girls, I think I might need a little help here," squeaked Robbie.

"In a minute, Dad. K3" said Jess.

"No girls! Now, *please!*" cried an increasingly piercing-voiced Robbie.

"What about my car?" shouted the neighbour.

"Are you coming Robbie?" shouted an oblivious Claudia, "I'm ready, an' that."

"Might be a delay, petal," screamed Robbie, "I'm kind of caught up in something here."

Emily looked up from her warfare-inspired game, and

caught sight of blood on the window ledge, and her father's tightly clenched buttocks just above the shredded glass/bollocks interface.

"Ooh Dad! Are you ok man?"

"Ooh, me knackers!" he offered. The third time's the charm.

"I'll get me mam!" Emily shouted, running.

Jess was still thinking tactics and had yet to look up, "Take your go first, our Emily!"

Police arrived first, all the officers from the station having a jolly good laugh at Robbie's predicament. Plenty of photos taken, massively brightening up a guinea pigs twitter account, and rapidly restoring his follower numbers.

Then the fire brigade, who decided – after updating their Facebook status – that the combine harvester might be best used to lower young Robbie, to the ground, as they'd never had a go on a combine harvester before, and the hay baler looked like fun.

The coast guards arrived next, for some unknown reason, then the AA and finally the ambulance service.

The neighbour, Mr Bristow, wanted to speak to someone about the damage to his car, and despite the offer, he refused to speak to the coastguard. As Hugh had already done a cracking set of pics on Instagram, he offered to speak to him.

After the AA had lowered Robbie onto the combine harvester – the firemen gave a favourable review, on Trip Advisor – and the coastguard and Jampton, who'd been called back from home, had helped him into the ambulance, it started off down the road before someone pointed out closing the doors might be an idea.

Claudia stood in the doorway, the light of the hallway turning her flimsy negligee completely transparent. Her face showed frustration and anger. "Well! I suppose that puts a shag right off the menu for tonight, then!"

The Deliveroo moped rider rode up the street, and hopped off, with a silver serving dish under his arm.

"Roast Cormorant, for a Mrs Harris?"

"Aw, thanks petal," she smiled, "Thought I'd have to do without this tonight, what with no husband, an' that."

"N13" called out Emily.

Aye, it was back to normal, an' that.

*****

"Robbie! Robbie! Robbie!" whispered an irritating voice in PC Gonemad's ear.

"No SIR, Sergeant Harris is in there having his 'nads sewn back on."

He stepped towards the door of the room indicated, pushing it open with the force of the desperate. He shouted, "Robbie! Robbie! Robbie!"

From his half-sedated state, Robbie Harris looked up and attempted to punch his Chief inspector in the face, but missed him by two miles. This was not due to the sedative, but due to the speaker not being Morose in any way shape or form. No, in fact, the speaker took the form of Hugh Jampton.

In Robbie's semi-conscious state, Hugh looked to be grinning manically and wielding an axe that he had conjured up out of thin air.

"Robbie! Robbie! Robbie! Anything strange happening at the station?"

What a strange question to be asked. And what a strange time to ask it. Curiouser and curiouser. Robbie blinked and Hugh had turned into two nurses and apparently while he was blinking they had changed the entire room into a corridor. Ridiculous, nothing at all like his previous room. The bollock pain seemed to have eased off while he blinked, too.

"You're not Hugh Jampton," Robbie stated, with all the certainty of the highly sedated.

"No I'm Nurse Gallagher," offered the first.

"And I'm really Colin Weird, just checking in on you, but this stupid Christian nurse thinks I'm saying Nurse Whittaker, go back to sleep Robbie."

"No man – Sir. I'm wide awake. Just…"

And during his next blink, a voice was in his ear:-

"Robbie! Robbie! Robbie! Lend's a tenner… make it £20. There's a sale on at Oddbins."

Robbie unblinked a single eye, "My Wallet's in my trousers."

Morose looked swiftly around the room. "I can't find your trousers Robbie, just this badly ripped pair of dung catchers."

"Aye Surr, they'll be on the stairs, at home. And no, you can't have any money."

"Oh, you're such a ball breaker, Robbie."

Robbie winced, the sedative was wearing off, as was his ability to cope with Morose.

*****

As a Porsche 711 spun a doughnut in the Oxford Road Police Station car park, taking out three police cars in its attempt to find the ideal parking space, so Colin Weird was busy in his office.

"Gonemad! White! The other one – the one with lady-bumps?"

"Franks, Sir" said White, closing the door behind him.

"No, I meant Brewis, but never mind, you'll do."

"Yes sir."

"Yes... now, what do you know about my office, matey?"

"Never feed it after midnight, is that the sort of thing...?"

"No, I see where I went wrong, a bit vague that. Not unlike yourself. Let's try again. How many doors are there in and out of my office?"

"Same number in as out, Sir. What a ridiculous question... Sir." He liked being able to breath.

"Alright smartarse, how many doors in?"

"One, that one," White said pointing at a window.

"Fuck off dolt, and send someone else in."

White fucked off and sent in Jampton, who was just taking his coat off.

"I'm just taking my coat off," he started.

"Off what?" asked Weird.

"Off some big bastard dog that I think has escaped from your dark dimension."

"Ahh good, something is happening then. I thought as much. I asked young White a moment ago, but he's a gormless turd at the best of times. So matey, what did this dog look like?"

"Well, you know, like a giant three headed hell hound. We've seen that sort of thing before, NFO – Normal For Oxford."

Weird smiled and nodded, "Yes, I thought something had

escaped. Oh yes, there's usually signs in my office, when the gateway has been disturbed."

"Rippling in the dimension stream? Quantum disturbances?"

By way of a reply, Weird pointed behind his desk at a massive steaming pile of dog porridge. Hugh considered a minute, before agreeing,

"Signs Sir…yes."

Weird nodded slowly. Very slowly.

*****

"Hugh? Hugh?" Mrs Jampton shouted up the stairs, "I've washed your uniform out as best I can. When are you back on duty?"

"Now Mum," Hugh shouted down the stairs, "I should be there, now!"

"Well, your trousers will still be a bit damp around the armpits. Oh, I do wish you'd speak to someone about your uniform sizing. Will you be straight home tonight?"

"No Mam, I'm going to pop in and see Robbie Harris in the hospital. He'll think I've forgotten all about him, if I don't go and see him."

"I thought you were going in this morning, you said you were."

"I said no such thing Mam, you're going nuts you are. Anyway, cheery-bye. I'm off to work."

As Hugh closed the garden gate with his face, his Mum called after him, "Hugh, you'll get awfully cold like that. Come in and get dressed first, you soft shite."

*****

Robbie Harris was having to do some serious thinking. Morose had had a motoring accident. Mr Chopper had destroyed the neighbour's sporty car piece of shit thing. Jampton had visited and so had that ghoul of a boss, Weird, alongside some God-bothering nurse.

But most important, how were his jocks? He decided to take a feel under the sheets. My God, where had they gone? They had been whizzed off! The miserable heartless bastards! Ah, no, wait. The pain from clenching them gently in his hand, reassured him that despite his own best attempts, they were still attached to him, and just as important, he was still attached to THEM. Ah, easy does it, chaps. A few days of care and you'll be back in fully working order. He made a mental note to avoid looking at anything female. Sleep on for now.

"Mr Harris?" asked a voice, "I'm Dr Hogg, your surgeon."

"Awright mate," Robbie replied, before turning over and looking straight at the massive norks of a young Jamaican doctor.

It was going to be a difficult stay.

*****

"......so anyway," Morose continued," I said to the fool, 'If you think I'm going in there without a member of the vice squad, you can blow it out of your bum!' By God, was he angry!"

The group of assembled idiots, halfwits, crows, and other neighbours of Morose's pillbox, all fell about laughing. He could tell a good story, especially one that was blatantly a load of lies and bullshit. Terry the idiot lad slapped his teeth, and thundered,

"The cow flies west tonight! Recycling bins versus Chelsea, on Sky Box Office."

There was a brief pause while everyone took stock of this, before Morose let loose a grass scorcher of a fart and announced,

"The Queen!"

"The Queen!" they all shouted, tried to stand to attention, and drank more vitriolic 'Forth bridge Paint Strength Special Brew' from various utensils, bird baths and hollowed out skulls of their enemies. At length, a crow spoke.

"What fucking Queen?"

Morose looked blank at first, swaying gently in the evening breeze that blew sparks around the campfire and up into the starry night sky. He recovered, took a deep breath, and managed to reply,

"Ahh, any old Queen. Fuck 'em all!"

There was a great cheer and more brew was consumed, while Morose honked up on the campfire and the alpaca curled out a canoe-sized turd.

Yes, all was well at Morose's monthly demolition drinking derby. Pissing it up with any passing creatures was a favourite. No doubt they would all pay for it in the morning, especially if that nice Mr Shark found out who'd burned down his new showrooms. Never mind. What was insurance for, eh? Just like the bloody thing that Harris had asked him to get on that car he'd nicked.

As a group of crows danced around the escaped orangutan, Morose's addled brain began to turn a few cogs. Insurance. Cars. Fire. Drink. Insurance.

"H'mmmmm," he said out loud.

"H'mmmmm," retorted everyone else, and toasted the incomprehensible noise.

The thought sat at the back of his mind all evening, and into his dreams. Insurance. H'mm indeed.

*****

"Harris?"

Harris opened an eye. Yes, it was him.

"Aye Surr?"

"You don't mind me bringing a few friends do you?"

From the door frame several crows, Terry the idiot, and a large bison peeped in at Harris.

"What is it Surr?"

"It's a large bison, don't you pay any attention to narration?"

"No Surr, what do you want?"

"Ahh yes, this cock awful sounding insurance thing, tell me more?"

It was easier to just go along with it.

"Aye Surr, well, let's say you have a house…"

"Or a second world war pill box, that isn't actually legally mine."

The crows sniggered.

"Aye Surr, what you can do, is pay a small amount each month, and if anything happens to it, or your cacking stuff in it, you're protected."

"I see, sounds great. What if you don't have ins… insurance wasn't it?"

"Aye, well your stuff is knacked and so are you, man."

"But if I had had insurance, the people I paid would have sorted it all out for me?"

"Well, they usually try to wriggle out of paying…"

"Sounds like a good pagga to me young Robbie…"

"Aye, why are you asking?"

"Ah yes! Well, young Billy here," he pointed at the bison, "Has just demolished my pillbox, and I was wondering if I could make a claim at all?"

"It's very hard to destroy a pillbox Surr!"

"Yes, he did have to try very hard, bless him. But he won that round. So, who's most likely to pay up do you think?"

The bison finished a can of Stella, as Terry opened another for him.

"Nobody Surr, you weren't insured."

"What if I take out insurance tomorrow?"

"Then I get to nick you for fraud, Surr."

Morose weighed this up, "I'll just stick with my pillbox, shall I?"

"Aye sir, and tell Hugh he can come into the ward, he doesn't have to stand outside."

Jampton, hearing his name, straightened his tie round Morose's neck and walked in.

"Hello Hugh, something you forgot?"

Hugh Jampton looked confused, "I've only just got here! Are the drugs still wearing off?"

Robbie laughed, "Don't be silly, I only had a few paracetamol, what have you left?"

"Er….nothing, I haven't been here before."

"Have."

"Haven't."

Chief Inspector Morose turned to the bison and the orangutan. "This is how humans interact without alcohol."

The bison muttered "Fuck that, then," and farted heavily, desecrating some wall plaster, and blowing up a baby incubator in the next ward.

*****

"Ah, glad you've come straight back Sergeant Jampton sir," said WPC Soames as she dragged a juvenile delinquent across the floor, "Could you get this little prick's mother on the phone?"

"Why, what's he done?" asked Hugh, getting the boot into the kid quickly, before pausing and adding, "And I'm just coming in on duty now, I've not been in since Sunday."

"Trying to walk past my car with an offensive haircut!" justified Soames, adding, "And you *were* in earlier, being a bloody nuisance with your new Porsche!"

"Aye, what does he say in his defence? I'd bring back the birch, myself. And I don't have a Porsche!"

"He says his mam did it for him! The lying rug wipe. That hot red 711 you were ragging up & down the carpark, bloody 'ell, Weird's furious at you!"

"Aye, what's your Mum's number, sprog? Just you wait til your Mum hears about this haircut she did! Yer little bollocks! Weird, furious at me? I've only just clocked on, even he can read that!"

"275-192" wailed the teenager.

Hugh dialled the number and noticed that he'd written up a load of rubbish in the station log. He scratched his head. A dead earwig fell out of his arse. He looked at the handwriting. 'Morose is a poo and Weird a trollop', he had written. Except he hadn't. His mum would back him up, wouldn't she? She'd said that he'd already seen Harris at hospital, and, er....erm....

As the wayward trash wailed at his mum down the phone, and tried not to scream at what WPC Soames was doing, so Hugh walked quietly to a back room. There was something funny going on here, and he wasn't laughing any more.

*****

"Knock knock!" said Hugh.

Weird tapped 'come in' on his desk.

As Jampton entered the room, Weird rose up to his full satanic majesty. His dark cloak removing all possibility of light in the room, leaving just the eerie afterglow of his dark presence to illuminate them. His head seemed to push back the ceiling as his fingers became claws dripping with blood, and his canine teeth became more prominent. His eyes seemed to draw on all the evil of several thousand years. He was simultaneously distant and somehow inside Hugh's head, tearing at his mind. The words that came from Weird, Hugh could not say with any certainty whether they were spoken, or projected into his skull.

"I hope you're going to clean those skid marks?"

Hugh gulped down temporarily the vomit that would shortly project unhindered into the disabled toilet bowl. "Me mam normally does me washing, Sir."

"In the car park!"

"No Sir, I don't keep me mam in the car park. We've got a Belling at home!"

"The skid marks in the car park. You and your Porsche left them. And I don't want to see them."

"Weird that!" muttered Jampton.

"Superintendent or Sir to you, you insignificant tool!"

"No Sir, I mean it's weird. It's like really, really strange. I haven't got a Porsche sir. I haven't been here. I haven't been to see Robbie, until recently. And I didn't order me mum's knickers. It's... it's weird. Is something going on?"

Weird came back to his more regular shape and appearance. It always left him with mouth ulcers when his teeth retracted like that. He winced.

"Like I explained to you this morning young Jampton, something has escaped from the dark dimensions..."

"The what?"

"Ahh the... golf club... At first I thought it was just the giant three headed dog currently roaming around Jericho, now it seems a clone of you has escaped and..."

The door opened, and Soames gave Weird a piece of paper. He glanced down at it, as Soames left.

"...And now apparently a half crazed girl with mad hair, is cornered in a block of flats in Blackbird Leys. St Aldates station are dealing with that. A group of lads going round in red jumpers apparently," he headed the scrap of paper into the waste paper basket. "Go and throw up Jampton, use the disabled toilet. And come back and see me when you're done."

Jampton went and broke up a standard lavatory and, having disabled it, got on with a good honk, while searching for his alter ego Rolf. Wiping his teeth clean on his trousers, he popped them back in his mouth, and returned to Weird's office, with his trousers in his mouth.

Weird had taken to hovering above his desk where he was muttering vile things in Swahili. A dark shadow that resembled a huge mouth, repeated the words, and again, it did seem that they were coming from inside of Hugh's mind. Weird pressed the "End call" button and the occult phone he was using promptly exploded.

"Fuck" said Weird as the smoke cleared, revealing all his hair singed grey, and his suit in strips.

"Sir, is all this escaped dogs and golf club portals anything to do with all the sightings of me? I mean, not me, but me, like me, as it were?"

Weird almost smiled, but remembered his Dark Majesty status just in time, and contented himself with a quick burst of flatulence in F sharp instead. A number of insects promptly fell over dead.

"I don't know, matey," he said, "But if I were you, I'd start keeping a record of all this."

"Will it make the charts?"

"I don't care. Just keep a low profile for now. I am making some investigations. Where is that fucking no brain, Morose?"

"Last time I saw him, he was trying to milk a bicycle."

"What the fuck for?"

"Something about it being lead–free."

"He is a colossal uncle frightener. Bring him here."

"Yes, sir."

"Now."

"I'll try his phone...."

"You humans are so slow...." cursed Weird, and, with a mighty effort, he summoned all his strength; and with supreme concentration, not only let rip another absolute corker, but managed to summon Morose, who looked utterly shocked, half dressed and stood on an unused portmanteau.

"Morose!" barked Weird, "You're on a new case. Watch over the comings and goings of Jampton here."

Morose snivelled, "You've summoned me to hold the hand of some washed out gimp like Jampton, sir?"

"Yes."

"But I'm busy filling in a fraudulent insurance claim!"

"Fuck off. Just do as I say or I'll roast you alive."

"Sir," replied Morose, in a "Go fuck yourself" way.

Weird watched Jampton and Morose leave his office, and together, immediately start a fight with a vending machine. As they did so, that tosser PC Gonemad waltzed into Weird's office.

"Sir, I've been contacted by the Ripoff Credit card company, about one of our officers, and a 1, 2, 2 and 2."

"Quit the dance routine and get on with it."

After a quick par de deux, Gonemad said, "They've asked us to track down and apprehend a sergeant Jampton? Surely they can't mean OUR Sergeant Jampton?"

"What's it over?"

"Fraudulent transactions on a sports car, a shop - full of women's underwear, and the services of an escort agency."

Weird glowed darker. "Escort Agency?"

"Yes! Doesn't sound like our Sergeant Jampton, does it?"

"It sounds like **A** Sergeant Jampton, you bloody useless wank sock, but I'm just not sure WHICH Sergeant Jampton."

Gonemad, puzzled, tilted his head to one side like a confused terrier, before asking, "Shall I comprehend this ape man, Sir?"

Weird thought. It was all going pear shaped and he was losing control over the powers that really need controlling from certain portals.

"May be best, for his own safety, matey."

Gonemad spoke into his collar, "Calling all units. Be on the lookout for a Sergeant Hugh Jampton. If seen, comprehend him at once."

There was a pause.

Weird spoke, shaking his head, and sending talcum powder across the room, "It's 'apprehend', you berk. And you're not wearing a collar radio."

Gonemad blushed, "Sorry, Sir, I'll get on the blower now."

He rushed out of the office and switched on the station loudspeaker intercom.

"Can all pigs be on the lookout for a Sergeant Hugh Jampton, if seen, apprehend him, you berk!"

There was a crashing sound and a scream, as nearly a dozen coppers dropped onto the hapless Jampton; and, after taking it in turns to beat him up, dragged him off to Cell seven, and locked him in. Weird shook his head, his left leg, and his knob. It was all getting very confusing.

*****

Well what a turnip for his boots, thought Jampton. Well, he had just received several good kicks to his head.

"Oi! Gonemad!" he shouted, "Can I have the lights on please?"

Outside the cell, Saul pulled a massive lever and the lights in the cell went on.

Hugh looked around, he knew what to expect, a bunk bed, a table, two chairs and a pack of cards.

It looked like he was getting the top bunk, the man he interviewed earlier in the week at the front desk – painfully thin, bowler hat, seventies moustache – was asleep in the bottom bunk.

"Sorry to disturb you, mate," he said stepping on the bottom bed to raise himself, "I just want to get up here, then I'll get that light out."

There was something about the way the painfully thin blue arm fell out of the bed, that told Hugh something was wrong.

He pulled back the blanket.

"Ooh blimey!" he whispered, then shrieked:- "Hello!! Come here, quickly! There's something dead in here!"

*****

"Interview commencing 11.15am, on Wednesday... Oh Robbie, I can't be arsed with this." So saying Morose began burping the theme to 'Emmerdale'.

"Aye Surr, well neither can I, frankly. Tell us what happened, Hugh?"

"I don't know, Robbie. It was in there when twelve of our force chucked me in, using reasonable levels of violence, after throwing me down the back stairs, twice. Oh, welcome back by the way."

"Cheers man, still getting a bit of an ache from the old 'nads, but I'm ok, like."

Morose coughed and spat out a cigarette that he had no memory of ever putting in his mouth. "We'll have to wait for Max before we can be certain, but it looks like the body of a painfully thin man with a seventies moustache. Just like in those porno films you have hidden under your guinea pig cage, Robbie."

"I've told you," muttered Robbie, "Mr Chopper, eBay."

"So, let me get this straight," said Morose, putting his spirit level on a shelf and adjusting it, before sitting a crow on it. "You were visited, young Hugh, at the sales counter..."

"Front desk Surr," interjected Robbie.

"Yes, the err... pie counter... You were visited by a man who said he knew you were going to kill him, and lo and behold, here you are with his corpse. Doesn't look good for your end of year review, does it?"

"I know Sir," pleaded Jampton, "But Weird said something about a double..."

"Oooh Jack Daniels for me, about time the ropey old twat got a round in."

"No Sir, a double as in a doppelgänger. Another me, if you like."

"No Hugh, I don't like. Another you? If I could write, I'd write a complaint letter."

There was a muffled squawk and a crash, as the crow fell into the waste paper basket, which it had been sliding toward since Morose had put it on the shelf.

"Always said you were a basket case," said Morose, before gobbing on it, and kicking the bin over. "Now then, where were we? Oh yes, doubles?"

"Very kind of you sir," Jampton replied, "Make mine a scotch."

As Morose poured a double and drank it himself, Jampton continued his rubbish story.

"Lads, there's another Hugh Jampton on the loose, except it's not me, it's like a really, really evil double of me, and its escaped from the portal in Weird's office, and now that it's loose, its causing havoc and really, really bad things, to happen all over Oxford."

There was a shout of pain as the crow made a bid for revenge, by headbutting its razor sharp beak into Morose's jap's eye.

"So, let's get this straight, Hugh," droned Harris, "You're

saying that all these crimes committed by you, aren't you, but another Hugh? A sort of Hugh two?"

The sickening thud of a small body into a wall, as the crow was hoofed into the plasterwork by Morose, failed to stop Hugh's reply.

"Yes."

Robbie bit his lip, "And you think no one has ever come up with that as an alibi, in the whole history of crime?"

"I don't care about history, I care about NOW!" shouted Hugh, losing his natural Brummie calm and charm, for the first time in living memory.

"Alright Hugh mate, calm down, ya cagey bastard," said Robbie, ducking just in time as a violently sulphuric cack was unleashed from the crow, to Morose's face, most of it getting to its target.

"Calm down? Youse don't believe me, do you?"

Harris, as well as Morose and the crow, all turned to shake their heads at him, before Morose dropped his pants, and attempted to launch one back at the crow.

Hugh sat back, dishevelled, beaten, and at the end of his patience.

"Ok. Up the lot of you. Get me my solicitor."

"You won't need one," came a familiar voice, and the familiar waft of rotten cabbage and over ripe stilton cheese in the air, "I've found the proof I need. Jampton, you're off all charges. Get back on the fucking desk and send these two tossers out to catch Jampton the second. He's just torched the city centre bogs and slashed a load of bus seats near Mill Lane."

There was a short pause before Weird, Jampton and Harris all jumped out of the way, and the body of Morose hurtled past, through the door, and landed in the corridor, tipping up WPC Soames and the teenage boy. The kid made a run for it.

Morose stood up and threw the crow after him. Both landed in a heap on the floor, that bloody bison must have left it there.

*****

The phone rang.

"Can you get that our Emily, I'm in the middle of trimming me bush. It's all got a bit out of control!"

"Aye mam, man" Emily shouted through the back door at her mum.

Claudia's Rhododendron was getting a rare seeing to, with shears and Weedol and a blow torch and that. "Right yer bastard, I'll have you back in shape in no time." The shears were a blur, briefly, as she commenced her assault on the hedge.

A head popped over the fence, Mr Bristow – the neighbour – Claudia sighed, he still hadn't forgiven Robbie for the combine harvester incident.

"I say, Mrs Harris?"

"Not now Mr Bristow, not a good time, man."

"You're making a good job there, Mrs Harris."

"You're embarrassing me Mr Bristow, I don't like being watched while I work."

"MAM?" screamed a voice from the back door.

"What is it our Emily, I'm just asking Mr Bristow to stop admiring my bush, can I not have a bit of privacy in my own garden?"

"Mam, there's a policeman on the phone from Blackbird Leys station. He says it's urgent that he speaks to you, it's about your daughter apparently."

"Ooh no! What's our Jess done now?"

"No, it's me, mam. Apparently, they've got me under arrest for smuggling and receiving stolen goods. Supposedly, I've brought in a fuck off big boat full off cocaine and Skol. I'm a right one, me!"

Claudia snapped, "Haddaway an' shite, ya little bitch, I'll fuckin' knack you when I get to yer in the pig pen!"

She paused to think about this. They looked at each other. Eventually, Emily spoke.

"Mam, what the fuck is goin' on?"

Claudia replied, slowly, "I've no idea worr lass, but someone's gonna get knacked. Don't worry aboot that bit!"

She went off practicing knacking.

*****

The front desk of the station was unoccupied... by humans anyway. A crow, not dissimilar to Morose's trouser tenant, was intently tapping away at the keyboard.

The Desktop Computer had two monitors, one seemingly for the bird, and one facing towards Claudia and Emily.

'Yes?' the bird typed by pecking away at the keyboard.

"Mam?" Emily pointed at the screen, the bird tilted its head, inquisitively.

"Oh! Erm. I've had a call that my daughter, this is my daughter, has been arrested and is in your cells. There's been a mistake, man... bird."

'Navy?' the bird tapped.

"No man, schoolgirl."

The bird squawked and tapped more aggressively, 'Bloody spellcheck, I meant, name?'

"It's our Emily you've arrested. Well, no, I mean this is our Emily..."

The bird looked at the ceiling exasperated, then took a quick stroll around the desk in frustration, before returning to the keyboard.

'I only asked for the name' he pecked.

"Sorry, it's Emily Harris"

'Hairy Slimer?"

Emily glowered, "No! Look, is there someone else we can talk to? Who are you anyway?"

The bird cackled and typed, 'I'm Ley, I own this estate'

"Well I'm Claudia Harris, an my husband's a pig, an' my daughter here – " she punched Emily in the face – "Has apparently been arrested and is in your cells, so, take me to her!"

The crow took a moment to digest all this, then typed in, 'What the fuck are you on about?'

Claudia grabbed Ley by the throat.

"I'm out to knack someone, an' at this rate, I'll be startin' wi' you, ya little vulture bollocks! Take me ta' me daughter noooo!"

Ley typed carefully.

'I must warn you, assaulting a police crow in the pursuance of his duty is a serious offence! #Ionlyasked'

By way of a reply, Claudia asked sweetly, "D'you know my husband's superior is Colin Weird, an' that?"

Ley tapped in, 'Follow me.'

He hopped off the desk, and Claudia and Emily followed him through a doorway, down a corridor passing the canteen where a number of officers where placing bets to see who'd be first to dive off the rim of the big tea cup, passing the broom cupboard and through a door leading to a holding tank marked 'The one'.

"Aye, this looks like the one," said Emily, I'll just go an' get me out."

She opened the door, and was flattened against the wall behind, as a huge festering thing rushed out, and down the corridor toward the exit doors.

'Stop that, that, thing!' typed Ley, but by the time he'd finished, spellchecker was advising of word repetition, and the thing was out of the building and down the street.

"Well!" exclaimed Emily, "I didn't know I could move like that!"

"Well at least we now know it's NOT you," said Claudia, "So now yer can relax."

"You mean I'm not gonna get me head stoved in, mam?"

"Nah, not now, yer a good kid wor Emily."

"Aye Mummy, man," came the reply.

They headed back to the front desk, but as they did so, they realised that all of the station force, every officer they passed, had stopped, and appeared to have been turned to stone.

Once Ley had hopped back onto the front desk again, all three paused and looked at each other.

"Is this a kind of, like, normal lunchtime activity, in Blackbird Leys?" asked Claudia, brushing some of the sandstone off a copper.

"It's like, they've all got stoned," observed Emily, "But I mean, really, REALLY stoned."

'Beats the shit out of me' typed out Ley.

Claudia's mobile phone rang.

"Fuckin what?" she rasped.

"Hi our Claudie like," came the voice of her husband, "Wor Jess said you'd gone wi' wor Emily to get wor Emily out of prison, an that, like?"

"Aye pet, aye."

"Any luck, like?"

"Aye, but we don't know what we've found, and it's turned everyone except us into stone."

"Into stone?"

Another voice came down the phone.

"Ah, Mr Harris, I think this may be my department...."

"Will ya fuck off sir, I'm talkin to mah wife, ya great transubstantiated cabbage."

"No, Mr Harris, I really need to speak to your...."

"No, you're not having a go of....."

There was a sort of smack in the gob noise.

"Mrs Harris?"

"Is that you, Weird, ya fookin tossa? I'll knack you in a minute down the foon!"

"No, let me explain, Mrs Harris, that thing you've let out of the cells there, I really need it back. Now."

"You expect me to go an' get it?"

"No, just tell me where you are!"

"Black bird Ley's estate Police Station."

"Right, put that black bird, Ley, on the phone."

Emily held the crow to the phone.

'Yes?' texted Ley.

"Now look, get all the rozzers you can after that creature, or it's Morose's trousers for you."

'On the job, sir' texted Ley.

"Good, well flush first and then carry out my orders."

'Ok k smiley face'

"Big thumbs up"

'LOL'

"Will you pair of turbo freaks stop pissin' about, an' get doon here!" yelled Claudia.

There was a renewed blast of cabbage flavoured air biscuits, and the crow had a beak bleed.

"And here we are," announced Weird, "Along with young Robbie, just for you."

"AW love, you finally made it!" Claudia clapped her hands and her husband's head, with delight.

"Ouch! Steady love, I've had a bit of a tough day an' that!"

"When you've finished all this cack, perhaps we can get after the demons and monster currently fucking up our city?" growled a just – emerging Morose, "And I can get back on the piss!"

Ley took one look at Morose's trousers and disappeared into the back room.

"I never said a word," Morose raised his eyebrows.

"Aye, but you did Surr, you said a lot of shite. But I don't think that's what's botherin' him. He looked at your troosers. He was petrified of ending up like your feathered pal."

Weird had finished studying the statues of the officers. "Petrified… hmm… yes. No, young Harris. He's not petrified, but all these officers have been. I'm starting to understand the shape of events now. You know Robbie, your wife, daughter Miss Harris, and the black bird, Ley, have all been very fortunate. The creatures loose in Oxford are transmutating Homunculi."

"Christ on a bike!" offered Claudia.

"They were puppets," Weird continued, "controlled by an external force; but the longer they stay on our physical plane, the more powers they gain, including sentience, and the ability to escape the chrysalis of their original form."

"Vishnu on a velocipede!" Claudia ejaculated.

"If I may," Weird glowered, "The one locked in here, the former fake Emily, has the ability to become a medusa. By now, she'll have grown snakes in her hair, and as we can see she has also gained the ability to turn people to stone..."

"Cool!" said Emily.

"One more interruption and I'll personally knack you all," Weird huffed, crossly, "Not cool at all, you three are very lucky to have seen the homunculus mid transformation, or you could have been the latest victims. From the sightings, it would also appear that the former fake Jampton, has the ability to become a hell hound,"

"What's that?" asked Claudia, ducking to avoiding severe knacking.

"A hoond as you Geordies might say, a Cerebus to be precise. A giant triple headed fire breathing dog. Someone must pay for this!"

"Why? asked Morose, "Has it shit on the pavement and no one picked it up?"

"And worse!" growled Weird, "but enough of this idling about! To battle!"

"To Battle," they all cried.

After looking up the train times to Hastings, he decided it might be better to head back to the police station, for a conference.

"Let's head back to the station, for a conference," Weird said, and so saying he stepped out of the door and trod in a massive turd up to his forked tail.

"And tell Ley to get a poo bag!" he fumed, "extra-large!"

*****

The streets looked post apocalyptical; Police vehicles exploding, a chip shop had a lorry driven straight through it, a light aircraft was strafing a shopping centre, and a traffic helicopter had been lassoed and was being dragged to the ground by fiends in hooded tops. A number of the dead had risen from their graves, and even now, were waiting for the 9.30 deadline, so they could use their bus passes into town.

This was the scene that confronted the Medusa, a typical day in Blackbird Leys.

"Fuck this," she muttered, "I'll only blend in here! If they're already like this, how am I supposed to scare the shit out of the population, before turning them into stone forever?"

A large, familiar figure leapt over the nearby wall, and screamed at her,

"Get on with it! I have already started plans to create fear and loathing by assaulting women, walking by the canal!"

"Okay, okay, springy pants," she muttered, and at once turned her attention to an 'inner city missionary' type, praising the Lord on his way to spreading the Word and false hope.

"Oi, Christian!" she hissed. The smartly dressed evangelist turned to look at her, and all the snakes in her hair repeating the words 'Oi, Christian!'

"Good morning ma'am, and what a fine day it is for...."

"Up yours, God botherer," she hissed as his skin cemented and he turned to stone. Yes, it was a good day, and she mentally chalked up one victim. As she turned, so a group of hoodies approached. They bunched up together, and tried to push her off the pavement.

"Outcasts! Lepers!" she cursed.

The lead hoodie pulled out a knife in a flash, "You talkin' to me, slag?"

The Medusa didn't miss a beat. "Yes, scum."

"Yes, scum," repeated the snakes in her hair, and as the hoodie pulled back his knife to slash her up a bit, so he had a split second to take in what he was looking at, and realise his fate was already sealed. He made to warn the others, but too late. One by one a similar fate befell them. The last survivor managed to grab his mobile phone and try to, ironically, call the police for help, but only managed to dial 999 and press 'call', before he realised that his end had come.

"Emergency services, which service do you require?" asked a disembodied voice. Medusa took a look at the modern device and snarled, but picked it up anyway, and carried on toward a set of tower blocks. THIS would be too easy.

Watching from a distance, a rival group of hoodies who had been engaged in a turf war with the first bunch, felt their collective blood run cold, as they became the next to realise what was going on. Medusa spotted movement and scuttled towards them. They made a tactical withdrawal to their gang leader's mutha's flat, and debated what to do, all the while watching as the Medusa trotted toward them, and their collective fates. Two went on Facebook, and updated their statuses with weedy things like "OMG," one – Joseph Bryson, or Jocka, as he was known to his 193 followers - had gone on to Facebook live, and began to broadcast. Slowly, word was spreading. Satisfyingly for both Medusa and Spring-Heeled Jack – for it was he - so was FEAR.

*****

Back at the main station, Jampton now used modern technology to turn the tables on his former tormentors. He'd been alerted by the operator, to a traced phone call to 999, that had been left running from a location on Blackbird Leys. He alerted Weird at once. Weird, acting on the GPS signal location, honed in on by Jessica and Emily Harris, began to prepare his net. On the ground, those useless pricks Morose and Harris, had been ordered to drive at top speed to the phone's location on Bong Boulevard. Even now, Harris was pressing the pedals as fast as the tuk tuk would carry them, while Morose stood on the roof with a bottle of scotch and a loudspeaker, shouting "Nee Nar" as they were roundly ignored by Oxford's traffic.

"Fuck this Harris!" Morose shouted down, "We'll never get anywhere like this! Give me your warrant card."

"Aw no, you're not going into that Bargain Piss Up shop, sir!" Harris shouted back, as he skilfully ran over a student.

"Bloody right I'm not!" replied Morose, "Just give me your card!"

Harris sighed and pulled over, and they were immediately hit by a bus.

"Blind bastard!" they shouted.

"Swallow it!" replied the driver.

Morose opened the doors from the outside and yelled,

"Swallow this!" and punched the driver through the assault screen, through his teeth, and halfway down his throat.

"Mmmmmffff!" replied the bus driver, before being dragged out of the cab by Harris, and being left at the bus stop with his fare home.

Morose took the wheel.

"Put the wheel back, we need that to point the bus," sighed Harris. Working with Morose could get him like this.

"Where are we heading?" asked Morose.

"Blackbird Leys," replied Harris.

"Okay, so we'll need to put number 5 on the front," said Morose.

"What the fuck for?"

"So we don't get pulled over by the traffic commissioner and lose our jobs."

"We're coppers, you cunt," Harris reminded him, helpfully.

"Oh, well that's okay then," said Morose, jumped into the cab, took a last swig of the scotch, and, selecting a gear – any gear - let go of the handbrake. The bus shot off in reverse while Harris sailed face first into the windscreen.

"Other way, knobhead!" screamed Harris, through his battered face.

"Ah, shit..." muttered Morose, "I hate this new fangled turd."

Harris waved at him as he sailed through the air, towards the back of the bus, and Morose rammed his foot onto the accelerator into "drive". There was a satisfying sound of Harris hitting all the grab bars - with his already fragile knackers - on the way to the back seat, like a human pinball. Harris found the back seat, face first. Spitting out the foam he'd collected, he managed to drag his way against the G force back up the bus, via several seats and old ladies colostomy bags, to direct Morose as best as possible.

They jumped a number of lights, and had clocked up an impressive score of pedestrians and cyclists, all of them whingeing and pointing at their helmet cameras, when Morose indicated left and, braking carefully, brought the bus to a stop.

"NOW what?" asked Harris, exasperated.

"Ticket inspector," whispered Morose, "Sit down and shut

it, we're running early."

"For fucks sake, the World on the edge of an apocalypse, and you're worried about that?"

"Tickets please!" The jolly voice of Billy the checker, who used to be a postman, rang through the vehicle, to be greeted by a chorus of tuts and sighs from the fossils and coffin dodgers who made up 95% of the passengers, "Driver, can I have your waybill?"

Morose punched him in the solar plexus, causing severe personality disorders, and he fell back out of the vehicle, landing in a grid head first.

"No, we're late, try the next bus," explained Morose, shut the doors and drove off at speed, ramming a white camper van full of hippy trash, into a traffic island in the process.

"Here Harris, you have a go, I'm bored now," accelerating the bus to 60m.p.h. on Howard Street East was never going to be a good idea. Getting out of the seat and leaving the driving to Harris was probably a worse idea. Especially as Harris was still trying to get off the luggage shelf.

"With respect Surr, fuck off!" Harris hinted.

The bus, totally out of control, screamed down the road.

"Oh, live a little Harris, you cheese favourer! I can smell booze in one of these fossil's bags. You're being highly irresponsible you know, most of these buses can't drive themselves."

Harris climbed into the cab while Morose eyed up a student sitting halfway down the bus. The student had his earplugs in, and seemed oblivious as Morose began shouting at him:-

"Oi! Dickhead? You know there's a parcel shelf for your rucksack, don't you.? Now I admit, my conscience, ol' Jiminy up there was sitting on the bastard thing a minute ago but your bag should be... right, you shit..."

Morose had had enough. He opened the rear emergency door of the bus and threw the rucksack into the traffic. It bounced off the road and hit another hippy-mobile, which then had to swerve to avoid the student, who was connected via earplugs and iPhone to the bag, now bouncing down Shelley Road.

"Anyone else got a bag on their seat?" shouted Endof. There were no takers. "Ok, who's got the whiskey then? I can smell it somewhere!"

A very brave university lecturer stuck his hand up. Morose raised an eyebrow.

The elderly lecturer swallowed hard, this might be tricky. "I think I've gone wrong, does this bus go to Kennington?"

Morose grinned, "You've gone very wrong, matey! But we can drop you off?"

The lecturer shook his head nervously, and looked with fake fascination at the shop windows hurtling past.

"Surr!" shouted Harris, "Can I have a word, like?"

"Of course, my dear boy!" Morose's usually drunken stagger seemed to mesh perfectly with the swing and jolt of the bus, giving the illusion for once of sobriety in Morose.

"Aye Surr, I just feel you probably need to know, the brake pedal appears to be knackered, or more accurately missing Surr. So I can't slow this bastard thing down, man."

"Hmmm, that is a Eartha Kitt of a problem isn't it. Now, what do you think Sherlock Holmes would do in a situation like this?"

"Cack his pants, Surr."

"Probably Robbie, probably. Don't you think he might also thank the person who set him this vexing puzzle?"

"What have you bastard done, Surr?"

"I said live a little, Robbie. I took the liberty of removing the pedal, pop quiz Robbie, how are you going to stop the bus with no brake pedal?"

"Oh you bastard, Surr" The sweat was pouring down Robbie's face.

"Come on Robbie, let Uncle Endof have a go." Morose rammed Robbie face first out of the cab window, and threw the hand brake on.

Robbie screamed as he hit a nun, the passengers screamed, Morose chuckled, the bus slid to a stop.

"Now, I think you'll find there'll be a good off licence around here somewhere, young Eric." Morose shouted out of the window, "I don't know what it is, but I've got a bit of a thirst on me today."

"Fuck that, man. We've got worlds to save," gasped Robbie.

*****

This was a strange day. Events taking place in Oxford were having exponential repercussions. Medusa still held Jocka's phone and curiosity had got the better of her. The snakes had originally told her to pick it up, it was showing an image of the pavement beneath her, which she couldn't quite understand. She put her hand to the back of it and saw the hand, magnified.

One of the snakes, who was a bit more pc savvy, told her to press the button that reversed the camera, so she could selfie the world. One of the other snakes called that one a dickhead, and reminded it that if she saw herself on the screen, they'd all do the statue routine.

"Oh yeah, bollocks to that," considered the first snake.

"No," the second snake pointed out, "If you let us two hold

the iPhone in front of your face, on non-selfie mode, we'll be able to get most of your face in."

Medusa was puzzled, "Why do I want to do that?"

Snake 2 took the iPhone out of his mouth, making sure his pal had a good grip,

"We need more people to see your face, luvvie. Maybe we can get you on 'I'm A Celebrity' or something. But for now, Facebook Live will get you mass audience appeal. See those numbers on the bottom of the screen?" He swung the screen around to show Medusa, "87 so far, that's people who are watching. Well… used to be people watching. They've all seen your face now so, y'know!"

Medusa grinned, "That's amazing. How do you know so much about this technology"?

"Followed it for a long time," 2 sniffed, "All early Nokia phones had Snakes, y'know."

*****

The hoodie Jocka's immediate circle of friends, were mostly from Blackbird Leys, a few were from other communities across Oxford. But, like ripples on a pond, the more these people connected to the Facebook Live image, the more people and communities it became available to.

From Oxfordshire, the home counties came next, the south of England, spreading up north, across the Irish Sea, and the Atlantic, soon it was crossing continents. Only the apathy of the average Facebook user toward "facebook live" could save the human race now… or maybe Endofleveldemon Morose…

*****

Morose himself, meantime, had managed to drag a protesting Harris toward the Windrush tower block. Shouts and screams were heard from within. The surviving officers from the pig pen at St Aldates on the estate, had broken out their heavy duty armaments, and were jostling for positions to dispose of the Medusa that was roaming in Windrush. Morose took stock of the situation and advised Harris accordingly.

"This is dangerous."

"Aye man, aye man,"

"Let's get out and go home."

"Sir, you're acting like a coward."

"I'm not acting."

"Stow it sir, we got this mess into Oxford, an' now we're going to get it out."

"Yes, out, that's us."

Harris managed to grab Morose by the trouser belt as he made to run off. Morose unbuckled his belt and it came loose in Harris' hand. Morose ran off another three steps before his trousers fell down, and he did likewise. Harris was at his side in a flash.

"Sir, man, we're doin' this, like, fer the lads this, er, thing had turned to stone."

"Oh, stop the dutiful heroics, you dildo, the pubs are open, we can watch the apocalypse from one of them! Unless they only have Fox News of course."

They took stock of the situation. Seven piglets, themselves, and a line of stone people leading them to the Medusa. Morose, ever the detective, suggested,

"Lets try to follow the line of corpses."

"Brilliant thinking sir," squealed a constable.

"Shut it, creep. Follow me," ordered Morose.

He headed off the other way. Harris threw a brick at him, taking a chunk out of his skull, and he turned back with a resigned sigh.

"Okay, now follow me into here, and if it all goes wrong, blame my sergeant, Wong, here."

They crept in single file into Windrush. It was dark and stank of piss.

"Harris! Its dark and stinks of piss!"

"Put in back in, then, sir, and get back in front."

"Ah! Right–ho!"

They made their way along one corridor, past a stone granny, up a flight of steps past a couple of stone slags, a stone cat, up another flight of steps, and then Morose asked, "Why don't we just use the fucking lift?"

"We might go past it, sir," explained Harris. They found the lift was jammed anyway, as a drunk had been stood across the automatic doors pissing into it, and turned to stone across the door sensor, so every time it went to shut, it hit his petrified figure, and opened again, slowly giving the automated "Stand clear of the doors" voice, a full scale breakdown.

As they made their way up to the fifth floor, so Harris remarked,

"That medusa thing's been busy, sir. Even the stairs have been turned to stone!"

Everyone else stopped and glared at the stupid fucking muppet; then, having run out of glares, carried on. The stone statues got more in number. An alarming number seemed to have been wearing hoodies, and were turned to stone at a point of advancing toward the Medusa.

"Sir," whispered a useful–looking WPC, "What's that noise?"

Harris glared one back at Morose, "Have you got it out again?"

"Not me, Edward!"

"Its Harris sir....yes, WPC Horne, what IS that noise?"

"It's a sort of wailing noise, like someone's trapped," muttered PC O'Toole.

"And a pissing noise too, this is all very strange," Morose heaved up for good measure, before adding, "Where's that cockhead Weird when you want him? Curling one out at his bloody Freemasons club, I suppose."

The smell of cheesy cabbage heralded the lie to this idea.

"I'm right behind you, you septic boil on the arse of humanity."

"Thank you sir, nice to see you too," snorted Morose.

"I suggest young Robbie Wong goes ahead," hissed Weird, "He's good at this sort of shit."

Harris snapped back at once, "Ah get the fuck out, think of my wife an' kids!"

"Must I?" asked Weird, genuinely pained; and suddenly added, "Wait! Footsteps approaching."

They all held their breath; except Morose, who just held one in.

Someone, or something, was walking, or even shuffling towards them. Agitated breathing. A sigh. The footsteps came nearer. The coppers and their soul-less leader all pressed themselves back into the wall as far as they could, hardly daring to breathe. Harris found himself trying to dig into the concrete with his fingernails. The footsteps stopped almost next to him. Why had he not worn camouflage?

A breath inward heralded a voice. He couldn't stand the tension.

"Dad, yer can all come out, you silly bastards, the Medusa's got herself stuck behind a line of bodies."

They all stepped out into the light again.

"Young Slimer?" asked Weird.

"Aye man, an' don't you forget it!"

"But what's caused the medusa to get stuck?"

"Come an' see, you bunch of big girls' blouses."

The Medusa had certainly got stuck. Not only had she stood in a corner demanding that all the neighbourhood "Come and get me, you mortal shitbags," but as they turned into stone before her gaze, so they had gradually blocked the silly cow in.

"So, you dozy trollop!" Weird managed to hiss out loud, "Stuck in a prison of your own making!"

"I will turn you to stone!" screamed Medusa.

"Not me, you silly moose!" laughed Weird, "Don't you remember me? I was your second husband in Hades! I'm not even remotely mortal!"

"Colin 'The cabbage' Weird?" she squealed.

"The same."

"I'll pick your bones, you pillock!"

"The CSA have already done that, you vile dog! Meantime, if you want freeing, pick the bones out of this!" and with that, he let loose a cabbage soup of flatulence that would later see the Windrush Tower block condemned as 'unfit for human habitation'.

"Free me at once, you old fart bag!"

"Certainly, donkey breath, but first," – he produced an Ipad from Christ knows where – "You'll need to sign this."

Medusa grasped it and looked at the screen. It was a facebook live feed of herself.

There was a general groan of dismay from all the snakes, in unison, "Oh cock cheese"

Then a sort of explosion, and the smell of sulphur; and the Medusa was gone, back to Hell.

Colin Weird reached down to Jocka's still functioning iPhone, now lying on the landing, and switched off the Facebook Live feed. "Very satisfying that," he said. He switched his iPad onto notes, "Note to self. Cancel maintenance payments."

By now, Harris, Morose and the officers had joined Weird on the landing and were examining the carbonised remains of the former residents of Windrush Tower.

Harris blinked, "It's not just Windrush Sir, there'll be bodies all around the world. And we still haven't sorted out who is behind this, but I'm sure we will by Chapter 6 or 7."

Weird nodded. "We'll need a sanctified explanation for all these deaths, but it's certain that these people will be missed."

"Aye Sir, will there be a tribute to them?"

"Possibly," said Emily, "There could be a statue put up to them."

*****

And so, the day came to an end, and as is the way of things all the officers made their way home.

"I'm home Mum," shouted Hugh, before deciding to go into the house first.

"I'm home," he tried again, walking into the front room. Oh good, his Mum had lit the coal fire.

She smiled over at him, "Look our Hugh, I've found a wee timorous beasty! Awl alone he was, so I brought him in for a warm. He seems to like the heat of the fire. I'm going to call him Laddie, say hello to him."

From by the fire a pair of brown eyes looked up at him; then another pair, then another pair.

CHAPTER 5 – IT'S ALL OVER

(Dedicated to PC James Sloan – Ian's dad – who made the same arrest, stopping a football match, in real life)

They drove at considerable speed into the courtyard of the college, pulling up in a cloud of stone chippings, tyre smoke and splintered wood, having failed to stop before the doorway to the Victorian college façade. Part of the restored medieval door lintel collapsed onto the police car following them, which shunted the 1960s Ford Anglia Estate into the stairs. There was a pause and then the staircase itself collapsed, bringing down part of the ceiling, and an entire upstairs room and the student contained within.

"Fuckin' ace!" laughed Morose.

Brushing off the dust and several badly injured students, Morose and Harris cocked their guns, gunned their cocks, grocked their cuns, clawed their way up the remains of the stair rail, and onto the surviving sections of the first floor.

"This is the room, sir!" shouted Harris, throwing himself against the wall, and dislodging more plasterwork and his shoulder blade.

"Right," snarled Morose, joining his sergeant against the wall so heavily that it gave way altogether, revealing a pair of students working away at their studies. As it were. These two screamed and ran out of the remains of the room, fell through the gap, and joined the pile of bodies on the Ford Anglia below.

"I'm going to count to three," Morose advised.

"Right Surr," Harris nodded.

"1...2...3..."

Nothing happened.

Morose sighed.

"I'm going to count to three, then we'll break the fuck out of the door," Morose added.

"Right, Surr," Harris nodded, hitting his head on the wall again. A lampshade further down the corridor fell onto an elderly deaf lecturer, who had come to see what all the quiet was.

Morose tightened his sphincter and hissed, "One.... two... er...."

"Three, sir," advised Harris.

"Yes, I know that, you ferret fixer; three!"

There was a click.

"It was open all the time," observed Harris.

"Its okay," growled Morose, "We'll go in, close it, and then batter the shit out of it, you know, just to make sure."

"Great thinking surr," replied Harris.

There was a sustained assault, and the door was suitably disarmed, as a door anyway.

"Good work sergeant, we'll make a quality pig out of you yet," Morose allowed himself a quick fart, before adding, "Ah, right, this.... THIS is what we came for."

They dropped down to the ground floor and jumped back into the Ford Anglia, revved the bollocks off it, and reversed out, causing most of the rest of the building to collapse in on itself.

Harris grinned as he drove out of the wreckage, "Fuckin well in surr. Let's get it back to the station."

"Ace, NOW I can have a shit."

So, with the toilet roll safely in Morose's carrier bag, they made their way back to the police station, so that Morose could get on with the rest of his dump.

*****

"You wished to scream at us, sir?"

Morose tried not to cower behind the desk in Weird's office, as Harris broke out in a horrifying cold sweat. Superintendent Weird hovered menacingly at 9 foot tall, behind his desk. He raised his head and hit it on the ceiling. His lack of eyes glowered menacingly, his hairs all stood on end out of his scales, a trick not many half lizards can pull off.

"You pair of turboturds are too much! Twelve million poonds worth of damage, most of it irreplaceable!"

"Surely they can salvage some of the bricks?" ventured Morose.

"Bricks, yes! Art work, possibly! Human beings, no!"

"Ah, I see," admitted Morose, not seeing.

"A right bloody tool I'm being made to look, down the golf club."

"Yes sir" the two coppers replied.

"Any more of this shit, and you two will be on the beat!"

"Aw now steady on sir, my legs are giving me trouble," whinged Harris.

"I meant, beaten to a pulp, you monstrous prick! Fuck my old boots!"

"What, now, sir?" asked Morose.

"OUT!!!"

"Before we go sir, any assignments need doing?"

"What???"

"Well, you know, any murders need looking into, any missing children, any nice prostitutes to question?"

*****

"You had to ask didn't you Surr?"

"Eh?"

"Ah mean, you couldn't just let it go with a polite 'yes Surr'. You had to wind him up."

"Oh Robbie, it's only until he gets bored or finds something else for us to do. And with Oxford so under-policed after all the Medusa statue business. They'll need us sooner or later."

"Aye Surr, but this…"

Robbie stuck another fixed penalty notice on yet another untaxed vehicle. He checked his hand-held tablet, and keyed in the registration number. By pure luck this wanker had taxed his car. He looked across the road, Morose had vanished again – he kept doing it – after a moment his head bobbed up again, as he walked to the next parked car.

"Surr, why do you keep bobbing down at the front and rear of these cars?"

"Just following orders young Robert."

"What exactly are you doing?"

"Just keying the registration numbers on all these cars. They're all scratched to fuck now!"

Robbie couldn't be arsed with this, "No Surr, what Weird meant was…"

Robbie's radio clicked into life:-

"Four five to three seven over"

"What's that four five shit?" asked Endof, endorsing another car.

"I think it means Jampton's been watching The Professionals again," Harris turned to the radio, "One nine for a copy, come in Hugh."

Morose nutted his radio on, "Breaker breaker come alive, rubber duck, what's your handle and how many candles you burning?"

"Surr, switch that off you git. I'm just getting feedback here."

"Right lads listen up, I've got very good news for you," enthused Hugh, "Stop harassing Oxford's motorists."

"Aww, I was enjoying that," sighed Morose, scratching an elderly lady's glasses, just to relieve the monotony.

"No lads, hush now. You're back on the case. Make your way to Foxleigh Road. To the football ground..."

"Oh not bastard crowd duty.." groaned Harris, handing the old nun her glasses back.

"No, will you listen. There's been a murder. Meet up with Max in the car park, he's on his way."

*****

The Ford Anglia screamed around another corner, as Harris explained the case to Morose.

"Aye, it seems the game was stuck at two all. Last minute of stoppage time Crowsnest Ironclads took a shot. It belted Oxford Wanderers' keeper in the face, and he went doon like a ton of bricks, man."

"How unfortunate!"

"Luckily, the ball deflected back to the feet of Ironclads Striker Howard, and he belted it in."

"Fuckin' ace" Morose muttered through an emptied out can of Stella.

"Aye, but I think the match has been abandoned."

"Harris, why are you telling me all this? I was with you when Jampton passed this info on."

"For the readers, man."

"Oh yes, sorry. Do keep reading, there's a good bit coming up!"

As they turned the corner next to the Dostoyevsky Towers - a 1960's block, now severely run down – Harris slammed the brakes on, just in time to avoid a battered white Audi, which flew out of the driveway at a speed inappropriate for the autobahn. The Anglia slewed across the road, and finished off half embedded in a hedge, while Morose finished off half embedded through the windscreen.

"Told you it was a good bit," he muttered.

Harris reversed out of the hedge, just for good measure he went back for the car. "Just keep your head doon Sir. I'm having that bastard."

A voice came from through the broken glass. "Murder takes priority, Robbie."

"Aye Surr!" reluctantly Robbie agreed, "I saw his face Surr. It was Barry Andrews. I thought that bastard was still in the army. I'll pop roond to his Mams later and pay him a visit."

"Yes, chin the fucker for me, won't you? Drive on young Robbie. I think I see Max pulling in!"

"What is he pulling in, sir? His car? Can't we get him for that?"

Morose punched young Robbie in the face, causing Robbie to punch his superior back where his face would have been, had it not been for the fact he was still part way through the windscreen. Instead Robbie just dislocated his fist on the side of the passenger seat. He stopped the reversing out of the hedge manoeuvre suddenly, and Morose shot back into the passenger seat, where Harris took the opportunity to punch him properly.

Thus, with both of them clutching their chins, they drove up to Max's beautifully preserved Mini Moke, failed to stop in time, and took part of it with them.

Max climbed out; well, slithered out, as his legs were in the portion of the car ten yards away on the Anglia. He gradually made his way over to them, looking for all the World like an over sized slug; and, chinning Morose one, muttered,

"They're MY fucking legs, you tit."

While Morose replaced his chin and cheek bones, Max reapplied his legs, took a quick snort of coke, and turned to Harris.

"How's it going, Fred?"

"It's 'Robbie', sir, and I'm just fucking ace, sir."

Max ignored this answer and, taking another blast, asked Morose,

"Well, where's the stiff?"

"I thought that was your department, we're just along for the ride."

"Being honest," Max started, "I don't know why any of us are here. A football hitting someone in the face, hardly the commensurate opening salvo of a crimewave, is it?"

"Aye," Robbie nodded, "but he is dead. Better check it out."

"I suppose so. Hey, that takes me back!" Max looked longingly across the car park.

Morose's ears pricked up, "Takes you back? What? A bottle of Macallan?"

Max waddled over to a beautiful relic from a time gone by. "Triumph Stag, Endof. Dream to drive. I drove one of these beauties up to the second time my licence was taken off me."

"Yes, I remember. Didn't I wreck it?"

"We never found out, did we? By the time we both came out of our comas, it was all a bit of a blur. Lovely little mover though."

"How long ago was that?" asked Robbie, as he hadn't said anything in a while.

Max looked up to the sky, searching for an accurate answer. "It must have been, ooh, in the past I should think."

"Ooh, at least," Morose gave it a little more accuracy, "I mean, it has already happened."

"Aye man," sighed Robbie, "Shall we have a look at this goalkeeper, for giggles, like?"

*****

It was clear which goal they were to head to. It was the one nearest the tower block. Although they couldn't see the body yet, they could see the small crowd gathered around, and the repetitive chant of 'you're not breathing anymore'.

"Let us through, I could pass for a police officer on a good day," Morose held out his old Blockbuster Video card. The crowd obligingly separated to get away from the smell.

"Don't anyone leave," Robbie ordered, "We'll have some questions in a moment."

A man walked past carrying a large bottle containing a yellowish liquid.

"Are you taking the piss?" asked a replica kit wearing hoodie, "He doesn't half ruddy well honk!"

"Fucking right he does!" chorused a pair of nuns.

"I'll pour some Brut on him later," promised Max, "But first, we need to spend a while ridiculing the deceased. Right, let's start with yer actual body. Achingly dull, same for the legs and arms... Ahh!"

Robbie perked up, "Found something Max?"

Max looked around, Morose – he noted – was busy insulting the nuns. He turned back around to Robbie, "Don't tell his Nibbs, but I've just remembered what I did with a particularly lovely crate I started on Friday. Although fuck knows how I'll get it down, from the top of the conning tower, now!"

"Aye Max, focus man!"

"No, it's no good Robbie. I might as well go back to the corpse here. I can't keep calling him corpse, do we know his name yet?"

Endof punched a nun, "Ooh you fucker!" she screamed, throwing her match program to the floor as she made ready to give Morose a right good pagging.

In a dive appropriate for the Premier League, Robbie was under the program before it hit the ground. Back page, there it was, in goal for Oxford was... Monsignor Bruce Kent.

"Right, pubs open in fifteen minutes, Max," observed Morose, "Let's get the natural causes this scene stealer died of, sorted, and get the fuck out."

Max dropped his guts; and thus turned the body over.

There was a collective gasp from both police and assembled supporters. Several tried not to retch, one nun lost her bladder control.

Morose spoke first.

"Max, can we just do the natural causes bit, without mentioning his face being shot off?"

Max stood back into an old dog turd. "I'm not sure that I can pin down a specific natural cause, that involved a low calibre bullet removing the front portion of this chap's face, without there being a few questions at the coroner's office."

"Cack! Robbie?"

"Aye man Surr?"

"Do some nominal police posing, 'til I get back from that Oddbins over the way, there, will you?"

Robbie sighed, "Aye man, over which way?"

"Oh you know, somewhere like Durham."

"I'm giving you two minutes, you addled old knob, otherwise I'm grassing you up to Weird."

"Fuckin' snitch," muttered Morose.

Robbie called Hugh to send in a few cops, scene of crime johnnies, and the photograph crew. He then took the small throng of fans from both teams to one side, and announced,

"Aye! Looks like we'll be here for a time. So, while I wait for a few of the lads to help me interviewing you all, can I just ask, did anyone see exactly what happened?"

"Me!" squealed a nun.

"Who are you, sir?"

"I'm sister Tiggiewinkle of the Order of the Hedge Botherers."

"Oh aye, the ones my boss is waging a guerrilla war against?"

"Yes, that's us."

"I'm a little surprised to see your lot here at the

match, man?"

"Oh, we're not here for the football, sergeant."

"No?"

"We come for the racist, homophobic chanting, and the coin throwing and a bit of mindless violence. Then perhaps one or two of us can go home with a sailor afterward."

"Sailors in Oxford?"

"Well we can stretch to one of your snotty piglets, what are you doing, later?"

"Whatever it is, it won't be you!" cried Morose, lurching back into the very thin of the action, with half a bottle of Vole Stopper lager.

As Franks and Soames turned up with fresh notebooks, and that idiot White got out of the boot with his binoculars to photograph the corpse, so Morose settled down next to the body.

"No you don't," tutted Max, "You won't be able to do the old Archie Andrews routine with this one, especially with half his face blown away."

"Can't they photoshop another face on him?" asked Morose.

"Perhaps you can interview me, Sergeant Harris?" asked a young man in a tracksuit.

"Aye, and who are you?" asked Harris.

"I'm the team coach and physio."

"Aye well, it's a bit late now, isn't it? Yer magic sponge isn't gonna be much good in this case, is it, like?"

"Well it's wiped the smile off everyone else's face."

Morose sighed. "Can we please have a moment of silence."

Robbie scratched his chin, "What? Respect for the deceased you mean?" This was a new high for the Chief Inspector.

"Don't be silly, Robbie. I just want to appreciate the effort that's gone into making this marvellous can of terminal strength piss juice."

Robbie sighed and paused, while his chief necked what was left of the can.

"Alright Surr?"

Morose gave a vague thumbs up sign with his middle finger. Robbie returned his attention to the man in the tracksuit.

"Aye, and why would we want to talk to you, man?"

The physio put his Zimmer frame to one side, and looked darkly at Robbie.

"I've trained Bruce Kent, our star goalkeeper, since he arrived at the club as a talentless no hoper."

"That's right," chipped in a bloke with an Oxford shirt on, "And thanks to Les here, Bruce is the number one goalie in the Shark's Motors Second Division South."

Robbie turned his attention to the new voice, it was attached to a man who was also new.

"And who are you?"

"I'm Chas Arsehole, team manager." Chas took Robbie's hand and shook it. He then twisted it, threw it, and passing it through a mangle, wrung it out.

"Thank you," said Robbie, "I think you two gentlemen should come over here, I shall take a full statement from you both."

While Robbie got on with the boring bit, and WPC Soames battered a confession out of a police horse, Morose watched with interest as that balloon head White took photographs of the body and crime scene. So far, he'd taken a picture of a chip paper, a passing swallow, and WPC Soames being shat on by a police horse. Morose strolled over to White, and asked nonchalantly,

"What the fuck are you doing, you pig snorkelling toss rag?"

"Oh hello sir," grinned White, "I'm jolly glad you've turned up, there's been a murder here."

"There'll be another in a minute, you fish lipped spunk chariot. Just photograph the corpse and fuck off, you useless cow nosher."

"My sir, you're in corking good form today!" beamed White.

Morose contented himself by beating White's brain out with a compacted can of Newt Death, and lurched off to abuse Max's Mini Moke.

Harris consulted his notes and counted heads. According to the ticket office, they had sold 12 tickets today. Ignoring match officials, team staff and players, there were 11 spectators here. Someone was missing. He asked a very cheerful though now brainless White, to make sure that he took a picture of everyone, and got names, addresses and contact details, while Harris himself, approached the ticket seller.

"Possibly you can help Surr? We seem to be missing one spectator, did anyone leave early?"

"I wouldn't have a clue. I don't stand guard. After kick-off I normally come and watch the match. I was only saying to... ooh, now 'ang on. He's not here!"

"Who, Surr?"

"The fellah who's not there!"

Harris briefly thought of shooting him for a laugh. "What did he look like, and where was he standing?"

The ticket wallah pointed towards the stand adjacent to the car park. "We were stood in that stand. Had the whole stand to ourselves. He kept checking this big case he was carrying, checking inside it like. Anyway I had a curry..."

"When was that?"

"Last night, beef and some very nasty looking vegetables..."

"What has that got do with..."

"It was rotting my guts constable, so I went off for a shit. While I was off on the log flume, the goalkeeper collapsed. I wondered if it was the drains again at first. Anyway, meladdo with the big case. He's missing."

"Aye Surr. Description?"

"Two Cleveland steamers, and a little bit of pebbledashing."

"No Surr, of the missing man."

"Oh sorry. Well, about average height, two legs, two arms, one head I think."

"Any distinguishing features?"

"Yes. Bore a startling resemblance to that fellah off the telly. The one that's always on that thing."

Robbie closed his notebook. "Thank you, we should have him in no time."

Morose stumbled over.

"Yes, that's the fucker!" said the ticket man.

"Great, you've been a big help," smiled Robbie, pushing him under the horse that was busily trampling on WPC Soames.

"Get anything?" asked Morose.

"Aye, a few germs and the urge for a slash, hold this will

you?"

He gave Morose an empty bottle to hold, pissed in it; and, remembering to fasten his flies up, made for the sanctuary of the scene of the crime, it was bound to offer some peace and quiet an' that. He studied the 6-yard box, unusually large underwear the bloke had. He checked the goalmouth, he checked the back of the goal area, and the large hole in the nylon covering that was draped across it.

"Found anything, Harris?" asked Morose, taking a swig from the bottle.

"No sir, I think he's slipped through the net."

"They need these goalposts renewing. This one is splintered to fuck!" exclaimed Morose, "Get White to photograph it, will you?"

Harris glanced up at the damaged goalpost and crossbar. "Aye man. What's today's official insult for White?"

Morose consulted his copy of Wisden for 1998. "Er... Putrid fart wagon."

"Thank you Surr. Hey! Putrid fart wagon!"

White consulted his copy of the Beano Annual 1984. "Yes Sir?"

"Get this goal post photographed will you. It's knacked, man. Just make sure we don't get the blame for it!"

"Yes sir, I'll date the photograph last Thursday, that'll confuse them."

"Good lad," Robbie patted White's head patronisingly.

They made sure all the evidence was collected, that could be collected; they managed to revive Soames by pouring a bucket of water over her; they stapled the front back onto Max's car. Thus ready, they then arrested everyone at the match, and hauled them in for Jampton to sort.

*****

Harris knocked on the door and coughed the 'I'm important' cough.

The door was abruptly opened by a very unimportant older lady.

"Yes?"

"Mrs Andrews?"

"No, I'm Mrs Andrews."

"I know that, man!"

"Why did you ask then?"

"Look, just fuck off will yer? Is your Barry in?"

"Barry?" she shouted. "Are you in? I think it's the filth!"

A voice came from inside, "Are you sure, mam?"

"I think so," she shouted back, "I'll just check." She smiled back at Robbie, "You *are* a pig, aren't you?"

"Aye, how did you know, like?"

"You coughed the 'I'm important' cough at the start of this section. Look, just below the asterisks at the top of the scene. When you knocked on my door." She shouted back through the door, "He says he is with Oxford Scum!"

"Tell him I'm out, mam."

"He's out, officer. Can I give him a message?"

"Well… probably. You are his mam after all. I think I can trust yer. Just tell him to come to the door now!"

"I think he knows you're in, love. Come and tell him you're out."

"Yes Mam".

The same young man who was driving the Audi earlier, came to the door. He supported himself on the gas meter cupboard and looked Robbie in the eyes. "I'm out, like me mam says."

"Aye, can I leave a message for you then?"

"Yes, I'll make sure I get it when I'm back."

"Aye. Look laddie, y'kna that awld Ford Anglia you nearly knacked coming oot from by Dostoyevsky Towers?"

"Yes... I mean I don't know anything about it."

"Aye well I saw you driving your Audi man. And it was me driving the Anglia. At the very least I could do you for dangerous driving."

"Sorry... it's Constable Harris isn't it?"

"I've been promoted Barry. I'm a Detective Sergeant now."

"I know, I've read the books."

Harris nodded. "Do you want me to sign them?"

Barry laughed, "No thanks, they're shit."

"Anyway, I thought you were still in the Army. What you doing back here?"

"Medical discharge."

Robbie looked embarrassed, "Well, just make sure you wipe it up, man. What's wrong with you?"

"The doctor says I've got Parkinson's Disease. I get the shakes you know."

"No I'll get them, you'd only spill them." His joke wasn't appreciated, "Aye man, I do understand, actually. My uncle had it. I'm sorry to hear that, Barry, man. All the more reason not to drive like a fuckin' maniac, eh?"

"I suppose so. You're going to tell me I shouldn't be

driving at all, aren't you?"

Robbie shook his head. "No man, as long as it's controlled well by your medication and your doctor's happy, you can keep driving for now. But not like a maniac, eh? Just take the warning, I divvn't want to have to drag you in, behave yourself man."

As Barry closed the door, Robbie could hear Mrs Andrews, on the phone, arranging for a posse to come to the house. Robbie quickly keyed the Audi, and left.

*****

There was the usual clattering of breakfast plates, cups and cutlery at the Harris household. Which was odd as the Harris's weren't up yet.

A head popped around the bedroom door, "Mam? Mam?"

Robbie opened an eye, it sounded like Emily had a bad throat. "Aye Emily, let your mam sleep, what do you want love?"

"The key to the bastard whiskey cabinet, Dad. Any idea where the chiselling cheapskate… sorry Dad. I mean do you know where it is?"

Robbie's eyes were wide open now. His head did a wonderful 180 degree swivel like Regan from The Exorcist, or indeed Morose, from some shit books Barry Andrews hadn't wanted signing. It wasn't Emily at all.

"What are you doing in my house, again Surr?"

"Looking for the key to your whiskey cabinet young Robbie. Where have you hidden it?"

"I don't have a whisky cabinet, sir."

"Well, your lovely wife, then?"

"She also doesn't drink whiskey, sir."

"I don't suppose the girls have a small stash?"

"No."

"Oh piss! Well, I might as well tell you about the call then. While I was checking your kitchen for anything happy, your phone rang."

"I didn't hear anything." Robbie pondered, taking Claudia punching him in the groin as a hint that they were disturbing her sleep. He got up and headed to the door. Morose held out his pyjama bottoms, but Robbie decided to put on his own instead.

"You didn't hear your phone ring Robbie, for the very good reason that I didn't want it to disturb you. I threw it out of the window."

Indeed, there was a window broken in the front room, and on the lawn the house phone lay next to Robbie's work mobile, from when he threw it out with a guinea pig attached.

Robbie looked out of the undamaged glass section of the window, opposite the broken one on the left.

"This is a right pane, sir," noted Robbie, "My fuckin phone's on the grass and you're goin' doon stairs to get it back."

Morose laughed mockingly, "I'm doing no such....."

....and with that, Morose was launched out of the window. Robbie quickly threw on his shirt and trousers, he threw on his socks, his threw on his shoes; fed up of throwing them he donned the lot, and slid down the drainpipe to join his boss, catching his knacks on the grid cover en route.

"Here, it says, 'missed call', that'll be the one I was telling you about," Morose said from the middle of the rose bush.

"Cheers, petal," said Harris, kicking him in the balls for good measure, with the added result that Morose fell further in and ingested a community of aphids.

The missed call was from that permanently on duty clot, Jampton. This could be important! He pressed the 'recall' button, but still couldn't remember what he'd had done with his life. Never mind. Hugh answered anyway.

"Fuckin what?"

"Aye Hugh man, you'd rung me up at fuckin' five in the mornin, ya useless horn stopper, what is it noo man?"

"Aw Robbie, its really important, have you seen this mornin's Oxford Gazette?"

"Hugh, its only half five in the mornin now an' I was asleep at five, you fucking buffoon, but anyway, do tell me about the newspaper."

"It's just there's a load of photos from the match!"

"And?"

"Well, there might be something important in there. You just don't know."

Robbie looked at the dull grey slash in the sky that marked another dull, drizzle laden day beginning in Oxford.

"Hugh?"

"Yes?"

"Thanks. I'm going to ring off now."

"Okay mate! I hope I've not woken you up or nuffin!"

Robbie pressed "end" and wished that Jampton would do just that. Still, there may be something in the photographs, as he ripped Morose out of the rosebush, he told him,

"We'll take a look at the Oxford Gazette photos now sir, there might just be something in them that clot White may have missed."

By way of a reply, there was the sound of a hornet's

nest apparently coming straight at him; Morose opened his mouth, and the highly pissed off colony of aphids hurtled out. Morose belched, dropped a substantial air biscuit, and spoke,

"Okay."

They made for the Anglia and hopped in, a right pair of berks they looked too, on one leg.

*****

"Hullo?"

"Aye man. Oxford Police…"

"No."

"What do you mean 'No'?"

Robbie was pissed off with this conversation already. The fine drizzle outside his house had now turned to sheets of rain. The heaviest rain Robbie had seen in many a year. The water was bouncing off the road, and the drains were flooding already. In the distance he could hear thunder approaching, it was 5.45 and this berk on the other end of the intercom outside the Oxford Gazette, was saying 'no' to him.

"No, as in no we are not Oxford Police, we are the Oxford Gazette. We don't solve crimes, we just profit from people's inherent nosiness about crime, celebrity news and sport. If you want the police I suggest you go to…"

"Aye man. Y'see we're the police. I'm Detective Sergeant Robert Harris of Oxford Police. Can we come in please?"

"I don't think so…"

Robbie was exasperated. "Why not?"

"Well, I think the door's locked. Try giving it a push."

"No man, can you let us in?"

"How do I know you're really, really Police?"

"I've got a warrant card, man. And my boss has got his Blockbuster membership card…"

"Sorry, I can't see that from up here. I think you'd better come back later…"

A sodden figure stepped up from the overflowing drains and staggered over to join Robbie, "Did you tell them I can drive a Ford Anglia straight into their reception and then do them for wasting police time? I can do that, because today I am a police officer."

The voice on the other end of the intercom shouted, "Mr Taylor…" and there was the sound of running feet.

A deeper, slightly more authoritative voice came on to the intercom next. "Hello, yes?"

"Aye man. Just open the fuckin' door. It's pissing doon, and we're the pigs."

*****

Mr Taylor, chief editor of the Telegraph, looked at the two soggy, dripping wet men, each stood in a four inch deep puddle which had caused the carpet in his office to sag, in front of him.

"Is it raining outside?"

Morose uploaded another colony of aphids onto the carpet, before saying,

"No. What the fuck makes you think that?"

"Just a hunch."

Robbie Harris cleared his throat, and added it to the aphids now drowning on the carpet.

"Sir, having a hunch in the presence of the police, can lead to your arrest."

"Robbie, I think that's 'firearms', not 'a hunch'", Morose pointed out.

Robbie considered this, before revising his approach.

"Sir, having a firearm in the presence of the police, can lead to your arrest."

"Well this is your lucky day, sergeant, as I don't seem to have a firearm on me, at the moment."

Morose patted Mr Taylor down, not to check for firearms, just cos he rather enjoyed it.

"You're right out of luck Harris, he really doesn't have a firearm on him."

"Cack!" spat Harris, "We'll come to the point, Mr Taylor"

"I wish to fuck you would."

"Have you seen this morning's Oxford Telegraph?"

"Funnily enough, as I edit the frigging thing, yes. Why?"

"There are some pictures of the football match, between Oxford Wanderers and Crowsnest Ironclads, on the sports page."

"Should they have been in the used cars section?"

Morose managed to get a few words in.

"Do you mind if I get a few words in?"

Harris groaned, "What is it, sir?"

"Nothing, I just wanted to get a few words in. Carry on sergeant, you're doing a great job, and that's what I'm off to do right now."

So saying, Morose proceeded to lay cable across the carpet, which after all was fucked anyway by now.

"Gentlemen please, you were asking about the morning's newspaper?"

"Ah yes," remembered Harris, "Can you tell us, who took the pictures, and do you have them all, like?"

"Well that was our sports photographer, and yes, I have them all, like. Would you like to see them all….like?"

"If we could," Harris replied, in his most annoyingly patronising voice.

"I'll do that sergeant, as I am doing so, would you kindly ask your chief inspector to stop wiping his arse on the coffee machine, and not to use the photocopier to despatch the results all over the office?"

"Aye sir, I'll have a word while you're busy an' that."

"I say, thanks!"

As Morose stopped producing his own brand of 'cappuccino', and Mr Taylor skipped off to get the proofs, Harris took a look round. Not a great place. The carpet was fucked and full of drowned aphids, some horrible individual had shat across it, and the coffee smelled simply awful. He'd have to have a word with somebody about this, somebody like Sting.

Mr Taylor returned.

"I have returned," he announced, "with the photos as requested. Now can you both please fuck off?"

"Aye man," said Harris, "And as for the firearms, we'll just say that was all a mistake, and we'll all forget about it, eh?"

"Well done Harris, that's kept that wanker in check," added Morose, "Now, do you think we're best to reverse back out of the reception area or power on through the back doors?"

Mr Taylor thought long and hard about his reply.

"Please just go away. And could you take that carpet with you? Some filthy bastard has dumped their load all over it."

Harris rolled it up and for good measure took the coffee machine with him too.

"Always pleased to help out, man!" he smiled, as they walked out through the plate glass doors without opening them.

*****

Back at the station, Morose went off to check if Oddbins were having a closing down sale yet, while Robbie called all the other officers to the meeting room.

"Right lads," he said looking at Soames and Franks, "take 10 photos each..." he dropped the file of photos on the desk, "...we're looking for any faces not accounted for at the ground on Satadee. Remember we had someone leave, when they knew the police were coming..."

"Oh fuck!" said Brewis, "when are they coming?"

Harris continued, "We need to identify this chap, carrying a case, remember. Could be a weapon. Stood in the right stand to shoot the goalies face off. Did we all get a look at the goalies face? Put me right off me Coco Pops man! Right fuckin' mess! No consideration... I mean our Claudie's doing Chicken Tikka for tea. I'm right off that, man!"

The 'phone rang.

"'kin what?" enquired Robbie.

"You'll fookin' eat what you're given, ya little cock bubble," shouted Claudia, and hung up at once.

Immediately, Robbie's mobile rang.

"I'll have your Chicken Tikka, you stay at the station with Soames for the night," ordered Morose.

Robbie pressed "end call" and sent his boss a photo message of a baboon's arse.

*****

After twenty minutes Franks shouted, "House!" She was having one of her bingo dreams again. Soames elbowed her in the left airbag to shut her up.

"Sir!" Shouted Soames, "I've got something!"

"Is it contagious?" asked White

"Do I need to get myself checked out?" asked Brewis, sticking his whole head inside his flies.

"I mean on this picture, I've found someone different. Someone we didn't see at the game, look!" Soames clarified.

"Who's had me bastard readers?" Harris looked accusingly round the room, particularly at Jampton, specifically at Harris' readers on Jampton's nose.

In the ensuing pagga, the glasses had to be filed as 'lost in friendly fire', although there wasn't much friendliness in the severe kicking White received.

Yes, "White received" - it started as Harris versus Jampton, but, well, White was there, and in the absence of Gonemad... well, you can see how these things happen, can't you.

After Franks had brought the accident log book out and accidentally logged in it; and the criminal injuries book out, the disciplinary log book out, and the Viz annual out (Morose was back), and they'd all posed for a few pictures for the Oxford-Pigs Facebook page.....Jampton spat out another tooth, and reminded everyone that Soames had a picture to show everyone.

"Where's me bastard readers?" asked Harris who was still slightly concussed. Morose punched Harris unconscious and reached for the picture.

"Who's this unaccounted-for turd with the case?" he asked the room, who didn't reply.

In the absence of a response, they left a note stapled to Harris's forehead, requesting that when he wakes up he should pop out, and get some copies made up of the picture, so they could all ask around. Morose gave Harris an extra kick for good measure, and went out for a slash.

THIS was policing done proper.

*****

WPC Soames knocked on the door, took the obligatory step back, and waited. There was a fumble, a bolt being drawn, and a key turned. The door opened.

"Good morning, sorry to bother you sir, but....."

"Can't you read? No hawkers, no circulars, no pigs!"

"We're conducting door to door enquiries after...."

The door was slammed in her face. A fine start.

She went to leap the piss poor attempt at a fence between the two former council properties, now privately owned, although between them, the economic reality of mortgages had seen both properties repossessed several times – the score was currently 10 to number 7, 8 to number 9. Unsurprisingly, the fence collapsed, and she fell with a heavy crunching sound.

Both sets of doors opened; Soames addressed the owner of the next house.

"Good morning, sorry to bother you, but we're....."

"Oi! Francis! This fat cow has trashed our fence!"

"Fakkin 'ell Rick, she 'as 'an all!"

"Well don't just do something, stand there!"

"Oi! Pig! Have you knacked our fence?"

Soames addressed them both but just in case, put her hand on her taser.

"Sorry about the mess, my chief inspector will pay for the damage!"

Francis got Alan next door.

"Oi Nuff, look at the mess this sodding pig's made of the fence between mine and Rick's place!"

Alan got a chair to stand on and took a look.

"Fakkin 'ell lads!"

Soames addressed all three.

"I'm conducting door to door enquiries, asking if anyone's seen this bloke in this picture."

"But you've smashed Rick and Francis' fakkin' fence!" exclaimed Alan.

"Collateral," explained Soames.

This stopped the current homeowners in their tracks.

"Fuck me, Fran, what's 'collateral'?" mused Rick.

"Isn't it what them vicar types wear round their necks?"

"Nah, that's choir boys," explained Alan, who was the less unintelligent of the three.

"Have you read that stuff in The Oxford Picture Post? All about all those pigs looking for gunmen?" Francis arsked.

"No?" asked Alan and Rick.

"Apparently there was some geezer down the match the other day and he was all collateralled up all over the shop, real nasty do it was, and ...."

"..... and I'm asking if any of you have seen this man we want in connection with the shooting!" Soames jumped in with this and stunned the three men into silence.

"Fuck me Fran," said Rick after scratching his head, "She needs us to see if the collateral man is connected to us."

"Or just have you seen him?" Soames encouraged. She was getting somewhere.

All four stood on the flattened fence and examined the photo.

"Can't imagine him down the boozer," observed Alan.

"Can't imagine him down anywhere, he looks a right dodgy one," agreed Rick.

"Gentlemen, this is an urgent enquiry, lives may be at risk!" Soames kept up the pressure.

"Is he a connected collateral then?" asked Rick, "What's he connected to, the terrorists or the other ones, or somefin?"

"Nah, just a lone kinda gunman," said Alan, "Look! He's on his own even in the picture!"

Francis suddenly stepped forward and the last of his fence disintegrated. He took the photo and looked at it hard, like, real hard.

"Are you trying to scare him into submission?" asked Alan.

"Nah, shut it! Lads, look, look real close! Isn't this what's it?"

Rick tore the photo off Francis.

"Ah fuck, look it is n all!"

"Come on chaps, let me in on the secret, who is it?"

"Well... he was on that thing wasn't he on the telly..." offered Alan, unhelpfully.

"What thing on the telly," asked Soames eagerly,

"Pointless? Channel 4 News? Dads Army?"

"No… that thing on me mam's telly… that framed picture…it's me dad."

Rick looked at Francis in astonishment, "I thought the picture on yer mam's telly was the Pope?"

Alan was aghast. "France! You mean, your Dad's the Pope?"

"No yer daft sods!" explained Francis, "Not the fakkin Pope! The old geezer next to him!"

"Cardinal Richelieu?" asked Alan.

"Fucks sake, you've never been the same since Margueritta Time, have you? The photo, next to the fakkin Pope, on me mam's telly, is of me Dad!!"

"Yeah, right got it," nodded Rick, "But isn't he kinda dead?"

"Not really," sighed Francis, "That's just what we told me mam, innit? Just to claim on the……"

"Lads, the pigs are here," Alan reminded them.

There was an embarrassed pause. Soames put it gently.

"Let's forget the insurance scam, eh chaps, just tell me about the old man?"

Francis sat on Alan's chair, and Alan was reduced to standing on the dead cow on the lawn to see properly.

"Well it's like this……"

Soames quietly switched on her collar radio, "Pink five to base, think I've got something."

There was a crackle on the radio. Brewis's voice spoke.

"Do I need a check-up, then?"

*****

The doors of the inn swung open, as a really imposing figure approached the bar, slow steps and a threatening gait to his strides. Those trousers were REALLY shit. He walked up to the bar. "Is there a Mr Coughlan here?" he called around the hushed room.

A stubbly man stood up from the barstool nearest the toilets, dropping his empty whiskey glass onto the counter. "I'm Coughlan," he whispered.

"Morose," replied the newcomer, dropping his guts in the ashtray.

"No, I just enjoy a drink," said Coughlan

"No, I'm Morose."

"A whiskey for this man" Coughlan called the bartender, in fact he called him a frog faced fool, and demanded a drink for him too.

Morose gratefully drained the bottle and threw up with relish.

"Must have been that relish I ate," he explained, "It disagreed with something I drank."

"Must have been some heavy shit?" asked Coughlan, "Why don't you pull up a stool?"

Morose promptly dropped one, and sat on it anyway, the flies all made a bee line, well, fly line for him.

"Mr Coughlan," began Morose.

"Who did you say you are?" asked Coughlan.

"Morose"

"Barkeep!"

The frog faced fool brought out two fresh bottles.

They took a sip, and threw the empties at the jukebox in the corner, that was playing some Level 42 shit.

"Morph, you say? Weren't you in Take Hart?"

"No, Morose."

"Frog Face? Two more bottles."

By the time that they had established who the other was, both had forgotten who they actually were themselves.

"What happened to me after I parted ways with Tony Hart?" asked Morose.

Coughlan scratched his head, "You became inspector Morph?"

"By the way, what happened after Marguerita Time?"

"I'd already left by then, still keep the old drumming up, but I'm mostly working for the Football Association now. Tracking fraud, and you know, stuff."

"What about the Oxford game the other day, eh?"

"What a shot, eh? Killer! First shot missed, second hit the wood work but that third one went right in!"

"Mr Coughlan, are you saying…"

"One all, and the Ironclads on the attack and then somebody took out the goalie. Definite black card offence, if you ask me!"

"Oh, you're talking about the first goal? Right! Why did you leave, Mr Coughlan?"

"Well, she was getting me down, all those pictures of the pope and Cardinal Richelieu all over the telly. Couldn't even watch bleedin' Catweezle!"

"No Mr Coughlan, and get another drink in while I'm talking to you, why did you leave the football match?"

Coughlan tapped his nose, secretively, took a swig of

Morose's fresh Ruby Port, and fell down unconscious.

*****

WPC Soames decided that enough was enough. She'd managed to carefully nail together Francis and Rick's fence, and had even put Alan's fence back into the right shape. They thanked her profusely with a profuse, and she stepped back to admire her handiwork. Sadly, she tripped backward over the dead cow on Alan's garden, and fell into the fence, which began a dominoes effect collapse of the entire street's fences. As the one at the end of the street fell over into the house, so that house collapsed sideways into the next house.......

Soames quickly got up, and taking away the dead cow as evidence, got into the squad car and drove off quick.

*****

"Bastaad!" said Harris getting to someone's feet, they certainly didn't feel like his. Possibly it was being punched unconscious by his boss, but he didn't really feel like working at the moment. Add to that he had a cow's fanny of a headache for some reason. It felt like someone had been stapling notes to his forehead, add to that he was seeing double...well, A double... of himself!

"Oh good! You awake noo? Canny man!" said Harris

"Errr... I'm not sure, man. Me man!" said Harris.

"Aye man, you're awake man, canny good, like you said."

"No, man, I think... *you* said..."

"Aye, but I'm you... canny good."

"Aye... are you one of those visitors that came with the Medusa last time? Because if so, you're kind of giving the game away by being with me, man. I mean, I know you're a double because well… I'm me 'n' shit."

"Aye but I'm not one of them man. I'm you, but from the future like."

"Aye, Aye… how far in the future? Cause if it's twenty years I'm looking canny good like!"

"Hadaway man, only next week, like."

"Can you tell us the score on the Newcastle game on Saturday, like?"

"Aye 2-0. That's right isn't it?"

"Divven't kna man, until Saturday."

"Oh aye, any way bonnie lad. I've got a message for you."

"Aye?"

"Aye. You know when people say if you could go back in time, and give yourself some advice?"

"Aye…?" This must be important, if he'd risked time paradoxes by presumably necking a bottle of Macalan '46…

"Aye, well, don't ever go back and give yourself advice. We've been caught out by that before."

"Aye" he must throw that bottle of whiskey away.

He blinked, his eyes opened to an empty room. His head hurt. He took the blood-stained note and the staple out of his forehead, and read it. It said:

"You are a piss gargling spunk weasel and a Quisling, PTO."

He turned it over. The writing was a little more blurred, but it said,

"This statement is my honest opinion E. Morose end of annual appraisal."

The wanker!

Still, there was always the door to door enquiries, now where was that dozy mare Soames?

He went to the door to look for her, and was predictably flattened against the wall as she rammed her way into the office.

"Coo – ee! Sergeant Harris!"

There was the sound of a body gradually extracting itself from the plaster wall, and a set of lungs re inflating, a quick de-rending of bones, and then a few teeth being re set. The door was pushed open from the wall.

"Ah sergeant, there you are, we've got some great leads for you on this shooting!"

"Fer – ching, oh shit there goes me gold filling, aye lass, great work, aye."

"Tell you what Sergeant, you get the coffees in, and I'll set my results up!"

"Aye man, woman, man," muttered Harris as he pressed the "Coffee an fuckin hurry up" button on the vending machine.

They sat at the table as the day began to fade, lights on, spare sets of glasses on.

"Well its like this, Sergeant," Soames took a big slurp of coffee, "I'd made a few enquiries at…….Jesus bastard Christ, this coffee tastes of shit!"

"Ah fuck!" cried Harris, "I used the newspaper office machine!"

Having both made themselves ill and cleaned up, and topped up on fresh coffee from the approved 'Offya Face Coffee' machine, Harris and Soames sat down to go through her results.

243

"......so you see, while Inspector Morose is still out there interviewing this Coughlan type, I've not only repaired three sets of fences, but looking at the photos, have you noticed, that the keeper isn't even watching the ball? No wonder he let the bloody ball in the net, sir!"

"Aye? Let's have another look." He punched her in the face to increase the speed of her passing the photo over. Soames yelped.

In between repeated punches to various parts of his anatomy he did spot that she was correct, the keeper wasn't even watching the ball, he was presumably looking at the man in the stand with the gun, about to shoot him…

"Hang on a minute, Soames. This is important. What's he looking at?"

Soames stopped herself mid punch. "You can't really see from the picture, can you?" She took a deep breath and finished the punch.

*****

By the time they'd finished with the various accident report books, Health and Safety Logs and disciplinary reports, located the first aid box, found it was empty, located an all night Tesco's and stocked up on emergency beer, it was hardly worth the thirty minute drive home, when they'd have to be back early in the morning.

And so, a mere fifty minutes' drive outside Oxford, they found a lovely four-star hotel, and chained their bikes to the car they'd driven there in.

"Sorry we're havin' to slum it, lass," sighed Harris, "but it's this or my house, an' I'm not sure how wor Claudie would take t' me bringin' another lass home fer the night, y'see."

"Another lass?" asked Soames, "How many do you normally take?"

Robbie scratched his compact disc. This could be an uncomfortable night, and it would need tact, care and diplomacy to keep Claudia happy and in the dark; and Julie Soames happy and preferably staying in the dark at the back of the cupboard. H'mm.

"Singles or double?" asked the inn keeper.

"Double," Soames jumped straight in.

The inn keeper brought her a huge vodka which she downed in one.

"Thanks," she wiped her mouth on the guest book, "How about you, Robbie?"

"We'll have a room with twin beds, and I'll have a cocoa," smiled Harris, "And it's sergeant Harris, we're still on duty."

"Not when I get you upstairs," she smiled.

"Here we go, gentlemen," said the inn keeper, handing over the key to the sole twin bed room in the inn. "No shouting, no drinking, no breathing after ten, and if you need anything in the night...."

"Yes?" asked Soames and Harris.

"....all you have to do is go and get it yourselves, you lazy bastards, I'll be asleep."

With that he lurched off and fell over his Zimmer frame.

WPC Soames and Sergeant Harris were coming at this from opposite intentions. Harris needed a night's rest and time to get over his recent trials and stapled head. WPC Soames had been waiting for a chance to leap on him and this, she felt, could be THE chance.

While she undressed to her underwear, he made himself another five cups of cocoa and took an anti-inflammatory. He crept back round the door and asked, "All okay?"

"Ready when you are, Robbie," came the reply he didn't want.

"Look, Julie, I'm off limits, married, snared, got me slave bangle on, spoke for, tied up elsewhere, and her name is Claudia and she eats lesser mortals for breakfast, and that's that," he explained, staying behind the en suite door as he got down to his long johns and then hurled himself past her and under cover.

"Playing 'hard to get, Robbie?" she smiled.

"Shut it and get to sleep," he growled.

The wind blew hard, and the temperature in the room dropped.

"Sergeant Harris," came a suspiciously low voice, "Its cold here."

"Aye man, constable."

"Won't you warm me up?"

Harris threw the hot water bottle at her.

Hailstones battered the window.

"Sergeant Robbie, it's still cold," she called.

"Aye man, Julie, shut the window."

"I cannot," Robbie could almost hear her smile, "I am undressed."

"Then I'll look away."

"Can you shut the window?"

"Are you kiddin? If I go past you, I'll be a different man in the mornin'."

"Don't you want that?"

"Divorced? No."

The hailstones were finding their way into the room.

"Sergeant Harris, its cold and I need warmth," complained Soames.

"Aye, shut the window," groaned Robbie, and tried to bury himself under the duvet.

"Please shut the window for me? I'll be ever so careful with you after," she smiled sweetly.

"Over my dead body, and if a word of this gets back to Claudie, I'm fuckin' dead, man."

The window began rattling and slamming as the wind and hail simply got worse.

"Sergeant...."

"Aye man, now what?"

"Please shut the window. I'll make it worth your while."

Robbie sat up and put on the bedside light. He looked hard at her.

"Constable Soames, how would you like to be Mrs Harris for the night?"

Julie Soames sat up with her hands already pulling her bra strap off.

"Oh Mr Harris, I'd love to!" she beamed.

"Great," retorted Harris, "Then you shut the fuckin window."

And with that, he turned off the light and turned back over and fell asleep.

"Loser," muttered Soames, as she shut the window and walked quietly out to give the inn keeper a cardiac arrest.

*****

It was a cold crisp morning as Harris and Soames left the pig mobile, bicycles still attached, and walked the short distance back to the pitch.

"Ok Soames, let's do a reconstruction, you be the keeper."

"Do you want me alive or dead?"

"We'll start with 'alive', shall we?. Let's see, where was he standing?"

"Between these two posts, sir."

"Aye…aye. You stand there then. Just see what he was looking at."

Soames looked. "The car park sir."

Harris scratched his head. "Why the fuck was he lookin at the car park? Didn't he know there was a match on?"

"Maybe it was the highlights?" suggested Soames.

"Aye, man, maybe it was, cannae good thinking. Now, if he's seen all this before, what's so important about the car park?"

"Had he spotted his car being stolen?"

Harris pondered before deciding, "Nah, he'd have reported it stolen after the match."

"Sergeant Harris, he was dead after the match!"

"Aye, any excuse to make our job difficult, the cunning stunt."

"But Sergeant, if his face was shot off as he stood here, the gunman would have to be….. over there!"

BACK ON THE LASH WITH INSPECTOR MOROSE

She pointed behind the goal.

"Well, we'll put your little theory to the test, just stay there a few ticks, love."

Harris got his mobile phone and rang home.

"Aye man, its me, aye. Oh, hello wor Jessie. Aye. Can ye get over here wi' yer high- powered Elephant Gun? Aye, bring Emily too in case we mess up first time. Aye. And a few hankies to mop up after."

There was a sonic boom and the girls stood there, along with the elephant they'd borrowed the gun from. Soames was getting a tad concerned.

"Aye, now take your first shot at Soames from just behind the goal, an' see if her face falls off at the same angle as the goal keeper, there's a good lass."

"Sir...." began Soames, but was silenced by the hail of splintered wood off the goalpost in her face.

"Nah Dad, that's the wrong angle," complained Jess, "I'm at the wrong trajectory an' that."

"Well, stand on wor Emily's shoulders?"

She did but they both then sank into the mud.

"Nah dad, it's all wrong, we need height."

"Aye Daddy man, hows aboot I take a squint from up on them flats that just happen to be nearby, and at the correct angle of elevation to around 24 degrees and 3 minutes?"

"Aye, whatever," said Robbie.

"Sir..." began Soames, "Can I have one last request?"

"Now just stay there a bit longer, we'll be through wi' yer in a moment. Jess, can ya just google 'Local Funeral Directors' for me? Aye yer a good lad."

"Ready?" came a shout from the flats.

"Sir?" asked Soames.

"Aye lass, give it both barrels man."

"Sir!" began Soames, and then noticed that the peak of her cap had fallen to the ground.

"Great shot wor Emily!"

Still singeing, the front of Soames' cap was retrieved from the halfway line by the elephant. Emily returned with the gun cocked and handed it to her dad.

"It was just as I thought Daddy man," she explained, "Wor Jess here had the angles all ready an' by using the parapet of the fourth floor, ye can shoot the balls off a gnat wi' nae problem."

Pausing only to pick up a shocked to shit Soames and carry her on the elephant, they made their way back to the police station and a waiting Morose.

*****

"So, what was he looking at?" asked Morose.

"Apparently the car park... Sir"

"And what, pray, was worth throwing the cup for? What I mean is, what was he looking at, in the car park? What was distracting his attention?"

"Well, there was nothing worth looking at when we were there." Robbie looked up from the Divorces section of the Oxford Gazette, just in case.

"When the match was on, what was there, you gimp rest!" Morose pondered and added, "What was there when we arrived?"

Robbie thought, long and hard, "Erm... Max."

"Yes, but he only arrived after the shooting. He was occupied looking at that car..."

"Aye Sir, you could see where that car was parked from the goal mouth..."

"It's a nice car Robbie, not worth throwing the cup run for though..."

"Has anyone been called about that new coffee machine? It's really shit." Jampton stood in the doorway.

"It really is, isn't it?" said Morose, removing a piece of bog roll from the back of his trousers. "Tell me, young Hugh, in between playing this game of gambling with dysentery, have you given any thought to looking up any criminal record our - until recently - goalkeeper might have had?"

"Sorry lads, he's as clean as a sterilised whistle. Only record we had was of him reporting a crime, nothing against him."

Morose got out a big piece of paper and drew a blank.

"Out of curiosity, and for no other reason, what was that crime, Hugh?" Harris asked, curiously and for no other reason.

"Car theft lads, two weeks ago he had a..."

"Triumph Stag" completed Morose, "The one Max was admiring..."

"Aye," Harris continued, "You and Max were drooling over it..."

Morose looked at his watch, "Let's pay Max a visit. It's 2pm, he should be sober enough to remember the car by now."

*****

"Of course I do, Endof old chap. Lovely little motor. She only had 65,000 on the clock. To be honest, I keep having dreams about it. Woken up quite excited a few mornings I can tell you..."

Morose sighed, "If you can quit frothing at the mouth Max, can you remember the reg? Or anything distinctive?"

Max pondered, "Sorry lads no, I'll try again after my memory loosener this evening, if you like?"

Harris looked incredulous, "But you remember the mileage?"

Max nodded, "Well yes, I remember, on the dashboard there was a copy of a magazine. I had to duck down to look under it to see the numbers."

"...and the magazine was..." Harris prompted.

"Not going to be much help I'm afraid, it's a nationally published thing, wide circulation figures..."

Robbie again, "Called...?"

"What?" said Max, "Oh, what was it again... that's it, yes, Refereeing. Sorry I can't be more help..."

Morose sighed again, putting Max back to sleep with a well-aimed punch. "I'll put a call through to my dear friend Mr Coughlan. He was at the match to investigate the referee on behalf of the FA. Bribery charges apparently, match fixing. That's why he had to slip away, before he was spotted. He should be able to give us all we need to know about the ref and his car."

*****

"Yeah, well, we've had the little trouser snake under observation for a few months," explained Mr Coughlan.

Morose took a quick blast, before asking,

"Anything solid on him?"

"Just a few pigeon droppings, but we found he has a poor record of sticking to Football Association rules."

"Such as?"

"Oh the usual professional 'sportsman' bollocks, teenage waitresses, coke dealing, church burning, the odd donkey smuggling run......."

"Anything that may be of interest to the police?"

"You mean teenage waitresses and coke an' stuff isn't your thing?"

Morose groaned as his arse let another one escape.

"Sorry, that may need a clean-up soon, anyway, what I meant was, anything actually criminal?"

"Match fixing."

"Where can we find this clap hangar?"

Coughlan got out his diary and hit Morose over the head with it, before thumbing through the contents, and relieving him of £50.

"Ah, here you go, mush. You'll find him this evening refereeing at the South Liverpool match, they're up against Newcastle."

"Thank you, Mr Coughlan, you've been a great help."

With that, he bought John a fresh pint of water, and stumbled off to Gonemad who was waiting outside in the squad car, on the parcel shelf.

"Where to? asked Gonemad.

"South Liverpool Football Club, and step on it."

"Why?"

"I'm dying for a dump."

*****

Harris had been putting two and two together, and for

once getting four.

The shots had come from the tower block.

Morose and Robbie had passed the tower block shortly after.

Their car had been driven off the road by another car.

A car driven by Barry Andrews.

Barry Andrews was ex-military.

He knocked on the door. "I can see you Barry, come and talk to me, man!"

After a lengthy delay the door was opened slowly.

Barry was clearly having a bad day. He could barely stand.

"The condition's a bit further advanced than you said, isn't it, Barry?"

"Y-yeah" Barry mumbled.

"That why you missed the first two shots Barry, lad?"

"I, I don't know what you mean."

"I've been looking into your record, man. You came out of the army a year back on a medical discharge. What was it you specialised in? While you were serving, I mean?"

"I, I was..."

"You were a sniper weren't you man? SBS trained an' that weren't you? And what did you do when you got out?"

"I..."

"Went to work for a local thug didn't you. Used your training, to polish off a few dodgy characters. I bet you saw it as just cleaning the streets eh?"

Barry looked at the floor.

"So, what made you miss the target eh? Bad day with the Parkinsons?"

Barry's shoulders drooped. He knew the game was up. He nodded.

"But why man? What had he done to warrant a hit?"

"He... owed a lot of money to match fixers and they were giving up on ever seeing it again..."

"The keeper? He wasn't into anything dodgy Barry. What are you talking about?"

Barry Andrews looked baffled. "Why are you talking about the keeper?"

*****

Gonemad parked the car up in the nearest available space, and walked the short distance to the Triumph Stag.

"Now Saul, I'm going to need those papers."

Gonemad searched his pockets and found the requested papers.

"Crime log for the stolen vehicle, sir."

"Indeed. Now, it says here that the underneath of the car was sealed and after that the exhaust was replaced. So logically, if we look under the car the only part unsealed will be the exhaust. As the plates have been changed, that is our only way of identifying the car. Now Saul, my dear chap, you know I'd look under the car myself, but frankly I can't be arsed. Have a peek won't you?"

Saul peeked, it was as described.

To enter the football ground, Morose waved his Blockbuster card, and made his way down to the pitch side. There was a small police presence at the ground, every single officer under five foot tall. Fortunately, Morose's reputation carried even this far from Oxford.

Newcastle were on the attack as Morose walked onto the pitch, slipped in the mud, and was trampled underfoot by three of the attacking players. Gonemad held out his hand. Morose wearily hauled himself up and pushed Gonemad under the return waves of attacking South Liverpool players. Dusting himself down, he walked across Gonemad with a firm stride, over toward the referee, Gonemad struggling to get up.

The spectators knew a piece of drama when they saw it, and a scruffy looking man accompanied by a freshly trampled police officer approaching the referee, definitely counted as drama.

"Get off the pitch," shouted the referee.

"That's my line!" Morose shouted back, producing a red card from his pocket. "Albert Stebbins, I arrest you on charges of car theft, match fixing, and donkey smuggling. Anything you say can and will…"

"Sir," Gonemad looked around, "You do know the match is still in progress, don't you?"

"I'm sure you can help out, Gonemad." He passed him Stebbins' cards, whistle and watches, and as an afterthought his shorts, meaning he could also be done for indecent exposure as well. "See you back at the station later."

*****

After the match finished, it suddenly occurred to Saul that Morose had abandoned him in Liverpool, without a ride home.

*****

Harris was settling down, snuggled up to Claudia, debating how to tell her he couldn't face a cup of cocoa tonight, when his phone rang – Gonemad.

"Alreet Saul man. A believe you got Stebbins eh?" He scratched his leg ineffectually, before realising he was scratching Claudia's leg, and receiving a punch in the bits as a result.

Responding to Saul's droning whinge down the phone, Robbie replied, "Aye man, and I've brought Barry Andrews in...... Good result...... Aye, I'll drive up and get you. Eh! One more thing, what was the score? Someone very close to me promised it'd be 2-0!" He wasn't ready just yet to tell Claudia that he'd put this month's wages on that result.

His face dropped, 2-0 was right, 2-0 to South Liverpool.

He fetched his car keys, and explained to Claudia he just needed to pop out to southern Liverpool. Well, it would give him a few hours to think of how to explain to Claudia about a hotel bill that was coming through for a room for Mr and Mrs Harris, and that this month's wages were up the creek.

Never go back in time and give yourself advice: he needed to tell himself that!

CHAPTER 6. 12,000 MILE SERVICE OF ALL THE DEADED

The bells could be heard chiming across a large portion of the city of Oxford.

The doors were open at St Ozzy of Osbourne's parish Church, Jericho.

Inside, the organist was practising, ready for the expected small congregation. Indeed, the organist was shortly joined by his wife and son, a church warden and couple of cleaners.

In the confessional box at the back of the church, the priest was giving his bell a quick polish, well he was a leper. This was, after all, a special service; for it was the celebration of the feast of St Mongo McMongo, son of Mongo, the patron saint of something or another.

The priest checked his watch, yes, it was still on his wrist. That last bunch of Scouse tourists looked a bit dodgy, you couldn't be too careful.

The bells stopped, signalling either that it was time for the service to start, or that one of those Scousers had come back for the scrap value.

There was a rap on the confessional door. He got a cloth to clean it off. Someone had a heavy burden to unload, there was some sighing and several attempts to clear their throat. The priest gave a polite rap back, to let the confessioner know he was ready for them. As he did so, a familiar voice came back,

"There's no point knocking mate, there's no paper in this one either."

"That's not the kind of burden I expect you to unload in my confessional, you little prick," the priest whispered.

"Suck it up buttercup," replied the gruff voice, "Any chance of a quick tipple before the service?"

"I will utterly bash you, just shut it and get into the body of the church."

"As opposed to the bodies of all the...."

"Just go, you need some saving."

"Just your life savings will do."

"Move!"

There was a brief scuffle, and the whole confessional tilted violently to one side, and fell over. The cleaning ladies sprang into action. The minor commotion passed, and the service began.

*****

A stolen Jaguar hurtled down the side streets of Jericho.

"Thank buggery that's stopped!" Morose looked like vomit wasn't far from his mind... or his throat.

"Thank buggery what's stopped, Sir?" Harris asked.

"Those bastard church bells. Don't they know I've got a hangover? And it's your fault!"

Harris looked exasperated, "My fault, Sir? How do you work that out?"

"I'm sobering up Harris! That hasn't happened since 1952. I need you to open an off-licence, now!"

Harris settled back into his seat, and contented himself with just muttering,

"Aye man, aye man."

It was easier than actually having a discussion with Morose. The chief inspector 'floored the bitch' and they rocketed down Slime Road, narrowly hitting a student on a zebra crossing as they went. The second-hand record dealers at the end of the road, was where Morose was headed, and he collided with it head-on.

The owner calmly walked out.

"Ah, Mr Morose, the usual damages forms, is it?"

"You know the drill, Blenkinsop," replied Morose, "I was after the new album by that grime rapper chappie, Mr Fruitcake."

"Ah yes, I think I have it in, for you!" smiled Mr Blenkinsop, and, taking Morose by the neck, led him in. Harris sat back in the sumptuous plastic seats of the Chinese-made Jaguar replica, and settled down for a bit of "away from Morose" time. He was able to text his wife, and check his ebay account for that pair of cool, grey trainers that had just an hour left to go before they got set on fire by the seller, who was that desperate to get rid of them.

Morose liked his violent music – all political punk, black metal or grime rap. Speaking for himself, Harris didn't really 'get' it, he preferred 7 club S or that gender-confused soul artist girl, boy, man, whatever, man.

There was the sound of a knife fight and Morose came back out of the shop head first, followed by his CD of choice, and a voice shouting,

"And take your fucking Special Brew with you!"

....before it joined him via the back of his head.

"Mother fucker," shouted Morose back at the window, where Mr Blenkinsop stood repeatedly raising two fingers at him. Morose clambered back into the car via the sunroof, and, having sat on the horn for twenty seconds, causing a nearby cat to have a nosebleed. He pressed 'eject' on the car stereo, threw Harris' copy of Phil Collins "Repetitive Hits" album back out of the sunroof, and slipped his new disc in. Having thus fucked his back up, he then played the new CD.

"Sir," cautioned Harris, "Can I just remind you, we don't HAVE a sunroof."

"Oh, never mind all that shit," replied Morose, shutting the sunroof, and screaming as he jammed the remains of his hair in the catch. He pulled out a massive pair of sunglasses, tore his shirt open, put a heavy gold chain round his neck; and, with Mr Fruitcake's new album on full blast, released the handbrake, and eased the car into a passing nun.

"Fuckin' bang on, sir," observed Harris, also donning shades and a trilby hat.

Thus, looking like a right pair of tossers, they began a kerb crawl of the neighbouring colleges -with an upturned police light under the car they looked just the part. All it needed was the suspension lowering, and that was provided courtesy of a passing truck.

Their cruise was interrupted by a message on the radio.

"Calling Inspector Morose, come in please."

Morose coolly grabbed the hand-held radio and, elbow on the window ledge of the car door, cleared his throat of yock, and then replied,

"Fuckin' what? Over."

"Incident at St Ozzy's church, sir, get over there. Over."

"Okay, I'll be twelve minutes, over."

"Fuck off sir!" cried Harris, "We're only round the corner from it!"

"Yes," replied Morose, "But I need a can of brew and a cack first, here, hold this will you," and with that, he shat in Harris' lap.

"Oh man," said Harris, "That fuckin hums!"

"Oh man up, you loser," growled Morose, and knifed the covering off the back seat, "Wipe it off as best you can do, with that."

One wiped up shit later; and with the offending turd in the glovebox, and Harris having assaulted a passing Methodist minister for his trousers, changing them, and leaving his soiled pair on the remains of the back seat: and with Morose two cans of Special Brew under, they drove at considerable danger to everyone to a small business a few roads along. They got out of the car and went into the business.

"Here's your car back, we don't want it after all," said Morose to Mr Shark, and left him with the keys and a further parting gift on the counter.

They flagged down a taxi and dragged the driver out. Leaving him a small tip of a pair of smalls, they roared off back to the Church of St Ozzy's, arriving in just under the 13 - minute mark.

*****

"You're late," snapped Max.

Morose took in the full splendour of the church interior, the majestic stained-glass windows, the ornate font, the stone carvings and religious iconography, before focussing his attention back on Max.

"Ah, swallow me knob," retorted Morose, and fell over in a stupor.

Max turned to Harris, "Keeping well, Tommy?"

"It's Robbie, sir," sighed Harris, "Sorry we're late, but, actually, no, fuck it, I don't care if we're late."

"That's the spirit," growled Morose from the floor,

"Chin the fucker from me!"

"Oh, hello, Endof, old chap. I tried not to see you down there, you insignificant little onanist." Max smiled, showing where two thirds of his teeth used to be. "You still holding my embalming fluid hostage?"

"I let most of it go this morning." Morose looked wistfully skywards. "Good vintage that shit."

"With what? Ice? Lemon?" pondered Max.

"Max, you old anal cyst! You know that makes less room for anything silly! I like to take a spoonful of the good stuff and swiftly follow it with the rest of the bottle." Morose grabbed himself by the scruff of the neck, and helped himself to his feet, a trick not many people can replicate.

"Time for a wakener now?"

Harris cut them off at the pass, "Sorry gents, crimes to solve first."

They all stood looking at the recently carked body on the floor, in front of them.

Max spoke first. "Has anyone rung the police?"

"Do you think that's wise?" Morose swayed dangerously toward the floor, passing through 50 degrees of tilt before gradually straightening himself up again, another thing most people can't do, either. And why would they? Harris grabbed the notes off that tool White, and informed them,

"It's apparently a Harry Ramp."

"By the fact he looks like he's wearing Endof's Sunday best, I had already figured he was a gentleman of the road," chortled Max.

"No!" corrected Robbie, "He's a *Mr* Harry Ramp. That's his name…like."

Max took his coat off, disgorging a plague of flies; rolled

up his sleeves, and got out his knob. Remembering, he quickly put it away again, and instead produced his stethoscope. He began a textbook examination, checking the skull for signs of abrasion, the neck for signs of haemorrhaging, the spine for signs of fracture, and the chest to see if there were any tits. Finding none, he began his assessment by announcing into his little tape player,

"Subject is male."

There was a murmur of consent from the little crowd of pigs and wannabees.

There was a dreadful wailing noise from outside.

"Ah shit, that'll be the deceased's spouse. I'll try to hold her up while you do the Lord Charles bit," offered Morose, adding to Harris, "Get it on your phone! The last one had over 20 hits on You Tube."

Max checked the hands, the wrists, the wristwatch, the blokes pockets for any change, and finally, worn out with the effort, sat back onto the curtain that was in front of the altar, causing it to tear in half, from the top to the bottom.

"Hang on Robbie, be right with you," Max gasped dropping the trousers and inserting the thermometer up the rectal passage.

"Max..." started Robbie.

"Don't tell me," said Max, "I'm supposed to do that to the deceased, aren't I?"

Robbie winced, "Aye man"

Two minutes later Max was helped back to his feet by PC White, as Robbie really couldn't be arsed.

"Well, Max?" quizzed Robbie.

"Quite well, thank you, unlike this chap."

"What's your findings then?"

"Well, this is only preliminary findings you understand, I'll know better after I get him back to the lab. But I'd say he's dead."

The assembled crowd of filth and pig support teams gave an impromptu round of applause. Max took a bow and accepted the flowers WPC Franks presented him with.

Robbie heaved up a multicoloured sigh, and accepting the interview notes White presented him with, left the church to find that trollied old toss outside.

*****

Morose found the braying woman sat on a bench, being comforted by some other hog.

"Ladies," he began, "do I take it from your awful racket that you are in some way related to the fly attractor in there?"

"If you mean Mr Ramp, yes this is his wife, oh sorry, I should say widow, shouldn't I? Takes a bit of getting used to, doesn't it?" the lady not crying responded.

"Right, first things first, I'm going to give you a fixed notice penalty for littering. You can't go leaving shite like that husband, just anywhere, you know?"

He passed her the slip of paper. She examined it.

"This is blank."

"Business is bad."

"Maybe you should sit down then, on that pew," she suggested, pointing past the approaching Harris, at a pew in the church.

Harris strode up to Morose with his strode, and, pulling out his lighter, set fire to some of the excess wax in Morose's ear. Such was the conflagration, that one of the wailers was able to light a cigarette off it, on the other side of Morose's head.

"Sir," reported Harris through the smoke," It seems that our Mr Ramp didn't even get as far as the vestry, there's nae poonds in the safe."

Morose swore, "Arse bollocks, there goes my trip to the bookies."

"Seems the poor blerk died of a massive blow to the head."

"Well done Harris, can't you do the same to yourself?"

"....AND, you great toad burglar, there's evidence that some friggin' gentleman of the road, has absconded with it all."

"Better get on the blower to central sty, then."

"I'll do better, sir, I'll radio HQ."

Robbie called up Jampton.

"Fuckin' what?" Jampton answered.

"Hugh mate, have you any record of a down and out type derelict character, name of Swan or Swannie, sleeps rough, probably got a lot of cash on him, witnesses say he was up to no good just before the carking. So, if he did it, and has taken the money, he'll be likely to be in a pub or off his face in the children's playground?"

"Let me check.....no Robbie, just the same name of Morose."

"Well keep checking just in case."

He returned to find Max trying to relieve the widow of any booze she might just keep hidden about her person. Morose, having already done this, swayed alarmingly from side to side as he managed to blurt out,

"We just need you to identify the body, dog face."

"Which particular body would you like me to identify,

pig?"

"The one attached to your late husband."

Grabbing a rapidly-passing toy breed of dog, they took a quick peek.

"Yes, that's him."

"Ace! That'll save me having to call on you later."

The church organist, Mr Austin, took Mrs Ramp to his waiting mod scooter, and promised to make sure he got her home. Although to be fair, he didn't say whose home. Mrs Ramp's friend pulled her bicycle out of the open sewer nearby, and, using Morose's coat to wipe it off with, made her way back to her mother's house, to make sure she was secured down for the night.

Harris, Morose and the vicar, a Mr von Paulus, were left in the church alone to share a quick spliff, before locking up.

"All seems pretty straight forward," observed Harris.

"Hardly pretty really, was it?" asked Morose, "All that blood and bits of body, I'm surprised you haven't started whingeing about it putting you off your prawn fried rice or whatever." He turned to von Paulus, "How many people were at the service, then?"

Von Paulus thought, a first for him," Thirteen, all in the lady chapel."

"Thirteen eh? Hmm. No religious significance there then, eh? Twelve, plus one, to be ritually sacrificed...."

"Inspector Morose, the service was not intended to include a sacrificial offering."

"Hmmmmmmm!"

"Oh no!" Robbie paled.

"Hmmmm"

"Get him outside!" screamed Robbie.

"Hmmm!" added Morose before bowking up rich, creamy, Exmouth Gin, and what was left of Max's embalming fluid as a chaser.

"Christ on a bike!" uttered von Paulus.

Without pausing to draw breath, Morose continued, "No sacrificial offering you say? Where's the fun in that?"

"It was a religious service of divine Christian worship. Not a fucking ritual, you dickhead. There was only me at the altar, the others were faced the wrong way."

"What, to Satan?"

"No, for fuck's sake, there was no dark side stuff, I keep telling you!"

"So, what did you see?"

"Just a shadow. I assumed it was that pillock Swannie"

Morose took another toke, "Thirteen isn't many for a service?"

Von Paulus took a crafty drag, "It's a special service."

"What's so special about it?"

"Everyone stays away."

"But not this particular one?"

"Evidently not. It's the Feast of the Conversion of St Mongo McMongo, Son of Mongo"

There was a pause while Morose took this in, then a longer one while he took his waist in. Eventually he spoke.

"Thank you, von Paulus. I'll call you if I need you."

"What will you call me?"

"A God bothering Jesus freak."

Harris spoke up after popping a pill, "White passed me these, sir. They were in the deceased's pocket."

Morose studied the slips of paper carefully, "Betting slips, eh? White, check if these came in, will you, I'm in need of a bender of Christ-like proportions, tonight."

"Right away, Mr Morose," said White, and ran off to the bookies at high speed.

"Top man you have there!" observed Von Paulus.

Morose checked his hand, "The snotty piglet left the slips behind!"

"Right dickweed you have there. Anything else I can help you with?" asked von Paulus, dropping a bubbly fart.

"Not for now, but I'll just leave an offering in the collection box."

"It's through the doors past the vestry, flush twice, you smelly old shitbag."

With a quick exchange of punches, Harris managed to drag Morose out, and toward home.

*****

Harris got back home, to find his own family watching the latest thrilling instalment of 'The Great British Surgery Bee.'

"Aw Dad, you're just in time," cried Emily, "This contestant called Nina, has got to do an aortic by pass on Andrew Lloyd Webber!"

Harris got a helping of dinner from out of the fire, and pulled up his favourite chair to sit on the cat.

"Let's hope she get's it wrong, eh!" Harris crunched Claudia's homemade soup.

Robbie had managed to eat a pizza slice sized cut out of the soup when, like Alice, he began to find something curiouser and curiouser.

"Hey, wor Emily! How long have we had a bastad cat for?"

"Shh!" said Emily "Diven't make a fuss, Dad. I'll tell yer later, man!"

Robbie decided it would probably be easier to eat the soup with his hands. He scooped the remaining lump out of the bowl and took a bite, catching his leg on a nail in the chair as he bit in. "Aye! But who's cat is it?"

"Never mind Dad. I'll tell yer in a bit."

The cat looked up at him, but not right. There was something wrong in the way the head and neck seemed to wobble.

Robbie used the hard, outer edge of the soup, to hammer the nail back in. "That's got it! Emily man, is that a real cat?"

"No Dad, if you must know, Mr Chopper is going through a bit of an identity crisis. Ooh hush now, Nina is going in. And she got all her questions wrong, so she's only got a claw hammer to do the operation with."

"Aye, but she can still phone a friend," Claudia reminded them. "Oooh, that's not a great start," she added, as a fountain of blood shot up from an artery.

Distracted by the gory scene unfolding before them on the screen, Robbie took a bite out of the chair and sat down on his soup, to watch some great TV. "Fuckin' ace!" he muttered, as parts of Andrew Lloyd Webber were prised apart.

"Sounds like the soft bitch has forgotten the anaesthetic," mumbled Emily.

"Oh aye, so she has!" exclaimed Claudia, "He'll be a bit sore after the cameras stop rolling."

The patronising Z list celebrities talked over the ongoing operation, discussing just how wrongly Nina had removed the central aortic valve and sprayed it with WD40, rather than Tesco's own brand. Robbie Harris took a sideways glance at the 'cat' and noticed to his horror, that the cat was making notes off the televised operation. One to watch, this rodent, he thought to himself.

"Well Nina, you made a good start but dear oh dear, what is this?" asked the celebrity sexual deviant.

Nina tried to laugh as she cringed under the judges sneers and glares, none of whom had ever performed a bypass op in their lives.

"Well it started off as a surgical clamp....."

"A surgical clamp." sneered the token moose faced trollop. "Did you intend to sterilise it later? You know, after the operation?"

There were gales of laughter from the even less educated audience, who all thought that they were suddenly World-leading experts on the subject.

"What I like about the stitch work, is the butterfly design you've managed to incorporate into the wound," the over-sized closet Nazi droned.

"Aye, she'll never make the finals like this," muttered Emily.

"I wouldn't trust my giblets with her, I'm glad she's not my fuckin' doctor," agreed Claudia.

Robbie got a hatchet to open a can of beer with, knocked the fuck out of it, and poured the surviving bits into a glass. "Top class TV this, girls," he said, sat back and fell off the stool.

On the screen now, as they took a break and the REAL anaesthetists got mopping up and repairing the damage done, so the presenter who looked like they'd died the previous year, told us who was up next. The whole family cheered when the name of a well-known austerity favouring politician, came up for a liver transplant.

"Silly bastards got no liver left, too much booze!" chortled Emily.

Robbie Harris thought about that. Something resonated, he wasn't sure, but he thought it might be something to do with the current case.

*****

"Cock-a-doodle-fucking-do!"

That cockerel at number 47 was getting a bit past himself, thought Hugh, as he stretched and scratched his 'nads.

He could hear his mum busying herself downstairs. The routine had gone on so long now that he knew what every sound was.

PISH - that was the kettle being filled

CLANK - and put on the stove.

DUNK DUNK - two crumpets in the toaster.

CHUNK - toaster clicked on.

CHINK - Teapot lid opened

FIZZ - tea leaves poured in

PFFFT - His mum ripped one out. Always after the tea leaves.

THUMP - No, that was a new one!

He popped his dressing gown off, and made his way downstairs to the kitchen. His mum was stood looking at the back door.

"Lollypop!" she called.

THUMP

"Lollypop!"

THUMP.

She looked round at Hugh, exasperatedly. "He won't come in, Hugh."

Hugh rolled his arse cheeks. "Have you tried opening the door, Mum? It usually helps."

"Don't cheek me, our Hugh! I've had a dog flap installed. He was happy with it yesterday, but not today for some reason."

"Where's the door key, Mum?"

"Oh, piss sticks, I've just had it!" After a frantic search it turned up in the microwave, for reasons she was never comfortable explaining. She turned the key in the lock and there was Lollypop, six eyes looked up at Hugh and his mother. One tail wagged, expectantly.

"Oh, I see." Mrs Jampton started, "There's something blocking the flap."

A large red stone appeared to be blocking the doorway. Mrs Jampton reached a slippered foot out to nudge it away. It rolled a half turn away and lay, still.

Hugh and Mrs Jampton found there were now eight eyes watching them. Six eyes on one very strange dog, and a further two on the severed human head sitting on the outside mat.

Lollypop stepped over, and from inside the house took three mouthfuls of hair and dragged the object in.

"Mum," said Hugh, "I think I might have to phone this one in. Hide the booze and the very strong bleach, we might have an inspector calling."

*****

Morose dropped in on the friend of the new widow.

"Fancy a piss up?"

Mrs Joanna Nile took stock of the thing called Morose in front of her.

"I'm afraid not, you smelly git, you see I look…."

"Well how about just a few pints? I've brought a couple of bottles of rosé anti-freeze with me?"

"I can't, I think the drains are up, or is it you?" She took a lungful, "Yes, it is, you. Anyway, I look after my mother, she can't sleep if she eats late."

"I'll get her a few cans of Special Brew, the daft old bat will be out like a light."

"No."

"Well, I've just got a few questions for you."

"If it involves me getting my kit off, you're wasting your time."

"Well in that case, a few police questions."

"Fucking hell, okay. What can I possibly help you with, you addled old cork abuser?"

"You're a regular at St Ozzy's?"

"Yes, I've been in the choir since I was twelve."

"Wouldn't they let you out?"

"I'm also the church cleaner."

"Well, you missed that body yesterday, you blind dope.

Did Mr Ramp like the horses?"

"Well you've met his wife. It's not something I wish to discuss."

"When people don't want to discuss something, I do."

"Well I also don't wish to discuss Dark Ages literature, Game of Thrones or Sardine sandwiches. Have fun with that lot, cockwomble!"

"Was he in any sort of trouble?"

"He was an ex-Marine. I think its awful the way society treats its heroes. He was in the Marines for years. After he left, no one would employ him, with his damaged mind. After his pension dried up, he felt trapped by society, and gambled to get out of debt."

"He won a few thousand yesterday, that's good isn't it?"

"I don't think anything will console me for Harry's death."

"H'mmm..." began Morose, but was stopped from his usual hurling session by his phone ringing.

"Fuckin' what?"

"Ah hello dick brains, it's me, Max."

"You want sympathy?"

"No, I want you here, now. I've got some pretty odd stuff for you, here."

"Okay, I'll be there before you can say Jack Robinson!

Just don't say it til three this afternoon."

"Just move it, you….."

Before he could finish, Morose hurled the phone at a passing nun, hurled on her for good measure, and set off for Max's office.

There was a knock at the door. And the sound effects of a door opening.

"That was quick!" exclaimed Max.

Morose punched him, breaking several of his chins.

"That's for calling me whatever it was you called me down the phone. That poor nun is still in shock, you heartless bastard!"

Max shut the door on Morose's head a few times to get the message over, and then sat him down.

"Now look, Endof, old chap, this Mr Ramp of yours, he's been poisoned."

"I thought he'd been stabbed?"

"He was. AFTER the poison had killed him."

"You sure about this?"

"Yes, he'd taken it in some piss weak lager, he was probably dead in under five minutes."

"Should I inform the Guinness World Records?"

"I've got the contents of his stomach, here," and Max held up a bicycle.

"He'd drunk a bicycle?" Morose was incredulous. "No wonder it killed him."

"Oh, sorry, wrong thing, er, THIS is the contents of his stomach," Max held up a Tesco's bag with various fluids and a goldfish floating about, "I'll be drinking it later, you see."

Morose scratched the corpse's chin, "So he'd been poisoned and then stabbed. Why would anyone want to murder him twice?"

"That's your department. Why not get young Sid out asking a few questions?"

"You mean Harris? He's already busy at just that."

*****

"Next!"

Harris looked around, every eye in the betting shop was looking at him. He was next, it would appear.

The girl behind the screen looked up expectantly at him.

"Aye er... I'm Detective Sergeant Harris, from the sty on Oxford Road, like..."

"Can I see your warrant card?" she smiled brightly.

Robbie pulled it out, remembered, and got his warrant card out instead.

She took a moment to examine it, and also the warrant

card, before shouting "PIGS!" as loud as she could.

Harris looked around, expecting to see some members of the criminal fraternity sneaking out through the door, but no-one moved away. In fact, a large number moved into the queue behind him. He gave a curious glance at the cashier.

"Sorry Sergeant, you've called at a busy time. The 3pm Danish Streaky handicap from Chepstow is about to start. I need to take these bets before the kick off."

"Aye lass, but before y'do, can ya quickly tell me, who wrote out these betting slips?"

She took them and examined them, then remembered, and had a squint at the handwriting on the betting slips.

"Harry Ramp's writing, he's in here all the time. Is he okay?"

"He's had a kind of accident. Tell me, did he have a big win recently?"

"No, he never had any luck, is he okay?"

"He's been murdered."

"Aw, such a shame, are you placing a bet or what?"

"Aye lass, I'll have a tenner each way on that one that looks like Catherine Zeta Jones."

"Okay love, the race is about to start," she called out to the queue, "Any more bets for the 3pm oinks race?"

A few shady characters put their unsuspecting partners

life savings on likely victorious pigs. The runners were led out, led to the starting blocks; and, checking that the jockeys were all ready, the race marshal got the race under way.

Harris watched with detached interest as the pigs wandered off in all directions. This is really going to need some work, to catch up with the dogs, never mind the horses, he thought. He glanced back at the cashier, "How will we know who's won?" he asked.

"It'll go to an enquiry, it's all there on your ticket stub." She didn't even look up.

Robbie looked down at his ticket. Sure enough rule #5 said:- 'in the event of an indecisive result, the race will be decided by a Stewarts enquiry.'

She shouted through to the back room, "Stewart, who won the pig race?"

A voice came back, "I wasn't watching, say number 5."

Seems fair, thought Harris. Out of interest, he looked at the next rule, which read, 'in the event of Stewart being unavailable, the race will be decided by a stew.'

Harris, suddenly feeling unwell, made for the door.

*****

"So," growled Chief Inspector Morose, as he walked aimlessly around in circles to avoid Harris, "Where did the £200 he won, before he was stoved in, come from?"

Harris, walking around in circles the other way, managed to say, "Fucked if I know," as they passed.

"I'm going to need some inspiration, Harris."

"Aw no Surr, surely it's your round by now?"

Morose glared at someone else, "No, you hawk blaster, divine inspiration."

Harris stopped, "What? You want us to go to church?"

Morose, still walking in a circle, collided with him, "Yes. Scene of the crime. Dodgy clerical types. While you spent last night watching that dreadful 'Great British Jerk-off' or whatever it was, I was getting rat-arsed with a few gentlemen of the road. Apparently this Swannie chap was the vicar's brother. Or it may have been sister. Whatever. There's a church, we'll start there!"

Grabbing Harris by the collar bone, Morose and Harris walked quietly into the church, knocking over a font on the way in.

"Shh!" whispered a few God botherers.

Harris made for the furthest pew back, and Morose collided with a neat stack of hymn books, which fell to the floor with a loud crash.

"Shh!" came the reply, and a few discontented stares.

Morose sat on the hard-wooden bench next to Harris. Harris crossed himself. Morose double crossed him, and broke out a loud, rasping fart that resonated off the hard-wooden pew, and echoed around the church like a cannon shot.

Along with stares and "Shh!" came a number of tuts.

"Harris, look," whispered Morose. There was a line of congregation queueing for Holy Communion. "Free booze!"

Sure enough, the celebrant priest was muttering some shit about "The blood of Christ", with all the enthusiasm of a man recently bereaved.

"Aye man," replied Harris, "And look who's at the back of the queue, it's that dodgy looking church warden."

But he was speaking to an empty space, for Chief Inspector Morose was already pushing in near the front of the queue.

Outside in the churchyard, a few gentlemen of the road were also tipping back a Body of Christ bottle, for them it really was a life or death situation, not like the over ripe leeches in the church, piously living off the backs of the poor. No one seemed to mind, though, and the pantomime continued. Oddly, chief Inspector Morose was also, and simultaneously, pushing in at the queue for this bottle, too; another trick not many can pull off.

Infuriated, Harris ran outside and dragged the protesting Chief Inspector back in, before going to the communion rail at the front and dragging him back from there, too. He hit the Chief Inspector over the head with a hymn board, which broke (shh! Tut!) and sat him down again with a quick kick to the balls.

"if," observed Harris, "This guy was poisoned by something in the wine, the whole church would be dead, see? So, von Paulus here has to arrange it for the wine to run out before the last man in the line gets to it, right? Then he goes and refills the cup....."

"Chalice. The word is chalice, you ignorant cockhead."

"The word is fuck off, you patronising sociopathic fart. It's all so.... All so elaborate, it's almost mass murder."

Morose snorted, "High mass murder. Gettit! Hargh! Hargh! I haven't cracked one like that since my 'body of morticians joke!"

"That's your only joke since then, gobshite. We'll speak to the padre afterward."

"Vicar."

"Aye, whatever."

As each member of the congregation passed by, having partaken of the communion, Harris found himself wishing more and more that Morose had a dog collar, a proper one, with a choke chain and CS gas cannister. That way he could hold the Chief Inspector back a lot easier. By thunder, Robbie's arm muscles would be aching tomorrow from holding him back.

The last worshipper made her way back to the pew, and Morose bowed his head and began muttering. Robbie was mildly shocked to see an apparent religious conversion happening – Morose appeared to be praying! He kept looking towards the altar, then bowing his head, and the muttering would continue.

Robbie leaned in closer, to offer his supervisor a few well-chosen words of encouragement. If this was the way forward, he would not stand in Endof's way. As Robbie got level with Morose's bowed head, he could make out the words and the eyes looking at the remains of the bottle of wine behind the vicar, "Get it necked," Morose muttered, "Must get it necked!"

Von Paulus finished the service with the traditional blessing and "May the Force go with you!"

"And you!" they all muttered back at him.

There was a chorus of dropped hymn books and several dropped guts.

"Oh, it's okay NOW, is it?" cried Morose.

Several of the congregation muttered abuse at the vicar, one threw a bottle of piss that had been passed around during the service. One smashed a medieval stained glass window.

"That was shit", "I've had better shit sandwiches", "I'm off to the left footers," "Wanker" were some of the comments muttered, as they left. Von Paulus remained as the sole worshipper.

Morose slithered up to him, "Have you got it necked?"

"Yes."

"Twat. This service, was it the same as the one when the murder was committed?"

"No." Von Paulus shook his head, and for good measure, shook his socks too. "Today's service was a full Mass."

"What was it on the day of the murder?"

"That was a simple Mass."

Morose looked at the bottle of piss and the comments in the visitor's book, "Your flock didn't like today's service much, sorcerer?"

"No. It was more of a critical mass."

Harris and Morose broke off for a round of applause, before continuing.

*****

With freshly emptied guts and freshly picked flowers – the cemetery was nearby – Morose, with a whistle in his trousers, approached the house and decided to chance the steps.

Ringing the bell, he was introduced to the hissing noise of an activated intercom.

"Yes? Who is it? Have you come about the drains?" asked a slightly frail voice through the electronic witchcraft of the intercom.

"Oxford Police ma'am, any chance of a quick one?"

"A quick what?" came back the somewhat startled voice.

"I'm not fussy," Morose sniffed, "or failing that possibly I could talk to Joanna again?"

The door clicked open and Morose strode in, strodes at the ready. The succeeding door to the flat opened, revealing an older lady sat in an NHS wheelchair. The chair had been customised with Boadicea blades on both wheels, and a front fairing from a performance bike, possibly a Kawasaki, possibly a Budgie. On her head was a German World war Two S.S. helmet, a torn leather jacket festooned her shoulders with "Satan's Slaves" patches on the front and back, torn jeans and Doc Martens completed the picture. She had the obligatory "ACAB" tattooed on her knuckles.

"Morose", said Morose, holding out his hand, politely.

"Joanna's Mum," said Joanna's Mum, biting his hand, politely.

"Jesus….." Morose managed to hiss.

"Make your fucking mind up," said Joanna's Mum, "Jesus or Morose?"

Morose grinned and wrenched a wayward tooth out of his knuckles.

The tones of Sabbath Bloody Sabbath were blasting out of the sitting room, loud enough to peel the wallpaper three streets away, though why someone had wallpapered three streets is anyone's guess. Morose managed to shout,

"Can I talk to you?"

And got the answer,

"No."

With that he pushed her out of her wheelchair, strode into the room with his strodes again, and kicked the shit out of the stereo. The valuable "swirl vertigo" LP rocketed out of the window and shattered on the pavement three streets away, only the wallpaper saved it.

"Fucking pigs," said Mrs Nile the elder; and, pulling herself up and back onto the battle wheelchair, motored over to Morose and, pulling a wheelie, parked on his nose.

"You wanted to ask me some shit?" she asked.

"I was wondering if your daughter is in," Morose replied, gnawing at the rubber wheel of the wheelchair.

"In what? The flat? The church? The club?"

"In residence," finished Morose, "I need to talk to her about this murder business."

Mrs Nile the elder smiled, "By Christ, did she do that? I knew she had it in her."

Morose parked her wheelchair further toward the open fire, hoping she'd fall in, "No. But I do need to check up on a few gaps in her account."

Mrs Nile made a supreme effort and hauled herself out of the wheelchair, as it rolled nearer the fire. She stood, unsteadily, and looked Morose in the eye.

"Sherry, inspector?"

"Now you're talking!"

The atmosphere relaxed at once.

"I normally drink pints," Morose said. Mrs Nile promptly poured him a pint of sherry, and, gobbing in it, handed it to him. She poured herself one.

"You want me to gob in that, too?" asked Morose.

"No," came the reply, and Mrs Nile bit a chunk of the glass out and ate it, before downing the lot from the hole.

"Follow that, you mother fucker," she challenged.

Morose, never one to shy away from a challenge, strode to the drinks cabinet with his strode, and bit the top off a fresh bottle, drank half of it, pissed in it, and handed it to Mrs Nile. She in turn gave this to the budgie.

It was threatening to be an interesting meeting, but Joanna arrived back at just that moment. She took stock of the situation as both pugilists were about to drink and batter the shit out of each other. Both stopped dead in their tracks.

"Mother! What the bloody blue blazes is going on?"

Mrs Nile snarled, "I did never teach you language like that! You fuck witted gob shite!"

Pushing her into the fire, Joanna turned to Morose, "Really inspector, this is beyond the pale! Mother shouldn't have sherry, alcohol is a depressant."

"Maybe she should have a few beers and cheer up? Anyway, I've come to ask you a few questions."

"You've already done that."

"A few more. Is that vicar at your church a kiddie fiddler?"

"Who, von Paulus? Fuck off!"

"Well he's not married!"

"Neither am I!"

"Why, are you some kind of freak?"

"Inspector Morose, if I recall, you are also not married!"

"Are you calling me a puff?"

"No, I'm calling you a paedo!"

"Oh, that's alright then. Do you fancy some dinner?"

"I can't come out to dinner, I've got my mother."

"Well she should be quite well done by now, shouldn't she?"

Indeed, the smell of singed pensioner was filling their nostrils. Joanna went to the fire and pulled Mrs Nile out, while Morose went for some knives and forks. Sadly, the Satan's Slaves jacket had saved her, and Mrs Nile contented herself with throwing several bottles of claret at Jo and Endof before they managed to get out and nail the door up.

*****

Harris, meanwhile, had been following the deceased's widow, and made a few observations to Morose.

"Sir, this widow business."

"Are you about to bore me, you cockmunching wombat?"

"Aye, no, aye man, no, see, this Mrs Ramp, she was stayin' at the house of Mr Austin, the organist chap."

"While she got over the shock of the death of her beloved husband?"

"Aye, that's it, anyway, I stationed Gonemad over the road from his house, in the detection van, listening in! And they've been at it hammer and tongue all week!"

"What a surprise," deadpanned Morose.

"Poor Gonemad is worn out with listening!"

"I'm sure he is."

"And her a widow an' him a widower an' all!"

"Yes, thank you Harris! Welcome to the 20th century, you fucking square."

"AND I've checked the bank. Von Paulus has been paying thousands into Ramp's account."

"Did he know about the choir boys?"

"Blackmail?"

"And what about the tramp, that Swampy fellow?"

"Should we just file that with the Moyes case? Ah cannot be arsed lookin' for a missin' hobo, man. Oh, by the way, there was an emergency message from Hugh, something about his dog finding a head in their back garden. I think he's mistaken, me. Hugh hasn't got a dog. Anyway, I'll send Jampton round when he gets in. He knows the family, I think."

"H'mmm," said Morose stretching. He was sure there was a flaw in this idea somewhere, but his brain needed some lubrication to figure it out. "Right," he clapped his arse cheeks, "It's pub time."

Harris looked incredulous, "It's quarter past nine in the mornin', man!"

"Yes. It's pub time."

Grabbing Harris by the scruff of his knees, Morose stomped off to the awaiting Heinkel Trojan, stuffed him in it, and, climbing in, ordered, "The pub."

Harris drove to the nearest pub, the Fox's Arse. They walked in, and were flattened in the rush for the door. Dusting themselves down, they helped themselves to a few of the drinks left over.

"Quiet today?" Morose asked the barman.

"Fuck off, pig," came the cheery and inevitable reply.

"Ahh Geoff, doing a bit of bar relief here. What's happening at the Worm and Hammer?"

Morose's brother glared back at him, "It burned down."

"When did that happen?"

"In about half an hour, I'm just completing the claim form." He got a mallet out and smashed it over his arm, adding, "See? I broke my arm jumping out of the window! That's another thirty thousand."

Morose's complexion darkened, "Geoff, you are besmirching the good name of the family Morose. You shall not proceed with this dastardly plot, to rob an honest insurance company of their good, hard-earned cash, by breaking your arm. I challenge you to a duel!"

Geoff's complexion also darkened, "A duel, eh? I accept! Name your weapon!"

Endof smiled sourly, "A trombone."

Geoff looked at his shattered arm, "I've lost!" and went off to cry.

Morose surveyed the scene, deserted bar, stools all over the floor – obviously the bogs were out of order – and just a few people who had no criminal record remained. Suddenly his attention was taken by a couple in the corner.

"Harris?"

"Aye man, sir?"

"Is that Joanna Nile with..... with a man?"

Harris looked. With a fatalistic smile, he replied, "Aye."

Morose's face went crimson, the veins stuck out on his neck, he began to shake, and lightning flickered playfully round the horns on his head.

"What a slag! I've only known her as the latest hopeless messed up neurotic single bitch in my investigations for two days, and look! She's already being unfaithful to me."

"Aye sir, man, maybe ye'd better go."

"Fucking right," he dropped a violent wall bursting fart, and as the surviving clientele passed out, so Morose stomped off, muttering, "I'm off beer. And women. Oi! Nun! Where's the nearest Oddbins?"

Robbie Harris settled back and finished someone else's

lemonade. At least he could have the rest of the day off while Morose went out to get re-trollied. He rang home, and arranged to take Claudia out for lunch. WITHOUT Morose.

*****

"Oi vicar!" shouted Robbie at the seemingly empty church.

It was the following day, and Robbie had played the odds and driven to the nearest roundabout to Morose's pillbox, where he had struck lucky, finding Endoftreating passing vehicles to a makeover, with his empties.

Having coaxed him into leaving an ice cream van alone, and guided him back to the only vehicle they had access to for today – the canine division van – he had driven them back to the church.

By the time they arrived, Morose had been howling to be let out of the back and reluctantly Robbie had complied, noticing the teeth marks on the window bars and the Mr Whippy on the floor.

"Oi! Vicar man!" Robbie called again.

"If you don't come out now..." grumbled Morose, "...I'll set fire to yer pubes..."

The confessional curtain swished open. There was a sound of flushing and a hand dryer, as Von Paulus walked out, wiping his hands and his knob on the curtain.

"That's better! Can I help you gents?"

Morose parked some lunch in the font while holding a hand up, indicating that the vicar should wait.

"We have a few questions for you, gob shite!" said Morose, diplomatically, before casually yacking out his last slice of carrot.

Von Paulus looked slightly puzzled, "I thought you finished asking me questions yesterday. I am rather busy, you know!"

"A few more questions, then!" Morose breathed fire into the font, and smiled at Robbie. The satisfied smile of a child who had got a new trick right. "We'll be asking these questions back at the station... under caution. And under a filing cabinet, if you give me any lip!"

Von Paulus visibly shook. "I'd better get my clothes then," he muttered, wandering off.

"And get some church cleaners in, will you? Some dirty bastard's shit in this font." Morose shook his head in disgust, "I thought there was something odd about his appearance, couldn't quite put my finger on it."

"Aye man," muttered Robbie, "Best not to put your finger on it, we don't know where it's been."

"Meantime, I've got to see a wench about a job," said Morose, spotting Joanne in the church yard, trying to avoid him by hiding behind a grave. Harris waited for the vicar. Morose helped Joanne with her bike, by wrestling it to the floor in a headlock, while she stood alongside trying to stop him, and threatening to get the police.

Harris turned his head back to the vestry door, and was alarmed to see it was shut. He ran over to it, and found the vestry empty. "Fuck it," he muttered, and ran out to tell Morose, who was now getting a beating from Joanne, and about to start enjoying it.

"Surr! The vicar, he's run off!"

Morose threw the bicycle off, "Arse biscuits! Where to?"

"I dunno Surr, he's no in the church like!"

"Well he's not come out here......"

There was a scream from Joanna as she looked up. Morose took the opportunity to give Robbie a piece of on-the-spot coppering.

"Now Robbie, the dopey bitch seems to be distracted from my attempts to trash her bicycle. Using your powers of deduction, can you guess why?"

Robbie scratched his retina, "Well Surr, she seems to be looking in an upward direction...."

"Good start."

".....and her facial skin has suddenly bleached, as if there has been a constriction of the blood vessels away from the heart...."

"This is very good, young Tony."

"And she's looking upward to a point beyond our shoulders, sir, like it's all happening, ooh, I'd say, maybe, behind us?"

"Yes, top marks! Shall we take a nosey?"

"Aye man, I was just going to....."

There was a sickening thud, followed by a rending of flesh and bone hitting a mix of gravestone and bicycle frame.

"No," sighed Morose, "The woman is plainly utterly bats Joe, there's nothing up on the roof. Maybe we could ask this fresh corpse, that's draped broken across this symbol of Christian hope of eternal life?"

"Aw shit sir! It's von Paulus!"

"Cack! Well young Michael, you do know what this means, don't you? I only had interviewing the flying vicar in my diary for this morning, so that's my diary cleared! I'm off for a truckful and you're paying!" With that, he hopped onto the bicycle and with a cheery wave of his dick, cycled into a freshly dug grave.

While Harris restrained Joanna from filling it in, there was a screaming of sirens and two police cars, a Heinkel, and an ambulance raced up. P.C. Gonemad strode up to the gathering crowd of ghouls and Facebook photographers.

"Come on, move along now, nothing to see here!" he ordered.

"Oh, but there is, look!" squealed an elderly parishioner, "The Reverend has popped his own cork!"

"OH!" exclaimed Gonemad, "Well that's a turn up for the books!" and began broadcasting the grisly scene on twitter.

Franks and White took over crowd control, and the two paramedics made for the corpse.

"No use lads, he's a gonner," said Harris. The crowd was dispersed by Franks and White and Gonemad making several baton charges, and Joanna sat down to steady her nerves with a quick reefer. Harris sat down alongside her.

"You okay, Miss?"

"Do I look it?"

Harris was about to reply when from the empty grave behind them, came a voice,

"Robbie! This'll be fuckin' ace, watch!"

A plank of wood was pulled into the grave, and, with an effort, and a dodgy – sounding fart, there was a ring of a bicycle bell, and Morose slowly cycled out, singing 'Bat out of Hell' as he went. To add to the effect, a crow settled on the grave behind; but then ruined when he realised who Morose was, and, flying down, knocked him back off his bike.

"Fuck this," spat Morose, and stomped off, while Gonemad and Harris exchanged car keys – apparently Jampton needed the canine division van, to bring something in to the station.

*****

Using his powers of deduction, Harris followed Morose to the pillbox, and knocked loudly. Morose answered the door.

"What are you doing?" Morose challenged.

"Testing your door knocker," came Harris' reply.

"I don't have a door knocker."

"Aye well y'see, that's okay, I've brought one with me."

"Well thought out, young Trevor, but why have you come around here and disturbed my gentleman's excuse me?"

"I've managed to track down von Paulus' boss, sir."

"Are we arresting the tip rat shithouse?"

"No sir, not yet, he's given me a bit of lowdown on the late, low flying reverend."

Morose sighed. "Must you?"

Harris ignored him. "He told me that while Linus von Paulus was ok as a shaman type, his brother was better."

Morose stopped what he was doing and fastened his trousers properly, "His brother?"

"Aye man. His brother is called Simeon, and was a totally fuckin' great vicar, but took to the piss bottle too hard, an' became a man o' the road."

"Christ! The tramp chap!"

"Yes! And he was threatening to expose Linus as a tosser an' a womaniser an' fiddlin' the church accounts!"

The phone rang. Both men looked at it.

"Harris....."

"Oh, NOW it's okay to call me by my name?"

"Yes, funny shit, what's the drill for getting the phone?"

"Leave it to me."

Harris got the phone and answered it.

"Hello?"

He was felled by a punch to the neck.

"That's MY phone, you bastard," swore Morose, and barked into the receiver, "Hello? Yes? What?"

He slapped Robbie in the face and said, "It's for you."

"Aye, fuckin' what?"

Jampton's voice came down the line, "Ah, Rob, two things, I've chased up that dangerous dog report, its all okay, they're friends of mine."

"Great, and the other bit?"

"Mr Austin the organist, and that piece of stuff he was knocking off, Mrs Ramp, have vanished."

"Shit."

"Great news about the dog, eh?"

Morose was waving.

"Aye man, hang on, the trollied shit wants a word…"

Morose shook his head, "No need for me to be arsed getting up. Just ask that desk monkey how he made this call to me… I don't have a phone."

Jampton's voice could be heard clearly, "No idea Rob, Weird made the call and just put me on to speak to youse! By the way, the filth have been in touch about the dog, I'm to bring the head in whenever I can. Bloody liberty, pigs eh? I'm thinking of making a complaint. Anyway, cheery bye!"

After a moments silence, Morose clicked his fingers at Robbie, "Eh, Beppo! Throw it over here!"

Robbie ignored the slight, "Throw what, Sir?"

"The phone, you flat battery dildo."

"That's wrong on so many counts, Sir. How can I throw the phone, man? We don't have a phone."

"Yes 'canny good' young Kevin, just chuck it over."

Exasperated, Robbie mimed throwing a phone at Morose, who caught it expertly and cradled the handset between his face and his shoulder, while tapping a finger downwards in the air in front of him.

"Yes…yes please, could you possibly get me Superintendent Colin Weird, at the Oxford Sty…. Yes, it's Fuckall 1212…. Thank you," then to Robbie, "IT is just connecting us."

There was a 'ring' tone and a whiff of sulphur, followed by a familiar, and totally unwelcome voice. Colin Weird.

"Fucking what?"

"Ah good day to you, sir, and what a fine day it is, too."

"I said, 'fucking what', I expect am answer, you toad burglar."

"Very original, sir, we've not done that one before. Are you well?"

"Yes, I am well pissed off that you have rung me. I can barely get the hang of all this new fangled horse shit, never mind talk down the ruddy thing."

"It's about the von Paulus case, sir."

"Don't tell me he's come back to life again?"

"Not yet sir, though I'm sure he's lodged an appeal with the Almighty."

"He'll not get back past the Archangel Eric, he's a right piss weasel, literally. You wished to grind my bollocks to death with boredom, on some obscure aspect of your insignificant case?"

"My goodness sir, you're sharp today."

"Watch it, you slimy shit."

"I was wondering, could you get von Paulus' solicitor on the line?"

"One moment."

There was a brief pause, then a distant knocking on a door, a scream, the sound of a body being dragged, and then a voice.

"Hello? Captain Cack, solicitor, here."

"Ah, thank you for coming to the phone."

"It wasn't easy, I was in my office in London 30 seconds ago, when suddenly a huge tentacle...."

"Yes, I can guess, tell me, Cack, what did Linus von Paulus leave in his will?"

"Well, he left the parish thirty pieces of silver, on the grounds that they're a bunch of Judases, he left his Morris Minor to his mistress, and a huge hole to the church yard."

"What did he leave to his brother?"

"The stipulation, as I remember it, was that 'my brother gets fuck all', and so he has."

"Thank you, Captain Cack, you've been a huge help. I'll hand you back to the tentacle."

He rang off to the sound of Captain Cack being strangled at high speed.

Morose looked at Harris. Harris looked at Morose. Morose looked at the painting on the wall of Adolf Hitler.

"Back to church, Robbie, I think. The scene of the crime. Something's bound to turn up."

Wearily, Robbie drove them both back to the church. They livened the journey up by taking it in turns to spit at pensioners and students as they drove past. Sadly, as they were driving rather quickly, most of the spit simply ended up back on their own seats. Harris stopped the Heinkel in the still unfilled grave and, as both men climbed out, so they both took a look at the tower.

"We'll start there," snarled Morose.

"Don't talk shit man, you hate heights."

"I hate you even more, so you stay here and trip up any God botherers, and I'll take a nosey upstairs." With that, Morose spread his bat-like wings, rose two foot off the floor, mis cued, and fell back to Earth again.

"I think I'll use the stairs," he snorted at Robbie, before kneeing him in the balls as a token of thanks for helping him up.

As Morose started up the stairs, the rustle in his flies told him that the Crows were up to something. By the end of the first flight they had all taken the decision to fly solo. Endofleveldemon Morose hated heights. He had to take flying lessons blindfolded, so he didn't panic. He managed to look out of the top of the tower, and found that the ground was further away than he'd thought. "Fucking floor," he muttered to himself, "This is worse than being off my face!" He took a peek at the bell tower, he took a looksee at the clock, he took a leak over the parapet at Harris. Finally, he took a gawp at the roof. Something there. The crows were marking an area out with scene of crime tape. There was something beyond the tape. A body. A very dead looking body. Lots of blood and pieces missing, being fed on by rooks.

Heights. Dead messy stiffs. It was all too much.

*****

"Looks like he had a really big, bad fall," said Max, as he wiped his hands on Harris' shirt.

"Aye man," replied Harris, "But what about the dead body?"

"Ah, him! Yes. Another murder, you'll be pleased to hear."

"Are you sure? I thought he'd fallen."

"He had been pushed, AFTER he'd been garrotted, gnarled and mangled, keelhauled, castrated and head bashed in by a rock."

"So, we can rule suicide out, like?"

"And rule murder in." Max walked to a nearby tombstone and after examining it, turned a tap on the side and filled himself a pint glass. "Any idea who he was?"

"I have," grunted Morose, lurching back into the action with his head in a sling. "It's the missing Mr Morris."

A 'phone in a nearby bush rang. Morose picked the receiver up.

" 'kin what?"

"Morose. It's Weird. A right fanny I'm being made to look at the golf club."

"I'm surprised anyone noticed the change, sir."

"Watch it, matey. Now listen. There were thirteen people at that fucking service, five are now dead, and people are saying you're an incompetent spunk guzzling mutant with shit for brains, and virtually no policing skills at all!"

"Very kind sir, I just need one lucky break."

"Then hurry, or I'll be forced to return you to the menders."

Morose paled. "Out of interest, sir, why the increase in the body count?"

"The five deceased are Harry Ramp, von Paulus, Mr Austin, Mrs Ramp has just been found submarining in the canal, in another murder made to look like suicide; and... Inspector Morose."

"But I'm not dead, Sir!"

"You will be very soon, unless this mess is sorted out, matey!"

There was a thunderous sound down the line, from Weird's end of the call.

"What the hell is that?" gasped Harris

Weird sighed, "HST going past. That High Speed Tentacle that dropped Captain Cack back to London."

The line went dead, as did Morose's heart.

"Harris."

"Sir?"

"That pair of delinquent dogs, that you call your daughters?"

"Aye man?"

"I've got a job for them."

*****

Jess Harris was busy pushing pins in a voodoo doll of her younger sister. Due to a lack of response, she was considering using a pneumatic drill next, but was interrupted by her fatha.

"Wor Jess! How's it hangin'?"

"Aye daddy man, aye," she muttered.

"Cannae grand, now look, I've got a quick job fer ya, ter help wi' all this moorder business aroon the toon, y' knaa."

"Aye man, Daddy, what is it?"

"Call wor Emily."

Jess hit the doll with a mallet and a few seconds later, Emily appeared at the bedroom door, with a massive sling on her head.

"Some fooker chinned us, fatha," she began.

"Aye Emily man, now listen, the pair of yez, y'know this latest set of murders an' that, goin' on in the toon?"

"Aye man," they both chimed in unison.

"Well here's a job for yez, get yer chemistry sets oot."

They both did.

"Aye yer both a good 'un. Find out, where's the best place to hide a body, from the pigs like?"

"We'll have the results in noo time," promised Jess.

"Aye ye' can rely on us," agreed Emily.

Robbie went downstairs and sat on the soup, while Claudia got him a bag of beer and a pint of chips. The lynx walked in.

"Mr Chopper, ya soft shite, get that fookin' disguise off, no one's fooled," said Robbie.

"Have a heart, luv," pleaded Claudia, "Ye must have seen all this three-headed dog scare, that's goin' aroond the toon, 'n' shit? An' it's all over three faces book!"

"Aye Claudia man?"

"Well he's like really, really scared, an' this is his way of wardin' it off, see?"

"Ah, I'm a right daft cunt me, aye Mr Chopper man, carry on."

The lynx carried on and curled one out on the floor. There was a thunder of hooves on the stairs, and a faint whiff of sulphur as the girls burst in.

"Dad, we've found it!"

"Aye well done, what does your crystal meth say?"

"Wor Jess was just takin' a bong hit," explained Emily,

"When like a fookin' massive flash, it comes to her!"

"Aye that's great, what's the answer, Jess?"

"Well I found that by mixing a solution of like, cocaine and water-based paint, an' adding three slices of Mum's soup, that the best place to get bodies out of the way in Oxford, is in a church yard!"

Robbie dropped his guts with amazement.

"This is sensational!"

He got his jacket on and made for the door, "Don't wait up luv, I'm off to the sty an' shit, there's a possibility that I can prevent the next murder!"

He ran out of the door and was in the Vauxhall Viva in one bound. There was a roar, but that was from Mr Chopper.

Back in the room, the girls and Claudia looked at each other in astonishment.

"What the fuck was all that about?" Claudia managed to stammer.

"No idea, Mummy man, "said Emily.

"I just made some shit up while sticking pins in me doll, an' he's taken it all serious, like!"

"Just goes to show," noted Claudia, "Just how much of this police work is sheer guesswork."

*****

Harris drove rapidly down to the church, with Morose in tow. Not in the car, mind, he'd just lashed him to the back. Having thus run the Chief Inspector sober, Harris untied him from the rear bumper, and after beating him violently with a crow, told him,

"Sir, the best place to hide bodies and even bump people off is in a church. That bint you're after, she cleans churches, an' she was at the service where the warden was killed - we should be with her now, and she's on her own in there!"

Morose took this all in, and asked, "What?"

"Just get in the church an' make sure she's safe!"

Morose started to walk off the wrong way, Robbie turned him round, and they managed, after pulling the door the wrong way for ten minutes, to get into the church.

Inside, all looked normal. Joanna was cleaning the lady chapel. A church warden was polishing the organ. A Scouser was polishing off the lead pipe work behind the organ.

"Well that's pissed on your chips," Morose said to Harris, "There's fuck all amiss here. Maybe you should go home and have a carraway seed?"

"Nah, ya daft shite, shhh, there's someone else coming up from the crypt below."

"Bloody Hell, you're right. Quick. Duck down."

Harris ripped open a quilt to get some, but Morose hit him with a pew, and they took refuge from the eye of the mystery arrival. As the two organ grinders were out of sight of Joanna, so the shadowy figure moved swiftly over to her, and, with a chord of some sort, slipped it round her neck and rapidly began choking the life out of her. Morose made the first move,

"Quick! Let's get out while the going's good!"

..... but Harris gripped Morose's 'nads, and dragged him back in by them.

"Quick sir! Or you'll never see Jo alive again!"

"Oh shit, yes, I'd overlooked that!" agreed Morose, and, releasing his balls, ran over to the rapidly expiring girl, and with an ancient martial arts cry, that no one understood but sounded like "Socky Fo!", lashed out at the assailant. There was a scream as he missed and hit the wall. The assailant looked round, a right fat bastard he was too, and this gave Morose the body mass advantage, and his next thump landed on the assailant's glasses, breaking them inward, to a cry of pain.

The assailant, blinded, lashed out at Morose's general direction and hit his teeth, fortunately his teeth were in a glass of water alongside, and with a howl of rage, he staggered to the bell tower stairs.

"Oh fuck off, not the stairs again!" cried Harris, and began to chase up after him. Morose, seizing his chance, managed to loose off the tie from Joanna's neck, and he bravely began the kiss of life on her. Suddenly she began breathing, and realised who had got her back to life, and tried to kill him so she could die all over again; but it was no use. He'd revived her.

Up on the tower, Harris' job was made a lot easier by the fact that the assailant was blind. Attempting to brush off a sudden formation attack by the crows, who could smell Morose on him, the assailant took a swipe too far, and, inevitably, fell off the tower to land on the escaping Scouser and his lead piping.

"Thanks for that!" Harris waved at the feathered ones, "A real murder of crows!"

They performed a victory fly past and went off to eat the corpse.

*****

Chief Inspector Morose knew how to reward the help of the Harris family, in solving the case of the church killings. Emily and Jessica were busy getting trollied in the children's area. Claudia was on her fifth pint of Frog Vomit real ale. Robbie Harris had just started his second bottle of Panda Pops, yes, this was the life, he thought, an' that. And their jovial host was just preparing 'punch', from ten bottles of fortified rum and ten of Scotch, and a load of blueberry gin that happened to be to hand, and an absolute shitload of Port to "give it some flavour".

The pangs of guilt Robbie had originally felt about them breaking into Victoria Wines at night, had subsided, and all were thoroughly gorged on crisps and peanuts.

Morose lurched back to the display stand with a wheelie bin full of 'punch', and sat everyone down with a kick to the shins.

"So," he farted, "I suppose you're all wondering how I got to the bottom of this case?"

"No," came back the firm reply.

"Well," he ignored, "The main problem I faced, was in accepting that there had been a service, at Saint Ozzy's church, celebrating the feast of St Mongo McMongo, son of Mongo."

"Aye?" slurped Robbie, through his straw, as he drained the last of his bitter lemon.

"Well, I asked that bishop chap, you know, Linus von Paulus' employer, about this ridiculous pantomime of a service, and he told me," he broke off to let out a damn buster of a pump, "He told me, that there is no such service!"

He dodged an empty bottle of vodka, thrown at him by Jess.

"So, the next question was, did von Paulus actually have a brother?"

Robbie grabbed a massive Cuban cigar and, lighting it, settled back to try to blot out Morose's incessant droning.

"Yes he did, and it was HIM that was murdered at the church, by the guy we'd all assumed was dead, Harry Ramp!"

He broke off for applause.

Getting none, he carried on anyway.

"So, you see.......ah, hang on....." He broke off for a piss in the cash register. "So you see, we were immediately hoodwinked into thinking some wanky Christian shit was going on, and that someone had been murdered. In fact, Ramp had already killed Simeon, and left to get on with Mrs Austin. However, the trail was getting back to him, and as each person began to suspect the validity of the whole fantastical story, so they were bumped off."

Claudia Harris was busy buying a new Jaguar and rocket launcher, that she didn't need off eBay, and roundly ignored him. Emily muttered, "Ah, shurrup ya fookin' borin' prick!" and fell into a bucket.

"Sadly for her, my interest in the story, the rather comely Jo Nile, has had to be taken in as an accessory to murder, as she was due to run off with our final corpse."

The lynx yawned.

"So that's it!" triumphed Morose.

"More thorough than the original," observed Harris.

"Yes, thank you, and now, to get utterly....."

He broke off, as the sound of several police cars approached.

"Ah fuck, it's the pigs!" cried Morose.

"Ah shit, some grass must have called them to see what's gan on in here!" said Robbie, "Quick you lot, round the back!"

Rounding up the girls in one arm, and Claudia in the other, he made for the back of the off licence, with Morose slobbering along behind, pushing the wheelie bin.

They burst out of the back door and were confronted by White, Gonemad, Collier and Turner all stood with batons, and Franks and Soames with C.S. gas cannisters and a taser each.

"Pardon me sir," said Gonemad, "Is this your piss up?"

"Here we go again," muttered Harris.

Morose calmly pushed his wheelie bin full of booze up to Gonemad.

"Yes. It is. It's all my fault. Arrest me. I don't care."

Jessica took out her voodoo doll and took a hair pin out, holding it to the doll's arse.

There was a pause.

"Good – oh!" shouted Soames, "We're coming in to join you!"

*****

Back at the station, the canine division van was parked up in the car park. Originally, it had been left in Bay 5B. but it had rocked itself out of that and was vibrating away from the station towards Oxford Road.

Jampton was inside the building, at his desk, trying to work out how many forms he had to fill out to bring in a three headed dog. He had sort of arrested one body... but three heads. Possibly Weird might have a better idea how to handle this one. He was about to go looking for him, when a honking of horns, an almighty crash and a roar of something Tolkienesque, prevented him from doing so. Quickly donning his own helmet, and putting the paperwork to one side, he exited the station house.

The scene outside was chaos, a bus had rear-ended a truck, the truck had rear-ended a milk float, and the milk float had hit the canine division van, what was left of it...

The van was shredded; the sides had been peeled back as though something inside had wanted to leave in a hurry.

That 'something' had vacated the vehicle. It had been Lollypop originally. The odd three headed hound. It... wasn't... Lollypop... anymore... The huge creature was tearing off the furry skin, that had embraced its body thus far, while two of its heads – protesting all the way – contracted back inside its body. The raw, torn flesh took on a deep red hue, while the remaining head elongated, and its roar exposed teeth the size of pylons. With a strangled scream two horns pierced the flesh on top of its skull and curled around, becoming something of a sick twist on the head of a goat.

It towered 60 foot over the road, smashing a bus into the top floor of a nunnery, and ripping out a nun or two to finish off later.

Hugh would need the lads back for this... and possibly Franks and Soames too.

CHAPTER 7 – IN NOMINE PATRIS

Liam Newbold stood back and watched as the match did its work. The brief and unspectacular explosion of striking it, had made his heart leap, but just as quickly the flame had faded, and its appeal was lost forever. But it had done its work. The newspapers doused in petrol took hold with a much more alarming "whoof". The inside of the gothic style building seemed to shake, and felt as if it was trying to pull away from the conflagration within. The extra fire lighting blocks that he'd brought, in case of a failure, would not be needed. Out of a sense of sheer malice he tossed a few of the books piled up on the nearby shelf, onto the thrilling blaze.

They had the effect of retarding the fire. Cursing, Liam grabbed a few of the nearby cushions, that his unknowing hosts had left scattered about the place. Fools. Idiots. The cushions, being made of a mix of foam and stuffing, wrapped up in muslin, had a much better effect. For good measure he threw in the firelighters anyway, it's not as if he'd be needing them now. The less evidence, the better. The pigs might stop him. They usually did anyway: "How are you, Liam? Got any drugs on you, Liam? Where are you going, Liam? Do you want a lift home, Liam? Do you want a lift to *my* home, Liam?"

Wankers. Fucking pigs.

The kerosene that he'd laid out around the choir stalls erupted into life, with a flash that would have done their accursed god credit. The organ caught quickly and burned very well. The altar was casting clawing shadows of itself up the walls, as it began to catch. Soon would come the bursting of the windows under the intense heat, the heating system and the boiler exploding, and hopefully, if all went to plan, the joists of the roof falling in on the main body of the church.

The temptation was always to stay. The crackling whispers seemed to speak to him, cajoling him, begging him. 'Stay' they asked him, 'stay with us'. There was always the desire to watch the flames leap up to the ornate ceiling, and to take hold of the chapel. To watch the whole destruction to its perfect, glorious conclusion; but he wasn't finished.

Best to get away now, and watch on the news tomorrow.

No one knew it was Liam Newbold. But everyone in Oxfordshire, if not across the country – the country! – knew *of* him. He had left the side door leading to the graveyard open, to make sure he had his escape route fail safe, and also, so as not to cause a back draft and possibly get himself caught up in the blaze. A blaze in the sky, the northern sky for some people. Lucky bastards, being able to watch this from their homes. He looked back just once, enjoying the moment, before walking out into the black of night, doing up his Black Metal styled hoodie; and thus, blending into the shadows, he slipped away, joy in his heart, as the classical style eighteenth century Anglo Catholic church of St Ozzy of Osbourne burned, burned on to its full spectacular collapse. By daybreak tomorrow it would be a blackened, skeletal wreck of destroyed Christianity, those people of pious hope, pompous do gooders, and self-righteous clowns.

This would be his Easter tide offering to the brotherhood. To the Dark Ones. Third church this year and not even Easter day. The bigoted losers would be calling it God's judgement on homosexuals, liberals, the permissive society, those foreign types.... the poor, the unwanted, the downtrodden, the unloved, the druggies, the prostitutes. The kind of people that their ridiculous Jesus had wanted them to help. Blame anything except themselves and their lousy superstition. But that wasn't his concern. Triumph was his tonight. Fear walked victorious with him. Let the fuss die down, and people's guard would slip and vigilance slumber; and then – oh glory! – and then another target.

He turned the key in the door to his flat, bolted the door behind him, took a glass of water to bed with him, and fell asleep to the sound of emergency service vehicles heading to the lost cause of a third church burning.

It had been an honour.

*****

Robbie Harris was not happy. "Aw man, Surr. That's made me heave man. I'm not happy. Why did you have to show us that?"

Morose looked up from the floor behind his desk, "*You* told me I should involve myself on social media, more. Get a life *you* said. *You* gave me some ideas of what to post, and I..."

"Aye Surr, when I said some people post pictures of their dinner and that on Facebook, I meant before they've eaten it, not just before they flush it, man."

"Oh, I see, well... you never said..."

"Shouldn't have to man. That's... not normal..."

"Oh, fuck off, you garrulous piss weasel, always putting obstacles up in my way! I thought you'd be proud of me, Rudy."

"It's Robbie, sir," sighed Robbie.

"It's had 5 'likes', and one heart, and someone's even shared it," sighed Morose.

"Aye man, that was Weird."

"Weird on Facebook?" exploded Morose, "Where's me 'cancel account' app? And who's he shared it with, anyway?"

Robbie glanced at his phone, "Probably someone higher up in Chad Valley Police, or... Oh, no. It's not a hundred percent clear, but it looks like it's gone off to the dark web... very odd! It's getting more likes over there."

Morose was incredulous, "I'm incredulous, Rabbi," he said, "It's a picture of a turd, and people actually share this?"

"Aye man, yer average facebook user man, no brain, man. Some people use it to actually do stuff, yer knar, spread a little happiness, make a serious point, but they're usually the ones who get hoofed off. "

Morose took a look at Robbie's 'dark side' facebook page.

"What does that little speech bubble mean?"

"Ah, now that's more interestin', that means someone has sent you a message."

"To me Rudi? Couldn't they have just rung me?"

"But as your account is 'live', they thought they'd get you this way, I mean, you might be busy takin' a shit or asleep...."

"Or maybe shitting IN my sleep? I do a lot of that."

Robbie battled on regardless, "But this is like, another way of gettin' hold of you, so as not to immediately disturb you, but so you'll see it, an..."

Morose's snores stopped him. Robbie's punch awoke him.

"Sorry Roby, but I really couldn't care less. What's this message thing?"

Harris fumed silently, "I'll open it fer yer, man."

"Very good, that'll save me doing fucking anything."

"Aha, yes, ah, this is important actually sir, you might need to take note."

"I doubt it."

"It's from some joker calling himself 'Superintendent Weird.'"

"Oh?"

"Aye, its sayin like, ' I know what you were doing last night you hopeless vomit drinking wank cloth.' "

"They know me, then?"

"Aye man, it also says, 'if you are not in my office by now, yours shall be a slow, painful death."

"What, that cliched cack again? Send him a reply, 'Fuck off you stool chewing oxygen thief', and sign it with your name, just in case it's genuine."

"Aye man, done that."

"Any reply?"

"Not yet, you deficient, it'll have to be….ah, er, okay…. It seems to have been replied to before it was sent."

"Maybe it is Weird?"

"It says, 'Of course it's me, you pair of trouser snakes, get here now."

"Should we go, Robbie?"

They ran out of Morose's office and, ploughing down WPC Soames and her lunch trolley, made it past Jampton's front desk. Harris held the front door open as Morose scuttled through; he felt the outside air, crisp and cool on his face just before discovering he was in Superintendent Weird's lair.

They took a moment to consider their new position.

"Ah. You came," said a disembodied voice.

"Don't worry sir, it'll brush off later," retorted Morose.

"Your feeble attempts at belittling my threats, are as a fly farting in the face of an onrushing train, you lollipop jockeys. You are both being demoted, and returned to The Beast… I mean, the beat."

Harris and Morose looked at each other, then back at the empty space where Weird might sit.

"What?" they both managed to gasp, in unison.

"While you were arranging a mammoth piss up in the Victoria Wines branch in Sesame Street or wherever you think you live, in your tiny pox ridden minds, there were a few developments in Oxford last night."

Morose glared at the empty desk. "Nothing the pigs can't sort."

"Nothing at all, in fact, that they could sort, as they were all out pissing it up the wall with you! Meantime, I had to drag out Blackbird Leyes station to deal with a fuck off massive Demonic force in what the press are calling, 'The battle of Oxford'! A right wang I'm going to look at the flower pressing club later. I was going to sack the entire station…"

"Except me!" called a brummie voice through an invisible intercom system.

"Yes, except for that turd on front desk, who was the only officer from this…"

"Sty?" offered Morose, helpfully.

"…precinct… no, that's American isn't it? Oh, what is the bastard word?"

"Station, Surr," offered Harris, more helpfully.

"Hmm?" Weird pondered, "Yes, if you like… anyway, the point is, you were all on duty and should have responded to the call… mates!"

"Yes, I see that," mumbled Morose, "but the thing is, when an off licence has been broken into, the booze is awfully cheap… an absolute steal you might say, and I've never been able to resist a bargain."

"Well, I think you're all due a disintegration… let's have the entire…err…"

"Station" offered Robbie again.

"Sty," completed Weird, "down in the cellar, come on. Let's get a bit of discipline going here."

"Aww man, I thought you were just going to demote us?" Robbie whined, in that annoying Geordie way of his.

"I'm thinking on my cloven hooves here. No, I think some right evil discipline is needed to get this station back in line. Come on."

From the ceiling Weird materialised into a corporeal form, and caused the door of his office to open. Harris and Morose found themselves back at the front desk.

Having passed through the doorframe, Weird, in defiance of the laws of gravity floated towards the ceiling, causing one elderly couple to decide to give it one more night before reporting their cat missing.

"Everyone!" Weird's voice boomed, "Join me in the cellar for your disciplinary hearings…"

Soames, Brewis, Gonemad, White and the other characters that Ian and Howard can't remember right now, all gathered in the reception area, while Weird pushed his way through.

"Hold on, sir!" shouted Jampton, "emergency!"

Weird visibly deflated, the smell was ghastly, "Can't it wait until after I've finished hammering these bongs…"

Jampton didn't enjoy disobeying his supervisor, as his mother would testify to when she washed his underwear.

"No Sir, not if you're going to kill them. We need them… for the emergency…"

Weird pondered, the smell was worse, and sighed, "Well, I might kill you all later then. See how you get on."

"You're a good lad, Colin," said Jampton, forgetting himself and then almost forgetting to breath, "Er, St Ozzy's church, on Oswald Road, blazing away merrily apparently, full turn out required."

He was talking to an almost empty room. The entire station force had vacated, Jesus, the smell, leaving just Jampton and 'good lad' Weird.

Another clean up job for Mrs Jampton and her long-suffering washing machine, and the station would need some industrial strength pot pouri.

*****

By the time the entire station force had loaded into the various defective station vehicles; and discovered most were awaiting post Morose treatment by Terry, and found the only vehicle available was a twelve seater tandem, or 'dodecadem' ; and no-one knew the way to Oswald Road: it was almost a pointless act to stop at the newsagents and buy a map of Oxford, especially after Gonemad insisted on buying some sweeties 'for the journey'.

The firemen had begun toasting the marshmallows by the time the dodecadem pulled up and all twelve fell off, as no one knew how to stop and dismount. There was still a fire burning but it was contained, as they say, and the fire lads were topping up on the overtime by letting the lot re-ignite.

"Ohh, marshmallows!" cooed Franks, Soames, Brewis, and White.

Gonemad offered sweets round, and was immediately arrested, as he'd wandered into the children's playground area, the cupid stunt.

"Is this your child, sir," he protested as he was led away by local vigilantes who rather enjoyed knocking the shit out of him. Morose filmed it to put on his facebook page later.

"Any clues?" Morose sneered at the Fire Chief.

"Ten down, four letters, anagram, use a lightbulb to measure this man's popularity."

"Ah, I'm good at crosswords, let's see…."

"It's about you."

"Let's see now….."

"What can you tell us about the fire, Dixon?" Harris asked the junior fire officer.

"Oh, well! It was jolly hot, and we had the deuce of a job getting it all wet."

"How was it started?"

"Looks like some thoughtless individual soaked the main aisles and the transept, the cloisters, the choir stalls, the bell tower steps and the vestry, with petrol, and threw firelighters and the entire stock of kneeling cushions into the mix, adding some kerosene and homemade bombs around the walls."

"Do you think it was deliberate?"

"Do popes shit in the woods" sniffed the fireman.

"Er…." began Robbie.

"The answer is 'yes', you cockhead," said Morose, stumbling over to him, "This seems to bear all the marks of our unknown fire starting friend, who's already accounted for two churches in the Oxford area this year. I'd better see Weird about this."

"I wouldn't recommend it, man," Robbie said, "He was in a twat of a mood when we left."

"Oh fuck him and his woolly communist thinking," replied Morose, "You watch Columbo and that crap, wouldn't he build up some cringe worthy 'profile' about this church burner?"

"Profile, sir? You mean he's on facebook?"

"You see, Fire Chief," observed Morose to Captain Dixon as he punched Harris in the face, "This is the sort of cretinous piglet I have to work with every fucking day!"

"You should come over to the fire service, we hate the pigs here, cunts. By the way, put the word out, the barbecue starts in ten minutes, just as soon as one of your lads can nick some steaks from Iceland."

"Iceland? Are there no shops nearer than Reykjavik?"

A slightly warm fireman approached, and farted.

"That's all under control now, captain, we can claim our overtime sheets for the next four hours and fuck off home in twenty minutes."

"Fuckin' ace," said Captain Dixon. "Well we're off, Morose, you can call in the forensics and the other nutters now, been nice talking to you."

He extended his hand, Morose in return extended his kitchen.

"Selection," said Morose.

"Pick," said Captain Dixon, and with those choice words, they went their separate ways.

Harris sighed as the fire engines drove off, only stopping to soak a local scrote on his stolen quad bike. "They're leaving a bit early man. That church is still blazing away merrily."

Morose looked through the brown haze of the whiskey bottle he had acquired from somewhere. "They said it was under control. HAWK. Mind you I think he might have been talking about the overtime claim."

"See that building next door Surr? That's an orphanage, that blaze is heading right for it!"

"Hmm," Morose pondered, "I can never really enjoy the smell of burning orphans. Tell you what Robbie, just to be on the safe side, put a call through to the Oxford coastguard service. They're never too busy, probably be glad of something to relieve the monotony."

"Aye Surr," Robbie grinned, "you called me Robbie!"

"Sorry Rudy," Endof murmured into his bottle.

*****

After the Oxford coastguard service had dealt with the fire, and made a few new recruits, employing the government approved press gang methods; and after Oxford Mountain Rescue had relocated the orphans to Cowleaze Wood – just to be safe - Morose approached the embers of the former place of worship.

"Everything's gone, Robbie. Nothing left."

"What were you hoping to find, Surr?"

"Well... a visitor's book might have been helpful."

Robbie looked up, in that smiling, disbelieving way that Kevin Whately carried off so well in the TV series he did after Auf Wiedersehen Pet. "I don't think the Firestarter would have signed in, Surr!"

Morose gave that smiling, 'possibly you're right' look, that John Thaw used to do in that detective series he did after The Sweeney. "Criminals always make that one camel bending sized mistake, Robbie. Remember that."

"Aye Surr, actually, I DO remember."

Morose paused. "DO remember what?"

"That criminals always make that one camel bending sized mistake, Surr."

"Well done, you hopeless turd," complemented Morose, and tipped him into the embers.

*****

Liam Newbold took a look at the news on his mobile phone. Aside from some pathetic and entirely predictable political scandal, his church burning exercise had taken top billing in the national news. It was on the telly, too. And in that free paper they always stock on the buses. He felt an inner glow as he watched the hysterical outpourings of crocodile tears and grief, beamed into his room, so that he didn't have to move from his sofa. He was tired after his exertions. Getting up hadn't been easy, getting past the front door an impossibility.

Main thing was, he'd made his escape. What Liam feared most wasn't so much being captured and exposed as the greatest church burner of the century. Oh, no. Not even of going to prison for some considerable time, as some piss weak excuse to "bring him to justice" and all that crap.

No, Liam rather more feared going back to *that* place. You know, with the analysts, the doctors, the corridors, the treatments to make him better. He'd first been exposed to this twenty – first century version of St Mary's of Bethlehem, at the age of ten when his step father had battered him and he'd been taken away by social services as his mother couldn't guarantee his safety. He'd not meant to take the claw hammer to his step-father. It had felt good, though. That was his first hospital stay. He'd been frightened then. He was frightened now, of the memories. He'd been regularly propelled back into treatment, just as he was starting to enjoy life again, for some so-called misdemeanours at school, like trying to strangle Beth Steele, or torching Robin Devon's tie, while he was still wearing it.

The policy though, was care in the community; and he had used this to gradually sharpen his mind to The Dark Path, and to find comfort in his revenge. Sharpening his mind to Darkness had resulted in his rejection of drink, drugs, meat, and life with friends. Friends can hurt. Stick with what you know. Bring fear, terror, and a little notoriety for yourself, after death; for you can't leave anything in this world but a marker of your life, and the bigger the markers, and the harsher the punishment of the weak, the longer the notoriety would live. "They do not know me: but, they fear me," he paraphrased Colonel Britten. In this way, and this way only, would true immortality be made. Not though goodness, kindness or other limp notions. He didn't want to be liked and respected. He wanted to be hated and feared.

THAT lasts longer.

*****

After the Oxford coastguards had left, having damped down the fire considerably, and the Scene of Crime Officers had said they couldn't be bothered coming out tonight (as there was a good dirty film on Film4 that they all wanted to watch, with lots of quality nudity in it), eventually all twelve officers mounted the bike and left the scene. A few community support officers – Morose's celebrated 'plastic pigs' – remained to guard the mess.

Inside the church, the last crackling of the burning wood could still be heard. As dusk settled, and limited light made its way through from outside, via the now partially missing roof, the darkened interior was further lit by the redness of the burning embers.

It would have been unsafe to keep walking on; but if you cared so little for your own safety and had made your way through the nave towards the pulpit, you might just have beheld a strange sight. Through the glowing remains and crackling noises the pulpit could be seen – gently at first – to vibrate, to rock from side to side.

Like a child's swing, that keeps rocking, swinging wider and wider, eventually it must reach a point of no return. And like a swing, the pulpit crossed that point and crashed to the ground, falling through the fire-darkened floor to drop into the crypt below, leaving a gaping hole.

From the resulting cavernous hole, a high-pitched gasping came, as a pair of red hands reached up through the floor. The elongated fingers stretched through to grip the wooden boards, giving support to the figure raising itself up.

A pair of glowing yellow eyes peered through the chaos, as a chilling voice laughed in a painfully high cackle.

If you cared so little for your safety as to be in the remains of the church that night, your sanity would also have been unprotected.

*****

Chief Inspector Morose sat back and lit up a fag. Deep clouds of carcinogenic smoke were sucked into his lungs and he gave an involuntary cough.

Ahh, that's better, he thought.

His mind fogged up a little as the nicotine hit home, so he steadied it with a quick swig of his scotch.

Yes, all good so far. He popped a fresh strong mint or three into his mouth, sat back, and began to relax.

"Mr Morose."

The voice demanded his attention.

"Eh? Fuckin' what?" he demanded back.

"I must ask you again, to desist from smoking, drinking, and sweets. Just for now."

"Why?" he demanded.

"Because I'm trying to see to your bastard teeth!" shouted the dentist.

Morose sighed, and, smiling at the pretty dental assistant nearby, chucked the bottle at her, and stubbed the fag out in the mouthwash. Swallowing the rest of the strong mints in one go, he smiled back at the dentist, "Okay, nuts, carry on."

Taking a small rock hammer, the dentist did just that, removing most of Morose's teeth in one go.

"Wanker," muttered Morose.

"Bet you're sorry you came here today!" laughed the dentist, sweeping up.

"Not really, I just needed my current false one replacing."

"False ones? What the fuck are you doing here, you retread?"

Morose stood to his feet, just for good measure he nutted the dentist in the face.

"Just passing a bit of time, while my sergeant finishes going through your records. We're on a man hunt, you see."

"For what?" asked the dentist, spitting out a few of his own lovely teeth, while the pretty dental nurse crept quietly out of the door to hand in her resignation.

"That nut job who's busily torching churches all over Oxford. We've got some dental prints in the pulpit handrail."

"Mr Morose, shouldn't I be going over these dental records? Seeing that I'm a dentist, you know?"

"Don't talk shit," replied Morose, "You're busy seeing to my teeth, aren't you?"

The dentist made a few notes and advised him accordingly, "Get out, you tosser, and take your bastard sergeant with you."

"Ah lick me rim," said Morose.

The door went, Christ knows where it ended up, but anyway Sergeant Harris walked in.

"Ah, think I've found what we're after, Surr," he grinned

in that pathetic, smug way, known and hated by millions.

"You have?" asked Morose.

"Aye, it seems that our unknown fire starting chappie....."

He paused for effect.

The effect of the pause was, Morose swung the dental lamp round into Robbie's face.

"Well?????"

"Aye well, he's likely to have his own teeth still."

Morose picked up his mobile phone and dialled Jampton.

"What?" Jampton answered.

"Arrest every fucker in Oxford with their own teeth."

He pressed 'end call' and threw the phone at Robbie, narrowly hitting the pretty assistant, who had popped back to insult a random pig, and they don't come more random than Gonemad. As he wasn't there, she left a message.

Morose continued, "You fucking moron, we've wasted nearly half an hour of valuable pissing it up time, at a tooth quack, for you to tell me that the biggest arsonist in Oxford's history, most likely has his own teeth?"

"Aye, wel,l these things can't be rushed."

"Perhaps to save time we can assume he also has his own hair, skin, and bollocks?"

"Aw Surr, no wonder you're a fuckin' Chief Inspector!" lauded Robbie.

Morose pushed him into the dentist's chair, injected him with too much anaesthetic, and pausing only to gob on the dentist, lurched out and toward the pub, pushing the pretty nurse into the canal on his way. He pushed open the door of the next pub, that didn't have a 'no Chief Inspectors' sign hurriedly made up, and stormed in.

He sloshed his way to the bar, a cloud hanging over him, and rained on the barman.

"How dare you storm in here, like that," said the barman.

"Ah kiss my sit-upon," replied Morose, "I suppose you don't want to see my impression of an early aviator, next?" and with that, he got his knob out and started swinging it round, shouting "Contact!" as he did so.

"Yes, I'll put your drinks on the tab, just put it away, you turbo freak."

"Once you pour it, I'll put it away," he grinned, through his new teeth, a trick not many of us can pull off, but, being only part human, Morose could.

"What are you having, sir?" asked the barman, through his old teeth.

"Probably a coronary before the day's out. Oh, to drink you mean?"

"I *am* a barman, Sir."

"I refuse to hold that against you, some of my best friends start the night as barmen."

"To drink sir?" asked the barman, patiently.

"Ah yes... to drink!" Morose raised his hand, "You know, it's difficult to toast drinking if you won't pour me a drink..."

The barman sighed, and wondered if it might be easier to just drink the dregs tray and end it all.

"And *what* would you like to drink, sir."

"What a good question! I'll have.... Everything please... and as quick as you can, before I lose my ability to stand up. Start with the very naughty shelf and keep them coming. And I don't expect to see anything... at all when I've finished drinking, but especially nothing without a percentage proof."

The barman got a four-pint jug and started emptying a

bottle of Jack into it; but Jack objected, so the barman put some good ol' Tennessee whisky in, instead. He paused, as a thought crossed his mind. He looked over his shoulder and remembered back to his bar training days. They had said this day would come, but he had always thought it was a myth – you know, something to tease the new starters with, but this showed all the signs. He had to test his theory.

"You finished work for the day, Sir?"

"Less talking, more pouring or I'll have you arrested."

He paled. "Mr... Morose?"

"That's my Dad's name... not strictly true, he was called Spring-Heeled Jack."

"Inspector Endofleveldemon Morose?"

"Does everyone in this twatting town know my name, except me?"

The barman pressed a button under the bargirl, and excused himself to look for a safety helmet and the riot shield, that were kept in the back.

Endof pondered, the smell was rank by now. He vaulted the bar and emptied the jug. He had seen the barman's hand reaching under the bar, and could now see the button, it didn't take an expert to realise that button meant trouble.

No time to lose; he grabbed a handful of top shelf riot, and while pouring some into the jug, used his spare hand to mainline straight into his mouth. At times like this, breathing was just an obstacle, he had some serious necking to do before the filth arrived.

He was on his fifth quart, quite an achievement in his state, when he heard the sound of a vehicle approaching at speed, and screech to a halt outside. A few shouts, a taser loaded, and running footsteps approached the door. Damn those pigs! He just about made it, as the door was flung open, and in they came; as he blacked out, he could hear the shout go up, "War Cry! Buy your War Cry issue from us!"

*****

"Well, come on, Morose, how do I explain this to the Pig Handlers, eh?"

Morose's fogged brain cleared a little bit, just enough to ask, "Pig Handlers?"

"Yes, you goat fucker, you know, the Police Complaints Commission?"

His fogged brain cleared a little more, "Oh, those frigid gimps?"

Weird sighed, this was hard work. He tried to relieve the strain by breaking wind violently, adding, "Twist!"

Morose replied by dropping his trousers and shitting in the waste paper bin, adding, "Stick!"

After opening the usual windows, and sweeping up the flies which had expired with the smell, Weird continued,

"We have a double header of a problem, Morose, and I need results with both of them!"

"Just remind me of all three, Sir?"

"Three?"

"Yes, who am I again? The mists in my mind are clearing...."

"You're that remedial, Morose. There is some loon on the loose burning down churches, which I personally think is an ace idea, but sadly, the rest of society don't see it that way. AND, there is some vile creature ALSO on the loose, from that place that you and I both know, and bears a distinct resemblance to that idiot Spring Heeled Jack".

*****

Tom, the barman, had just finished headbutting those salvation army bitches out of the door. There were copies of War Cry everywhere, in amongst the broken glass, upturned tables, smashed pool cues. It had all kicked off after that police officer had staggered out, bloody god botherers.

Still, shift nearly over. He reached for his brush, and began sweeping up the debris.

It started as a feeling on the back of his neck. Something primeval made the hairs stand up, his bladder emptied and as if taking the hint, so did his bowels. He sensed, rather than heard or felt, a presence behind him.

Although his entire body was screaming not to, he turned around.

The door had not opened, but a large figure stood there. Its head brushed the ceiling. Tom couldn't see how he could have come through the door, anyway.

The figure coughed, making sure he had Tom's full attention. As if the flaming yellow eyes and forked tongue snaking in and out of his mouth, was not enough of an attention grabber.

Once sure he had Tom's attention, he spoke, "A four-pint jug of the top shelf please." He paused, and thought, before adding, "And a copy of War Cry, I need to catch up on the tits."

"Oh fer fucks sake," replied Tom.

*****

It was time to go door to door with their enquiries. Morose had reluctantly accepted the point Weird made, as they had no other leads.

The problem was, Oxford is a big city, and only had a handful of officers. It had been suggested that the Superintendent might join them, a suggestion that provoked a lot of very nervous laughter.

Besides, Weird could probably be of more use by exploring lines of enquiry within the Golf Club. They certainly needed more people out asking questions, though...

*****

Liam opened his front door to see a giant hairy freak standing, looking at him. The freak had oily overalls on, and had a hand raised ready to knock on the door. He was carrying an engine cover off a Fiat 126 for some reason.

He knocked three times on Liam's face.

"Windolene in both barrels," said Terry, holding out a freshly made up police warrant card.

"No, I was in all night."

"Monkey's been sick in the toast rack again!"

"Yes, I heard... a real tragedy."

Terry said, "Yes", and shook his head, adding as an afterthought, "The camera dipped into polo mints".

"I'm not sure... if I hear anything, I'll phone your station right away."

"You'll need the dromedary bending through a hundred and eighty degrees, for that."

"Goodnight!"

"Hmm"

With that minor scare over, Liam returned to his book about famous torchings across Europe. He'd have to beware of the pigs doing random door to door enquiries like that, though. Before this year, his paranoia would have started to nag him, sending him into random panics about roadblocks, and police marksmen keeping watch on his front door and window; but time had matured him into a cold calculating machine, and he was now able to dismiss such insecurities. The pigs had been. The pigs had interviewed him. The pigs had failed. And now, to carry on as if they'd never existed.

*****

Sergeant Robbie Harris walked up the front path, to the respectable looking house. Aye, here was class, style, and a well-presented family house for the better off. The rose bushes, the neat privet, the well-kept borders. Nice. He knocked, and waited for an answer.

The door opened nervously.

"Aye, what is it man?"

"Hello, young lady, is your Mummy in, an' that?"

"Howay Dad, ya soft shite, ya know she's in work, ya daft bastaaad!" said Emily, "Why didn't ya just use ya key and walk in?"

"Aye Emily man, sorry, me head's all mashed up at the moment wi' this case. Or rather, set of cases!"

"Aye, well come on in, I'll get ya a brew an' that. Yer look fairly shagged out, an' that!"

Robbie walked through the house, reminding himself not to admire it too much, as it was actually his an' Claudia's, aye man.

"Nice place you're got here," Robbie said to Emily, as she poured the kettle over their nosy neighbour.

"Daddy, sit the fuck down, you're comin' over all weird

an' strange!"

"Aye, sorry pet, I've just got so much goin' on!"

Emily walked over with his cuppa, a few biscuits and a hardcore mag.

"Now just take ya time, an' don't keep goin' on about the place as if you've never seen it before, fer fuckssake! Mam'll go off her fookin' trolly!"

Robbie ate his biscuits between alarmingly loud slurps of tea.

"Now look Dad, why don't ye tell me all aboot it, an' I'll see if I can shed any light an' shit on it?"

"Well, it's these church burnings, that sloshed old fart Morose wants us to build up a profile of the arsonist, an' then go after him."

"What's wrong with that idea, then?"

Robbie sat back in his chair and dropped a silent one, "I think we need to wait until he makes another move."

"What, burns another church down?"

"Just keep an eye on all suspiciously large sales of firelighters, matches, petrol in cans, y'know, all that. I do like those curtains, by the way, nice touch."

"Daddy, you're doin' it again!"

"Cack! Sorry."

"Anyway, I'll tell ya what we'll do, me an' wor Jess will keep tabs on all unauthorised sales of firelighters and explosives an' that, an' all you have to do is get the lads in the station t' swoop, an' his cook is goosed!"

Robbie relaxed for the first time all week.

"Ah, tell ya what wor Em, I feel like I've relaxed for the first time all this week! You're a good un."

"Aw cheers Dad, I'll inbox wor Jess now, she's upstairs workin' on that Moyes case, an' we'll be right onto yer as soon as the little prick makes a false move!"

"Cannae fuckin' great."

There was a moment's pause while Emily messaged her older sister.

"Reet, well I'll be off now," said Robbie, with a smile, "But first, just get these on, will yer?"

He took Emily's wrist and snapped handcuffs on her, before cuffing her to the door, racing upstairs and dragging a protesting Jessica down the stairs after him. He then took each by the neck and frog-marched them outside to the riot van.

"What's the charge?" asked P.C. White.

"This pair of gobshites playing truant from school! Down the station an' caution them, then phone their parents."

"Daaaad...." sighed Emily, as she was thrown in after her older sister.

*****

"Do yow want a double cell or two singles?" asked Jampton, booking the girls in.

"Double please," Jessica decided, "It'll be easier to carry on wor research for Dad."

"Bustin'!" Jampton laughed. He gave them cell 17, "You'll find that one's got an excellent view of the abattoir and the old flogging yard."

"Aye, we had that cell last time Dad went crackers. Has it had wifi installed yet?" Emily punched Gonemad for no reason.

Jampton checked, "Ahh no, not yet. But your dad's installed why aye fi."

"That's not funny," said Jessica, in that way teenage girls do, taking the break in conversation to chin Gonemad for good measure.

*****

Alf was annoyed. It was becoming harder and harder to get a bit of peace and quiet on the banks of the canal to enjoy a day's peaceful fishing. Bad enough that there had not been a single fish in the canal for the last fourteen years, unless you counted brown trout - which he did not – but now Chief Inspectors chucking young dental assistants in the water. There was no chance of him catching anything after that noise and disturbance of the river.

By the time he'd packed away his fishing gear, finished his sandwiches and his flask of coffee, it became increasingly clear that the pretty young woman was not going to make her own way back to the riverbank.

Alf pondered. In an ideal world, he would have caught on film the notorious Police Inspector throwing her in, and could share a video on yoohootube, or whatever the youngsters called it. Too late for that now. Still, he might catch her climbing out, if he was lucky.

It took him several minutes to fetch his camera from his car, which was in Coventry; set up the tripod, and screw the Box Brownie on top into position. No... she was still struggling, she was shouting out some shit about "Help," this was no time for popular Merseybeat music! The woman was clearly mad, she kept making gestures about a mobile phone, and something about "999", shouldn't she be phoning a local boatyard, and asking them to build a barge for her, so she could row to safety?

He was clearly going to have to "Help" her out himself, if he wanted a picture. If she kept going under the water like that, she'd do herself a mischief. Someone should speak to her about it!

Thinking hard, didn't they pay for such things on the telly? "You've Been Drowned", or something like that?

"Hello!" she screamed, disappearing under the water again.

Hello what? That's no way to start a conversation! Shout 'hello' and then disappear.

"I'm not going to wait all day!" he called across. Just for good measure, he put his head under water and repeated himself, just to make sure the silly moo had heard him.

She reached out and held onto him, as if her life depended on it.

"Christ on a bike woman, steady!" he scolded, "You almost dragged me out of this boat!"

Strangely, she still refused to let go. Obviously hysterical, probably a socialist as well. Oh well, he was stuck now, as she'd managed to drag herself across the side of the boat, using his gonads as a lever, and would probably be claiming squatter's rights, or some such Bolshie rubbish, any minute.

"Well, by Gad woman, as you evidently have no respect for others' property OR person, I feel I have no alternative, but to row you all the way to the bank, and deposit you there! And I hope you feel jolly rotten about it, on the morrow!"

She went to reply, but instead hawked up six fish and a cow.

"By Jupiter! You didn't say that you're a fellow angler! Do you have a permit for this stretch of canal?"

"Just get me to shore, you garrulous hog nosher."

"Right young lady, if you'll be kind enough to furnish me with your name, I'll see you're banned from ever going near this water again."

As the small boat reached the bank, she staggered out and gave him a non-verbal reply, pausing only to bring up a shopping trolley from Timothy White's. With a pound coin freshly inserted into it, she wheeled her way off, and along the tow path.

It was alright, he'd report her anyway. To Mummy. That badge on her chest told him all he needed to know. His sister Caitlyn's days of fishing this stretch, and stretching this fish, were over.

*****

Caitlyn left Alf as the light began to fade, and began her walk along the towpath. That fucking spine case of a brother needed a good battering, with a railway sleeper preferably. Tosser. Fortunately, both parents had already disowned him as being a waste of air, rations, and space. If he went to them, banging on about her littering the canal or some other cockwombling story, at least they'd have some useful target practice for their anti-tank guns, and those crocodiles could shift some by now.

As she squelched her way back to her flat – she'd really have to have it properly pumped up one day – she became aware of the fact that someone was following her, probably that tool Alf trying to bill her for wetting his boat. He had crept up rather rapidly mind you; one could usually hear Alf from a hundred yards away, as he fooled around between chain-smoking cigars and muttered abuse at anyone left wing of Hitler. And pedal bins. And rain.

"Fuck off, Alf!" she called out, just to be clear.

The steps behind her sped up slightly, she increased her stride. That smell of burning hedge didn't really match Alf.

She took a deep breath and looked behind. No Alf... no

one.

Unnerved by now - and this had started as *such* a normal day – she started walking again, soon finding her steps matched by the consistent clipping of steel bottomed shoes, tapping along the footpath behind her still.

Ahead was a bridge, the towpath disappearing into darkness underneath. She tried telling herself to be brave, it was only two lanes of traffic wide, she could cross it to safety in seconds.

Accelerating to a fast step, she strode purposefully into the dangerous shelter of the bridge. At first, she became aware of a moment of comfortable release. The footsteps behind her had ceased. Was it safe to...? She glanced behind; the footpath was clear.

She breathed a sigh of relief, and turned to step back out into the dusky light.

Her way was blocked by a figure from a nightmare.

Roughly eight-foot tall and wearing a black suit, cloak and top hat, the creature grinned demonically at her, his pronged tongue reaching into the darkness of the tunnel. His face was white as a ghost, with lips smeared blood red, and eyes of yellow fire.

She tried to say 'let me through', she tried to step back, she tried to scream. She was like a rabbit in the headlights, she could neither speak nor move as he opened his mouth wider. As time seemed almost frozen, everything was recorded indelibly in her mind's eye. As his mouth opened to a surely impossible width, something clicked and sparked near his tonsils. Instantly, the inside of his mouth was replaced with a searing flame, that arced out, past his tongue and out towards poor Caitlyn.

She screamed, finally she screamed! - and the demon cackled to have caused such a reaction. He was back... Spring-

Heeled Jack was back in England, and let them all pay for that.

There was a moment of silence.

"Hey mate?"

Jack looked into the darkness of the tunnel, "Huh?"

Caitlyn was shaking, but had found her voice, "Look thanks for that... you've dried me front up. If I turn around, will you dry the back of my uniform, please. That's lovely, that!"

Jack looked aghast, crestfallen. He whimpered slightly. This girl was supposed to be terrified, instead, the dopey cow was about to commend him on his dry cleaning skills!

The manic grin faded, she was reaching into her pocket. She held up something small and shiny that flashed a white light at him.

"Oh.... Fuck off" he half cried, leaping into the air. There was a crunch and a muffled scream, as he hit his head on the underside of the bridge. Cursing, he took a few steps back, and with another leap, disappeared from Caitlyn's sight.

*****

Caitlyn Nolan had changed her half-dried clothes and slipped on her Converse, well, they were a bit greasy. Now, with the purpose of a woman going to do something, she strode up to the Pig Nest in central Oxford and walked through the doors, pity they were shut. That was not about to stop her. This had to be fixed.

"Be with you in a min, luv," said the sergeant on the desk, a man who looked like he hadn't slept for a week, which in fact and as usual, Jampton hadn't. He finished typing up his report on how to type reports, and lifted his shades up to his forehead so he could see her clearly, which he could anyway as both lenses had popped out.

"'Allo, can I help? I'm a coppa, y'know!"

"I want to report a halfwit."

"So, which officer is it you want to complain about?"

"What? No, I've been assaulted."

"Oh right, you'll want one of our female officers then…"

"No, not like that. I think it might have been a student prank gone far too far…"

Jampton paused, "Someone acting the giddy goat, eh? Sounds like a case for our PC Gonemad. SAUL!" he shouted.

"No, I left a message for him earlier, can I speak to someone else?"

Gonemad, having been summoned, walked through a wall from the back of the station, eating a prune, as Harris walked in through the remains of the front door.

"It's alright Saul," said Jampton, "you're not wanted."

"Oh, before you go, Saul man. Some bint at the dentist told me to call you a turd guzzler, left a message, like."

Caitlyn turned around, "I beg your pardon?"

Harris clocked her, "Aye man, that's her. Called you a turd guzzler and a rancid cheese fondler, man."

Saul looked lost, "And?"

Harris shrugged, "Fair point."

Jampton took the initiative, "Robbie, this lady wants to make a complaint about some prank which seems to have mis-fired, can you deal with her? I'm sorting out Inspector Morose's sick leave."

"Is he unwell?"

"No, he keeps yacking up all over the shop, some poor sod's gotta mop it all up, and we've run out of cleaners with the relevant chemical warfare suits."

Harris scratched his head, and for good measure, scratched the wall before shitting in the litter tray. "Aye, Miss man, come this way, eh, why aye etc."

"Thanks," smiled Caitlyn, and followed him, after kicking Gonemad up the arse.

Harris shut the door, "Now Miss, what seems to have been the trouble?"

Caitlyn opened the door and stepped into the office.

"Well, corporal, I've had the afternoon from Hell."

Harris battered a fly that had come to investigate his smell, "Aye, they all say that."

"No, I was not only shoved into the canal by your arse jockey of an Inspector after I'd quit at the dentist's that he was wrecking, but also, some dick weed of a student thought it would be funny to try to follow me home! He leapt out on me! Fair scared the pony and trap out of me!"

Harris shrugged, "Probably just rag week, Miss."

She shook her head, "No, I'm not due for a couple of weeks yet."

Harris shook her head. "Stop fucking around and get to the point, Miss."

"Well, my would-be assailant was about eight-foot tall, and did a very convincing fire-breathing act, and.... Are you alright?"

Harris had stopped mid-breath and was looking at her very intently. "Aye, I'm alright, man, do you mind repeating all that, what you've just said, in front of a couple of my superiors?"

"Er, well...."

Harris pressed the special 'Get Weird' button under his

arse. There was a short delay and then a sudden drop in the temperature, as if Jampton had left the iceberg unattended again.

Emily popped her head around the door, "Hey, Dad, its fookin' freezin', and me an' wor Jess have just found a....."

Harris shoved her back out of the door and gave Miss Nolan a quick prep talk:-

"Keep these dark glasses on, and only speak when it – er, the Superintendent, like – speaks to you. Sorry about the iceberg, Jampton really needs to train it better."

She started to reply, "Er...."

"You summoned me, wretch?"

"Aye man, the lady here has a complaint...."

"Hers' shall be a slow and painf...."

"Nah, ya daft prick, listen will ya! See if this has a like, familiar ring?"

"H'mmm."

Caitlyn told her story. Weird glared at Harris. Harris glared at the pedal bin.

"So. It has happened," hissed Weird, "Young woman, return to your accursed dwelling and thank your pitiful beliefs, that you have survived this experience."

"Aren't you going to prosecute? Or even investigate?" she complained.

"We have been investigating for years. Centuries even. As for prosecution, that may be a little beyond even our powers. We will, however, inform you of his fate."

"His what??"

"His, er, pre-trial hearing. That is all. Evenin', all."

A small imp scuttled into the room, placing safety cones

in front of and behind Weird, then nodded at him.

And with that, through a cloud of black smoke, Weird dematerialised, and the temperature returned to normal.

The imp collected the cones and scuttled away, taking its Hi Viz jacket off as it left.

Harris looked down at the floor, "Well, now we know who's been torching the churches, then!"

*****

Robbie Harris made his way home, this time remembering that he lived there, and that he need not pass patronising comments about the décor, walls, vomitorium etc.

"Is that you?" called Claudia as he shut the door on his hand again.

"Who wants to know?" he asked her.

"Oh, some mad woman."

"Did you tell her I've already got one? Just my little joke," he added quickly, as she appeared with a carving knife.

"Just my little fist," she replied, and Robbie had to duck fast as his wife removed several chunks of wall plaster with missed punches.

Greetings over, Claudia uncorked a fresh bottle of port, and drank the lot as Robbie got a couple of sandwiches out of the bin and ate them with relish (which was in the cupboard).

She was about to hurl the empty bottle at their neighbour, when she suddenly noticed the silence.

"Robbie! I've suddenly noticed the silence, are the girls both locked in their rooms?"

Robbie had a nasty feeling.

"Ah, reet, I'm glad you've asked me that.... Er...."

Claudia's expression, despite the alcohol, changed noticeably as Robbie struggled for words.

"Rob, ya soft prick, hic, Ah said, where's the girls, man?"

"Aye well, er, it's like this luv…"

"What have ya done wi' wor Jess an' Em?"

"Well you see, we had this idea……"

Having swum her way into an upright position, Claudia swayed slightly as she fixed her stare at a point just below Robbie's throat.

"If wor girls have been locked up again….Ah swear, I'll fuckin' stove your head so far up your arse that it comes back out of its own teeth…."

"Aye Mummy, what's fer tea, man?" asked Jess as she breezed through from the stairs.

"Aye, I'm fookin' starving me, it had better be good or I'll yack it up afterwards, like" added Emily.

Claudia tried to discreetly put down the baseball bat, but dropped it. Both girls turned roond.

"Aw Mum, I've been lookin fer that all week," exclaimed Jess, "I've been wantin' ter fill that bitch Olivia in at school, an' since they've now banned assault rifles, I've been lookin' fer that wi' some barbed wire!"

Claudia was shocked, "Jess, ya fookin' trout faced moose, how dare ya even consider such action!"

Jess was crestfallen, "Sorry Mum."

"Anyway, what the fuck's for tea?" asked Emily again.

"Er….. yer dad's just off to make some, why not go an' help him, ya pair of homicidal clowns?"

"Yes," added Robbie quickly, "Come an' giz a hand? Like, now?"

Claudia collapsed back down into the settee, and Robbie shut the kitchen door as his wife cracked open another bottle of port.

He popped some bread in the toaster, and turned at once to the girls, and hissed, "How the blazes did ya get out? Ah thought ah was in fer a battering from ya ma."

"Aye Dad, ya soft tit," explained Jess, "Ya forgot to get any of those hopeless pigs to lock us in!"

"Aye," added Emily, "And guess what, whilst in there, we've put a tracker in Mr Morose's jacket, so we can track him, an' checked on all illegal volumes of sales of explosives an' shit, and found nothin'."

"Really nothin'?" asked Rob, as the toast bounced off the ceiling and onto his head.

"Aye daddy man," confirmed Jess, "Emily did however, manage to locate Morose."

"And, where is he?" asked Robbie.

"In some dodgy boozer down by the red light area," sighed Emily, "Probably off his fookin' face again."

"Back on the fookin lash again," complained Jess, "You'd think he'd invite Mam every so often."

"Well," smiled Robbie, "Ah think ye can both have a can of Special Brew wi' yer toasted cat food on toast, as a small thank you from me, fer keepin' yer traps shut."

Both girls put their arms round him, "You're the fuckin' best," whispered Emily.

"Aye," confirmed Jessica.

Meanwhile, in the dining room, Claudia was wondering who put the room on 'spin'.

*****

Also wondering who had put a different room on 'spin,' was Inspector Morose. "Stout yeoman!" he called, to get the barman's attention.

The 26 stone barman glared across at Morose from the other end of the bar, "Stout? Who are you calling 'stout?' Are you calling me fat?"

Morose harrumphed. A gentleman sat at the other end of the bar harrumphed too. It was really the only thing to do.

Endof smiled his sweetest smile, as two fresh teeth clicked into place – he must have spat two out earlier, "My dear tubby, I wouldn't dream of offending you. Why, you hold the key to all of the sweet things in life. And, a dray comes regularly to restock your shelves. Why, oh why, my dear lard bucket, would I say anything to offend you?"

"Hear, hear!" chimed in the tall chap from the other end of the bar.

Morose continued, "Now, stop being such a grumpy blubber mountain and pour me another gallon of your finest, please."

The barman waddled over to get another bucketful for Endof. Morose noticed the other barfly's bucket seemed to be running low, too. the man looked longingly at his empty pail.

"Can I get the fat fucker to top you up, too? I hate to see a good man running on empty."

The man nodded, "I could do with one, I've got a proper thirst on me... my throat's burning. And after the day I've had..."

Morose clicked his fingers at the barman and pointed at the empty bucket. The barman nodded.

"What, problems?" asked Morose, "I get the impression, I'm supposed to care. Never get used to these things."

The man nodded, "Just had a bad day in work. Had to

do a demonstration for a lady, to start a new campaign, and... well, it just went awfully wrong... I fear, that I might be losing my touch."

"Burn out, eh?"

"Very dry response."

The barman lifted the two buckets onto the bar. "Make these your last gents, I'm closing up shortly."

"Surely not that time already, Lardarse?" spluttered Morose.

"It's nothing to do with the time," the barman responded, "You've drank me dry! I had a Salvation Army mosh up arranged for later too. They'll be well pissed off."

Both men drained the top three pints off their whiskeys in silence.

"You fancy going on somewhere?" asked the tall man. "I mean, I really fancy burning up this shitty clapped out student town tonight, you up for it?"

Morose smirked, "You know, my mum told me, that my old Dad used to say 'Donec id induretis,' in times like this."

The man smiled, "Get it necked! Yes, that's my motto too. Let's get these finished! I'm sure there must be a good brewery somewhere near here, where we can get a proper session going."

As they stood up, Jack let rip with a force that blew his barstool through a stained-glass window.

"Keep the change," said Jack to the barman.

There was a moment of slightly embarrassed silence, before Morose evened the score by forcing his stool after it with an Earth moving trouser ripper, adding, "There's a tip from me, too."

The barman stood there going almost purple with a

mix of rage and feeling sick.

"And what am I supposed to do with these stools?"

"Oh, I'm sorry," smiled Morose, "I don't suppose you have any proper bog paper I could borrow?"

A moment later, both men were being deposited on the cobbles outside The Jolly Nag.

"Fucking fat knacker," observed Morose, to his new drinking companion.

"Ah never mind him, let's get going," declared Jack, and added, "But check this out first!" and fair broke a few cobbles with a massive boff. "Here let me show you something," he continued, "This'll teach him not to throw us out." He looked for a moment like he was going to deliver an industrial strength yakking, Morose braced himself for splashback.

With a small clicking noise in the back of his throat, Jack hurled flames at the door of the pub, which although now free of any flammable alcohol, still caught fire remarkably easily.

"Fucking ace!" laughed Morose, "I've been working on a trick like that."

Somewhere in the air was the smell of a distillery. They followed their noses towards it.

"I say," questioned Morose, "You are *awfully* pale you know, are you getting enough alcohol?"

"Just been out of the Sun for a long time. Never mind, I'm back now. I say, I never did find out your name."

"Awful thing... never use it, my bastard of a father cursed me with it before he left. A bit like 'A boy named Sue'"

"Ok then Sue, let's find that distillery, possibly we can open an off licence on the way, just to keep us going."

Morose pointed at a corner paper and booze shop, "Let's

open this one!"

"What a zinging idea!"

The corner shop owner was surprised, having locked up some ten minutes earlier, to find himself being dragged out of his kitchen, and rammed back behind the counter.

"But why are you doing this? I'm just trying to make a living, and you threaten me with being arrested if I don't stand here and shut the fuck up!"

"I said shut it!" barked Morose, "You're staff, aren't you?"

"Yes, that's my name, Mr Staff."

"So, we're robbing your store, and you need to call the pigs as soon as we've made our escape!"

"Can't I just find my shop broken into, tomorrow morning, as l stumble out of bed, like every other day?"

Morose and Jack looked at each other. Morose muttered something and went out to yack in the pile of returned newspapers on the pavement.

"That's made a splash on the front page," he quipped.

"Can't you just fuck off?" asked the shop keeper.

"You never said that in Mr Benn," complained Morose.

"Anyway," added Jack, "We're back on the lash, me and my new friend. Actually, he's my new best friend. Ever."

"So watch it, fanny face, or we'll arrest you for having an offensive fridge."

"There is nothing offensive about my fridge!"

"Yes there is! Its got no booze in it!" retorted Morose.

"Try the fucking Booze Fridge, you blind twat," said the shopkeeper.

"Oh yes! Thank you so much!"

After they'd carried the whole fridge outside, Jack hailed a passing taxi, into which he pushed the fridge, and out of which Morose dragged the driver.

"I'll drive," said Endof.

"Great!" laughed Jack, "I never got as far as driving tests."

"Neither did I," said Morose, "Never stopped me tearing up the Woodstock Road to my pad."

"Pad?"

"House. Fortress. Okay, it's a bloody pillbox. Hold on!"

And with that, Morose put both feet on the accelerator and they took off for chez Morose.

Back in the corner shop, Mr Staff dutifully rang the pigs.

*****

Liam walked calmly down the side of the New Baptist Church in Redbridge. A few days of careful planning had resulted in him building up a veritable supply dump of flammable material, and this should really be a synch, doing this place over. His slight frame belied the fact that he was also very strong; the side door to the church was pathetically protected by a single door lock, and the crowbar he had concealed up the sleeve of his Emperor hoodie, was quickly out. A quick wrenching move and the doorframe cracked, the hinges sagged, and the door moved freely enough to let him enter. He squeezed through the gap. He went to put the door back into place and noticed that the pathetic lowlife, whose church this was, had even left the key in the lock. Onanistic fools.

There was a light in what seemed to be the vestry, or the celebrant's office, or whatever this bunch called their priest. Probably their idea of a security light. "The Lord will protect us," or some other pious platitudes. He won't be protecting against this, Liam thought.

Liam re opened the door and brought in several cans of petrol, that he had earlier hidden around the churchyard and in the verger's hut, adjacent to the church. He deposited them by the altar. He got a couple of packs of supermarket firelighters – the best – and set them by each door, except the one he had the key to. Moving with alarming speed and silence, he poured the petrol over the doorways, the floors next to the internal walls, the altar, and set a good line of gunpowder from fireworks through the lot. His heart leapt as he noticed that this bunch of fools, had a kitchen built in to the main church building. Brilliant. He poured some of his last can of petrol over the gas stove, and turned the gas on, on each ring, so it would seep out. Some kneeling pads, nice and flammable, were soaked in the rapidly decreasing supply of petrol, and put lovingly by the Christian book shelf corner. That lot would be going up quick.

There was a movement behind him. A firm hand on his wrist.

"Got you."

He looked into the eyes of Pastor Homer Fobe, the minister.

"Hello," was all he could reply.

"You'll be the arsonist."

"Did you work that out for yourself? Or did God tell you?"

Fobe was stunned by the viperous words, but only for an instant,

"God has evidently enough love for His flock and His church, to see that I am here tonight, to ensure that you will no longer carry out your unspeakable acts of blasphemy and persecution against His people."

"Too late."

Again, Fobe was caught off guard; again, he recovered.

"May you live to regret your ill words. I'm calling the police. Now. And don't try anything silly, I'm a former boxer."

"I can tell by your formidable build. But physical strength is nothing to me. You can let me go; I have no intention of stopping you ringing 999."

Fobe cautiously relaxed his grip. This man had some nerve, he thought. Keeping just out of reach, Pastor Fobe rang 999, stated which service he wanted, and simply said, "This is Homer Fobe of the new Baptist church at Redbridge. I think I've caught the church arsonist. Yes, I'm at the church now. He's here, I have him under citizen's arrest. Yes. Make it quick, I don't trust him."

Fobe ended the call. He looked at Liam. Liam looked indifferently back. There was a silence. Finally, Liam spoke.

"Would you permit me a drink from my bottle?"

He slowly produced a bottle of water from his hoodie pocket, and, unscrewing the cap, gave Fobe a quizzical look.

Fobe kept that arm's length, "Go on, then."

"Thanks."

Liam took a mouthful, smirked, and spat it with alarming accuracy into Fobe's eyes. Fobe screamed in horror,

"My eyes!! What have you done?"

"Petrol, you loser," came the reply, before a kick in the lower abdomen region and a punch to the throat, laid the pastor out flat.

Liam thought quick. He ran back to the kitchen, and turned the gas rings up to full pressure. Out of malice, he ramped up the main oven gas tap as well, and scattered as much cutlery as he could across the top. Shrapnel bomb, anyone? He could already hear the distant, but fast approaching sound, of sirens and engines. He made his way to the side door, and then noticed the screw-in light bulb, just inside the door. He reached up, unscrewed it, and grabbed it quick; cracked the top of the bulb, and poured the rest of the petrol from his 'water' bottle in. He reached up, and screwed it back in, again. As he became aware of the blue lights, he managed to summon all of his frame's strength, to drag Fobe's unconscious, damaged body near to the side door. Liam left at a run, and made all haste to the hedge at the back, getting cuts but also getting through, just as four huge coppers made their way down the side of the church. Liam could hear them, even as he ran.

"This door?"

"Yeah, quick, we've got to get him before he makes his escape."

The door, unlocked, was flung open.

"Quick!" shouted a third voice, "Get that light on, there's somebody out cold here!"

The light switch must have been deployed, and as Liam threw himself face down and flat, so he heard the initial explosion, followed an instant later by the gas igniting. He felt the pavement lurch, and the air seemed to reach out and knock the breath out of him. Debris and body parts rained down; then that awful silence before anyone in the houses nearby, was able to react.

Before the shouts, the screams, the full horror was absorbed.

Liam, at a safe enough distance now, did react, simply by getting up, and walking unsteadily away.

For a short time, the sounds would be peaceful. The noises in his head more passive.

He would sleep tonight.

Pastor Fobe's God willing.

*****

"Aye surr, I know." Harris could still feel the heat of the church on his face. He opened his mouth to respond to Weird on the mobile, when the breath was pulled out of his lungs by yet another deafening explosion, this time from the rear of the building.

Harris' ears were ringing, he couldn't tell if Superintendent Weird was still talking. In the end he said, "I'm sorry Sir, I can't..." before realising his phone was dead. A kitchen knife blade was wedged in the back of it, saving it wedging in his head. Another casualty of the explosion.

The firemen were rushing to the back of the building, from reading their lips he could make out something about a hut.

Oh man, Morose had really carked his career this time.

The ambulances were just arriving. There was apparently at least one body inside and one outside, and nothing had been heard of the other three officers, who had been first on scene.

Harris felt a tapping on his shoulder, and turned around to see the normally nightmarish sight of Colin Weird.

"How many inside?" Weird asked.

"No Sir, I think we'd better stay out here until the fire bobbies put the blaze out, man." Robbie rubbed his ears.

"No, you malingering fuckwit! I asked, who's injured."

"Well Pastor Fobe would know all about the insurance sir. We're just looking at the injuries and deaths, just now man."

"Where's Morose, you dung hamper?"

"He's not got a camper van, he's kipping at his pillbox as far as I know."

"So, Spring Heeled Jack torched this church, while on a bender with Morose?"

Soames was approaching from her police bike, as she affectionately referred to Franks. "Sir... sirs... I've just been on the radio and..."

"That phone-in show?" asked Weird "Win anything?"

"No sir, I..." Soames attempted to continue.

"Hmmm, they can be very difficult questions..."

"No sir..."

"Well, you didn't win anything did you?"

"With respect sir, shut your fucking pie hole! I was saying, I've been on the radio to Sergeant Jampton, he says Morose and Spring Heeled Jack were seen earlier this evening getting right mashed up. Now, thanks to Robbie's daughter's tracking device, we know he's at the pillbox, but we have no idea what has happened to Jack."

"Right," said Weird, "I want a full assault team presence to Morose's pillbox. If Jack is there, they are both to be arrested after being beaten with a shitty stick. Preferably a fresh one. Do I make myself clear?"

Robbie shook his head, "It's no time for a beer man."

Weird picked Robbie up by the trouser belt.

"I realise that the explosion has affected your hearing. Lip read this. GET. MOROSE. NOW!"

"Anyway," Harris said, re fastening his belt, "I canna waste me time here, I'm off to get Morose and Spring Heeled Jack, if it's all the same to you, Sir."

Weird sighed. "Canny good man."

"Theirs shall be a slow and painful death, rest assured of

that, Sir!"

*****

At the side of the road was a field. Up against the fence at the edge of the field, was a pillbox.

The first rays of the morning sunshine began the slow process of illuminating the sky, the field and indeed, the pillbox. From inside the pillbox could be heard the strangest sounds.

From outside it sounded like someone was setting fire to a small newsagents. Inside, the contents of Mr Staff's shop were being repeatedly ignited and put out.

"Show me again! Show me again!" Morose bounced up and down.

"Watch closely," the tall demon suggested. He opened his mouth wide. Again, the faint, clicking noise was heard from within and less than a second later, flames gushed out across the room, setting fire to everything except Morose and three wide eyed crows.

"Now, the other bit!" urged Morose.

Again, Jack's mouth opened, snake-wide; and after another clicking sound, he took a deep breath and the flames, the smoke and even the heat, were gone.

The crows began the round of applause this time, closely followed by Morose.

"Oh, bravo Sir," clapped Endof. "I can do the flame bit, not as well as you. But, that extinguisher bit... that's bloody marvellous."

One of the crows nudged Morose, "Have another go."

"Alright," said Jack, "Wait for the click though. We'll get you sorted in no time."

Morose drew a deep breath and clicked...

*****

Harris looked around. His hearing was starting to clear a little. He had heard Soames' last fart loud and clear.

"Right everyone, can yez all hear me?" he asked into his radio.

There was a confusion of squeals and rumble noises, as everyone tried to speak together.

"I'm just going take that as a yes. On the count of 73, I want us all to storm the pillbox. There's only one way in, so..."

"Why 73, Sir?" Unmistakeably Franks.

"My lucky number." Harris replied.

From the air around each of them came the voice of Colin Weird, "73, fucking go... now!"

From all sides camouflaged officers appeared and moved in closer to the door of the pillbox.

The explosion caught them all by surprise, flaming brick and concrete lit up the scene and flew as much as fifty feet into the air, catching the police helicopter a good one, causing a crash landing in the next field... and the one next to that.

The Pillbox, what was left of it, was ablaze and with the power of that explosion, nothing from inside could possibly have survived.

"FUCKING ACE!" came an unmistakeable voice, "Go on Jack, do your bit!"

A whooshing, wind-whistling noise next, and the flames were out. But still, the pillbox that had survived a world war was gone.

Morose drained his bottle, "Fucking great! Robbie, you've brought all the piglets to my housewarming. This is my dear friend Jack." He pointed at his glass and then looked at the demon, "I'm sorry, I don't know this dear fellow's name."

Colin Weird floated forward, "This 'dear fellow' Morose, is also Jack, Spring Heeled Jack… your father. And I am placing you both under arrest for murder. You don't have to burn anything, but anything you do burn will be taken down for public safety…"

Morose looked at Jack, and muttered darkly, "Fuck bollocks."

Spring-Heeled Jack looked at Morose, and shook his head.

"Alas my son," he said quietly. He shook his head again.

"Father?"

"No, keep your distance. I…… I need you to know…"

"Need me to know what?"

He shook his head again, and pointed, "Alas, I have dandruff."

*****

Liam looked shocked, "It's all over the papers."

Mr Staff looked up from behind his counter, "No, those are the returns. Today's papers are over here. Clean and fresh."

"No." said Liam, "I mean it's all over the papers, they've arrested someone as the church burner."

"About fucking time… that's good news for a change."

Liam thought about his response. The madman in him cried out against these fools, for taking him out of the limelight. The rather more cold, calculating Christian-baiter in him, was pleased, for the same reason of taking him out of the limelight. After considerable thought, in the end he simply said to Mr Staff,

"Isn't it."

"Isn't it what? Fucking hell, you haven't spoken for two hours. Get out of my shop you freak!"

"Freak?" he thought to himself as he walked away through the still charred doorframe, "Just be thankful that you're not in charge of a church. Or that you're not a priest. Come to think of it, what religion is Staff? Should I diversify and burn up a temple as well? I mean, now the heat is off me…. Hahaha, funny, that, the heat is off…."

Humming 'The Heat is Off' to the tune of 'The Heat Is On', he made his way back to his flat, he really did need to pump it up again one day.

*****

The door to cell seven clanged shut, and was immediately locked. Morose looked at Robbie, patiently –

"Robbie… my dear boy…"

"Ah, I see you remember my name when it suits you."

"Yes, now Robert, please listen carefully. I think we may have worked out why so few of our arrests result in custodial sentences."

"Aye man," Robbie didn't bother to look up from his phone, as a text had just come through.

"Now, you've just closed and locked the cell, yes?"

"Of course, man"

"Yes, or indeed aye. Where should I be?"

Robbie glanced up, "Oh bastard! Aye man, sorry." Robbie unlocked the door and Morose walked in.

Endof smiled out at Robbie, "Be an angel Robbie, bring me a crate of Macalan and an industrial strength wank mag, please."

Robbie smiled, "Aye man," and turned to walk away.

"Robbie," Morose called after him, "Don't forget to lock me in. I'm a dangerous man, apparently."

Robbie came back clutching his keys, "I'd forget me bastard balls, if they weren't stitched on!"

*****

In cell three, two rockers were looking in amazement at the occupant of cell four. They had seen him brought in, all white faced and breathing fire at the arresting officers, before he collapsed on his bed and passed out.

The occupant was still asleep, but they couldn't wait to tell Gene Simmons what a god he was.

'Gene Simmons' was actually in some degree of trouble now. Whilst still able to breathe fire and generally cause alarm to the populace, he only had a limited repertoire, and only had a limited amount of time to wander the world of the living, before having to return to the world below. Being locked up in a 21st century police cell, was not going to do his powers any good.

Confound these fools, he thought constantly in his dreams.

In the cell next to him, 'Ace Frehley', aka Morose, was sat chewing over the fact that his Dad was some kind of semi demonic loon, who he'd previously only heard of in cheap Victorian novels. And he, Morose, and dad Jack, had been pissing it up all night, and still not got so far off their faces, that they could cause any REAL distress and damage! Yes, blowing up an 80 year old pillbox and causing casualties to plenty of his colleagues was hilarious, but, that chap burning down churches and killing coppers – that is, yer actual coppers – was top drawer stuff! Why couldn't he be related to *him*?

Morose went to reach for his mobile phone, but of course it was with that massive bell end Jampton, at the front desk. He went to reach for his flask, but that would be with Max by now, who'd be face down in a pile of corpses. He then went to reach for his house keys, but, no, they'd be with Harris who'd be making out some limp wristed toxicology report on them, coming to the grand conclusion that they are keys, or some other arse bollocks. He thought of going for a piss, but on this run of form, felt he'd rather not go looking for his cock just yet. White probably had it framed.

Oh, what was to become of him? Those dildos in King Richard 3rd Street police station would be loving this, Morose arrested and chained up by Weird, that dreary turd Harris taking over as acting inspector til his dullarse promotion came through, those gimps White, Gonemad, Franks and Soames all getting increments and applying for higher things...... the whole lot made him shudder and feel positively sober.

Of course, there was always the chance that his friends would spring him from prison! A daring raid here, a blast bomb there, a helping hand and freedom! Then he remembered he didn't actually have any friends. He would have asked for a solicitor but they all knew him. Bah, what could they charge him with anyway? Being drunk in charge of his own dad? Being drunk and orderly? They couldn't get him on that drink driving crap, he'd sold the car to that tosser Shark, and just to make sure, he'd pushed them both into a swamp.

A cough alerted him to a presence, behind him. A fluttering of wings gave a further clue. It was little Vel. Vel, the crow had landed on the window ledge and was looking in at

Morose. Vel cocked his head to one side, which in a Disney film would probably look quite touching, as though Vel was asking a question, 'can I help you, mate?', or something like that.

"I'm sorry Vel old chap, I can't get you anymore booze. I'm… running on empty myself."

Vel turned around and crapped on the window ledge, and Morose watched Vel Crow fly away.

*****

"Interview commencing 11.15 a.m. 14th April. In Attendance, in order of Importance Detective Sergeant Robbie Harris, WPC Franks, WPC Soames, PC White, PC Jampton and Superintendent Colin Weird…"

"Surr… perhaps as you are the suspect, maybe I'd better do this bit," interrupted Harris.

"Knob cheese," offered Morose, as a comeback.

Weird glowered, "Perhaps you'd better do it again, young mortal. And if I don't get my proper place in the pecking order yours shall be a…"

"Slow and painful death," everyone else chorused to much applause, laughter and a refused High-Five from White.

"Aye Surr, it's just not very funny to do again, so can we take it as read?"

Weird harrumphed but said nothing, while Jampton reached for the air freshener.

"Now," began Harris, "Perhaps we can start with an easy question, what is the capital of Mongolia?"

"Fuck's sake," hissed Weird.

"Robbie, you're at it again, you dickhead," confirmed Morose, "It's a fucking High Grade Pig interview, not a fucking quiz, you wazz bucket."

"He has a point," observed Jampton.

"Aye okay," Harris conceded, "We'll give you just one point for that, but as a bonus question, can you tell us your whereabouts on the night of the last church burnin'?"

Morose cleared his throat and gobbed on the ceiling, "Do you know, I really couldn't say. I was out with my new father, and we abused and assaulted this newsagent chappy for having a really poor fridge, but after that it all went a bit pear shaped."

The gob on the ceiling started to droop down like a stalactite forming.

"So yer cannae tell us which of yez, started the fatal fire? Not that I'm pinnin' that on you, cos that would be against police procedure, but we know ya did it, like."

"Yes, so stop piss–balling about," began Weird, "We just need to make the punishment fit the crime, and….."

There was a hiss of steam from the tape recorder and it blew up, dropping bits of tape and grill over the walls, and adding to the weight on the gob hanging off the ceiling.

There was a brief squabble as Soames and Jampton tried to get out of the door at the same time, only resolved by them both falling out, along with the doorframe.

"Marvellous," smiled Morose, "I'm glad to see the old place running so well. You know, I could quite get used to being on the wrong side of the law, it's much more entertaining. Ah, welcome back, losers!" he added, as Soames and Jampton crushed their way back in with a 1970's reel to reel tape recorder.

"Can we just fucking get on?" asked Weird, with a tape recorder spring hanging out of his eye still.

"We're all getting on just fine, except you," grinned Morose.

"Stow it, tit head," snarled Weird, "Start the interview, I can't hold off squashing this duck all day."

"Aye man, aye," said Harris, patting the microphone and releasing a fair cloud of asbestos, which floated about for a while before getting stuck on the stalactite, that was now lengthening off the ceiling.

Jampton took the mike.

"Well that's ruined that recording," sighed Franks, as Jampton walked off.

A very long arm shot after Jampton from Weird's side, followed him down the corridor, lifted him up by the Alberts, shook him, grabbed the mic back, and retracted back to Weird.

Superintendent Weird now took over proceedings.

"Right, mother fuckers, this is Colin Weird, interviewing the guilty party Morose, can anyone smell burning?"

Sure enough, the 1970's equipment wasn't up to consuming 2020's electric; Soames went to get some bread to toast, and the janitor was summoned to bring a fire extinguisher. He rushed in, pulled the trigger, and blew up, as no one had thought to take the plug out of the mains.

"His was a fast and painless death," grinned Morose.

Weird banged his fist on the table, which gave way, spilling the reels all over the floor and catapulting coffee and Soames into the air. Fortunately, Soames was able to grab the stalactite of gob, and slid down to safety.

Weird, by this point, was seething and close to the boil.

"Can we in the name of all that's unholy and Satanic, get this absolute horse shit of a job done? Just record the bastard interview and let's go?"

Harris quickly texted his elder daughter, and asked her advice.

"Aye well Daddy," she said, as she walked into the interview room at that very moment, "I'll record it on me phone, then use the wifi connection to put the recording into a cloud, and send it to yer phone an' the main piglet's file source at the I.P. address, an' that."

"Reet love," said Harris, not understanding any of that, "Is it up an' runnin'?"

"Aye man."

"Interview with, oh, him, also in the room, the others, go, just talk will yez?"

"Tell us about the church burning, Endof," demanded Weird.

"Well," sighed Morose, "To be honest, I can't remember. Me and Jack - that is, my new found father – were on our way to our tenth barring from a pub in town that night, when we were vaguely aware of some calamity, somewhere; but thought we couldn't be arsed, and anyway we couldn't move, so, there you are."

Weird broke the silence with a prolonged boff, which so shook the room, that the stalactite of gob fell off the ceiling, bringing down a sizeable chunk of plaster, along with a main supporting beam. The police station shook, and dust settled in the room, while outside in the road a sink hole opened up.

"So, you're saying it wasn't you, then?" asked Harris.

Morose shook his head, "No."

Harris turned to face the camera, "Well, we'll take a break for now, but we'll be back after this word from our sponsors."

He was aware of Weird's fist slamming into his face, but lost interest at once as his world turned black and he inexplicably fell over onto the upturned table.

*****

Some time had elapsed; but, sadly, not Morose. He was still sat in the interview room, and had now been joined at the interrogation by his late father, who had joined them late.

Superintendent Weird paced the room with his paste, very nice it looked in a sort of smeggy off-white. Harris and Jess had the recording equipment ready, and Harris was sat with a pile of prompt cards, and a gun held to his head by Weird. There was a fire officer, a paramedic, an electrician and just for good measure, a Buddhist monk, all on standby.

"Tell us about the church burning," Harris read from the cue card, adding, "Is that alreet?" quietly at Weird. Weird sort of glowed a bit darker.

"I can't," replied Morose.

"Why not?" asked Harris, reading off the reverse of the cue card.

"Cos I wasn't fucking well there, as I keep telling you, you rat stomper."

"Well if you can't answer, I'll have to pass it over to...." he was aware of the trigger of Weird's gun suddenly getting tighter, ".....er, I mean, I'm going to ask your fellow prisoner, er, Mr Jack, tell us about the church burning."

"What about it?"

"Why did ya do it, like?"

"I didn't. WE didn't. WE were too far off our faces to burn our dinners, never mind a church."

At once, Harris saw his chance, and leaned forward to ask, "Tell us about the burned dinner, then."

Weird's trigger finger suddenly tensed, but as it did, so the main support joist for the room gave way, and the rest of the ceiling fell onto Jess' mobile phone.

"Marvellous, fuck this," snarled Weird, and contented himself with a honk of suspicious strength.

The door that was barely staying in place - as the supporting RSJ moved – grumbled, as something outside tried to push the door open, then gave it up as a bad job.

The voice of Sergeant Jampton could be heard through the steady fall of plaster from the ceiling.

"Ow lads! I've had a call, might need some of yow!"

Weird floated upwards on a cloud of his own making, "Make yourself clearer, minion" he hissed.

"Y'know the St Thomas area? Well a little bird has told me one of the churches is on fire…"

Harris at once thought he had the two suspects by the Niagras, and went in for the kill "Where were you a few minutes ago when this fire at this hitherto unknown church, started?"

Weird gritted his teeth with a specially made gritter.

Morose cleared his bum. "We were here, you piss gargling horse fellonist,"

Harris pushed his final button.

"Aye so ya say, but can you prove that?"

Weird rolled his eyes across the floor and fell over.

*****

"Faster!" they ordered Soames, "Floor it!"

The Ford Popular ground into top (ie, 3rd) gear, as it hurtled Harris, Morose, Jess, Spring Heeled Jack and that cretin White taped into the engine bay, towards the blazing church, with Weird floating above the roof. Soames was actually standing on the accelerator pedal to milk the last few miles per hour out of the distraught old car; added to which she had to stand anyway as that hatstand of a mechanic, Terry, had taken the seat out, owing to an invasion of seal pups. Using Morose's really useful machine, she gritted her teeth and as the veins stood out on her forehead, she skilfully rounded the last corner on the approach to the new conflagration, and drove them straight into a tram.

They all staggered out. Robbie looked at the tram.

"How long has THAT been there?"

Jampton examined the tram, "Seems they forgot about this one when they dug the system up in 1940. Shit, imagine the parking fine now!"

Weird was rather more scathing.

"You idiot!" he hissed at Soames, "That was one shit piece of driving! How fast were you going?"

"Almost 30 mph, sir!"

"And what gear were you in?"

"Just my usual slacks and T shirt, sir!"

"Shut it, you hog," snarled Morose, "Just push the tram, we'll all get there together."

They all piled into the tram and Soames, heading for her first major coronary, managed to move the creaking, rusted up scrap heap all of five yards, before the front wheels buckled and the whole thing fell over.

"That's great!" shouted Morose, "We can run the rest ourselves now," and they all ran off laughing into the burning church, which was after all only another ten yards away.

The altar area had caught the worst of the pyromaniac's

glory. Although, it was clear to look around that it wouldn't be long before the rafters caught, and then the building was finished.

Jack looked around the nave and transepts and held his large arms out to block everyone else from advancing any further. Without looking back he called out, "Hey Colin! The guy who did this must be brilliant, look at the clever way he's got those curtains alight!"

Weird floated over to Jack, "Very smart, only a genius could do this."

"What are yez talking aboot?" asked Robbie, before a swift boot to the 'nads sent him floor wards.

Morose removed his right boot from Harris's baby making area to steady himself, but kept the left in place, just in case Robbie opened his mouth again.

Morose cleared his throat, "I'm thinking of adding a piece of my own to the theme. Do you think the artist would mind, or...?"

"No!" came a shout from the back of the church. A small, thin young man, dressed in black and carrying two petrol cans, stepped out of the shadows. "This is my work pig! You start your own fire."

"Ahh, I'd like to," carried on Morose, "but you seem to have all the petrol. Can I maybe borrow some?" Endof pushed his father's arm out of the way, and stepped down the aisle, towards Liam. "You see, all the petrol stations will be closed now, as these stories are set in the 1980's. So, if I could just have a borrow of some..."

Liam carefully placed one of the cans on the floor.

Morose took a few steps closer to the proffered can as Liam reached into his jacket pocket, revealing a flare pistol.

"Hold it," whispered Liam.

Morose unzipped his flies, flopped it out and after a long pause, said, "Right, I'm holding it, now what?"

"Put it away, matey," hissed Weird. As no-one heard the hissing over the crackling of the flames, we'll never know who he was talking to. Weird turned to Harris, "I want you to get everyone out of here, we haven't got long."

Reluctantly Robbie nodded.

There was a meeting of eyes, between Liam and Morose, both of whom were now stood there with a nasty weapon in their hand. There was a loud crash from the sanctuary, as the altar window burst in the heat, and part of the supporting wall gave way with it. The 19th century Catholic church was starting to break up.

"Now look," began Morose.

"I have been," snarled Liam, "It really isn't impressive."

"Its all over," said Morose, "Give up. This God bothering hole is surrounded by pigs, and the only ways out are blocked by things that even you will be scared of."

As if to prove his point, Weird manifested himself nearby, the filthy swine, as Jack joined them.

"I am fully aware of your association with the Dark Side, Mr Morose. Sadly for you, I'm on a one-way ticket there, and you're coming with me."

Morose sighed, "That cliched crap?"

There was a horrible rending sound, and as the supporting police, led by Harris, ran back out of the building, the bell tower support floor gave way; and the large, heavyweight cast brass bells crashed to the floor and buried themselves in it, blocking the main aisle.

"Only one way out now, Matey," observed the totally detached Weird.

"I'll soon see to that," said Liam, and with worrying accuracy, fired the flare pistol at the far end of the building, where the main doors were. There was a ghastly whooshing sound, and the petrol-soaked doors and cushions there, went up in a horrifying blaze.

"Jesus wept!" grinned Liam.

Morose looked at the blocked exit, "Yes, I'm... I'm feeling a little weepy myself," but instead contented himself with throwing up on the lectern.

Liam sat on the floor and began muttering things that were incomprehensible.

Jack was looking around for another exit. It was no use, there were none. Blue lights could be discerned through the windows, though the sirens were barely audible over the noise of the (by now) substantial holocaust.

Morose, deciding now that it didn't matter, tucked it back in, as he glanced over at his father, and began, "Tell me something..."

"'kin' what?" asked Jack.

"Why... why Endofleveldemon?"

Jack spun around to face Morose, "You want to know that, *now*?"

Morose smiled, "It would appear that NOW, is all we have."

Jack took a deep breath, "I knew I wouldn't be around and if you were..."

Morose interrupted, "Don't give me the Johnny Cash version. Why?"

Jack looked Morose in the eyes, "To identify you."

Morose paused, "Identify me as what?"

"Something big is coming, and you were left here to

deal with it... I don't know what will happen now..."

"I do," said the quiet voice of Liam Newbold.

He pointed upward. Jack, Morose and Weird, all looked upward. They all simultaneously became transfixed by the scene, and watched in morbid fascination as the ceiling buckled, wavered, paused; and then fell in on them.

*****

"Aye, that's cannae grand that," burped Robbie as he pushed his plate away, and it fell on the floor and shattered.

"Aw Dad, ya soft shite," groaned Emily, "You've gone an' made us look like a family of lower class origin, now!"

"Aye well," said Claudia, "Anythin' ya can do, Ah can do better," and she stood up and threw her plate on the floor really loud.

The diners in the Greek restaurant all stopped eating and watched.

"Mam," Emily tried to slide under the table in horror.

"Haddaway, ya softie shites," declared Jessica, and grabbing her plate, hurled it out of the open window, where it struck a passing nun in the face.

"Reet, that does it," shouted Emily. She finished off her Special Brew, and grabbed her own plate, and launched it at the waiter, who ducked, and it went straight through the mirror.

There was uproar. Everyone grabbed a plate and smashed it, and all the waiters ran out shouting "Dolofonia!" and other such weedy things.

Robbie grinned at Claudia, "Aye, when the Harris family gan oot on tha' toon, we make a reet fuck up of it!" He added

"Cacking Jesus!" as Emily downed a bottle of claret and buzzed the bottle at a coppa, who'd come over to see what all the racket was.

"Fookin greet idea, this, Daddy!" shouted Emily.

"Aye, you're a good lad, wor Em!" he shouted back.

"Just fookin' neck it!" she laughed, throwing a cactus plant at him, knocking him clean oot.

Claudia glanced down at her husband from between mouthfuls of scotch, "Aye, he could never hold his drink."

Jess punched a retired colonel as she made her way through a second bottle of gin, "Aye Mum, he's as soft as shite!"

Yes, the Harris family knew how to hold a wake for their happily departed friend Morose. He'd have been proud of them!

They didn't realise, however, just HOW proud......

ALSO AVAILABLE BY THE AUTHORS...

BEING MOROSE
BY
Howard White & Ian Sloan

In a dystopian parallel world, Oxfordshire Police have a hopeless drunk and an over worked Geordie novice, working on crime solving mysteries, along with a cast of shady characters in the force, and very dodgy residents, their families, pets, and gardens.
Anarchy alcoholic fug and rude words abound

Amazon 5 Star

"very funny, very clever would certainly recommend it as a very good read."

"it's bloody brilliant, funny, witty and all together a fantastic read, why are we waiting so long for volume 2?"

"Very funny & witty book. Didn't realise it was possible to solve crimes after drinking so much alcohol! Can't wait for the next book."

Available on Amazon Paperback and Kindle

RAISE A GLASS TO INSPECTOR MOROSE
BY
Howard White & Ian Sloan
(Inspector Morose Book 2)

Finally! A sequel to the hysterical Being Morose

"You pair of hedgehog graters, this evidence is utter cack!" Chief Inspector Morose, the miserable b**tard, returns as Oxford Police's most useless and most plastered detective in six new stories.
THRILL as he survives a stay in hospital.
GAPE as he deals with unusual smuggling activities.
BE JOLLY IMPRESSED as he falls over a lot.
Warning. Contains rude words and cartoon violence. Squares, Royalists, lefties, dullards, whingers, OCD freaks and Health & Safety officials, will hate it.

"On a par with Milligan, Cleese and Adams at their best" – Russell Woodward

Amazon 5 stars

"THIS has to be one of the funniest books ever written. A madcap mix of "Inspector Morse" and totally off-the-wall comedy, I was given a copy to read by a friend who'd read it several times, noting that it helped him drag himself out of depression"

"I can't believe some of the things I find myself laughing at, sometimes I feel I shouldn't be, but can't help myself! You need to try it for yourself and you'll see what I mean!"

Available on Amazon Paperback and Kindle

Printed in Poland
by Amazon Fulfillment
Poland Sp. z o.o., Wrocław